DESTINATION:
Romance

JULANE HIEBERT
K. MARIE LIBEL
ROSE ALLEN McCAULEY
KIM VOGEL SAWYER
CONSTANCE SHILLING STEVENS

Five inspirational love stories spanning the globe

DESTINATION:
Romance

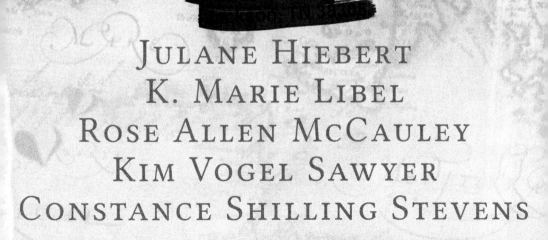

JULANE HIEBERT

K. MARIE LIBEL

ROSE ALLEN McCAULEY

KIM VOGEL SAWYER

CONSTANCE SHILLING STEVENS

Published by Wings of Hope Publishing Group
Established 2013
www.wingsofhopepublishing.com
Find us on Facebook: Search "Wings of Hope"

Hiebert, Julane; Libel, K. Marie; McCauley, Rose Allen; Sawyer, Kim Vogel;
Stevens, Constance Shilling
Destination: Romance
Wings of Hope Publishing Group

Digital edition
ISBN-13: 978-1-944309-19-0
ISBN-10: 1-944309-19-5

Cover artwork and typesetting by Vogel Design in Hillsboro, Kansas.

TABLE OF CONTENTS

BARE FEET AND WARM SAND

KIM VOGEL SAWYER

For *David*,
who loves sea turtles;

and for *Kendall*,
who loves going barefoot

"So God created the great creatures of the sea
and every living thing with which the water teems and that moves
about in it, according to their kinds...
And God saw that it was good."

GENESIS 1:21 NIV

CHAPTER 1

Tamiera Davison kicked off her flip-flops and crossed the warm, white sand bank. Glistening particles coated the bottoms of her damp feet and caught between her toes, but what did she care? Back in North Dakota, people could be wearing boots and trekking through snow. As much as she missed the people from her childhood home, she didn't miss November's snowstorms. She'd gladly take the island's sunshine and tropical breezes instead. Besides, there weren't any green sea turtles in North Dakota.

She examined the drag marks extending at least a dozen feet from the farthest reach of the tide to a patch of disturbed sand. She crouched and ran her fingers lightly over the slight mound, certainty making her chest go tight. A turtle had nested during the night. Her pulse sped into double beats—part excitement, part worry. If she'd found the spot, predators would, too.

She stood and waved both hands over her head, her signal for her helper, Manny, to bring down a wire cage and netting.

The young teen came running, arms laden. His broad smile formed a slash of white against his dark skin. "Success, Miss Tamiera. Yes?"

As usual, he over-emphasized the "meer" consonant of her name, giving it an island lilt. She'd never liked the unusual pronunciation—*Tameera* rather than *Tamra*—until she heard it from the lips of the Jamaican people.

She offered the lanky youth a smile and nod. "Absolutely success." She took the mesh frame and moved behind the mound, scowling against the bright sunshine. "Now let's do what we can to make sure these babies hatch, huh?"

"Yes, ma'am!"

Using her hands as scoops, she gently dug. About twelve inches down her fingertips encountered the pile of round, white orbs. She carefully excavated the circumference of the nearly perfectly round hole, then she and Manny pushed the wire mesh tube around the periphery of the eggs. "Careful—don't disturb them." She didn't need to warn Manny. He'd helped her with at least a dozen nests and knew what to do, but the instructions left her lips without conscious thought. "A little deeper, I think. No sense in taking any chances."

Perspiration beaded on Manny's dark skin. "If people would keep their dogs at home, we wouldn't have to worry, would we?"

She shot him an approving grin. "You've learned well, Manny." How many lectures had she given about the importance of pets not being allowed to roam free on the island? And yet people refused to heed her warnings. The sea turtles had fewer wild predators than domesticated ones. And out of all the domesticated predators, humans were the worst.

With the wire completely surrounding the nest, they pushed sand back over the eggs. Tamiera draped netting over the frame, and Manny secured it with wire ties. When they finished, Manny sat back on his heels and sent an expectant look across the top of the enclosure.

"You gonna pray now, Miss Tamiera?"

Some might think her foolish for praying for sea turtles. But in her opinion all of God's creatures—human, mammal, reptile, marine, or fowl—were valuable in His eyes. Why else would He have placed them on the earth? She nodded and bowed her head. She offered gratitude that they'd found the nest, she asked that the protective measures she and Manny added would hold the entire seven or eight weeks needed for the eggs to hatch, and she finished on a rasping plea. "Let these turtles live long lives in the sea. Amen."

Manny echoed, "Amen."

She brushed the sand from her feet and donned her flip-flops. As they ambled up the rise to her Jeep, Manny nudged Tamiera's arm. "It's pretty quiet along this stretch of beach. Do you think all the eggs will hatch and the turtles will make it to the water?"

Another hundred or so turtles added to the wild population would make Tamiera turn cartwheels of joy. Yet it was unrealistic to expect all of them to make it. Sadness settled on her as she considered the odds against this batch of turtles living long enough to grow to adulthood and possibly return here in twenty-five years to lay their own eggs in the sand. But she wouldn't defeat this young man who cared about the sea turtles as much as she did.

She slung her arm across Manny's narrow shoulders. "We've done our part. Now it's up to God and nature to do the rest."

Joe Phelps stayed at the rear of the group of people listening to the tour guide's instructions for holding baby sea turtles. He doubted he'd hold one of the year-old turtles himself. Couldn't a person get salmonella from turtles? But others were certainly eager to take advantage of every opportunity available at the sea turtle farm. Their eagerness filled him with excitement. Surely Dad had made a wise choice for the location of his corporation's next resort hotel.

Dressed in a tropical print shirt, khaki shorts, and sandals, he fit in well with the tourists who'd signed up for a Caribbean Sea Turtle Farm and Conservatory tour. No one would suspect he held ulterior motives for joining the excursion. He'd never been one to engage in subterfuge, but his dad's last words before he boarded the plane for Florida still lingered in the back of his mind.

"It's your time to shine, Joe. Listen well, learn much, and choose wisely. I trust you."

Not once in the six years since he'd joined the family's resort business had Dad placed his full trust in his youngest son. It made him determined not to disappoint his father.

The group swarmed behind the guide to a basketball court sized concrete pad containing what looked like a dozen hot tubs. He peeked over the edge of the closest one. Perhaps fifteen turtles, a little bigger in circumference than the salad plates used in the hotel's dining room, swam around each other, as graceful as ballerinas. For a moment, he stood, transfixed by their seemingly choreographed dives and swoops.

The teenage girl next to him reached into the tub, her long brown braid dipping within an inch of the surface of the sparkling water. She caught a turtle, lifted it from the water, and held it over the tub the way the guide had directed. The turtle flapped its flippers, nearly clapping above and below its head.

The girl squealed. "Oh, quit that! I don't want to drop you, little guy!"

Joe instinctively reached to help steady the wriggling turtle.

A woman with a floppy straw hat and huge mirrored sunglasses held up a cell phone. "Tickle its neck, Casey. Remember? The way you'd tickle a cat's jaw."

Grimacing, the girl extended one finger and stroked the underside of the turtle's wrinkly neck. The wild flapping slowed, and then its flippers sagged. Joe could have sworn he heard the little reptile sigh.

The woman clicked the phone several times and beamed at the girl. "Got it!"

The girl lowered the turtle toward the water, but she flicked a sideways glance at Joe. "Did you wanna hold him?"

Joe shook his head and backed up a step. "No, thanks. Go ahead and put him back where he belongs."

She shrugged and placed the turtle in the tank. It darted underneath the other milling turtles. The girl trotted to the hand washing station, and the woman followed, both of them jabbering about the fun excursion.

Joe used a squirt of the hand sanitizer at the washing station even though he hadn't actually touched the turtle and then ambled along a winding concrete pathway to a large enclosure with a sloping sand bar leading to a pool of water. Turtles as big as the turtle-shaped sandbox he'd bought his nephews for Christmas a few years ago lazed in the sun on the sand or swam in the crystal blue water.

He stacked his forearms on the concrete block wall surrounding the enclosure. The sun beat hot on his head, but a breeze kept him comfortable. He watched the swimming turtles, smiling at how they managed to maneuver around each other even though the water teemed with activity. Did they have some inner radar that prevented them from bumping into each other?

Someone tapped him on the shoulder, and he straightened. A young couple stood close. The man held out his camera—a smaller, digital model with a telephoto lens attached.

"Would you mind taking a photo of us? I'd do a selfie, but she wants more of the background in the pic." He gave a long-suffering sigh, but his eyes twinkled with humor.

The young woman aimed a crinkling grin at the man. "Thanks, hon."

Joe took the camera and backed up several feet. The two positioned themselves next to the wall, looped their arms around each other, and smiled.

Joe centered them against the backdrop of sand and turtles and snapped the photo. As he handed the camera back to the appreciative pair, a clumsy movement at the edge of the pool caught his attention.

He resumed his observation spot and focused on a turtle struggling to climb the sandbar. None of the turtles moved as gracefully on land as they did in the water. Their weight obviously affected them. But this one's progress seemed especially laborious. He squinted through the lenses of his sunglasses and examined the turtle. To his shock, he realized it had a stub where its right front flipper should be.

"Well, I'll be... Wonder what happened to you, buddy?"

"A fishing net."

Joe zipped his attention to the blond-haired woman leaning on the wall only a few feet from him. He hadn't realized he'd spoken out loud, but now he was glad he had. The woman wore matching khaki shorts and a safari type shirt with a sewn-on patch on her left shoulder announcing Caribbean Sea Turtle Farm/Conservatory and her name.

He slipped his sunglasses to the top of his head and grinned. "You must know a lot about the turtles here..." The spelling of her name threw him, but he made a guess. "Tameera."

She grinned. "Yes, I do." She pointed to the turtle, which now positioned itself in a sunny spot and dug its snout in the sand. "Her name is Vera, short for Perseverance, an attribute she certainly has. We found her a couple of years ago, washed up on the beach and half dead from a festering wound. She'd gotten tangled in a fishing line, and who knows how long she swam out there, suffering, before a storm blew her in."

Joe shifted his attention from the turtle to the woman. The pain in her blue eyes was evident, and he experienced a twinge of guilt even though he hadn't had anything to do with the turtle's unfortunate circumstance.

"Our staff veterinarian amputated the flipper and treated the infection, all of us on staff teamed up and gave her around-the-clock care, and I did a lot of praying. Her recovery was slow with a few setbacks, but four months after the surgery, we released her into the general population of adults."

"Not back into the wild?"

Tamiera pushed a strand of hair behind her ear and sighed. "Although we work hard to replenish the wild turtle population by releasing about a hundred turtles a year into the ocean, Vera wouldn't survive in the wild. But here, she's able to live a fairly normal life, and a few weeks ago, she laid her first nest of eggs in the sandbar. That was a major celebration time for all of us. We've already transferred the eggs to our incubator, and when they've hatched, we'll take some of them to the ocean's edge and let them go. So at least part of Vera will swim free." She grimaced. "And we can pray they'll have the chance to grow to adulthood."

Curiosity caused Joe to blurt a question. "What would keep that from happening?"

She turned a somber look on him. "You."

CHAPTER 2

The man drew back and gaped at her. Tamiera couldn't blame him. She'd been accusatory, and not completely by accident. People needed to understand how their thoughtless behavior affected marine animals. If shock value would get their attention, then so be it. Even so, she didn't want to scare off a paying guest. The ticket purchases helped fund the biology side of the tourist attraction.

She extended her hand. "Forgive me for being so blunt. In my years as a marine biologist, I've seen the harm that man's garbage and inconsideration for animals has wrought. I suppose I'm a little prickly and defensive about it."

"A little?" He chuckled, and the look of shock faded beneath a grin of amusement. He shook her hand—a firm but not pinching handshake, the kind her military foster father had taught her. His dark brown hair was cut military short, and his trim physique spoke of one who was accustomed to long jogs. But his cheeks bore a heavy shadow, as if he'd skipped a day of shaving. Something the military wouldn't allow.

She slipped her hands into her pockets and squinted at him against the afternoon sun. "I'm Tamiera Davison, one of the three marine biologists who live here at the farm and care for the turtles."

"I'm Joe Phillips. It's nice to meet you." He slid his mirrored sunglasses into place, hiding his blue-green eyes from her view. "You said you live here?"

She nodded. "Right on the compound in staff cottages. It lets me track the turtles' growth, their habits, their mating behaviors. The more we know about them, the better chance we have to increase their population."

He settled his weight on one hip and tilted his head slightly. "I guess I hadn't thought about marine biologists taking care of turtles. I figured they'd focus on whales, seals, dolphins...that sort of thing."

She smiled. "I like whales, seals, and dolphins, too, but my main focus of study was on endangered marine life, and sea turtles—especially the green sea turtles, like we have here at the farm—won my heart. They really are such majestic creatures. I enjoy educating people on their contribution to our ecosystem and how we can insure they don't become extinct. I—"

A representative from one of the many tourism companies connected to the cruise industry jogged up to them. "Are you Mr. Phillips?"

Joe nodded.

"The driver sent me to tell you the time here is done. The bus needs to leave for the rum factory."

Joe glanced at wrist watch. Tamiera glanced, too. A face as large as a fifty-cent piece contained four small dials in addition to the time dial. It reminded her of the control panel on a small airplane. To her surprise it was after two thirty. She needed to get to the theater for the three o'clock lecture.

She took a sideways step away from the men. "It was nice meeting you, Joe."

He raised his hand, and she stopped. He turned to the rep. "If I skip the remainder of the excursion, is there a way for me to get back to my hotel?"

"You could take a cab, but you'll have to pay for it yourself, and you won't get a refund for the parts of the tour you didn't see."

"That's not a problem." Joe pulled out his wallet, withdrew a five dollar bill, and pressed it into the rep's hand. "Thanks. I'll see to myself from here on."

"Suit yourself." The young man trotted off.

Joe aimed his smile at Tamiera. "Okay, that clears my afternoon. You were saying...?"

For a moment, she found it difficult to form a reply. She couldn't remember any other tourist giving up a rum factory visit to stick around and talk about turtles. The choice immediately endeared him to her. Admittedly, it didn't hurt that he was as handsome as a young Tom Selleck, her foster mother's favorite actor.

She cleared her throat. "I was going to say I give lectures about the sea turtles every weekday at three, and it's..." She pointed to his watch.

He jolted. "Oh, I need to let you go."

She took a step in the direction of the theater.

"Are the lectures open to anyone, or do I need a ticket?"

She turned to face him. "You want to come?"

16

He shrugged, a very boyish gesture, and pushed his sunglasses on top of his head again. "Yeah. I'd like to hear what you have to say."

Tamiera couldn't stop a smile from growing. "Okay then. They sell lecture tickets in the gift shop, but I always carry a few complimentary ones in case I meet somebody I think could benefit from the information." She dug in her fanny pack and pulled out a ticket. Then a worrisome thought struck. "Um, do you need more than one?"

"For...?"

"Your wife, or girlfriend, or..."

He shook his head. "It's just me."

Just him, vacationing on Grand Cayman Island. Interesting. And more of a relief than she wanted to admit. "Here you are." She handed him the ticket and began a slow backpedal. "The theater is on the other side of the incubation hut. Follow the signs. Hour long program beginning at three o'clock sharp."

"Got it." He saluted and grinned.

He really was way too cute. She turned and hurried off.

Joe would say one thing for Tamiera Davison, she knew her stuff. Using slides on a huge screen and touches of humor, she'd held the attention of her audience for every minute of the half hour lecture. Even the youngest of those seated in the wooden, old-fashioned movie theater-type chairs hadn't fidgeted. Then she'd opened the floor for questions. Here they were, twenty minutes into the Q-and-A, and not once had she so much as hesitated before giving an answer. Joe's brother Justin was in the habit of saying pretty girls had empty heads, but not this one.

Although he'd never been terribly interested in the ecosystem or in endangered species—his major was business, not biology—by the end of her lecture, Joe was trying to find a way to incorporate biology into business. Why not? If the new resort was going to be built right here on the island, in close proximity to where the wild sea turtles made their nests, it only made sense to capitalize on the ecological happening and allow it to boost visitors to the place of business.

A boy maybe ten years old shot his hand in the air, and Tamiera pointed to him. He stood. "If I wanted a sea turtle for a pet, what kind of habitat would I need for it?"

A few people laughed, and the boy slunk into his seat.

Tamiera folded her hands in front of her and pinned the boy with a serious look. "Although many reptiles have been trapped and sold into the pet industry, it's my personal belief that wild creatures should be allowed to live in the wild. Creating an appropriate habitat for a turtle that will eventually grow to weigh 350 pounds would be a greater undertaking than an individual could manage."

Finally, a smile curved her lips. "But if you'd really like to have a pet turtle, I suggest visiting your local pet shop and searching for an aquatic turtle. Fitting a 55-gallon tank in your bedroom is easier than putting a 55,000 gallon simulated ocean in your backyard."

A few chuckles rolled.

She winked at the boy. "But keep in mind, aquatic turtles can live as long as 15 to 25 years, so this is a pretty big life investment." Sadness pinched her brow. "Too many people take in these exotic pets unaware of the responsibility. When they grow weary of it, they release the pet, thinking it will survive on its own. Sadly, many do not, and those that do can disrupt the natural ecosystem into which they're released. So always do your research and carefully consider the pros and cons of adopting a 'wild' pet."

The man seated next to the boy raised his hand. "You said wild creatures should be allowed to live in the wild, but you have how many turtles here living in captivity?"

Joe sucked in a breath. The man's question seemed more inquisition than inquiry. He experienced an unexpected shaft of sympathy for her. Joe observed Tamiera under the harsh light from the track of bulbs above the stage.

"We have between thirty and forty adults capable of reproducing, and of course countless turtles in various stages from babies to juveniles. Of the turtles hatched here on the farm, twenty-five percent are released into the ocean in the hopes of rebuilding the wild population. Another twenty-five percent are sold into the food industry."

A few people groaned, and a small boy near the front said, "Yuck!"

Tamiera laughed. "If you aren't accustomed to eating turtle meat, you might think so, but it really is quite popular in many cultures. Over-hunting for meat is part of the reason the green sea turtle is considered endangered.

Since it takes twenty-five years for a turtle to mature enough to reproduce, many are caught and killed before they reached maturity. By selling turtles specifically into the food market, we can protect those in the ocean and let them grow up and become mamas and daddies someday."

Joe raised his hand. "There are fifty percent unaccounted for. What happens to those?"

She aimed her smile in his direction, and he couldn't deny it had an effect on his pulse. "Some are kept here to use as breeders in the future, some are released to zoos or biology programs elsewhere, and some..." She sighed. "Some don't survive. But in the wild, of the roughly hundred hatchlings in a nest, fewer than ten percent make it to adulthood. Here on the farm, closer to ninety percent survive since they aren't exposed to predators or pollution. So our efforts are very valuable to preserving the future of green sea turtles."

She glanced at the wall clock. "And that's all the time we have today. Thanks so much for coming, and I hope you'll visit the Caribbean Sea Turtle Farm and Conservatory again soon."

The attendees ambled out, some stopping to shake Tamiera's hand or thank her. Joe stayed in his seat until the last ones departed, then he stood and made his way to the front, clapping softly and rhythmically as he went.

She folded her arms across her chest and tilted her head, a half smile lifting one corner of her lips. "What?"

He slipped his hands into his pocket. "Very well done, Miss—" He glanced at her left hand, but it was tucked under her elbow. "Are you Miss, Ms., or Mrs. Davison?"

"Miss."

Never married. Such a shame. Or was it a blessing? He gave himself a mental shake. "Miss Davison. Your knowledge is commendable, but more than that, you have a natural delivery style. I'm surprised you didn't choose to go into teaching. You seem to have an innate ability."

She hit a switch that plunged the room into darkness. She gestured to the exit door, and he followed her into the small, glass-walled foyer. "Funny you'd say that." She kept talking as she locked the theater door with one of the keys dangling from her belt. "My foster mom was a teacher, and she encouraged me to go into education—job security and all that. But I guess I was too restless back then. I wanted something...bigger."

She laughed, and pink crept into her cheeks. "And I can't believe I told you that. I'm not usually so open with people I just met."

"Then I'm flattered." He meant it, too. The longer he was with her, the more he liked her and the more he wanted to know about her. Was coming to the sea turtle farm on the first day of his month-long stay on the island chance or providence? Either way, he wasn't ready to tell her farewell. "You know, there's a really nice restaurant on the beach next to my hotel. I was told they serve terrific steaks and sea food. Would you be interested in meeting me there?"

She bit down on the corner of her lip and gazed at him so intently he wondered if she could see underneath his skin. "Well..."

He held up both palms, as if under arrest. "Dinner only." He lowered his hands and smiled. "I'd like to hear more about your work here with the turtles and how they play into the ecosystem on the island. Why not satisfy our hunger while you satisfy my curiosity?"

CHAPTER 3

Tamiera examined her reflection in the full length mirror attached to the back of her closet door. She'd donned one of her church outfits—floral skirt, pink silk tank, and white lace cardigan. In the States in November, she wouldn't have worn white, but here on the island the rules were different. She reached for her beaded wedge flip-flops, the fanciest shoes she owned.

As she popped them onto her feet, she released a nervous giggle. Had she really agreed to a date? And with someone she'd met in passing at the turtle enclosure? Her foster parents, Don and Carol, had always required any boy who asked her for a date to spend an evening with the whole family in their home before they allowed her to go out on her own with him. They would probably shake their heads in dismay at what she was doing tonight. She sat up, frowning. Or would they?

Joe Phillips was clean-cut, polite, well-spoken, and respectful. An awful lot like Don. She'd encountered some men, including some who wore three piece suits, who gave her the heebie-jeebies. But she had been at ease with Joe from the first minutes. Even when she pretty much told him he personally was the reason why her beloved sea turtles were endangered, he hadn't gotten defensive or angry. He'd listened. Seemed to care.

Her heart fluttered, and she pressed her hand to her chest. "Stop that!" He was here on vacation. He'd be around for a few days and then gone. Getting attached was not a good idea. She repeated the admonition to herself at least a dozen times on her short drive to the Sandbar Grill about three miles from the conservatory. But the moment she spotted him waiting outside the restaurant's carved front doors, her traitorous heart took wing like a sea gull.

Whoa, Carol, Tom Selleck's got nothing on Joe Phillips.

Her knees went a little wobbly, making crossing the paved walkway a challenge. Watching her feet—getting her focus off of his muscular frame

21

showcased by trim-fitting tan trousers, a pale mint button-down shirt, and paisley tie—helped. By the time she reached him she could meet his smiling gaze and offer a casual greeting.

"Hi. You're early. Or am I late?"

"You're just on time." He slid his fingers down the length of the tie then held to the tip, his eyes crinkling slightly in the corners with his smile. "I intentionally came early so you wouldn't worry you'd been stood up." He pulled the door open. "I already put our names in, so we should have a table before too long."

She crossed the threshold, getting a whiff of his aftershave as she passed him. Something fruity yet spicy—an intoxicating scent that was too quickly overtaken by the savory aromas coming from the restaurant's kitchen. He'd no more than stepped in behind her when the woman behind the *maître d's* desk called, "Phelps, party of two."

Never had an announcement felt so personal.

Joe touched her spine with his fingertips and guided her forward. They trailed a server across the plush carpet between linen-draped tables lit by flickering lanterns to a small, square corner table next to windows overlooking the beach. An L-shaped, padded bench provided the only seating, and Joe held out his hand in invitation for her to slide in first. When she was settled, he hitched his pant legs and slid in on the opposite side, putting them at right angles to each other. Not as intimate as side-by-side, but definitely less formal than across.

The server handed them their menus, listed the evening's specials, which included two different alcoholic beverages. Somehow Tamiera wasn't surprised when Joe ordered water with lemon for both of them.

The server nodded. "I'll be back in a few minutes with your drinks. Please feel free to peruse the menu, and let me know if you have any questions." He hurried off.

Joe snapped his menu open and smiled at her over the top of it. "Have you eaten here before?"

She'd lived on the island for more than three years and joined co-workers for dinner at various restaurants, but she'd never gone to what her roommate Paula called a *take-a-date place*. She opened her menu. "No, but if everything tastes as good as it smells, we ought to enjoy our dinner."

"I came in yesterday evening after I checked in at the hotel. The grilled halibut was the best I've ever tasted. I might have it again."

She glanced at the entrées and located grilled halibut. Her mouth began to water when she read the accompaniments. "That sounds perfect." She set the menu aside, and so did Joe.

The waiter arrived with their water glasses. "Are you ready to order?"

"Yes. The lady will have the halibut, and I'll have the shrimp and scallops scampi."

"With fettuccini or angel hair pasta?"

"Angel hair, please."

"Tonight's soups are turtle with shell pasta in a tomato base or creamy clam chowder." The server's gaze flicked from Joe to Tamiera.

Although it was technically Fall, which was always soup season in her foster home, soup didn't appeal in this tropical climate. Besides, she couldn't bring herself to eat turtle soup and, in her opinion, eating a clam was too much like chewing on a pencil eraser. "None for me, thank you," Tamiera said.

"What about salad? Our house Caesar is very popular."

Joe looked at Tamiera. "Would you like a salad?"

The halibut came with garlic mashed potatoes and sautéed spinach, so she really didn't need a salad, but she loved a good Caesar. "Well..."

Joe grinned. "Two Caesars, please."

The server nodded, picked up their menus, and departed.

Joe took a sip of water then linked his hands on the edge of the table. "I have to ask...have you ever eaten turtle soup?"

Tamiera fiddled with her napkin and tried not to grimace. "No. After working with the turtles all day, I'd feel like a, well, a cannibal eating turtle meat."

He laughed, but not in an offensive way. "I kind of figured that. You wrinkled your nose when he mentioned the turtle soup."

"I did?" Her face went hot. If she still had the menu, she'd fan herself.

"You did. Which let me know how much you love the turtles. So tell me, where did your interest in green sea turtles begin?"

Not a hint of humor tinged his expression. Tamiera pushed aside her embarrassment. "When I was a first grader, my teacher gave us all books for Christmas. Mine was a picture book about marine life. I grew up in North Dakota in the middle of an agricultural community, so whales, dolphins, and sharks all seemed so glamorous compared to horses, pigs, and cows. I guess you could say my fascination began then, but not until my foster parents took me on a K-Love cruise—"

His forehead puckered. "A what cruise?"

She released a short laugh. "K-Love. It's a Christian radio station. They host a cruise every year to various locations, and the ship is packed with Christian music artists." Worry struck. He was a very nice man, but if he didn't know about K-Love, was it possible he also didn't know about Jesus? If so, she'd need to get her interest in him in check. She chewed her lower lip for a moment and gathered her courage. "Do you listen to Christian radio?"

Joe took another sip of his water. "I rarely turn on the radio. I'm pretty busy with my job, and I'm also easily distracted—I was one of those wiggly kids in school, so the radio playing would have a negative effect on my productivity. But if the artists sing contemporary Christian tunes, I'd probably know some of them. My church back in Florida has a worship band that plays before every service, and they do mostly contemporary Christian music."

The flutter in her heart returned. "Joe, may I ask you a personal question?"

"Sure."

"Are you a Christian?"

Without a moment's pause, he nodded. "Yes. I became a Christian when I was fourteen at a youth camp. How about you?"

"When I was sixteen in Sunday school."

"That's great." A genuine smile lit his face. "Sure makes a difference, doesn't it? I—"

Their server arrived with two crisp Caesar salads. He placed them on the table and then whisked a wooden pepper grinder from his back pocket. "Pepper?"

Both Tamiera and Joe nodded, and they leaned back to allow the server space to operate the grinder. When he finished, he bobbed nods at them by turn. "Enjoy. Your dinners will be here soon."

Joe stretched his hand to her. "Shall I say grace?"

Tamiera battled a lump in her throat as she listened to him offer a brief yet heartfelt prayer. None of her co-workers had ever offered to pray with her. She hadn't realized how much she missed holding hands at the table and listening to someone thank God for their food.

"Amen." Joe released her hand and picked up his fork. "I interrupted you.

You were saying your foster parents took you on a K-Love cruise to...?"

He might not listen to the radio, but he sure listened closely to her. She smiled as she stabbed her fork into the bed of Romaine lettuce. "To celebrate my seventeenth birthday. We booked an excursion to the turtle farm, and I fell in love with the turtles. From that moment on, I knew I wanted to be a marine biologist, and I knew I wanted to work with sea turtles."

The remainder of the evening flowed smoothly, with none of the awkward pauses she'd experienced on first dates with other men. Not that she'd dated a great deal. Her foster mother called her reserved, but Tamiera inwardly admitted she was cautious. Her early years in a volatile household—so volatile the state determined she'd be safer away from her parents—still impacted her even after her dozen years with the Wagners, who'd provided a secure, loving home for her. She marveled that she felt so at ease with Joe, as if she'd known him for months rather than hours.

They both declined dessert, Joe paid the tab and left a generous tip, then he escorted her to her car. He leaned against the hood, crossed his ankles, and slipped his hands into his trouser pockets, the picture of ease and charm. She held the fob to unlock the door, but she hesitated, reluctant to leave his presence just yet.

"Tamiera?" His voice emerged softly, almost hesitantly, in contrast to his intense gaze, which never wavered from hers. "I really enjoyed tonight."

A gentle, salty breeze tousled her hair, and a delightful shiver wiggled through her. Was it the tropical air or his presence creating the pleasant sensation? "I did, too."

"Is the turtle farm open tomorrow?"

"Yes. We're open seven days a week to accommodate tourists."

He sighed. "Ah. I was hoping maybe you got Sundays off."

She released a soft laugh at his crestfallen expression. "You didn't ask if I was working tomorrow. If you had, I would have said no."

His eyebrows shot up, and he straightened like a soldier coming to attention. "So you're free tomorrow?"

Tamiera shrugged. "It depends on what time. I attend service at one of the Baptist churches from nine until close to noon."

"Where is it located?"

Another shiver, as sweet as the scent of plumeria, descended. She gave him the address, but she couldn't resist asking, "You want to go to church?

Even though you're on vacation?"

His smile went straight to her heart. "Of course I want to go. Even when I travel, I look for a place to worship on the Lord's day. Why should He bless the work of my hands if I don't carve out time for Him?"

She couldn't wait to tell Carol and Don about Joe. He was rapidly meeting all the characteristics they prayed her future husband would possess. *Christian, gentlemanly, honest, kindhearted, unselfish...* She gave a little jolt. What was she thinking?

"Could I talk you into giving me a personal tour of the island after the service?"

Still reeling from where her thoughts had taken her, Tamiera didn't answer.

His grin turned teasing. "Do you accept bribes? I'll buy your lunch...and even your dinner if the tour runs long."

She shook her head, laughing. *Impish* might not be on Don and Carol's list, but it made for a perfect addition. "No bribe needed. I'd enjoy showing you the island. It really is beautiful. God did some of His best work here."

"All right then." He plucked the fob from her fingers, hit the unlock button, and opened the door for her. "I'll see you at church in the morning. Good night, Tamiera."

CHAPTER 4

Having Tamiera close to him on the creaky wooden pew during Sunday morning's worship service proved more distracting to Joe than any blaring radio ever could. Her perfume, something light and flowery, invited him to lean close and breathe it in. If he hadn't known better, he'd think the delicate aroma came from the trumpet-shaped, bluish blooms climbing on vines all over her knee-length skirt. Morning glories? Or honeysuckle? Mother would know. Tamiera's pale blue blouse with a ruffle circling the neckline brought out the baby blue in her eyes. Her sunshine colored hair went perfectly with the sky blue shirt. She looked so wholesome, so classy, so—

He gave himself a shake. He needed to pay attention to the service. By keeping his gaze forward even when Tamiera crossed her leg and smoothed the skirt over her tan knee, a feminine gesture that begged to be observed, he heard every word of the last half of the pastor's sermon on Jesus using only a few loaves and fishes to serve the multitudes.

The service closed with a hymn, and sharing a hymnal with Tamiera offered a feeling of oneness he wanted to experience again and again. He caught her eye as they sang the final line, *I'm standing on the promises of God*, and her smile sent his pulse into double beats. He'd better be careful. He was supposed to be here on business. Dad wouldn't approve of him getting tangled up in a romance instead.

They grabbed burgers and fries at the requisite Mickey-D's—was there anywhere the franchise hadn't reached?—and took their lunch to the stretch of beach fronting his hotel. The entire expanse of white sand and frothy, turquoise sea milled with swimmers, sun-bathers, and seagulls.

Tamiera sat at one of the picnic tables and pulled the food from the bag. "This table doesn't have an umbrella, so we'll have to be careful."

He laid out napkins in lieu of plates. "I put on my long-lasting sunscreen this morning."

"That's wise, but I wasn't talking about the sun." She glanced skyward. "Look out for the birds. They're pretty brazen. They'll swoop in and steal food out of your hand. Sometimes not even an umbrella keeps them at bay."

Joe laughed, envisioning it. He bowed his head to say grace, and something fluttered next to his head. He ducked and opened his eyes. A seagull flew off with one of his French fries in its beak.

Tamiera's merry laughter rang.

He scowled at her. "That's not funny. My favorite part of the meal is the French fries, and that bird robbed me." He examined the remaining fries. "Do you think the bird dropped feathers or mites on the rest of them?"

She stopped laughing, but her blue eyes twinkled. "Here—trade with me." Two more birds circled above them. "Put your napkin over the food and your hands over the napkin while we pray."

He made the prayer short, determined to eat what was left of his lunch. They ate quickly, him scanning the sky for more feathered thieves and Tamiera choking back chuckles. She didn't eat the French fries, though, so she probably didn't trust them to be mite- or feather-free. When they finished, they wadded the wrappers and put them in the sack. Tamiera scattered the French fries in the sand, and a horde of birds swooped in.

Joe grabbed the sack and ushered Tamiera to a trash barrel. He eyed the squawking birds. "Should they be eating fast food?" If it wasn't terribly healthy for people, it seemed to follow that it wasn't healthy for seagulls, either.

She sighed. "Probably not. But it's better than some other things I've seen them eat."

They ambled toward her car, the sand pulling at their shoes. "Like what?"

"Bits of tinfoil, cigarette butts, rotten food..."

The sadness in her tone took some of the shine off the day. "People are careless, huh?"

"Careless, yes, and sometimes deliberately destructive." Her blue eyes clouded. They reached her car, and she hesitated next to the driver's door. "God created this beautiful place for us to live, and too often we abuse and misuse and waste what we've been given." She shook her head. "And this is supposed to be a day of excursion, not of ruminating. I'm sorry."

He touched her shoulder. "No apology necessary. You love this place and you want to see it cared for. There's nothing to be sorry about in that."

A smile curved her lips. "Thanks, Joe. Are your shoes meant for walking?"

He blinked twice, confused. "What?"

She pointed at his feet. "Are your shoes comfortable enough to wear for a lengthy walk? If not, you might want to go to your hotel room and change."

He checked out her footwear—flip-flops with strings of dangling beads on the toe straps. "What about you?"

She grinned. "I put my slip-on sneakers in the car before I left this morning, so I'll be fine."

He grimaced. "I probably ought to change."

"Okay. I'll wait here."

He jogged across the parking lot and entered the hotel lobby. Cool air washed over him, enticing him to slow down and enjoy the minutes out of the sun, but Tamiera was standing out in the heat. He took the stairs instead of the elevator—only three floors up—and kicked off his leather loafers inside the door. He changed into a pair of tan shorts and removed his tie, but didn't swap his short-sleeved button down for a T-shirt. Tamiera was dressed so nice, he didn't want to look like a slob next to her.

In less than five minutes, he trotted across the parking lot on tennis shoes-covered feet. She'd changed her shoes, too, and waited in the driver's seat with her door open. He darted to the passenger side and slid in. "Ready. So where are you taking me?"

She closed her door and turned the key in the ignition. "To Queen Elizabeth the Second's Botanical Park." She eased out of the lot into the flow of traffic. "It's one of my favorite places on the island, because they work so diligently to preserve the natural environments of the island." She flashed a quick grin. "There are some great panoramic views that'll take your breath away, and it's the only place in the world where you'll find Cayman blue iguanas in the wild."

"Are Cayman blue iguanas considered marine animals?"

"Nope, they're lizards, but they're endangered, like my green sea turtles. Can you believe in 2003 there were only about a dozen blue iguanas left in the wild?" She shook her head and huffed. "Most of their habitat was taken over for pastureland for cattle, and my turtles' predators, feral dogs and cats, nearly wiped them out."

Her cheeks blazed pink despite the cool air blasting from the vents. He gave her shoulder a quick rub. "But they're making a comeback?"

The bold color faded. "Yes, thanks to efforts from environmentalists who placed them in a protected area, although they'll never be as plentiful as they once were." She turned a thoughtful glance on him. "You might never get another chance to see a blue iguana living free of a zoo enclosure."

"I'm glad I'll have the chance today then."

Her smile rewarded him. He settled back and watched the green landscape outside the car window, occasionally glancing at Tamiera's sweet profile. He admired her passion for God and His creation. He approved her unpretentious appearance. He marveled at the wealth of knowledge she possessed. Granted, they'd only been together for a few hours, but he hadn't yet encountered anything he didn't like about her. He sensed it wouldn't take much for him to fall headlong into love with her, the woman. But love led to marriage, and marriage led to establishing a household. Tamiera was a marine biologist. Marine life existed in abundance in Florida, but the state couldn't offer her green sea turtles. Her home was here, and his home was there. He'd be wise to steel himself against falling in love.

They spent an enjoyable two hours roaming the beautiful gardens and visiting the information stations at the botanical park. He snapped photos with his cell phone, and Tamiera kept up a steady stream of chatter, feeding him as much or more information about the island's history, flora and fauna, and wildlife than he'd have learned from a paid tour guide.

From the botanical garden, she drove to the Mastic Reserve for another lengthy hike through the subtropical forest, another area fast disappearing due to man's encroachment. Tamiera pointed out wild orchids, various bright-plumed birds, and lizards smaller in size than the blue iguanas and able to move much faster, thus giving them an opportunity to escape predators. Seeing the island through Tamiera's eyes gave Joe an appreciation for Grand Cayman's beauty and rich history. More than that, it gave him an appreciation for the woman herself.

Joe checked his cell phone as they left the reserve and discovered it was already past six o'clock. Little wonder his stomach had been growling. Although sweaty and tired from hiking the trails, Joe still offered to take Tamiera to a restaurant.

She stopped at the edge of the parking area and tipped her head. Remorse glimmered in her eyes. "I hate to say no because I've really enjoyed the day, but I'm on duty at six tomorrow morning in the incubation hut, so I should probably go home. Besides"—she gestured to her limp skirt and wrinkled blouse—"I look a fright. No maître d would welcome me into their dining room."

He grinned at her wind-tossed hair and held up one finger. "First, you don't look a fright. You're adorable. Really."

Even more so when she blushed.

Two fingers up. "Second, you need to eat, especially since you gave away half your lunch to the greedy seagulls."

She ducked her head and giggled.

"And third..." His hand with three fingers raised trembled slightly. Should he say it? "I'm not ready to say goodnight to you yet."

Her gaze met his. "Joe..."

He shoved his hand in his pocket and sighed. "You fascinate me, all right? You're so smart and so funny and so cute. I'm feeling...what's the best word? A crush. Like I have a crush on you."

She turned her face aside, giving him a view of her delicate profile. "That's nice, because, well, I kind of feel that way, too."

He stepped into her line of vision and searched her face. "You do?"

She nodded, the becoming flush staining her cheeks again.

"Then can I take you to dinner?"

She shook her head. "Not tonight. Not with early duty, and not while I'm all sweaty and stinky."

He grinned. "You smell okay to me."

"Probably because you've become immune to it and can't really smell the reality anymore." She sniffed her armpit and grimaced. "I shouldn't be in polite company."

He threw back his head and laughed. "All right, Miss Stinky, I'll let you off the hook tonight. But when is your next free evening? I still owe you dinner for the great tour."

Her eyes widened. "But I haven't shown you nearly everything yet. There's still the Seven Mile Beach, and the reefs, and Pedro's Castle, and—" She clapped her hand over her mouth.

"What's wrong?"

She lowered her hand. "Am I presuming?"

"Presuming what?"

"That you want me to show you the rest of the island? Maybe you'd be better off joining the different excursions offered by the tourism bureau. Because I don't have a lot of free time, and your vacation time is probably limited, too."

He needed to clarify his purpose for being on the island, but a strand of hair drifted across her cheek, completely derailing his intention. He tucked the silky wisps behind her ear. "I don't want any other tour guide than you. Whatever free hours you have, I'll grab them. That is, if you don't object to reserving them for me."

"I don't object."

He'd never heard sweeter words.

CHAPTER 5

For the next three weeks, Joe's schedule revolved around Tamiera's schedule. If she was free, he set aside his work and spent the hours with her. Saturdays and week days offered limited time, but she gave him all of Sunday. He'd expected her to be off duty on Thanksgiving day, but she explained the islands were British territories and therefore didn't celebrate the American holiday. The islanders celebrated Christmas in addition to the British Boxing Day, but Joe wasn't sure he'd still be on Grand Cayman that far into December.

When he wasn't with Tamiera, he viewed parcels of land available for purchase. He researched business licensing, requested bids from three different construction companies based on his speculative blueprints, and gathered information about taxes and building permits and average salaries for hotel employees.

By the end of the first week in December, he had all the information necessary to make a resort hotel in Grand Cayman a reality. All he lacked was a piece of land on which to build the resort. He shared the results of his research with his father from his hotel room during a FaceTime chat.

Joe gestured to the files of paperwork on the large desk in the corner of the executive suite. "Even though Grand Cayman is considered a tropical paradise, the actual construction costs will be less than we paid to build the hotel in Miami—and that's taking into consideration shipping in the materials. Of course, the resort here won't be as big as the Miami hotel, which means the number of rentable rooms will be fewer. But that shouldn't affect the profit because we'll conceivably be able to ask double what a Miami room brings."

"So the potential for profit margin is higher than average." Dad's forehead pinched into a thoughtful scowl. "What did you determine about suites versus rooms?"

"The resorts I toured have an equal number of each available, and the rooms fill the fastest. Some family groups visit, but most of the people who come are looking for a private get-away with one special someone." The special someone who'd been filling his dreams the past several nights crept in and stole his focus. "I wrote out a...um..."

He cleared his throat, chasing Tamiera to the back of his brain, and leafed through a stack of papers. "Ah. Here it is." He held the paper aloft and scanned the numbers. "It's no surprise rooms take up fewer square feet than suites. Basically we can fit five rooms into the same space as two suites. Given the square footage of the entire structure and the higher demand for rooms, I suggest we designate the top and bottom floors of the resort for suites and put rooms only on the middle three floors. Keep in mind, the first level will also house the restaurant, kitchen, spa, gift shop, and lobby, so that'll eat up a significant portion of the floor space."

"Wait, back up... Five stories?" Dad nearly barked the question. "The Miami hotel has seven."

"I know, but five seems to be the limit around here. Hurricanes being one concern, and blocking the view of the ocean another. Every commissioner or big-whig I talked to was very firm about the number of floors."

"All right then." Dad leaned back in his chair and finally smiled, the lines on his forehead and those along his mouth relaxing. "You've done well, son. As soon as you settle on a location, we can put the construction team on our payroll. If all goes well, by this time next year, Phelps Grand Cayman Resort will be open for business."

Joe propped his elbows on the desk and leaned close to his tablet. "Dad, I had an idea...something that might appeal to guests. A lot of resorts are named for something specific to what they offer, such as Atlantis, building on the mythical undersea city, or Sandals, reminding guests of the sandy beaches. Several beaches on Grand Cayman are nesting grounds for sea turtles." He shared some of what he'd learned from Tamiera about the sea turtles' habits and their status as endangered. "What would you think about naming the resort something other than Phelps?"

Dad's frown returned. "All of our hotels bear our name."

"I know, but Grand Cayman is so far from the United States. It's so... different here."

"You want to name it the Turtle Resort?"

When said out loud, it came across as humorous. Childish. Ridiculous.

Joe rubbed his temples. "Not necessarily the Turtle Resort, but something that brings to mind turtles, like..."

"Like what?"

He sighed. "I don't know yet, Dad. But it seems a wise business ploy to capitalize on some of the natural and unique elements of the island. Sea turtle nesting is certainly unique to most people's everyday experiences."

"I can't argue with you there."

Mom's smiling face appeared next to Dad's. "Hi, Joe. How is it going over there?"

"Good," Joe said. "Dad can fill you in."

"Oh, I'm sure he will." She slipped her arms around Dad's shoulders and pressed her cheek to his. "You're not spending all your time working, though, are you? It would be a shame not to take in the sights while you're there."

Joe grinned. *All work and no play makes Jack a dull boy...* How many times had Mom used the adage to convince their hardworking Dad to let up on him or his brothers? "Don't worry, I'm taking some time to enjoy the surroundings. I've had the privilege of being escorted around by a marine biologist from the Caribbean Sea Turtle Farm and Conservatory."

Dad released a sound that was half snort, half laugh. "So that explains it."

"Explains what?" Mom flicked a look from Dad to the screen, pinning Joe with her curious gaze.

"Joe wants to name the Grand Cayman resort after turtles."

Joe rolled his eyes and groaned.

Mom gave Dad's upper arm a light smack. "Don't make fun. You put Joe in charge of this project, and if he thinks the resort should be the...the..."

"The Turtle Resort," Dad said.

Mom wrinkled her nose. "Maybe Dad's right on this one, Joe."

"I usually am."

Joe couldn't resist laughing. He loved witnessing his parents' repartee. They reminded him of couples half their age, still honeymooning. He and Tamiera joked with each other that way, too. "I admit I haven't been able to settle on a good name for the resort, but my designated tour guide might be able to help come up with at least one that you'll find appealing. I'll give you some better options the next time we talk."

They briefly discussed Thanksgiving and proclaimed he'd been missed even though his three brothers, three sisters-in-law, and seven nieces and nephews had crowded around the table. Joe assured them he'd wrap up everything and be home in time for Christmas.

"I'm glad," Mom said, her eyes misting. "It's been lonely here without you."

"I miss you guys, too." Joe hadn't realized how much until he'd seen both of them on the tablet's screen. "Love you both. I'll be in touch again soon."

They said goodbye, and the screen went blank. Joe linked his hands behind his neck and let his head fall back. His thumbs encountered knots of tension in his neck. He'd spent too much of the day hunched over a desk. But tomorrow there'd be no desk time. Sunday... Worship with Tamiera and then an afternoon of exploration. Last Thursday when they met for supper she'd told him about a quiet stretch of beach largely undisturbed by houses or businesses.

"It's so unspoiled there—still very natural. It'll give you an idea of what the island looked like before the tourism industry swooped in and commandeered much of the area." She'd touched his hand and added, *"There's something extra special there I want you to see."*

He envisioned her fervent expression, and his heart gave a lurch. Unspoiled... Natural... Special... And best of all, devoid of businesses. That meant no hotels. Would Tamiera guide him to the very piece of land for his family's newest resort?

Tamiera left her cottage and headed for her car for the drive to church. When she was halfway to the staff's small designated parking area, the pound of footsteps behind her brought her to a stop. She whirled around, fingers sliding into her purse for the little can of mace Don insisted she carry, but she recognized the person approaching. She released the can and smiled.

"Manny, hi." She hadn't seen the lanky Jamaican teen for at least a week, and she'd worried about him. "Where've you been keeping yourself?"

"My gran'ma had some sickness, and I been keeping her garden. She has a big garden with lots of vegetables she sells in market."

She squeezed the boy's narrow shoulder. "That's kind of you. I wish I'd known. I would have prayed for her. Is she doing better now?"

His smile flashed. "Much better, thank ya." His gaze whisked up and down her sundress. "You lookin' pretty, Miss Tamiera. You goin' to church?"

She nodded. "Do you want to go?"

"Yes, ma'am!"

She loved this boy's enthusiasm. She'd never met a sunnier 14-year-old. "Well, c'mon then, let's go."

As they settled into the seats, she sent a grin in his direction. "You've picked a good morning to go with me, Manny. After the service, I'm driving a friend to the dune where you helped me set the wire and mesh. Do you want go with us to check the nest?"

"Yes, ma'am!"

She laughed. She hadn't expected anything else. "Let's get going, huh?"

CHAPTER 6

By the time Tamiera reached the church, her stomach was knotted with worry. The few men she'd dated in college got possessive after a handful dates—and not in the protective way Don had added to her list of future-husband attributes. Although she couldn't exactly classify her excursions with Joe as official dates, they had spent quite a bit of exclusive time together. How would he would react to Manny's unexpected presence?

Joe was waiting outside the doors of the church, and his smile didn't dim even a smidgen when she introduced Manny and told him the boy would be spending the afternoon with them. Instead, he shook Manny's hand and gave him a genuine welcome.

Friendly, kindhearted—definitely on the list. She couldn't have asked for a better response.

She sat between the two for worship service, and midway through the sermon she realized her heart was aching. She identified the source. For the first time since she'd moved out of Don and Carol's house, she was experiencing a sense of family. Usually she sat by herself in church. Even though she shared her days and most meals with co-workers, she'd still remained alone. Single. Solitary. Having Joe on one side and the teenage boy on the other filled her with longing to end her solitary existence and be part of a family again.

Her mind tripped through the list she and her foster parents had made when she turned sixteen and was deemed, by their standards, old enough to date. After Don left the room, Carol had taken Tamiera's hand. *"Remember to be careful about dating. Yes, it can be fun and exciting to have a boy want to spend time with you, but dating comes with responsibility. Dating is the precursor to marriage. If you can't think of the boy as a potential husband—someone you could give your whole heart to for the rest of your life—then be careful about dating him.*

And, no matter how much you like the boy, never sacrifice your standards for a few hours of fun that could lead you into regret."

At the time, Tamiera had inwardly rolled her eyes and considered her foster mother hopelessly old-fashioned. Now, almost ten years later, she appreciated the wisdom the woman tried to bestow. She risked a glance at Joe's profile. Chiseled features, unusual blue-green eyes, clean-shaven jaw, neatly trimmed hair. They hadn't put *ruggedly handsome* on the list. Joe exceeded expectation. If only he was an islander rather than a vacationer.

She gave a mental jolt. Was he vacationer? He'd been on the island for three weeks now, longer than the usual length of time for visitors. When she'd asked him how he spent his time when she was at work, he'd claimed he was making contacts for his family's business. Her heart took a little leap inside her chest. Maybe he intended to establish some sort of business on the island. Maybe he intended to make Grand Cayman his home. Maybe—

"Please bow your head for our closing prayer."

Tamiera inwardly groaned. She'd completely missed the last half of the sermon. She closed her eyes.

"Dear God, giver of life and bestower of blessings, please guide and direct us. Let us seek Your will above all things..."

A lump filled her throat. Not once during the past few weeks had she consulted her heavenly Father concerning her growing affection for Joe. She'd found herself contemplating a relationship with him, measuring him against the list of attributes she and her foster parents had created, pondering how a long-term relationship could work, but she hadn't asked God if Joe was the one He'd chosen for her.

Forgive me, Father, for not seeking Your guidance. Direct me now. Let me follow Your will concerning my relationship with Joe and in everything else in my life. I trust You to do what's best for me.

"Amen."

With the prayer's end, people rose to leave. Joe and Manny followed Tamiera across the grassy churchyard to the gravel parking area. The two chatted about the sermon, and her heart warmed as she listened to Joe patiently answer Manny's questions.

Manny caught up to her. "Miss Tamiera, Mr. Joe tell me even though Jesus has gone to heaven now, He still can heal people like He did in the Bible if we pray. I am going to pray for Jesus to keep the sickness away from my gran'ma so she can be in her garden the way she loves."

Tamiera flashed an approving smile at Joe then focused on Manny. "That's a very unselfish prayer. My foster father told me that Jesus is still in the miracle business, so Jesus certainly can keep the illness away, and He'll do it if it's His will for your grandmother."

Manny's face clouded. "How could it not be His will for my gran'ma to be well and able to dig in the soil?"

Tamiera leaned against the car. "The thing is, Manny, God's thoughts are a lot higher and deeper than ours because He doesn't only see today, the way we do. He sees tomorrow and all the way into the future. He sees how things that happen now affect things that will happen later."

The boy still looked confused.

She sought an example, and an idea struck. "For instance, God's will might be for you to spend more time with your grandmother, like you did last week. If she's able to do everything herself, you might not be as likely to go to her house every day. Am I right?"

The boy grimaced. "Ya."

"So even though we don't like to think of your grandma not feeling well, her illness might be something God uses to bring the two of you closer, or to make her even more dependent on God to give her strength."

Manny nodded in slow motion. "I think I see what you say, Miss Tamiera. Thank you for explaining to me God's will." He grinned. "Hooph, to think like God might make my head hurt."

Joe laughed and put his arm around Manny's shoulders. "It's a lot easier for us to trust God than try to think like Him. So how about we all agree that His will is best and then do our best to follow it, huh?"

"Yes sir, Mr. Joe."

Joe's gaze latched onto Tamiera's. His blue-green eyes, almost the color of the beautiful sea water that lapped against Grand Cayman's shores, seemed to search her very soul, and she couldn't look away. Did his words to Manny hold deeper meaning concerning their blossoming relationship? She held the car fob in her hand, and her fingers tightened on it, inadvertently hitting the unlock button. At the *click!*, their gazes broke apart, leaving her oddly close to tears.

Joe reached for her door handle with a jerky motion. He cleared his throat and bounced a half-smile across Tamiera and Manny. "I don't know what you had in mind for lunch today, but I'd prefer something other than fast food. Is that little cafe in the shopping district open on Sundays? I really enjoyed the lobster hoagie and slaw I had there earlier this week and wouldn't mind a rerun."

Manny licked his lips. "Mm, I like the way you think, mon."

The boy's comment broke the tension. Joe burst out laughing, and Tamiera couldn't resist joining him. She gestured to the car. "Get in, you two. If we want an outdoor table, we need to get there as quickly as possible."

Tamiera parked her car at the edge of the road above the beach. Her stomach was so full it ached, but what would she have left on her plate? The sandwich and coleslaw tasted so good, she couldn't bring herself to waste even a bite. Then Joe ordered creme brûlée for each of them. The creamy vanilla custard with its caramelized sugar and cinnamon topping paired with a cup of strong Jamaican coffee had perfectly finished the meal.

She groaned as she pulled herself out of the vehicle. "Okay, if I waddle down this slope, it's all your fault, Joe."

Joe and Manny grinned at each other. The two of them had formed a fast friendship during their hour-long lunch, and although she teased them about leaving her out, she secretly celebrated. Manny needed male influences in his life. Even if Joe was only here temporarily, it still benefited the youth to spend time with a Godly man. Joe's ease with the young teen gave her a glimpse of what kind of father he would be. Joe Phelps grew more appealing by the moment.

They followed Tamiera down the sandy slope, still joking with each other. She dodged tufts of thick grass and a few spiny cacti. She pointed at the latter and peeked over her shoulder at Joe.

"An island folklore is that Christopher Columbus visited and planted cacti during one of his explorations. I don't know if that's true, but it does seem unlikely that the desert plants are indigenous to the island."

Joe raised his eyebrows and nudged Manny. "Did you hear her? Indigenous... She's pretty smart, huh?"

Manny's smile grew. "She very smart, mon. An' she strong, too, so don' be dissin' 'er." He only spoke slang when he was very comfortable. Joe had obviously won over the islander.

She shook her head, giving both of them a teasing scowl, then laughed. "Manny, do you want to show Joe the nest?"

The boy's whole face lit. "Yes, ma'am! Come on, Mr. Joe."

Manny grabbed Joe by the elbow and pulled him past Tamiera to the smooth patch of sand where the wire cage and its cover of mesh still stood. He began gently untwisting the ties holding the mesh in place. Tamiera crossed to the opposite side of the enclosure and helped Manny lift the mesh from the wire circle.

"Miss Tamiera and me put this here to keep dogs from digging up the eggs. The dogs, they will eat the eggs before the turtles can hatch. Sometimes cats will, too. But not this batch. Our wire cage stayed strong, and that means these turtles will grow big enough to push out of the shells and try to reach the water, right, Miss Tamiera?"

How Tamiera hoped the entire batch of hatchlings would reach the safety of the sea before birds or other predators caught them. Of course, there were other dangers in the ocean, too, but she didn't want to squash Manny's enthusiasm. "That's exactly what we prayed for."

Joe crouched and seemed to carefully examine the enclosure. "Do you put these things around every turtle nest?"

"No." Tamiera ran her finger along the top edge of the wire. "I don't always spot the nests. But as often as possible, we try to protect the nest and give the turtles a fighting chance to develop and hatch."

He stood and scanned the beach in both directions. He whistled through his teeth. "You were right about this area. Completely unspoiled." His brow furrowed, and he aimed a thoughtful look in her direction. "Do you happen to know if this patch of ground is available for purchase?"

Her heart turned a somersault. If the land was owned by a private citizen who cared about the turtles as much as she did, then the beach could be made off-limits to human encroachment, allowing the turtles to nest undisturbed. "The land survey at the city offices would give you that information." Hope made her pulse beat hard and fast. "Why do you want to know?"

He slipped his hands in his pockets and smiled. "Because this would be the perfect spot for my business's newest resort hotel."

CHAPTER 7

Tamiera's expression changed from sunny to stormy so quickly Joe took a backward step. "What's wrong?"

She gaped at him. "What's wrong?" She pressed her palms to her temples for a moment and then her arms flew in wild gestures. "Did you really ask what's wrong? Haven't you listened to anything I've said when we've talked about the turtles? They need protection. Do you have any idea what harm it would do if you built a hotel along this beach?"

Joe put up both hands. "Whoa, slow down. I wouldn't build right on top of the nesting grounds."

"It doesn't matter, Joe! You could build it half a mile away and people would still walk to this beach. They'd get close to the nesting turtles and take stupid selfies. They'd interfere in the hatchlings progress to reach the sea. We've encroached on every other piece of this island where the turtles return and try to lay their eggs. This is the only— Oh!" She groaned and sat in the sand. Elbows on her knees, she gripped the sides of her head and hung her head low. "Why did I bring you here?"

Manny scurried close and knelt beside her. "Miss Tamiera, don't be angry at Mr. Joe. He didn't know. He knows now, so he won't put a hotel here." The youth raised his troubled gaze. "Will you?"

Joe turned aside from Manny's questioning, hopeful expression. He couldn't give an answer. Not yet. In his three weeks on the island, he hadn't found a piece of land this perfect. He could already envision the building covered in peach colored stucco with aqua window awnings and gray-green portico tile so it would blend seamlessly into the landscape. The location was close enough to town for easy shopping but far enough away to escape the city's noise and busyness. Dad would approve this patch of ground in a heartbeat.

"Mr. Joe...?"

Joe turned to the pair on the sand near the wire cage. Manny looked unwaveringly into Joe's face, but Tamiera stared across the water. Tears quivered on her lower lashes. The boy's disappointment and Tamiera's sadness pierced him, but what could he do? He was a businessman sent to secure the best spot for the newest Phelps resort hotel. Dad was counting on him.

He swallowed hard. "I'm sorry, but I have to make inquiries about this plot of land."

Tamiera rose stiffly and reached for the mesh, which flapped in the light breeze. "Help me refasten this to the wire, Manny."

He obeyed without a word, his gaze flicking from Tamiera to Joe and back. Betrayal shimmered in his dark eyes. She understood how he felt. She'd been duped. She could cross through one qualifier on her list of attributes—*honest*. Joe had misled her, using her knowledge as the springboard for his business venture. A venture he'd never bothered to explain. He wasn't a visitor to the island, he was an intruder. He had no desire to protect her turtles, he wanted to exploit them for his own selfish gain. Her chest ached so badly it was agony to draw a breath.

She and Manny finished securing the mesh. She looped arms with the boy and turned toward the road without so much as glancing in Joe's direction. Anger surged through her, carried on a wave of deep hurt. She'd trusted him, and he'd taken advantage of her.

"Let's go."

Manny stayed next to her as they climbed the rise, occasionally glancing over his shoulder. Joe followed, and when they reached her car, he stretched his hand to her driver's door.

She stepped in front of him and glowered. "Don't."

He lowered his head. "I'm sorry, Tamiera. I know I've disappointed you."

"Disappointed doesn't even come close." There was much more she needed to say, but not in front of Manny. She wished she could take off with Manny and leave Joe stranded along the road. The miles long walk to his hotel in the midday sun might burn the memory of this stretch of unblemished beach from his mind. But she couldn't set such a poor example for Manny. "Please get in and I'll take you to your hotel."

He leaned close. "Take Manny home first so we can talk."

She shook her head. "I'm done talking. Clearly you don't listen to me." But he had listened. Attentively. Seemed to absorb her words as if each one was precious to him. How could she balance the Joe who'd seeped into the crevices of her heart with this cold businessman who'd shattered her? She shook her head hard, clearing her thoughts. "Manny, you ride shotgun, huh?"

No one spoke on the drive to Joe's hotel. When she pulled up to the entrance, Joe leaned forward and put his hand on her shoulder, but she shrugged it off. He sighed and left the car without telling either her or Manny goodbye.

Manny folded his arms over his chest and sat with his lower lip pooched out while she drove to the little house he shared with his mother and several younger siblings. She parked, and half a dozen dogs charged the car, barking. They sounded ferocious, but she'd learned they backed off quickly if approached. Manny reached for the door handle.

"Hang on a minute, please." She waited until the boy angled his gaze at her. "I'm sorry our day ended so abruptly, and I'm sorry I got so angry. I shouldn't have acted that way. It was childish, and I set a very poor example. Will you forgive me?"

The youth sighed and turned to fully face her. "I'm not angry with you, Miss Tamiera. I know why you got mad. The turtles, they matter to me, too." He squinted. "I liked Mr. Joe. And I thought..." He jerked his gaze to the side window.

"What is it?"

"Me and Mr. Joe and you talked about God's will. That bad things sometimes happen so God's will can be done." He gulped. "Is it God's will for Mr. Joe to build a hotel where the sea turtles nest, even though we think it is bad?"

Manny spoke so quietly, she had to strain to hear him over the muffled yips from the pack of dogs, but he might as well have screamed them directly in her ear for the pain they caused her.

"Oh, Manny..." She'd been neglectful in praying about her relationship with Joe. Then she'd spouted off without a thought about behaving in a manner pleasing to her Father. Now she floundered in answering a question that could very well impact Manny's fledgling faith for the rest of his life.

She closed her eyes for a moment, seeking guidance. Then she took Manny's hand. "Let's pray together right now. Let's pray for God's will concerning

Mr. Joe's hotel, the turtles, and the beach, okay?"

They bowed their heads and prayed silently. A tear slipped free and slid down her cheek while she shared her burden and concerns with the One who knew best. She asked God to direct her future relationship with Joe, to open both of their hearts to His will over their own, and ended by placing the expanse of beach and her beloved sea turtles into God's keeping. Even though neither of them spoke their prayers aloud, a calm settled around her—a peace in the middle of the storm. She opened her eyes and found Manny sitting quietly, his gaze pinned on her.

He smiled. "You no worry now, Miss Tamiera. Remember? We trust God knows best."

Over the next several days, Tamiera paused often in her duties to send up a quick prayer. *"We trust God knows best,"* Manny had said, and she claimed the statement for her own. Whatever happened—whether Joe built a resort on the beach or not—she chose to trust God would bring something good from it. When she was not quite seven years old and was taken from everything familiar, she'd thought her world was falling apart. But growing up as Don and Carol's foster daughter was a blessing beyond what her fractured home could have offered. God had proved Himself faithful in the past, why wouldn't He be faithful in the future?

On the ninth of December, the eggs Vera had laid hatched in the incubation hut. Tamiera and one of the other marine biologists, Scott, witnessed the little hatchlings breaking from the shells and lurching clumsily over each other on the incubator floor. She and Scott hooted with joy and high-fived and even hugged each other.

After counting the hatchlings—ninety-two in all—Tamiera darted to the door. "I'm going to go tell Vera."

Scott laughed and shook his head. "All right. Congratulate her for me, too."

She grinned and hurried off. Fewer tourists visited in early December, so she had a mostly clear pathway to the turtle enclosure. She caught hold of the edge of the cinderblock wall and pulled herself up on its ledge. Swinging her feet to the inside, she scanned the area for Vera. With so many turtles lounging in the sand or swimming in the simulated sea, it took awhile, but she finally located the turtle close to one of the palm trees at the far edge of the enclosure.

She hopped down and followed the wall to Vera. She crouched and cupped her hand under the turtle's leathery chin. "Guess what, old girl? You're a mama! Ninety-two babies." A lump filled her throat. "Ninety-two turtles that wouldn't have been born if we hadn't found you and brought you here." She scratched Vera's chin, and the turtle raised her head and released a little grunt of pleasure. "You have such great perseverance. I'm so proud of you."

"So am I."

The male voice took her so by surprise, she jerked. She lost her balance and fell on her bottom. Palms planted in the sand beside her, she looked up and met the blue-green gaze of Joe Phelps.

CHAPTER 8

Joe stacked his arms on the warm ledge and peered over the wall at Tamiera. How had he managed to last five days without gazing upon her sweet face? For a few seconds, he just

looked, admired, enjoyed. Before he could stop it, a chuckle rumbled from his chest.

She arched one eyebrow. "Is something funny?" The question could have been tart, but she ruined it by letting her lips quirk into a half grin.

"That wasn't a you're-funny chuckle. It was a I'm-happy-to-see-you chuckle." He sighed and braved an honest confession. "I've missed you."

She pushed herself upright and brushed off the seat of her knee-length shorts. He waited for her to make the same admission, but she pointed to the shortest part of the block wall. "If you want to talk, meet me over there."

Her invitation heartened him. Maybe she'd gotten over her anger at him. He hoped so. He'd hated having such animosity between them. They walked on opposite sides of the barrier to the lowest section, and he held out his hand. After a moment's hesitation, she took hold, and he assisted her over the wall. She brushed herself off again then aimed an impassive look at him.

"Did you pay to get in?"

He blinked twice. "Well, yeah. I kinda had to. They don't let you in without a ticket."

"Did you buy a ticket for the lecture?"

He shook his head and glanced at his wristwatch. Two thirty-five. He grimaced. "You've got the three o'clock lecture, don't you?"

"Monday through Saturday, like clockwork." She looked into the enclosure, and her expression softened when her gaze seemed to light on Vera. "It'll be so fun to tell everybody about Vera's hatchlings. It's a success story deluxe." She fixed her blue-eyed gaze on him. "If you want to come to the lecture, I'll give you a ticket. It'll probably be a small crowd today. December's our slowest month."

He wouldn't pass up the opportunity to watch her in action again. "Thanks, I'd like that."

Tamiera opened the theater at a quarter till three, but no one came to hear the lecture. He couldn't determine from her expression if she was disappointed or not by the lack of attendance. At three-fifteen, she turned out the lights and locked the door.

He grazed her arm with his fingertips. "I'm sorry no one showed up."

She shifted to squint up at him and shrugged. "It's not so unusual for this month. I'm glad you didn't waste your money on a ticket." She glanced left and right, chewing her lower lip. "Joe, I'd really like to talk to you, but I'm on duty until five. So..."

He understood. "Would you meet me at six at the turtle nest?"

Her brows pinched. Indecision played in her expression.

"Please?" He gathered his courage. "And if possible, bring Manny, too. I'll have everything we need for a picnic lunch."

She tipped her head. "Lunch? At six in the evening?"

He grinned, recognizing the teasing glint in her eyes. "Picnic supper then. Will you come?" He held his breath.

She seemed to cease breathing, too. "All right," she said with a whoosh of breath.

He blew out his held breath and smiled. "Thanks, Tamiera."

Tamiera stopped at the top of the rise and gawked at the scene below. This was a picnic? From what planet had Joe descended?

Manny's mouth hung open. He pointed mutely.

She nodded. "Yeah. Unbelievable." She kicked off her flip-flops and eased down the rise on bare feet. Manny followed close behind her.

Joe rose from the opposite side of the linen-draped table and smiled as they approached. "You're right on time." He took Tamiera's hand and raised it to his mouth. His breath, as warm as the sand beneath her feet, met her skin. Then his lips touched her knuckles, sending tingles up her spine. He released her fingers as he straightened and gave Manny a light clop on the shoulder.

"Glad you could make it, mon."

Manny snickered. He glanced across the snow white china and polished silverware shining in the sun. "This is no picnic, mon." He gestured to his ragged tank top, sagging athletic shorts, and laceless sneakers. "It's too fancy for me. I better go home."

"You sure?" Joe tapped one finger on the large silver dome covering a platter in the center of the table. "I've got jerk chicken, sweet potato wedges, grilled corn-on-the-cob, fresh pineapple, and—"

Manny licked his lips. "Okay, I stay." He plopped onto the closest chair.

Joe laughed and rounded the table. He pulled out a chair for Tamiera. "Have a seat."

Her knees went a little wobbly. His gentlemanly treatment always affected her. She'd tried to rein in her feelings during their days apart, but the flutter in her chest and the quiver in her knees proved she'd failed. She cautiously settled on the seat, concerned the legs would sink into the sand and spill her. Then she noticed the plywood platform supporting the table and chairs. He'd thought of everything.

She smoothed her hand over the chair's linen slipcover and watched Joe take three long strides to the remaining chair across from hers. "Where did you get all this stuff?"

He shrugged. "Some of it from the hotel, some from an events caterer."

Suspicion niggled. "You didn't pull this all off between three o'clock and now."

"No, which makes me really glad you didn't turn me down." His charming smile sent the tingles climbing her spine again. "Do you want to talk first or eat first?"

"I say eat," Manny said.

Tamiera laughed softly. She fingered the edge of the cloth napkin. "I'm not sure I can take a bite until I know what your plans are." *Your will, Lord. Let us do Your will.*

Joe aimed an apologetic look at Manny. "Sorry, mon, but she outranks you. If you want, you can eat while we talk. Is that an acceptable compromise?"

The boy nodded. Joe held out his hands, and she and Manny took hold, forming a circle. Joe bowed his head. "Dear God, bless this food to the nourishment of our bodies, and bless our hands to the betterment of Your kingdom. Amen."

She'd never heard such a short prayer, but somehow it was sufficient. Joe lifted the dome, and a wonderful aroma rose with it. Her stomach growled. She grimaced. "Maybe you and I should eat while we talk, too."

Joe threw back his head and laughed. "All right then. Dig in."

Despite the linen and china, they tossed convention aside and ate picnic style, everyone reaching at once and mostly using their fingers instead of the forks.

Tamiera's first bite of jerk chicken left sauce on her cheek, and she quickly wiped it away. Part of her feared the answer, but she needed to know. "Joe, did you buy this plot of land?"

He paused, holding a blackened corn cob beneath his chin. "Yes, I did. When we're done eating, I'd like to walk the entire expanse with you and make sure I went far enough to encompass all of the areas where turtles might nest."

Her appetite fled. She put the chicken on her plate and grabbed the napkin. She cleaned her hands in tense, jerky motions. "Oh."

"Tourism is the number one industry on the island, and frankly I'm surprised this stretch of beach hadn't already been purchased. I bought an entire mile of beachfront, but I'll buy more if I have to."

She wadded her napkin beside her plate and hung her head, battling tears and begging God to help her see the good in having the area taken over by a resort.

"Because if I don't, someone else with less concern for preserving the environment will come along and buy it."

Her head snapped up. Even Manny paused in eating and stared at Joe. Hope beat in her breast like a moth against a glass globe. "So...so you bought it, but you aren't going to build on it?"

He stood and put his hand on Manny's shoulder. "Do you mind eating by yourself for a little bit? I want to show Tamiera something."

Manny shrugged, smiling. "Might not be nothing left when you get back."

"We'll take that chance." He extended his hand to her. "Come with me, please."

She took his hand and allowed him to guide her up the rise and to a large, flat piece of ground where the land dropped sharply to the water and waves crashed melodiously against the exposed ground.

He released her and held both arms wide. "This is where Green Turtle Haven, a Phelps family resort, will stand." He took hold of her shoulders and turned her to face east. Roughly a quarter mile away, the lone wire cage stood sentinel, no bigger than a soda can from this distance. "On this side of the building on the upper level we'll build an observation deck with telescopes so guests will have a view of the nesting grounds and maybe have the chance to watch the hatchlings make a dash to the sea."

Her heart pounded so hard she could hardly draw a breath. "An observation deck?"

"Yes. I want people to be able to witness the wonder of the turtles' activities but keep the area as undisturbed as possible. So I'll protect it by constructing fencing, something like chain link so people can see past it but hopefully a little more attractive. I'm still exploring options."

"But—"

"Shh." He angled her to the west, where the sun was beginning its descent to the ocean. "We'll build a terraced staircase down to the beach on this side so guests can access the water, enjoy picnics, and have a clear view of the sunset." He gently turned her once more, so she was looking straight out at the turquoise water. "This is the view people will enjoy from the lobby. Breathtaking, isn't it?"

Was the view making her breath come in little spurts, or was it caused by his nearness—his hands resting lightly on her shoulders, his voice in her ear, the musky scent of his aftershave teasing her nostrils?

"Speaking of our lobby, it will have the requisite gift shop, but in addition to the typical island souvenirs, we'll sell books about the green sea turtles and keep a video of one of your lectures playing at 30-minute intervals. People who come to Green Turtle Haven will experience the wonders of the island as well as receive an education about the turtles, and they'll leave with a greater understanding of the importance of protecting our marine life for future generations."

Delight wiggled through her, and she hugged herself to hold it in.

His hands slid from her shoulders to her forearms, and he pulled her against his length. His chin brushed the top of her head. "I don't want to take you away from Vera and the other turtles at the turtle farm—that's your place of service—but I hope you'll have some spare time to spend with me. I'm going to need a friend on the island."

She broke free of his hold and spun to face him. "You're moving to Grand Cayman?"

His smile warmed her. "I still have to get approval for an extended stay, but I've submitted the paperwork. I want to oversee the construction, make sure we aren't tearing up any more of this wonderful, unspoiled landscape than is absolutely necessary. And my dad wants me to manage the resort for at least the first year after it's built."

She gazed at him in amazement, her thoughts racing. Her lips opened and closed, but she couldn't form words. It seemed as if God had chosen to answer her prayers about the beach and about continuing a relationship with Joe in one fell swoop.

He lifted his hand and tucked her breeze-tossed hair behind her ear, then let his thumb trail along her jaw. "I want to get to know you. Really know you. Because I think God has something special in store for the two of us. I—"

"Hey, mon!" Manny stood beside the table with his hands on his hips. "You gonna eat or not?"

Tamiera burst out laughing. She cupped her hands beside her mouth and hollered down, "Save me a corn-on-the-cob. We'll be right there."

Manny gave her a double thumb's up and plopped back into his chair.

She turned to Joe. Sunlight brightened the green flecks in his eyes and put a gleam of copper in his dark hair. She really needed to add *Drop-dead hunky* to her list and then put a big checkmark beside it.

She caught his hands and held tight. "I want to get to know you better, too. Whatever God's will is for us, I trust Him to make it known."

He nodded, kissed the back of her hand, and then aimed her for the rise. "Let's go enjoy our picnic before Manny finishes it all."

Hand in hand, they ran down the hill, their laughter adding harmony to the song of the sea.

SUFFICIENT GRACE

CONSTANCE SHILLING STEVENS

To *Judy Meyer*
My friend, my prayer partner, my encourager.
You have been such a godly example of grace.

"And He said unto me, 'My grace is sufficient for thee;
for My strength is made perfect in weakness.'"
2ND CORINTHIANS 12:9A KJV

CHAPTER 1

Nora Courtland slowed her steps. The normally sleepy town of Pine Ridge buzzed with excited voices as people hailed each other along the street. The unusual activity pulled her brow into a puzzled frown. What in the world was going on?

"Nora." Felecia Puckett, the proprietor of Puckett's Cafe, scurried in Nora's direction. "Have you heard the news? Well, of course you have, being the clerk at the courthouse and all. Isn't it exciting?" Felecia squeezed Nora's arm.

Nora glanced past Felecia where the pastor of their little church spoke with a couple of local farmers in an animated manner, obviously pleased about whatever had the town humming this morning.

She returned her attention to Felecia. "Isn't what exciting?"

"You're so silly, Nora. The new mill, of course. Everyone's talking about it." The woman fanned herself with her apron. "Just think what it will mean to Pine Ridge to have our very own mill." She leaned closer to Nora and lowered her voice. "Maybe I can contract with the people building the mill to provide meals for the workers." Her eyes sparkled. "Prosperity is right around the corner."

Felecia hurried toward the cafe, leaving Nora standing, open-mouthed, on the street. Yes, she knew about the new mill, had briefly met the man who planned to build it. Asa Bennington and his assistant, Donovan McNeary, had spent considerable time with Mayor Jarvis Gilbert over the past month. But no official announcement was to be made until the purchase of the land had taken place and the details were finalized. How did Felecia—and apparently everyone else—find out about it?

Mrs. Hollstead from the church choir, Mr. Deifendorffer from the feed and seed, and Udell Adler, one of the local farmers, all accosted Nora with similar questions, each one urging her to divulge information she was obliged to keep confidential. She begged off, saying she was not authorized to discuss anything.

Before she could reach the courthouse, Pastor Parkin approached with a broad grin. "The building of the mill is wonderful news for our little town. Families will be moving to the area. More commerce always brings in new folks. The church will grow, more souls will be won..." He rubbed his hands together.

Nora bit her lip. "Pastor Parkin, I'm really not supposed to talk about—"

He nodded. "Oh, I know. But it's hard to keep great news like this quiet. I'm gathering the church elders to make plans for meeting the needs of our growing community." He waved as he lumbered down the street, whistling "Praise God, from Whom All Blessings Flow."

How on earth did this get out? As the county clerk, Nora was well aware of the need for privacy until those in authority were ready to release the information to the public, usually by way of a headline story in the local newspaper. She increased her stride, hoping nobody else would intercept her before she could reach the courthouse.

She slipped in the door and blew out a breath of relief, only to draw it sharply back in. Myron Snead, publisher of the *Pine Ridge Register*, rose from his seat on the short bench outside the mayor's office when Nora entered. He pulled a notebook from his brown tweed coat and a stubby pencil from the graying fluff behind his ear.

"Miss Nora, what can you tell me about this new mill? What is the name of the developer? Where's he from?" He furrowed his brow. "He a carpetbagger?" He licked the tip of his pencil and held it, poised and ready, over the notebook like a vulture over a critter breathing its last. "How many jobs is this mill going to bring to the area? And what about property taxes? If the mill raises property values, taxes are sure to follow suit. I heard—"

The front door slammed and for one split second, Nora didn't know whether to jump or feel relieved at the interruption. She jerked her head toward the welcome intrusion. Mayor Gilbert's beady black eyes glared at Mr. Snead.

"Myron, if you have any questions of an official nature, you ask me, not my clerk." The mayor huffed across the room as if he'd had to escape the same town folk who had pelted Nora with questions. He nudged Mr. Snead toward the door to his office. "The *Register* is the only newspaper in the county. You're going to get the exclusive story anyway, so just wait until—" Mayor Gilbert's voice faded as he closed the door between his office and Nora's.

Nora sank into her desk chair as muted voices rose and fell behind the mayor's door. She sorted through the dealings of the past few weeks in her mind and kept returning to same determination. Nothing was finalized yet.

"So why does half the town know about the mill?" She could only be sure of one thing—she hadn't uttered a word about the tentative deal to anyone, not even to Grandpa. Failing to exercise discretion could result in immediate dismissal, and she needed this job.

Had Mayor Gilbert already discussed the coming mill with area business people? Surely he wouldn't do that if the deal wasn't near completion. Truth be told, she was as excited as everyone else. She tucked her lower lip between her teeth. Without having seen any final documents, she was obliged to keep quiet, despite wishing she could dance on the rooftop.

Donovan McNeary guided the carriage bearing his boss, Asa Bennington, and himself past the "Welcome to Pine Ridge" sign. Weathered buildings in sad need of paint and a main street lined with ruts recounted Donovan's original opinion of the town formed a month ago—unremarkable. Chattanooga or Atlanta would be a better location for the mill, but Mr. Bennington didn't pay him for his suggestions.

Bennington pulled the stub of his cigar from his mouth and used it like a pointer to gesture toward the town. "Look at this, McNeary. These people need us. They may not like northerners, but they'll sing a different tune when we bring jobs and business opportunities to this place." A snide laugh punctuated the man's comment. "You see the way they live. We won't encounter any opposition here."

Donovan slid his glance to catch a sideways look at his boss. Hair slick with pomade, belly straining the gold buttons on his fancy brocade vest, and an ever-present arrogant smirk defined the man. Donovan swallowed back the resentment he held for men like Bennington—men whose goal was to line their own pockets by working their employees fourteen hours a day, six days a week, for low wages. Bitterness filled his mouth. Would his parents be alive today if they'd not worked themselves to death in the factories up north, fearing to take time off when they were sick, lest they lose their jobs?

Bennington flicked his cigar ashes. "I hope the mayor has twisted the arm of the owner of that tract of land. He said they haven't lived here in years, so they'll surely be anxious to sell."

You mean they'll surely accept your ridiculously low offer. Bennington's shrewd business practices were laced with greed and disregard for sentiment. Being employed by such a man soured Donovan's stomach. He wished he had the nerve to quit, but as Bennington so often reminded him, there weren't many employers willing to hire an Irishman.

Donovan halted the carriage in front of the town's only hotel and hopped down. He grabbed the two bags and followed Bennington inside. Donovan recognized the short, skinny clerk with his pencil thin mustache from their previous visits.

"Morning. Mr. Cordell, right?"

The clerk nodded. "Henry Cordell, at your service. You gentlemen want the same rooms you had when you was here a couple o' weeks ago?"

Bennington snorted. "Can't you do any better than that?"

Mr. Cordell glanced from Bennington to Donovan and back. "I'm sorry, sir, those rooms are the best we—"

Bennington snatched the pen, dunked it into the inkwell, and scrawled his name in the register. "McNeary, bring the bags."

The clerk fetched the keys and handed them to Donovan. "I reckon you fellas must be the ones buildin' that new mill everyone's talkin' about. Seein' as how this here is the third time y'all—"

Bennington spun around so sharply, the clerk took a startled step backward. "What do you know about our business?"

Mr. Cordell's eyes widened. "I—I don't kn-know your business. But like I said, everyone's talkin' about it, so I just supposed..."

Donovan picked up the bags. "Thank you, Mr. Cordell. If we need anything else, we'll let you know."

"Yessir." The clerk tugged a frayed handkerchief from his pocket and mopped his brow.

Bennington scowled before preceding Donovan up the stairs. The worn carpet, wobbly banister, and faded curtains echoed the same impression he'd formed when they arrived. The town could do with a little prosperity.

As soon as they reached their side-by-side rooms, Donovan set Bennington's fine, tooled leather valise on the bed and turned to leave, but Bennington slammed the door, rattling the pitcher and bowl on the washstand.

"This deal hinges on putting every detail in place and pushing the paperwork past these ignorant, backwoods hillbillies before they can figure out the land is worth three times what I'm offering for it. Furthermore, I don't want to be delayed by having to negotiate. Absolute discretion is necessary."

Donovan wondered if Bennington's bark could be heard all the way to the lobby. "I assure you, Mr. Bennington, I have no idea how the hotel clerk learned of the mill. I haven't spoken a word about this transaction to anyone outside your offices."

Bennington jerked the straps that held his valise closed, pawed through its contents, and withdrew a flask. He removed the stopper and took several gulps. "Must have been that stupid mayor." He sat on a threadbare chair and kicked off his boots. "Go to the courthouse and tell that idiot to come here. Until the ink is dry, we can't risk being overheard."

"Yes, sir." Donovan turned toward the door.

"Don't forget who pays you, McNeary. And don't forget who it was that hired you when nobody else would." Bennington took another swig from the flask and belched before muttering a disparaging remark about Donovan's Irish heritage and waving him out of the room.

Donovan dropped his own bag in his room and hurried to do Bennington's bidding. The county clerk greeted him when he entered the courthouse.

"Good morning, Mr. McNeary." The young woman with hair the color of polished walnut glanced down at a paper on the right-hand side of her desk and frowned. "Was Mayor Gilbert expecting you? I don't see any appointments on his schedule."

Donovan waved his fingers. "We arrived a day early, Miss—" How embarrassing. She remembered his name, but he couldn't remember hers.

Her dark brown eyes sparkled when she smiled. "Courtland. Miss Nora Courtland."

Donovan gave a slight bow. "Miss Courtland. Is the mayor in?"

"I'm sorry, he's not. But I'll give him a message as soon as he comes in."

Donovan glanced to make sure nobody overheard, and lowered his voice.

"Please ask the mayor to come to Mr. Bennington's hotel room at his first convenience. Room twelve."

He allowed his eyes to linger a few extra moments on the lovely young woman. "If I may be so bold, may I ask you to accompany me to dinner one evening this week, Miss Courtland?" Her company would be a welcome improvement over Bennington's.

Her eyes widened for a moment before she responded. "I take care of my elderly grandfather."

Was that a refusal? He lifted his shoulders. "What do people do for amusement in Pine Ridge?"

A blush pinked her cheeks. "There is a fellowship dinner coming up at church."

Church? A bitter twinge bit his gut. "If you'll excuse me, my boss is waiting." He lit out the door without pausing to bid her a good day.

CHAPTER 2

Nora gave the pot of soup one last stir, then bent to pull the pan of cornbread from the oven. Soft humming floated in through the back door that she'd propped open to allow the breeze to cool their small house.

"Grandpa, supper's ready."

A minute later, the old man shuffled in from the back porch with bits of wood peelings clinging to his faded shirt. He gave Nora a peck on the cheek. "Can I help?"

The weakness in his voice made Nora cringe inwardly. "No, everything's ready. Have you been carving again today?"

Grandpa moved to the table. "Of course. Never let it be said Hosea Courtland sat idle."

Nora set the crock of butter where Grandpa could reach it. "Nobody would ever say that about you."

She sat and took Grandpa's hand while he prayed over their simple meal. As he slathered butter on a piece of cornbread, Nora watched his hands. They weren't as shaky today.

"Did you finish any pieces?"

He poked a bite of cornbread in his mouth and nodded. "Finished another jewelry box. That makes six now. Me 'n' the Lord started workin' on a chess set."

Grandpa always carried on a running conversation with God while he worked his carving knife. The thought brought a smile to Nora's heart.

Grandpa blew on his soup before slurping it from the spoon. "Pastor Parkin stopped by today. Word around town is there's gonna be a new mill built right here in Pine Ridge. A lot o' folks'll be happy about that, the farmers in partic'lar. Preacher's happy 'bout more people comin' to settle here and the church growin'."

Nora couldn't fault the pastor or her grandfather for talking about the new mill. She supposed there wasn't anyone in town who hadn't heard about it by now. Still, she side-stepped the topic.

"Did Pastor Parkin take your finished pieces with him?"

"Yep." He wiped his mouth. "His son-in-law's goin' to Atlanta end of the week. He's got a buyer down there for 'em. Preacher said if I finish that chess set by next month, he'd make sure it gets to Atlanta."

They finished their meal and Nora brought Grandpa a cup of coffee and two of his favorite oatmeal cookies. While he munched, she cleared the table and tackled the dishes, noticing the faraway look in his eyes as she worked.

"What's on your mind, Grandpa?" As if she couldn't guess.

A small smile tweaked the corners of Grandpa's mustache. "Reckon we can go out to the river Sunday afternoon? I'd like to have a visit with Eve."

Nora knew Grandpa's heart called him to return to the burial place of his love. Grandpa's Cherokee bride, his Eve, rested beneath a simple mound of rocks along the riverbank. The passage of fifty-two years hadn't erased Grandpa's grief. Nora heard his heartache every time he talked about raising their young son, Nora's father, alone.

Nora fixed her scrutinizing gaze on him. "If you feel up to it."

He flapped his hand toward her. "I'm just fine."

He'd never admit to the progressive weakness that was stealing his vitality. The walk wasn't easy for him, even if they took the buggy as far as they could. But if she tried to suggest he shouldn't go, she knew he'd just go by himself. "We'll go, Grandpa."

As with every visit she could remember from the time she was a child, they'd sit while Grandpa "talked" to his late wife. Then he'd reminisce and tell Nora stories—most of which she'd heard many times before—about when he was a young man and fell in love with a Cherokee girl, and the animosity and bigotry they faced. Even after his wife died and the Cherokees were removed by way of what some called the Trail of Tears, many people still treated Hosea Courtland with disdain over the years.

"We'll make sure nobody sees us."

The painful thoughts must have shown on her face. Grandpa rose from his chair and brought her his empty coffee cup. He squeezed her shoulder. "Nora girl, it's been more'n fifty years. Most folks've forgotten all about those times."

She slipped her arms around his neck. "But you haven't."

"No." Grandpa's shoulders sagged. "I'll never forget."

He walked over to his rocking chair by the fireplace and settled himself while Nora finished cleaning the kitchen. She wiped her hands on her apron and came to sit near her grandfather while he read their evening scripture out of Second Corinthians.

His eyes softened when he read of God's mercy and faithfulness. "And He said unto me, 'My strength is sufficient for thee, for My strength is made perfect in weakness.' Most gladly therefore will I rather glory in my infirmities, that the power of Christ may rest upon me."

Guilt pricked. Trusting in God and resting on His all-sufficient grace is what Grandpa had lived all his life. Nora dropped her gaze to her folded hands in her lap. How she wished she had the faith to do the same.

Nora picked up a stack of papers to be filed and rose from her desk just as the front door opened. She looked up. Donovan McNeary stepped in, his sandy brown hair slightly askew from the brisk breeze. When his eyes connected with hers, her breath caught.

He ran his hand over his tousled hair. "Good afternoon, Miss Courtland."

His smile set off strange flutters in her stomach. "Good afternoon, Mr. McNeary. How may I help you?"

"My employer, Mr. Bennington, has sent me with a message for Mayor Gilbert. Is he in?"

"Y-yes, he is." Her voice hiccuped. *For goodness sake, he's going to think you're a silly twit.* She pulled in a breath and swallowed. "I'll let him know you're here."

Her face warming, she scurried to the mayor's door and tapped. In response to his grunt, she peered in and informed the mayor of his visitor. Instead of simply instructing Nora to show him in, Mayor Gilbert strode to the door.

"Come in, come in, Mr. McNeary. Is Mr. Bennington with you?"

Nora stepped aside as the men shook hands, and she caught a whiff of Mr. McNeary's shaving soap.

"No, sir. He had some paperwork that required his attention."

The men retired to the mayor's office, but the door didn't fully close and their voices floated out to Nora's office. Mayor Gilbert said something about the surveyor's report being available in the next day or so.

Nora's interest piqued. Like everyone else, she'd speculated over the location of the new mill. Most likely it would be close to town, a centralized point for the farmers bringing their cotton and hemp to be processed. But despite the news of the mill spreading like wildfire, the building site remained anyone's guess.

Nora shrugged. In all likelihood, the mayor was planning on a grand announcement. But when Mr. McNeary spoke, his statement surprised her.

"Mayor, with all due respect, it seems to me you've gotten things out of order. Surveying land we don't yet own is premature. Mr. Bennington wants to know when you expect to get a response to his offer."

The mayor harrumphed, and even though Nora couldn't see him, she could picture the way he always waved his hand in dismissal over things he deemed unimportant. "A minor detail, I assure you. If we have the survey report in hand, it will show them we are most anxious to expedite the matter."

Nora frowned for a moment, thinking over the events of the past weeks. Had she neglected to compose a letter for the mayor or send a telegram? No, she was certain he'd not instructed her to do anything of the sort. If communications had taken place with the landowners, the mayor must have done it himself. She glanced toward his office door. Strange. He normally dispatched chores of that nature to her.

The door opened abruptly and the mayor clapped Mr. McNeary's shoulder. "You tell your boss I'll let him know the minute I hear back from the owners. I'm sure it'll be any day now. Good day." And the door closed.

Mr. McNeary turned. When he caught her eye, his smile arrested her, hampering every effort to continue her tasks. The papers in her hands fluttered to the floor like so many butterflies newly freed from their cocoon prisons. Several of them glided gracefully before landing at Mr. McNeary's feet.

Arrows of embarrassment shot through Nora. For a fleeting moment, she considered diving under her desk. But his smile only deepened as he stooped to retrieve the pages.

She lifted her hand to her forehead. "Goodness, I'm so clumsy."

His grin disarmed her. "Not at all." He swept up the papers, tapped the edges on the floor, and held out the neat stack to her. With a quick glance over his shoulder, he leaned closer and whispered. "He annoys me, too. You must possess extraordinary patience to work for him."

A giggle rose in her throat, but she swallowed it back. "Thank you."

He cocked his head. "Perhaps you'd do me the honor of having dinner with me this evening."

"I'm sorry." Surprise quivered through her to realize she truly was sorry she had to decline. She shook her head. "I have choir practice this evening."

"Oh." He crossed his arms and his eyebrows arched. "You're a singer?"

"Goodness, no." She dipped her head and added the papers to the stack on her desk. "I play the organ for the choir."

"I see. Blessed with musical talent *and* patience."

Why was she breathing like she'd just run uphill? "I-I don't know that I'd call it talent. As for patience—" She heaved a sigh. "I need this job."

He nodded, as if in commiseration. "Maybe I'll drop by and listen to choir practice." One corner of his mouth lifted in a charming, lopsided smile as he exited.

Nora sucked in a breath, a tremble shaking the floor beneath her feet. But it wasn't the floor that shook. She sank down into her chair and propped her elbows on her desk, her hands covering her warming cheeks. "Oh, my."

Donovan walked away from the courthouse calling himself three kinds of a fool and questioning his own sanity. Did he really tell her he might drop by for choir practice? What was he thinking?

While the prospect of Donovan walking into a church might delight his mother—God rest her soul—he'd not darkened the door of a church since... well, since Ma's funeral.

How Ma had grieved over her straying son, begging him to "come back to the Lord." Shame bit him to think of the years he'd allowed to slip by while he neglected the things of God. He'd thought one day he might go back to church, but he'd always been too busy trying to be successful.

He hated to see how hard his mother worked, especially after his father died. Even when she was sick, she went faithfully to work. His plan had been to work hard and rise in rank so his mother would never have to work again. Well, she was at rest now. Except that she'd left this world without seeing the sole desire of her heart come to pass.

The day of Ma's funeral, the preacher berated him, barely stopping short of blaming him for his mother's death, saying Donovan had come to church too late. Now, as then, guilt skewered him. He couldn't deny his mother would have been overjoyed to see her prayers answered. If he fulfilled her wishes now and returned to the faith he'd been taught as a child, Ma would never know.

CHAPTER 3

Nora scooped apple cobbler into a small bowl and set it in front of Grandpa, smiling when he sniffed it with appreciation. She poured their coffee and rejoined her grandfather at the table.

"That was a mighty fine Sunday dinner, Nora girl." Grandpa smacked his lips.

"I could probably serve you cold biscuits and jerky and you'd still say that." She patted his hand. "Now slow down. You're going to make yourself sick eating so fast."

He gulped a bite of cobbler. "Don't wanna dawdle."

"We have the entire afternoon." But telling Grandpa not to hurry through his meal when he planned to go visit his wife's burial place was like telling the sun not to rise.

Disappointment had threaded through her two evenings ago when Mr. McNeary had not dropped by for choir practice. At the time, she'd speculated that perhaps his boss had altered his plans. But when he didn't appear at church this morning, disconcertment niggled at her. She could understand being hindered, but if he'd stayed away from church out of disinterest, her disappointment was better directed to compassion for his soul rather than any romantic interest.

Grandpa polished off his cobbler and rose. "I'm just gonna fetch my hat. We'd best be on our way."

The dishes and cleaning the kitchen would have to wait. Clouds had gathered to hide the sunny sky they'd enjoyed while walking home from church, but that wouldn't stop Grandpa when he wanted to "spend time with Eve."

Together they hitched their old mare to the buggy and drove as far as the river. The flat rocks at the crossing poked up above the water, providing dry places to set their feet to reach the other side. Nora held Grandpa's hand to steady him as the water swirled in lazy circles around the rocks. Once on the opposite bank, they hiked nearly a half mile through the trees and underbrush until they arrived at their destination—the abandoned Cherokee burial ground. Few people knew of the place or cared about it.

But Grandpa cared. The love of his life, Nora's grandmother, rested beneath a mound of rocks now overgrown with weeds and wild grapevine. A dozen more mounds scattered along the riverbank marked the graves of Cherokees who once called New Echota home. These were the lucky ones, Grandpa had said, because they didn't have to endure the brutal Trail of Tears. They'd died at the relocation forts before the forced march started. The graves were barely recognizable to anyone other than someone who knew what they were.

Grandpa pushed dead leaves and twigs aside from Eve's grave, and then settled himself on a nearby downed log. "Eve, my love, forgive me for lettin' so much time pass between visits. I know you don't miss me near as much as I miss you. After all, you're there in heaven with Jesus."

Nora quietly stepped away to give Grandpa privacy. Over the years, she'd come to love this place nearly as much he did. Every tree and stump, every mound of rocks and the souls that rested beneath them. It used to sadden her that these graves didn't bear crosses or grave markers like those in the cemetery in town. But as Grandpa had often reminded her, the animosity held by many of Pine Ridge's residents toward the Cherokees made this remote place a more fitting and tranquil spot for their cemetery.

It had taken several years, but eventually Grandpa had released his resentment of the man who had won this land in the lottery in 1835. Lemuel Weaver wasn't a bigot. He'd merely wanted the land to homestead, a place to bring his bride from Williamsburg, Virginia. By all accounts, he'd loved this place—perhaps not as much as Grandpa did, and certainly not for the same reasons. But after several years, Lemuel had come to visit Grandpa and promised him he'd leave the graves in this small section of his land untouched.

Nora whooshed out a grateful sigh—not only for Lemuel's compassion in not disturbing the burial ground, but also for Grandpa being able to let go of his bitterness. She looked over to where he sat, leaning forward with his elbows on his knees, sharing his thoughts with Eve. Her heart swelled. One day she hoped to find a love like her grandparents had.

A distant rumble of thunder growled through the hills and hollows. She hated to cut Grandpa's visit short, but she feared if they got caught in the rain, his frail body could succumb to illness. Dried leaves crunched under her feet as she walked back to join him.

"Grandpa, it sounds like a storm is coming. We'd better go."

He glanced up at the darkening sky and nodded. He rose stiffly, kissed his fingertips, and pressed them on the rocks. "Until later, my love."

They linked arms and made their way toward the place where they could safely cross the river. But before they'd gone more than a few yards, Grandpa halted and he pointed.

"What's that?"

Nora's gaze followed the direction of his finger and spied a small piece of red cloth tied to a short wooden stake, partially hidden behind some under-brush. She'd not seen it on their way to the burial ground. Grandpa went over and bent to take a closer look.

"Grandpa? What is it?"

He pushed back some blackberry vines. "It's a marker of some sort." He grasped it and wiggled it back and forth until the stake turned loose of the red clay soil. Grandpa straightened with the flagged stake. "It's a survey marker."

Alarm carved crevices across his brow as another rumble of thunder rolled through the woods. He pointed and swept his gesture along the river-bank. "Nora girl, look for others."

"Grandpa, it's beginning to sprinkle. We'd best—"

"Look! Look for more of these markers."

Grandpa rarely raised his voice, but the intensity of his command pushed her to obey. She tramped through the trees and underbrush and located another stake with a scrap of red material tied to it. She turned to see where Grandpa was and saw him pulling up another marker about a hundred yards downriver. He slogged through the tangled growth of weeds to her side. With more strength than she'd believed him to possess, he yanked up the stake.

Rain wept from the dark clouds as distress strained Grandpa's voice. "I don't know who put these here, but nobody—*nobody*—is gonna disturb Eve's resting place." He made his way to the edge of the water and heaved the stakes into the river. He turned and held out his arms as if embracing the burial site. "Nobody."

Yesterday's rain had softened the ground along the riverbank, making navigation hazardous. Donovan grabbed a thick vine for balance as his boss batted his way past him, intent on visiting the building site again. Despite not yet receiving word from the Weaver family regarding his offer, Bennington agreed with Mayor Gilbert about the survey. Both believed having the survey already done would motivate the Weavers to accept the terms and sign the sales agreement.

"*This is about money,*" Bennington had reminded him. "*I doubt these people have ever seen that much money, much less know how to count it.*"

Bennington halted and unrolled the paper in his hands. He studied it and sent his searching scrutiny up and down the riverbank. "According to this plat, the markers should be right along here." He thrust a sausage-like finger toward the area. "Check over that way."

Donovan moved downriver, searching back and forth for the survey markers the mayor said they'd find. He maneuvered around several piles of rocks, but didn't see anything that resembled a marker.

"You find anything?" Bennington yelled through the trees as he made his way in Donovan's direction.

"No, sir. I'm looking."

Bennington studied the plat again. "This is the place we paced off three weeks ago. I remember these rock piles." He pointed at the rock mounds with his elbow. "We can use them for the foundation."

After several more minutes of fruitless searching, his boss's impatience mounted. Experience had taught Donovan that he didn't want to be the target of Bennington's irritation, but presently there wasn't anyone else nearby.

"McNeary, where are those survey markers?" Predictably, Bennington's harsh tone sliced Donovan's ear. "Why didn't you come and supervise the calculations yourself? What am I paying you for?"

Donovan sorely wished to remind his boss that Mayor Gilbert had ordered the survey on his own, and neither Donovan or Bennington knew anything about it until Gilbert informed them it was done. But Donovan did remember where the mayor had indicated the corner of the property lay. If the mayor's surveyors marked it, he could find no evidence of it now.

"McNeary, you better find those markers, or else bringing the surveyors out here to recalculate the measurements will come out of your salary—if indeed you still have a salary by the end of the day."

It wasn't that Donovan didn't believe Bennington would fire him, but this wasn't the first time the man had threatened him with unemployment when things didn't go precisely right. He chose his words carefully.

"It's possible some animal knocked them down." The speculation sounded far-fetched even to Donovan, but it's all he could think of at the moment.

Bennington snorted in disgust. "What kind of animal would knock down all four stakes and carry them off? Unless it was a two-legged animal." He wielded the tube of paper like a sword and slashed it in Donovan's direction. "You get those surveyors back out here. And I'm making it your responsibility to see to it those stakes are in deep and secure."

His boss turned and tramped toward the rocks where they had crossed the river. Donovan hastened after him, still sending his gaze darting left and right for any sign of a surveyor's marker.

They climbed into the rented buggy and Donovan turned the horse toward Pine Ridge. He could feel Bennington seething in the seat beside him. His boss drummed his fingers against the side of the buggy, a sure sign of agitation. For all Donovan knew, he might be unemployed by nightfall.

A muted growl preceded Bennington's bark. "When we get back to town, I'm going to go see Gilbert. And he'd better have a copy of that surveyor's report. You start nosing around and asking questions. I want to know who is antagonistic toward the building of the mill. If you make halfway intelligent inquiries, you *should* be able to uncover something."

The man's emphasis spoke volumes. Donovan hoped he wouldn't let Bennington down, but nothing guaranteed he'd find the answers his boss wanted.

Bennington pulled a cigar from his inside coat pocket and bit off the tip. "In the meantime, you see to it that those rocks are moved down to the river's edge where the workers can begin building the foundation as soon as the land purchase is done." He stuck the unlit cigar between his teeth and clamped down.

Donovan drew a tentative breath. "Sir, should we begin moving the rocks and preparing the site if the land deal hasn't been closed yet?"

His boss snatched the cigar from his mouth. "These southerners can't be choosy about the price of their land. If they think I'll quibble over dollars, they're more stupid than I thought. This deal *will* go through."

He poked the cigar back into his mouth and spoke around it. "I'm leaving for Atlanta the day after tomorrow to order the gears and machinery. I'll expect your report when I return, and I want the name of the person who sabotaged those markers."

Donovan didn't nod, but he swallowed hard.

CHAPTER 4

Nora brushed her hand over Grandpa's forehead. The chill he'd taken in the rain on Sunday afternoon had resulted in a cough by Monday. Now this morning, he'd refused breakfast and limped as if his whole body ached. His feverish brow sent shafts of worry through Nora.

"You're going back to bed this minute." She took his shoulders and tried to turn him around toward his bedroom, but the old gentleman planted his feet.

"I can't go back to bed, Nora girl. We have to find out who's the no-good snake that planted those markers around my Eve's grave."

He teetered slightly, and Nora tightened her grip.

"Grandpa, you're sick. And if you don't rest and keep warm, you're going to get sicker." She used a bit more strength to turn him, and even though he resisted, she successfully maneuvered him back to his bed. She pulled down the quilt and helped get him situated, but the moment she tugged the quilt back up around him, he struggled to sit up. His hand shook as he pointed his finger at her.

"I don't have time to sit in bed. Eve's resting place is in danger." He tried to throw back the covers, but Nora held them firmly in place.

"Grandpa, if I have to, I'll stay home from work today to take care of you." Even as she spoke the words, she knew they couldn't afford for her to miss a single day's work. They needed every penny. But Grandpa's health was more important.

Grandpa's bushy white eyebrows dipped in consternation and a coughing spasm seized him.

Nora quickly fetched a cup of water. "Just listen to that cough. And your fever is getting worse."

Finally, Grandpa leaned back against the pillows, spent from the hacking cough. "All right, I promise I'll stay in bed. You need to go to work. But, Nora girl—" His raspy voice turned pleading. "You must find out who's responsible for puttin' those stakes out there around the burial ground. Tell me you will."

"Shhh." Nora brushed his hair off his forehead. "I will, Grandpa. I'm going to stop by Doctor Guthrie's office and send him by to check on you." She shook her finger at him. "But you stay in bed. You promised."

He nodded and caught her hand. "We have to go back out there, to the river, to make sure those scoundrels don't stick any more markers in the ground. Nobody's gonna disturb Eve's place."

Nora squeezed his hand. "We'll talk about it later." She refilled his cup with water and set it within his reach before hurrying to finish readying herself for work.

She peeked into Grandpa's bedroom before she left and found him sleeping, so she tiptoed to the door and slipped out. As soon as she stepped off the porch, however, she lengthened her stride and pointed her steps toward the doctor's office. The detour would make her late, and Mayor Gilbert would be annoyed, but Grandpa needed the doctor. She'd simply have to make up the time to appease the mayor.

Grandpa's insistence over learning the identity of ones who planted the surveyor's markers rang in her ears. Nora knew who was responsible for pounding in those markers. It had to be Asa Bennington and Donovan McNeary. To her knowledge, nobody else had planned to purchase any land around here. To think her heart had fluttered at Mr. McNeary's smile!

The only conclusion was that they planned to build their new textile mill on top of the Cherokee burial ground. Her breakfast churned in her stomach. The same mill that had the whole town excited, the mill that promised new jobs and greater prosperity, this mill of which everyone was in favor was going to desecrate her grandmother's resting place and give Grandpa apoplexy.

She could try to dissuade Mr. Bennington from building on the burial ground, but when he and everyone else learned the reason, she'd be shouted down as surely as day followed night. She couldn't think of more than a handful of people who would agree with her and Grandpa that the Cherokee burial ground should remained undisturbed. But Grandpa always told her sitting by and doing nothing when injustice occurred made her worse than the one performing the evil deed.

A small sense of relief eased some of the tightness in Donovan's shoulders as he watched Asa Bennington head out of Pine Ridge on the road to Dalton. Once he boarded the southbound train to Atlanta, he'd be in the city several days. Bennington's pressure to learn the identity of the person who sabotaged the survey markers before he returned hung over Donovan's head, so despite Bennington's absence, tension still roiled within him.

Naming the "culprit," as Bennington kept repeating, wasn't the only thing on Donovan's list, however. Quite aware that his boss was accustomed to having everything go his way—and at times was willing to pay whatever it took for that to happen—Donovan knew his tentative plan to privately consult a lawyer could easily backfire on him.

A few of the tasks Bennington had assigned to Donovan were premature at best, and possibly illegal at worst. If there were any legal repercussions, he wanted to make sure he didn't become Bennington's scapegoat. So he planned to stop by Mr. Lawrence Templeton, Esquire's office today for some wise counsel. If his mother was still alive, she'd hand him the Bible and tell him all the counsel he needed was right there.

Before he stopped at Templeton's office, however, he needed to check in with Mayor Gilbert to see if there was any word yet from the land owners. Just as he reached the courthouse door, Nora Courtland approached from the opposite direction, panting, hair slightly askew from her obvious hurry.

"Good morning, Miss Courtland." Donovan held the door open for her.

"Good morning." She ran her fingers over her hair. "I must look affright." She peered up at the courthouse clock that read twenty minutes past eight o'clock. "I'm late."

Donovan stepped aside for her to enter. The moment he followed her inside, the mayor emerged from his office, red-faced and scowling. "It's about time you got here, Miss Courtland. What is the meaning of this, coming in here twenty minutes late? You can expect your pay to be docked, and you can thank me for not firing you on the spot."

Donovan gritted his teeth at the way the mayor bellowed at Miss Courtland in his presence. Tardiness wasn't something Bennington tolerated either, but he had a gut feeling Miss Courtland had a good reason. He curled his fingers to prevent them from seizing Gilbert's lapels and teaching him how to speak to a lady.

Still out of breath from rushing, Miss Courtland twisted the ties of her reticule. "I'm sorry, Mayor Gilbert, but Grandpa is ill. I had to go fetch the doctor."

The mayor's expression softened immediately. "Hosea is ill?"

"Yes, sir." She clasped her fingers at her waist. "I'll work late, I promise. But I really need to run home at noon to check on Grandpa."

Mayor Gilbert harrumphed. "Yes, well, see that you make up the time." He waved his hand in a dismissive gesture.

Donovan relaxed his clenched fists. "Mayor, may I speak with you a few moments?"

The mayor tipped his head toward his office, and Donovan followed him.

Gilbert closed the door behind them and pointed to a chair facing the desk. "Have a seat." He took his own desk chair.

Donovan sat and cleared his throat. "Mayor Gilbert, my employer is quite distressed over the number of people who already know about the mill coming to Pine Ridge. This information wasn't to be made public until the deal was done. Seems like the whole town knows about it. Mr. Bennington was further troubled when we visited the property two days ago, and the surveyor's stakes were nowhere to be found." He leaned forward in his chair. "While I disagreed with having the survey done before the land is even contracted for purchase, the fact remains that someone has removed the stakes."

Gilbert's brows arched nearly to his hairline, and then plunged into a deep frown. "Is that right?" He rubbed his chin.

Donovan pressed his fingertips together. "Do you have any idea who might have gotten wind of the news regarding the mill and would be opposed to it?"

Gilbert rose and crossed the room to a map. He stood studying the plat, running his finger around the areas surrounding the land in question. "Why would anyone be against the mill? It means jobs, and commerce, and prosperity, and growth, and—"

"And re-election? Is that why you told people? So you'd look like a hero?" When the mayor turned around, Donovan nailed him with a hard stare.

Mayor Gilbert sputtered. "Now see here—"

"I do see." Donovan folded his arms over his chest. "The land deal is taking far longer than you anticipated, and you didn't want to wait for folks to know what a great mayor you are, bringing in this new business."

"B-but—"

Donovan rose from his chair. "May I remind you that Mr. Bennington was the one who first contacted you, not the other way around, and you assured him you knew of the perfect piece of land for Bennington Textile Mill. Since the Weavers haven't yet responded to several letters, you think you'll just push things along a bit, am I right?"

Gilbert's tone turned pleading. "I'm sure a letter will arrive any day now. The Weaver family hasn't lived in this area for years. Why wouldn't they want to sell?"

"Hmm, so you've said." Donovan hooked his thumbs in his belt. "So, do you have the surveyor's report?"

The mayor pawed through the clutter on his desk. "I think it's here somewhere." But after several minutes, he'd only succeeded in scrambling the mess into a worse tangle.

"Doesn't Miss Courtland file documents for you?"

Gilbert shook his head. "No, not papers of this kind. Too confidential."

Donovan ran his hand across his face in frustration. The report was so confidential the mayor couldn't even find it? "Look, I have some other errands. Find the report, and I'll come back later today."

The mayor bobbed his head, still bent over his desk. Donovan shook his head and let himself out. Miss Courtland looked up as he exited the mayor's office.

"Mr. McNeary, do you have a minute?"

Donovan pulled out his watch. "I'm sorry, I really don't. I have another appointment."

She twisted her fingers. "I really must speak with you."

Pleasure spiraled through him. Maybe his visit to the courthouse was worth the trouble of putting up with Mayor Gilbert after all. "I'd be pleased to speak with you. Perhaps I can come by at noon and take you to lunch. Puckett's Cafe has tasty food." Anticipation pulled a smile into his face, but his hope plummeted when she shook her head.

"I need to go home and check on my grandfather at noon."

"Yes, of course. You said your grandfather was ill." He berated himself for so quickly forgetting her distress this morning. "What if I come by at noon and walk you to your home? We can talk on the way."

She pulled her bottom lip in and caught it between her teeth for a moment before nodding. "All right."

A wide grin stretched his lips. "Great! Th-that is, I look forward to... speaking with you." His pulse hitched and thumped. "I'll see you at noon."

CHAPTER 5

Nora sent Mr. McNeary a polite, tight-lipped smile as he held the door for her. He beamed at her in return as if walking with her was the highlight of his day. A traitorous quiver wiggled through her at the thought. Knowing what she knew, she couldn't allow silly, schoolgirl flutters to distract her from the question with which she was about to confront him.

He extended his arm to her. A few days ago, she'd have been happy to stroll down the street on Donovan McNeary's arm. Today, however, angst over Grandpa's health and anger over the apparent building site for the mill clamored for center stage.

She drew in a deep breath. "Thank you for your gentlemanly gesture, but I really must hurry to check on Grandpa and get back to the courthouse since I arrived late this morning."

Without taking his arm, she hurried down the street, forcing Mr. McNeary to lengthen his stride to keep up with her. With every step, however, a niggling wish invaded her mind—one she tried to push away, but it stubbornly refused to let go. The idea of spending a leisurely afternoon with this man, getting to know him and allowing him to know her, wouldn't leave her alone.

No matter. When she told him what was on her mind, he'd view her stand against the mill being built on the burial ground as nonsense and, in all likelihood, scorn her heritage.

His long legs had no trouble maintaining the pace she set. "What was it you wished to discuss with me?"

His question prompted her to give voice to the question that had kept her awake for the past two nights. She halted abruptly and faced him. "Are you the one who stuck those stakes in the ground out at the—" She clamped her lips shut before she could blurt out *Cherokee burial ground*. "Uh...o-out there by the river?"

His smile faded and his eyes narrowed. "What do you know about it?"

Nora's breath hitched. How much should she reveal? She didn't know this man, not truly. His reaction would doubtless be like everyone else's, at least like those who knew there were Cherokee graves out there. Decades had laid much of the animosity to rest, and she wasn't willing to dredge up the hatred that would only hurt Grandpa.

"I really must hurry." She continued on toward her home, her thoughts warring within her. His response to her question incriminated him. The fact that his smile evaporated the moment she asked only reinforced her belief. But she'd need time to give consideration to her options. For now, her priority loomed ahead in the form of the doctor's buggy tied outside their front gate.

"That's Doctor Guthrie's buggy. I want to catch him before he leaves." She picked up her skirt and broke into a run, trotting as fast as propriety would allow. Whether or not Mr. McNeary followed wasn't important now. She'd confirmed what she wanted to know.

She scurried up the porch steps and rushed to Grandpa's bedroom. He was sitting up in bed as Doctor Guthrie bent over him and listened to his chest.

"Take a deep breath."

Grandpa scowled. "If I could take a deep breath I wouldn't need you here pokin' and proddin' me."

Nora moved to the side of the bed. "Grandpa, don't be such a grouch. Do as the doctor says."

Doc glanced up. "Ah, see there, Hosea? Reinforcements." He sent Nora a grim smile. "I hope you can remind this old goat he's no spring chicken anymore. He needs to rest if he wants to get better."

Nora sighed and eyed Grandpa. "I've tried, Doctor. You know how stubborn he is."

Grandpa aimed a boney finger at the doctor. "Pert near as stubborn as you." A spasm of coughing cut off further argument.

Doctor Guthrie rummaged through his bag and pulled out a gray box. He directed Nora to fetch her grandfather a cup of water and measured a spoonful of the box's powder into it. "Stir that up and let him drink it. Four times a day, and he's to stay in bed."

He returned to his black bag and produced a small bottle with dark liquid in it. "A spoonful of this every time he gets to coughing and can't stop." He handed the bottle to Nora.

The doctor aimed his steely look at Grandpa. "Now you rest, Hosea. If I have to, I'll take you over to my place where my missus'll sit with you all day."

Grandpa's scowl would have frightened a scarecrow. "Don't like sittin' in bed."

Doctor Guthrie snapped his bag shut and shook his head. "I've had two-year-olds who were better patients." He walked to the bedroom door and shook an admonishing finger at Grandpa. "You heard what I said, Hosea. Stay put and don't give Miss Nora a hard time."

Nora bit her lip. If she weren't so worried about her grandfather, hearing the doctor scold him might be humorous. She closed Grandpa's bedroom door and walked with the doctor out to the front porch.

Deep lines furrowed the doctor's brow. "I don't like the sounds of his chest. How long has he been like this?"

Dread bore into Nora's chest. "Just two days. He wanted to go out to the burial ground Sunday afternoon and we got caught in the rain."

"Hmm." Doc nodded. "I know he's like a hound on a possum's trail when it comes to visiting the burial ground." He paused. "If it's only been two days, the pneumonia isn't too deep yet. But at his age..."

The anguish in her heart intensified. Grandpa's frailty was indeed a factor. "What do I owe you, Doc?"

Doctor Guthrie flapped his hand and pursed his lips. "Hosea's my best friend. You make sure he rests and takes his medicine. And next time he wants to go have a visit with Eve, tell him to choose better weather. I'll be back tomorrow."

She managed a wobbly smile. "Thanks, Doc."

Donovan sat at the far end of the Courtland's porch with his elbows on his knees, waiting for Miss Courtland and the doctor to finish their conversation. After being lost in thought for the past twenty minutes, mulling over what Lawrence Templeton had told him, he'd debated whether to return to his hotel room to write out his letter of resignation. Some of the duties Bennington expected Donovan to do in his absence were, indeed, illegal in the light of the fact that the property was not yet contracted. The legal ramifications would come crashing down on his head despite Bennington directing him to perform such tasks as hiring men to begin felling trees and using the piles of rocks to dam up the river.

Before he could rise from his seat, however, Miss Courtland's conversation with the doctor nailed him in place. They obviously didn't see him in the obscuring shadow of a lilac bush. The pleasant scent of the lilacs had reminded him of his mother. He'd waited there, hoping to walk Miss Courtland back to the courthouse and inquire further of her knowledge of the surveyor stakes.

The pair walked to the picket gate together and the doctor tossed his bag into the buggy. "Can I give you a ride, Miss Nora?"

"Oh, I'd appreciate that. Mayor Gilbert wasn't happy with me this morning because I was late." The doctor gave her a hand climbing into the buggy and moments later, the two drove off in the direction of the courthouse.

Donovan stared after the buggy, his thoughts a muddled mess. Did they say *burial ground*? He ran his hand through his hair, aversion pooling in his stomach. Was Mr. Bennington planning on building his textile mill on top of a cemetery?

He covered his eyes with his hand. That would certainly explain why someone might be upset enough to pull up the surveyor's markers. But something didn't make sense. He'd walked past the church the evening Miss Courtland had said she had choir practice. Walked by, but didn't go in. The cemetery to the right of the church had, like the lilacs, reminded him of his mother. His heart couldn't handle the guilt, so he'd walked back to the hotel. But the town cemetery was there, beside the church.

Yesterday when he and Bennington had tramped around the wooded riverbank, he'd not encountered a single cross or headstone. How could there be a cemetery?

He set off for the courthouse, but before he'd taken a dozen strides he halted. Perhaps the man at the land office—what was his name? Dorsey. Wilbur Dorsey. If anyone would know of a second cemetery in the area, it would be the land agent.

Wilbur Dorsey sneered at Donovan's question regarding some kind of cemetery along the riverbank.

"Sonny, I'm near sixty-eight years old, an' I lived here all my life. My pappy a'fore me, an' his pappy a'fore him. I know ever'thing about ever'body hereabouts."

Donovan forced a smile. Sounded like he'd come to the right person, and it wasn't as if he was divulging confidential information. Mayor Gilbert had said Dorsey was the land agent with whom he'd arranged for the survey, so Dorsey knew the piece of property in question. "Then you know whether or not there is a cemetery there on the property Mr. Bennington wants to purchase?"

Dorsey's face screwed into a grimace as if he'd just taken a dose of castor oil. "Ain't no decent folks buried out yonder. Jest some dirty injuns buried somewhere 'longside the river."

Donovan lifted a single eyebrow and stared at the man. "We're talking about the same piece of property, aren't we? You ordered the survey for Mayor Gilbert for the tentative building site for the mill."

A half-hearted shrug lifted Dorsey's shoulders. "Yeah, I know the property. My pappy and gran'pappy knew Lemuel Weaver and his kin. So, some injun bones is buried out there. Don't make no never mind to me, and it shouldn't to you, neither."

The man's callousness clenched Donovan's stomach. "But we saw no headstones."

The land agent tossed his pencil on the desk and snorted. "I don't see no problem. Like I said, ain't no decent folks care a hoot about them stinkin' Cherokees."

Donovan gritted his teeth. "Well, apparently somebody cares, because the survey stakes were pulled up."

Dorsey retrieved his pencil and grabbed a scrap of paper. "Reckon you'll be needin' another survey, then." He jotted a note and stuck it on the spindle on his desk. Without another word, the land agent turned and went about his business.

Apparently dismissed, Donovan let himself out and looked down the street toward the courthouse. If Miss Courtland's grandfather was the one who'd removed the markers, that meant he cared a great deal. The problem now was figuring out how to look into the matter without offending the town folk like he had Wilbur Dorsey, angering Miss Courtland and her grandfather, or getting himself fired.

The notion of turning in his resignation fled. Bennington would replace him in heartbeat, most likely with someone who—as Mr. Dorsey put it—didn't care a hoot about who might be buried on that land.

CHAPTER 6

The front door of the church stood propped open. Odd that the place was open on a Tuesday afternoon. Donovan's curiosity sent him threading his way between wagons and horse droppings to see if perchance the pastor was about. He reached the church steps, and a cloud of dust propelled by a sturdy broom greeted him from the gaping door.

"*Pfft, pfft!*" Donovan waved his hand to shoo the dust and debris away from his face and clothing. "You certainly have an unusual way to welcome visitors around here." He coughed and batted dirt off his trousers.

A gentleman with white hair and a short white beard stepped through the doorway, wielding the broom. "I'm so sorry." He brushed dust from Donovan's shoulder. "I wasn't expecting anyone. Please forgive me."

Donovan chuckled. "It's a warmer welcome than I received at the last church I was in. No harm done." He extended his hand. "Donovan McNeary."

"I'm Pastor Parkin." He set the broom aside and gripped Donovan's hand. "It sounds as if I should try to leave you with a better impression of Christians than your previous experience."

"Sorry to interrupt. It looks like you're busy." Donovan gestured to the broom. "I was hoping to ask you a couple of questions."

The pastor laughed. "I welcome the interruption. Come in and sit down."

Donovan sat on the back pew. "Thank you."

The pastor perched on the edge of the pew across the aisle and tucked his hands under his arms. "I've been hoping to meet you and the other gentleman. I believe his name is Bennington, is that right?"

"Yes, sir."

"We're certainly pleased you've chosen Pine Ridge for the site of your new mill." The pastor's smile broadened. "Not only will the mill mean more jobs for the area, it will bring in new families. Our community will grow, and so will the church. Yes, we're all mighty glad you've come."

Not all. There was at least one person who wasn't happy about the mill. "Pastor, can you tell me if there are any other cemeteries around here other than the one beside the church?"

"Well, yes." Pastor Parkin nodded. "Many folks in the area have their own private, family cemeteries on their land, and there are a few Confederate cemeteries about a day's ride from here."

Donovan drew in a deep breath. "What about out along the banks of the Conasauga River?"

Caution staked a guarded veil across the pastor's eyes. "What exactly are you asking?"

There was no guarantee the preacher's opinion wouldn't be as jaded as the land agent's, but Donovan decided getting right to the point would save time. "Mr. Bennington is purchasing the parcel of land along the Conasauga belonging to the Weaver family. It has come to my attention recently that there may be a cemetery on the land. Would you know anything about it?"

He watched Pastor Parkin's face for any hint of disdain and detected none. Without blinking, the clergyman gave a slow nod. "It is my understanding that there's a burial ground along the riverbank on the Weaver land." His thick eyebrows dipped. "I wasn't aware the site of the new mill was along the Conasauga. Most folks have assumed it would be built nearer to town, along Granite Creek."

Donovan shook his head. "According to Mayor Gilbert, the creek is sometimes reduced to no more than a few inches of water during summer droughts. The mill requires a more dependable source of water power." He put his hands on his knees. "What about the cemetery, Pastor?"

The preacher leaned against the back of the pew and studied Donovan with an unblinking stare for a full minute. "I've been the pastor here for over twenty years, and I know most everyone for fifty miles around. Most are kind, generous, hard-working folks. You're young, but you've probably read how the Cherokee and Creek Indians were forced from their land back in the 1830s. Not many gave up their land without a fight."

He rose and walked to the open door. "Mr. McNeary, like I said, most of the people in this town are good folks." He turned to face Donovan again. "But there are a few whose forefathers had no love or compassion for the Cherokees. Those people were raised under the shadow of bigotry. Yes, there is a Cherokee burial ground along the banks of the Conasauga. Many of the residents of Pine Ridge—at least those under the age of forty—don't even know it's there. However, there are some so tainted by hatred passed down from generation to generation, they'd not hesitate to stir up trouble. While some may view the burial ground as sacred, others deem it unworthy of notice, much less protection."

Donovan suspected Hosea Courtland was among the former. "Tell me, Pastor, do you know Hosea Courtland?"

The preacher's perceptive gaze made Donovan squirm. "Of course I know him, and if you ask my opinion of the man, I'll tell you he's a fine, Christian gentleman."

The conviction with which Pastor Parkin stated his feelings for Nora Courtland's grandfather was clear and rang with principle. He'd not utter a single negative word against Hosea Courtland.

Before Donovan could decide how to phrase his next question, the pastor took his seat again and stroked his beard with his thumb and forefinger.

"As hopeful as I am about the new mill and what it will mean for this community, I will urge you to rethink any plans to build it at the burial ground. It makes no difference who is buried there. Knowingly disturbing the final resting place of anyone is not only disrespectful, it's deliberately hurtful to the loved ones left behind." The pastor's admonition stung.

"But wouldn't you agree that my boss has the right to build whatever he pleases on land he has purchased?" A twinge of guilt skewered Donovan at his insinuation that the sale of the property was already final, but he wanted to get the church leader's opinion. Knowing he had an advocate in the man to whom many folks looked for guidance would solidify his argument if he had to confront Bennington.

The pastor lifted one eyebrow. "Let me answer that question with another question. Have you ever lost someone dear to you?"

Donovan stiffened, his teeth clenched against the sudden burning in his eyes. He turned his gaze to the open door where he could glimpse one corner of the church's cemetery with its collection of headstones and crosses, many of which were adorned with flowers. His own mother lay beneath the sod of a small cemetery in Massachusetts. With him working for Asa Bennington in Georgia, there was no one to place flowers on Ma's grave. He held his breath and blinked, ordering the moisture in his eyes to retreat.

When the pastor spoke again, his tone was gentle. "I suspect by your silence and the sorrow I see in your eyes that the answer is yes. Care to tell me
about it?"

Donovan studied the toes of his boots. "My mother died a few years ago."
He cleared his throat. "I miss her."

"I'm sorry, son." Pastor Parkin's voice held genuine sympathy and comfort. "When someone we love passes away, our pain lingers a long time, often
for decades." He paused and his words settled in Donovan's chest like an an-
vil. "How would you feel if someone came along twenty or thirty years from
now and built a mill on top of your dear mother's grave?"

Hours later, as Donovan lay in bed with only the dim moonlight peeking
through his window for company, the pastor's question haunted him. He sat
up and curled his fingers into fists, ready to fight anyone who would do such
a thing. There were just as many people who despised the Irish as those who
hated the Cherokee, so it wasn't beyond the realm of imagination to picture
someone like Wilbur Dorsey or Asa Bennington casting such disregard on his
mother's final resting place.

He swung his legs over the side of the bed and leaned forward with his
head in his hands. "God, I know I broke Ma's heart by not going to church."

My son, you broke My *heart by pursuing success instead of following Me.*

He slid to his knees. "Lord, I'm sorry. Why was I so blinded? Help me find
my way back to You."

He searched the deep recesses of his memory for the scriptures his mother had taught him, but all that surfaced were bits and pieces.

In all thy ways...

For God so loved...

...supply all your need...

Trust in the Lord...

He remained on his knees for a time, relishing the embrace of God's un-
conditional love. If only Ma knew.

"I wonder what Ma would think of this mill." Perhaps it wasn't his mother's opinion that counted. He rose from his place beside the bed and stepped
over to the small desk. He lit the lamp and picked up the yellow paper—the
telegram he'd received from Bennington earlier today. There was a problem

with ordering the gears for the mill, but his boss expected him to have followed through on his instructions by the time he returned. How would Bennington react when he learned of the burial ground? For that matter, would Donovan even have a job once his boss found out the Weavers had still not responded to the repeated offers to purchase their land?

Nora exited the apothecary with the medicine for Grandpa and started toward home. One glance at the clock on the courthouse tower told her to hurry. Mayor Gilbert had grudgingly approved her taking time mid-day to run home and check on her grandfather, but she didn't wish to press her luck.

Across the street, she caught sight of Donovan McNeary waving his hand. Was he waving at her? A flock of butterflies turned loose in her stomach when he approached, and she berated herself. He was, after all, the enemy if he and his boss thought they were going to build their mill on her grandmother's grave.

"Good morning, Miss Courtland. How is your grandfather today?" His green eyes sparkled when he smiled at her, stirring the butterflies to more frantic flight.

She tamped down her own smile, chiding herself for her schoolgirl flutters. "He's a bit better, thank you. But I must get this cough medicine to him, if you'll excuse me."

"Wait, please." He placed his hand on her arm for a brief moment and a tingle shot all the way to her shoulder.

She halted her steps when her common sense told her to walk away. "I don't have much time. Grandpa needs this medicine, and I mustn't be away from my desk for too long."

His smile deepened and pulled a dimple into his cheek. Oh my, but he was handsome. She drew in a breath and forced her focus to the medicine in her hand.

"By all means, you must take the medicine to your grandfather. In fact, I'd like to speak with you both. May I walk with you? It's important." How could she refuse his request after he'd shown concern for Grandpa?

"Yes, of course." She bit her lip as he cupped her elbow and they made their way across the street. If he thought he was going to threaten Grandpa for pulling out those stakes, he'd better be ready for a fight.

She darted a glance up at him as they walked. "I don't want Grandpa upset."

He sent her a knee-buckling, soft smile. "Nor do I."

Moments later, they entered the house, and Nora pushed Grandpa's door open. He looked so frail against the stack of pillows. "Grandpa, there is someone to see you."

Mr. McNeary followed her into the room and Grandpa's eyes narrowed. He rose up from the pillows and clutched the quilt with one hand and pointed a bony finger at Mr. McNeary.

"You the one who's been out surveyin' around my wife's grave?"

CHAPTER 7

Alarm rose in Nora's chest and her glance ricocheted between Grandpa and Mr. McNeary. Caution told her to not allow her grandfather to say too much, but it might be too late. "Grandpa—"

Mr. McNeary's expression turned sorrowful and he hung his head. "I was afraid it might be something like that." He held out open hands. "I didn't know."

A thread of comfort spiraled through Nora at Mr. McNeary's admission. A secret desire hidden in the recesses of her heart wanted to believe he wouldn't be deliberately hurtful. He looked over at Nora.

"May I ask, if it's a graveyard, why aren't there any headstones?" His tone held no hint of disdain.

Grandpa's eyes softened. "There's no markers like you see in the church yard because it's a Cherokee burial ground. The Cherokee don't put up no fancy gravestones. But there's more to it than that. Sit down, young man."

Mr. McNeary pulled a chair over close to Grandpa's bedside. "I don't want to tire you, but if you're willing to explain, I'd like to hear it."

Grandpa nodded. "I married my wife, Eve, back in 1833. She was half Cherokee, her papa bein' a white man. We had us a son the next year. But even though she weren't full-blooded Cherokee, the way the law read, if anyone had so much as a drop of Cherokee blood, they was stripped of everything they owned and forced to go to a relocation fort. My Eve was in one of those forts, and I sneaked around lookin' for a way to free her. Almost got caught a few times, but I never stopped tryin' to get her out of there. I planned for us to go deep into the mountains where they'd never find us."

Moisture glistened in his eyes. "That fort was a horrible, filthy place. Little wonder so many of the Cherokee took sick before they even started marchin' toward Oklahoma. Disease, spoiled food, dirty water. My Eve got sick. She kept gettin' weaker and weaker, even though I tried to take her food and medicine." A tear escaped down his cheek and got lost in his white beard.

Mr. McNeary lifted his gaze for a moment and connected with Nora. Something deep but unspoken traveled between them. She saw nothing but regret and sympathy in his face.

Grandpa's voice softened, as if he spoke to no one in particular. "Jesus took my Eve home. She died before I could get her out of there. I woulda died myself but I had our little son to raise. When I looked at him, I saw her. He's Nora's papa."

Grandpa fixed his eyes on Mr. McNeary. "Out yonder along the riverbank is a Cherokee burial ground. My Eve's restin' place. No, there ain't no fancy gravestones. The Cherokees just use a pile of rocks to keep the animals from diggin'."

Nora sat on the edge of the bed and took Grandpa's feeble hand. "There were a lot of people who condemned and shunned my grandfather for his marriage to a Cherokee woman. It's taken over fifty years for the animosity to fade away. I don't want it stirred up again."

Grandpa's brow dipped and he raised his voice. "I don't care. I'll fight any-one before I'll let them desecrate Eve's grave." A cough rumbled up from his chest and seized him with a brutal spasm.

Nora jumped up and reached for him, looking over her shoulder at Mr. McNeary. "You'll have to go now."

But to her surprise and great annoyance, Mr. McNeary didn't leave. In-stead, he picked up a pitcher of water from the dresser and poured a bit into the tin cup beside Grandpa's bed.

"Sip this, Mr. Courtland." He held the cup to Grandpa's lips and glanced at Nora. "Get two damp towels and heat them on the stove."

Suspicion stalled her feet. What did he think he was doing? She had the medicine the doctor had prescribed, for all the little good the first bottle had done.

He arrowed his gaze at her. "The hot towels. Please?"

She moved to do his bidding, and when she returned, Mr. McNeary had pulled two pillows out from behind Grandpa and stacked them in front of him. He took the hot towels from her and laid one on Grandpa's chest. He then coaxed her grandfather to lean forward on the pillows while he placed the second towel on his back.

"Pull that quilt up around his shoulders to trap the heat."

She followed his instructions and then went to fetch a spoon to give Grandpa a dose of the cough medicine. But when she scurried back into the room, Mr. McNeary sat on the edge of the bed, rubbing Grandpa's back, and the coughing spasm was already beginning to let up.

Nora set the cough medicine aside. "How did you—"

Mr. McNeary continued to massage Grandpa's back. "I took care of my mother when she was ill with chest congestion."

The coughing spell gradually subsided, and Grandpa's strained, raspy breathing sounded easier. Nora heaved a sigh of relief.

She sent a curious look at the man who ministered to her grandfather. "Did this treatment work for your mother?"

Pain flickered across Mr. McNeary's eyes. "It made her a little more comfortable, but we had no money for medicine or a doctor. Ma insisted on continuing to go to work in a stuffy factory where the dust and dirt swirled around like fog."

Dread sliced through Nora—the same dread she felt when she heard Grandpa cough—and she feared asking what happened.

Mr. McNeary gave her a knowing look, as if he recognized her reluctance to ask. "Ma died for lack of medical care and because she was afraid if she didn't go to work, she'd lose her job."

He returned his attention to her grandfather and rearranged the pillows, easing him back to rest. His voice was stern, but gentle. "You listen to the doctor and your granddaughter, you hear? I'll do everything I can to protect your wife's resting place."

Nora released some of her pent-up tension as the lines of distress across Grandpa's brow relaxed and he nodded. Before Mr. McNeary could rise from the edge of the bed, Grandpa gripped his hand the best he could. He couldn't speak, but his message was clear.

When Nora's grandfather was settled and comfortable, Donovan followed Miss Courtland out of the room. "I think he'll sleep now." Donovan pulled the bedroom door closed.

"Thanks to you."

Her reply surprised him. When he turned, he found her with eyes brimming.

"Thank you for being so compassionate. The cough medicine he's been taking hasn't worked nearly as well as what you did."

Donovan shrugged. "I only did what my mother always did. She'd see somebody with a need and do what she could." He might never be the Christian man Ma prayed he'd become, but perhaps if he followed her example and listened to his heavenly Father, he'd make some progress.

Miss Courtland moved toward the front door. "Since Grandpa is resting, I need to get back to the courthouse."

"Of course." They stepped off the porch, and her dark hair caught the sunlight and shone with gold streaks. "Nora—" He nearly choked. Whatever possessed him to call her by her given name without asking her permission? "I'm terribly sorry. Miss Courtland."

Her soft smile robbed him of his cognitive ability. "You may call me Nora if you wish."

The boulder that momentarily occupied his throat went down hard. "Then I hope you'll call me Donovan."

She proceeded him through the gate and they walked down the street toward the courthouse. "Nora, may I ask you a question?"

The resentful suspicion that usually fringed her eyes was gone, and she nodded.

"What can you tell me about the Weavers—the family who owns the land?"

A tiny frown pulled her brows together and she cocked her head. "I don't know that anyone has heard from them in years. The man's name was Lemuel Weaver. He won the land in the lottery in 1836. There were already several Cherokees, including my grandmother, who were buried there. From the stories I've heard, Grandpa nearly came to bloodshed with Lemuel a few times."

One corner of Donovan's mouth quirked upward. "I can imagine."

They turned the corner and continued up the street. "Lemuel's plan was to build a cabin and bring his bride, Phoebe, from Williamsburg, Virginia. He built a sawmill upstream. Over the next few years, they had three children, two boys and a girl. Ellis, James, and Elizabeth. Their youngest, Elizabeth, was still quite young when Phoebe died. I remember hearing people speaking fondly of Phoebe, and it sounded as if the Weavers were nice folks."

Donovan glanced down at her. "You mean you didn't know them?"

She shook her head. "No. Lemuel was injured in a sawmill accident and couldn't make a living here. He and his children moved away. They might have moved back to Williamsburg, but that was before I was born."

Donovan halted. "So what happened to the sawmill?"

"Oh, it's still there." Nora slipped her hand up to smooth a lock of hair the breeze had tugged out of place, and Donovan's fingers itched to tuck the errant strands back himself. "The property was divided and the sawmill was sold. It's well upstream from the burial ground. But Lemuel wouldn't sell the rest of the land because he and Phoebe had loved it so."

"Hmm. You said Phoebe died. Is she buried out there as well?" If she was, then it only stood to reason that the Weaver family wouldn't want to sell the land for the same reason Nora's grandfather so fiercely wished to protect it.

"No, she's buried in the church cemetery." A faraway look etched her features. "When I was twelve years old my mother died. One day I took flowers to her grave. Phoebe Weaver's grave was just a few feet away from Mama's, and it looked so lonely. So I picked some daisies and buttercups and put them on Phoebe's grave because she didn't have any family here to bring her flowers. Grandpa saw me, and I was afraid he'd be angry. Later he told me it was a nice thing to do, but he never would talk about Lemuel or Phoebe."

They reached the courthouse and Donovan held the door open for her. "I'd like to stop back by your place later to visit with your grandfather if he's feeling up to it."

Her love for her grandfather showed in her smile. "I think he'd like that."

Disappointment nipped at him. He wished she'd said *she* would like it.

As he walked back to the hotel to make some notes, he reflected on Asa Bennington's undisguised opinion of the people who owned the property he wanted to purchase. He'd indicated they were ignorant, poor, lazy Southerners who he expected to jump at the chance to make some easy money, willing to sell the land at a price well below its value. Donovan had believed him at first and had accompanied Bennington here with the attitude that he must do whatever his boss wanted in order to keep his job. Now he was torn. A few days ago he'd been ready to quit, unwilling to push the legal boundaries by following Bennington's orders. But after meeting Hosea Courtland and hearing his story, he knew beyond any doubt he was needed here, if for no other reason than to protect Eve's resting place. The bits of information Nora gave him weren't much to go on, but he'd keep asking questions until he contacted Lemuel Weaver's family. He prayed he could reach out to them before Bennington returned.

"God, exactly what are You leading me to do?" Donovan grinned. He might not know the answer yet, but asking was exquisitely sweet.

CHAPTER 8

Donovan studied the telegram in his hands, considering a half dozen possibilities. The extra time afforded by Bennington's delay in Atlanta was an unanticipated gift. He'd expected his boss's return the day after tomorrow, but due to unforeseen circumstances, Bennington wouldn't arrive in Pine Ridge as scheduled. Donovan tapped the paper on his palm while his mind raced. After yesterday's visit with Hosea Courtland and Nora's recollection of what she remembered about the Weaver family, bits and pieces of a plan began falling into place.

His first order of business was to send a telegram to the courthouse in Williamsburg, Virginia. If his suspicions were correct, he hoped to secure new information regarding the Weaver family and their residence. The telegrapher at the Pine Ridge depot lifted a thick, caterpillar-like eyebrow when Donovan told him where he wanted the message sent but scrawled down the words without comment.

Donovan plunked down the coins and included an extra dollar. "Come and find me as soon as you get a reply. It's important."

The rotund man nodded his bald head and pocketed the dollar. "Sure thing, Mr. McNeary."

From the telegraph office, Donovan headed to the livery where he rented a horse. The riverbank property was only a couple of miles but riding was faster than walking. After securing the horse's reins to a tree branch, he picked his way across the river on the wide rocks. Bennington would be furious that he'd not arranged for another survey yet, but he had some hiking and poking around to do first.

As he tramped through the underbrush he tried viewing the landscape through Hosea Courtland's eyes. The mixture of hardwoods and pines along the gentle slope combined to paint a very different picture from that which he'd viewed with Bennington. All his boss saw was business opportunities and dollar signs. But today, as he approached the rock mounds scattered across the incline, he paused first by one and then another, wondering which one was Eve's. He'd not let this peaceful place be disturbed if he could possibly help it, but he'd undoubtedly have a fight on his hands.

"God, I'm going to need Your help. I can't do this without You."

He laid his hand on stones heaped together with wild grapevine crisscrossing them and sprinkled with pine needles. Whoever lay beneath these rocks, whether it was Eve or another Cherokee, should be afforded the same respect as Phoebe Weaver in the church cemetery.

After several minutes, he continued on downstream, taking note of the distance from the burial ground, the depth of the water, and the swiftness of the current, as well as the natural resources around him. His sketchy plan began to come together a piece at a time. But it would all be for naught if he didn't get the reply to his telegram like he hoped. He glanced upward at the patches of blue sky between the swaying tree limbs.

"It's in Your hands, God. Guide me, speak to me, steer me, show me what to do."

The current grew noisier as he proceeded. Rocks poked their heads above the water along the river's edge, giving the impression of shallowness. But upon closer inspection, the rocky bottom dropped off less than six feet from the bank. Donovan picked up a dead limb laying nearby and held it upright, reaching out as far as he dared to dip it straight down into the deeper water. It nearly submerged the entire limb. Getting his shoes wet was worth it. He paced off the distance from a rock outcropping to just past the point where the water deepened and then measured the rise of the slope with his eye. He was fairly certain this was still Weaver land, but he'd have to confirm it with Wilbur Dorsey at the land office.

He marked the spot by tying his handkerchief around a sapling, then he made his way back past the burial ground to the place where he could cross the river. The livery horse observed him as he stepped from rock to rock. Likely the beast was anxious to return to the stable and his feeding trough.

Just as he arrived at the livery, the man from the telegraph office waddled up the street toward him, red-faced and puffing. The telegrapher mopped his forehead with a red bandana and waved a piece of yellow paper. "Mr. McNeary. You got your reply."

Donovan dug into his pocket and extracted fifty cents. He deposited the coin in the telegrapher's palm. "Thank you."

"Yes, sir." The stout fellow touched the brim of his visor and set off toward the depot, his stride less urgent. Donovan opened the missive and scanned it. Just as he'd thought. Bennington had been sending letters to the wrong place.

The clock on the courthouse indicated Nora was likely back at work after having checked on her grandfather at noon. Perfect. He headed toward the Courtland house and was pleased to see Hosea sitting on the front porch in the sun. Donovan waved at the front gate and Hosea motioned for him to come into the yard.

"Come and set a spell, young fella. I can use some comp'ny."

The old man was still pale, but his eyes were brighter than the last time Donovan saw him, and no wheezing rattled his breathing.

Hosea nodded toward the chair next to him. "That were a right smart idea you had, usin' them hot towels. Worked better'n the Doc's tonic."

Genuine pleasure lifted Donovan's lips. "I'm happy to see you're feeling better. Does Nora know you're out here?"

A mischievous grin tweaked the man's white beard. "No, and don't you tell her." He shook his head. "I was goin' stir crazy in that bed."

Donovan chuckled. "I won't tell her if..." He glanced sideways at the old man. "You'll answer a few questions for me."

Hosea scowled. "What kind o' questions?"

"Well, let's begin with how many men can you name who might be interested in some back-breaking work moving rocks?"

Alarm mingled with anger pulled Hosea forward in his chair, but Donovan reached over and patted his arm. "It's not what you think. I won't move a single pebble from the burial ground."

Nora straightened from her bent position rearranging file drawers and placed her hands on her lower back, trying to push the ache away. She walked a few steps to the front window of the courthouse and peered out to the street. After allowing the fledgling feelings that had emerged in her heart for Donovan to take root and grow, a void now echoed within her. The note she'd found five days ago tucked into the picket gate in front of her house briefly explained his pre-dawn departure, but it didn't say when he'd return.

She longed to know where he was. How many times had she scanned up and down the street, hoping to catch a glimpse of him striding toward the courthouse? This time, however, it wasn't Donovan who made his way in her direction, but rather Waldo Fuller from the telegraph office.

Mr. Fuller's bald head glistened with perspiration when he opened the courthouse door. Nora stepped toward the mayor's office. "Just a moment and I'll tell Mayor Gilbert—"

The mayor's door jerked open. "I'll take that, Waldo." Mayor Gilbert snatched the telegram from the man's grasp, only to have Mr. Fuller grab it back.

"Ain't for you, Mayor." Mr. Fuller held out the missive to Nora. "This here's for Miss Nora."

Nora blinked. "Me? Whoever would send me a telegram?" Her heart accelerated and she almost closed her eyes in ardent prayer that the wire was from Donovan.

Mayor Gilbert blustered, but Mr. Fuller just grinned. "Ain't but one way to find out."

Both men eyed her, the mayor with suspicion and the telegrapher with glee. She took the paper and ran a finger over the seal, wishing for a few moments of privacy, but her wish remained unfulfilled with the men standing there watching. Uncomfortable warmth climbed her frame and despite her longing to tear open the folded paper, she slid it into her pocket. "I, uh, have work to do."

She spun on her heel to return to her desk when the front door of the courthouse opened. Mr. Bennington stalked inside, slamming the door behind him. He flicked a glance at Mr. Fuller, barged past Nora, and came toe to toe with the mayor.

"Where's McNeary?"

Nora sucked in a gasp and both men turned to look at her. Bennington narrowed his stare in her direction and twisted his lips into a sneer.

"What do you know of his whereabouts, girl?"

Her throat clogged and her lips froze.

"Well? Speak up. I've seen you walking out together, you hanging on McNeary's arm, no doubt trying to use your feminine wiles to lure him into your web. You two have been thick as thieves. What are you hiding?"

"Now, see here, Bennington." Mayor Gilbert took a step toward Nora. "I'll thank you not to speak to my clerk in such a discourteous manner."

If she'd not been quaking in her shoes from Bennington's browbeating, she might have let her mouth hang open in astonishment at the mayor's defense of her. Mayor Gilbert turned to her. "Miss Nora, do you know where Mr. McNeary is?"

She shook her head and tried to draw in enough breath to form words. "H-he said he'd be g-gone a few days, but didn't say where he was going."

The door opened again, drawing the attention of Gilbert and Bennington. Waldo Fuller stepped partway through the open door. "Reckon I'll just head on back to the telegraph office."

The mayor scowled and glanced back at Nora, his gaze coming to rest on the pocket where moments ago she'd slipped the telegram. She held her breath and her pulse pounded in her ears. Surely he wouldn't force her to open—

Bennington stomped toward the mayor's office. "Gilbert, we need to talk."

The mayor followed Bennington into his office and closed the door. Nora's knees weakened and she sank into her chair, her breath coming in short bursts. She slipped her trembling hand into her pocket and gripped the paper between her fingers.

Bennington's bark could be heard through the door to the mayor's office. "I gave orders for McNeary to move those rock piles to use for the mill foundation and to begin felling trees and clearing underbrush. Not only has nothing been done, McNeary's nowhere to be found, and nobody from your office will cooperate and tell me where he is."

Mayor Gilbert voice rose to match Bennington's. "I don't have any idea where your man went. He doesn't confer with me. Furthermore, we're still waiting to hear from the Weavers."

"I expressly ordered McNeary to have the contracts ready to sign by the time I got back." Footsteps clomped across the office. "You don't seem to grasp the gravity of this transaction, Gilbert. I can build my mill at any one of a dozen places in these hills. Perhaps I need to contact the town officials at Hendericksville or Varnell. I'm sure the good people of Epworth or Tellsford would be happy to have a mill in their community, and I am quite certain the administrations of any of those towns would be more cooperative and competent than what I've encountered here."

A chair scraped the floor. "Now, Mr. Bennington, you can't possibly fault me for your man's disappearance."

More footsteps. The office door jerked open and Mr. Bennington strode out toward the front door with the mayor on his heels.

"Mr. Bennington—"

The slamming door reverberated throughout the office as Mayor Gilbert stood raking his hands over his face.

Nora bit her lip and pulled the telegram from her pocket.

CHAPTER 9

Nora lost count of the number of times she'd re-read Donovan's short message. Mixed feelings churned through her as she watched her grandfather perch his spectacles on his nose and study the piece of yellow paper.

"What does it mean, Grandpa?"

He looked at her over the top of his spectacles. "'Pears to me like he's comin' back on tomorrow's train."

Impatience nipped her. "I understand that part. I wish I could warn him that Mr. Bennington is furious. He threatened Mayor Gilbert with taking his mill elsewhere. I'm afraid Donovan is going to catch the brunt of Mr. Bennington's wrath the moment he sets foot back in Pine Ridge."

"Hmm. Could be. But I think the young fella can withstand the storm." A hint of a smile pulled at the corners of Grandpa's mouth and wiggled his mustache.

Nora tipped her head. "Maybe. But what about the rest?" She ran her finger along the words. "It just says 'Sufficient grace.' Is it some kind of clue? That's the part I don't understand."

Grandpa lowered the paper to his lap. "You should. Hand me my Bible."

Nora did her grandfather's bidding and sat while he turned pages. When he found the place he wanted, he adjusted his spectacles and fixed a gentle gaze on her.

"One day last week, Mr. McNeary paid me a visit while you was workin', and we had us a nice chat. Said he'd had a meetin' with God durin' the night." Grandpa stroked his beard and smiled.

"Well, he says to me he was strugglin' with how to deal with that boss o' his and all his demands. Said he wants to protect the burial ground..." Grandpa's voice cracked, and he swallowed a time or two before continuing. "He knows how important the mill is to folks hereabouts, especially the farmers, but he wonders if it's possible to do both—build the mill and still protect the burial ground."

The prospect of the mill had the whole town excited, but if it meant stirring up the old resentment and bigotry or hurting Grandpa, she'd rather see Bennington carry out his threat and take his mill elsewhere. But her interest piqued at Grandpa's revelation. "I didn't know Donovan had come to visit you. Did he tell you where he was going?"

He gave her an apologetic smile. "Yes. But he asked me to keep it under my hat, in case he weren't successful. The boy has a plan but doesn't think his boss will agree. That's why he asked me to pray."

Nora's heart skipped. "Donovan asked you to pray?"

"Mm-hmm." Grandpa tapped the pages of his Bible. "And this here is what I read to him— 'My grace is sufficient for thee; for My strength is made perfect in weakness. Most gladly therefore will I rather glory in my infirmities, that the power of Christ may rest upon me.'" He closed the Book. "Second Corinthians, chapter twelve, verse nine, Nora girl. You 'n' me's read it more'n a couple times." He nodded his head slowly. "Him 'n' me prayed for God's strength and grace that's all sufficient. I reckon God will do the rest."

Hearing Donovan's request for prayer made Nora's spirit soar. Sufficient grace. There was nothing sweeter for which any of them could pray. She only wished he'd felt free to share his plan and his desire for God's help with her. "So where did he go?"

Grandpa's eyes twinkled. "I'll let him tell you about that. Reckon the two of you will have some talkin' to do when he gets here."

Warmth stole into Nora's cheeks, and she turned so Grandpa wouldn't see her blush. "I'll be praying for him when he has to meet with Mr. Bennington." She pulled the shawl up around her grandfather's shoulders. "Don't you get chilled now."

"Nora girl, I'm gettin' on just fine. No fever, and even Doc was impressed with the way them hot towels helped my coughin' an' eased the pressure in my chest." He wrapped his fingers around hers and drew them to his lips. "But you can't fool your ol' grandpa. I know what's going through your head. You're thinkin' 'bout that young feller." A chuckle rolled from his lips. "I never thought there'd be a man good enough for my Nora girl, but I reckon I was wrong. I ain't too proud to admit it. Never seen you light up around a man the way you do when Donovan McNeary's name is mentioned."

Grandpa was right, like he always was. She slipped her arms around him and hugged his neck. "I love you, Grandpa."

"An' I love you, Nora girl." His voice wavered. "I pray you can have the kind o' love me 'n' Eve did. Wish you coulda known her."

Nora cupped both sides of her grandfather's face, his scruffy beard tickling her fingers. "Grandpa, I know her. I met her through you. Through your stories and your memories. I'm so blessed to have grandparents like you."

The sun had only been up an hour when Donovan tapped on the Courtlands' door. Muffled voices and footsteps from inside soothed his angst. At least he hadn't awakened Nora and her grandfather.

The door opened and Hosea Courtland peered out, his countenance breaking into a smile when his gaze locked with Donovan's. "Come in, come in, young man. Nora girl, this feller looks like he could use a cup of coffee."

"Donovan." His name from Nora's lips touched his ears with the softness of thistle down.

His searching eyes slid past Hosea's shoulder and came to rest on her. Oh my, but she was lovely, standing there in the morning light. "G-good morning. Please forgive me for disturbing you so early."

"Nonsense." Hosea reached for his arm and tugged him in the door. The old man glanced at his granddaughter and back at Donovan. "Reckon the two of you have some talkin' to do, so I'll just mosey—"

Donovan caught Hosea's elbow. "Please stay, sir. I have some information for both of you." He sent Nora a look he hoped would convey his desire to speak privately with her at some point. But right now, they didn't have much time.

Nora gifted him with a tremulous smile and poured him a cup of coffee. "Have you had breakfast?"

Donovan shook his head. "I didn't want to risk running into Mr. Bennington until I had a chance to talk to you both."

She set the coffee on the table and nudged the pot of cream and sugar bowl toward him before returning to the stove. He followed her with his eyes until Hosea cleared his throat.

Donovan pulled his gaze away and found Hosea grinning at him. Heat swelled in his face and he quickly took a gulp of coffee. "I, uh, I got in rather late last night, and it wasn't appropriate to call at such an hour. But I do have news."

Hosea sat across from him with his own coffee cup and arched one eyebrow.

Donovan glanced at Nora. "Your grandfather already knows part of this. I did some research into the tax records for the Weaver property and found the taxes were being paid from an attorney's office in Williamsburg. I wired them and learned Ellis Weaver is living in Charlotte, North Carolina—a day's train ride from here.

"When I met with him, he was most gracious. He had been contacted by his attorney in Williamsburg regarding Mr. Bennington's offer. His attorney advised him to ignore it because the offered price was ridiculously low. He communicated with his sister, Elizabeth, who now lives in Roanoke. She deferred all negotiations to her brother."

"Wait." Nora set a plate of bacon and eggs in front of Donovan. "There were two brothers, weren't there?" She glanced at her grandfather, who nodded.

Donovan thanked her for the breakfast. "Ellis told me their brother James died in 1865. Their father passed away shortly after James did."

He bowed his head briefly and gave silent thanks for his meal. When he raised his head, moisture winked in Nora's eyes and she gave him an approving smile that grabbed his breath. He scooped a forkful of eggs. Between bites, he related his meeting with Ellis Weaver.

"Ellis will agree to sell for a reasonable price..." Donovan looked straight at Hosea. "But not the burial ground. He said his father taught him to respect that area. They weren't even allowed to play there as children. We discussed a plot of land downstream from the burial ground. I looked at it, tested the depth of the water and force of the current. It could be done, but it will require hauling in rocks to create a dam and spillway."

Hosea nodded like he knew the exact spot to which Donovan referred, but Nora frowned.

"Donovan, Mr. Bennington was spitting mad two days ago, and he threatened to take his mill project somewhere else."

"I'll handle Bennington." Donovan took one last bite and wiped his mouth on a napkin. "Nora, I need your help. Can you organize a quick meeting of the mayor, the town businessmen, some local farmers, and anyone else who would be interested in the mill?"

"We can do that." She glanced at Hosea. "When and where do want to hold this meeting?"

Donovan took a sip of coffee. "This morning, maybe around ten o'clock? I suppose we could have it at the courthouse since it will involve Mayor Gilbert. I know it's short notice, but you know everyone in town. Do you think—"

"Consider it done. Ten o'clock." She glanced toward the fireplace where a clock *tick-tocked* on the mantle. "I'd better get going if I want to catch all the regulars at Puckett's Cafe."

Donovan sucked in a deep breath and rapped on the door of Bennington's room.

"Come in! It's about time you—" Bennington jerked open the door. The expression on his face went from annoyance to unbridled fury in the space of two seconds. "I thought you were that fool from downstairs. I told him to bring me coffee more than a half hour ago." Bennington glared at him and cursed. "What are you doing here?"

Donovan folded his arms across his chest. "I'm not sure if I still have a job, but I do have some information I believe will interest you. Want to hear it?"

Bennington's glower spewed venom, but Donovan had grown immune to his boss's intimidation tactics. Moreover, he knew Bennington wouldn't be so foolish as to pass up information if he thought he could use it to his advantage.

His boss grunted and stomped back into the room and planted himself in an overstuffed chair. "Well? I'm waiting."

Donovan stuck his thumbs in his pockets. He didn't expect to retain his position anyway, so he had nothing to lose, but the people of Pine Ridge stood to lose a great deal if his effort failed. After a brief explanation of how he found Ellis Weaver, he described his meeting with the property owner.

Bennington sputtered. "Why didn't you give me the correct address in the first place, you ignorant, incompetent—"

Interrupting the man didn't scare him anymore. "I will remind you, Mr. Bennington, you were the one who got the contact information from Wilbur

Dorsey at the land office. Now, if you'd like to hear the rest of what I learned during my visit with Mr. Weaver, I will invite you to a meeting with Mayor Gilbert and a number of community businessmen that's due to take place in about an hour."

His boss's face reddened. He leapt to his feet and shook his fist. "Who do you think you are? You're not in charge of this project. In fact, you're fired!"

CHAPTER 10

Donovan stepped into the courthouse expecting to see a group of men waiting. Instead, the only person there was Nora. He leaned to see through the open door of the mayor's office but the room was empty. His heart sank.

"Weren't they interested? Didn't anyone want to come?" The hopes he had riding on the proposed meeting dimmed.

Nora caught his hand. "Everyone wanted to come. That was the problem—there wasn't enough room here, so Pastor Parkin suggested we use the church."

The wave of disappointment evaporated and renewed energy surged through him. "Is everyone there now?"

"Nearly everyone in town, including some farmers who happened to be at the feed and seed. More are on their way." Her brown eyes danced.

He wanted to grab her and plant a kiss on her lips, and although the idea was tempting, he restrained his desire. "That's wonderful." *She* was wonderful, but he'd address that later.

Her brow dipped. "What about Mr. Bennington?"

Donovan lifted his shoulders. "Oh, he fired me. But he'll show up at the meeting. You can count on that." He glanced around the office. "Can you write a sign and post it on the door? Say, 'Community meeting to discuss new mill. 10:00 at the church.'"

"I'll take care of it and meet you there." Her smile bolstered his confidence.

He brushed his fingers across her cheek. For the space of a few heartbeats, their gazes locked before he rushed out the door. Heart singing, he jogged all the way to the church.

A dozen folks loitered in the churchyard. He recognized a few of them, and they greeted him with handshakes. Myron Snead from the newspaper pushed through the crowd. "Mr. McNeary, what's this meeting all about?" He gestured around with the point of his pencil. "All these folks have been waitin' to hear some kind of official announcement about the mill. Is that what this is?" He poised his pencil, ready to record whatever Donovan said.

"There are a few details I think the people of Pine Ridge need to know. That's why I called the meeting." Donovan swept his gaze around the churchyard. More folks arrived by wagon. "Let's all go inside."

The moment he stepped inside, Mayor Gilbert grabbed his arm, his eyes darting back and forth around the room. "Is Mr. Bennington coming?" The man wrung his hands and dragged his handkerchief across his forehead.

The pleading in the Gilbert's voice poked at Donovan and he almost felt sorry for the mayor. "He's not happy, but I'd bet my last dollar he'll be here."

Donovan made his way to the front and held up his hands. "Everyone please take a seat."

Folks slid down the pews and scooted closer to make room for more, and a few stood along the back wall. As Donovan scanned the crowd, Nora slipped in the door. Doctor Guthrie rose and gave her his seat beside her grandfather.

He relished her reassuring smile. "Thank you all for coming. From the looks of this group, you all seem to be in favor of the mill being built here in Pine Ridge."

A cacophony of applause, shouts, and whistles filled the church. Donovan waited for everyone to quiet down. "I'm grateful for your support, but there are a few things you should know."

He sought out Hosea. The old man sat holding Nora's hand, his eyes closed and his lips moving slightly. Donovan's heart swelled with hope. Yes. Prayer was what they needed first. "Pastor Parkin, will you please open our meeting in prayer?"

A hush fell as the preacher rose and besought God for wisdom, truth, and sound judgment. At "Amen," Pastor Parkin gave Donovan a nod. "The floor is yours, Mr. McNeary."

Donovan licked his lips and swallowed. "As most of you already know, Mr. Asa Bennington has been working for the past couple of months to finalize the details so he can build a textile mill in this area. The proposed location is along the Conasauga River, on land currently owned by the Weaver family who lived here some years ago.

"At a recent meeting with Mr. Ellis Weaver, he told me that the plot of land Mr. Bennington has been trying to purchase is not for sale." Donovan's statement met with muffled groans. He held up his hand. "However, Mr. Weaver and I discussed another parcel, just a little ways downriver. It has good access, but will require some work to build a spillway to ensure consistent water power—"

The church door was flung open and Bennington stormed inside. "I don't know what this man has told you people"—he stalked to the front and glared at Donovan—"but he is no longer in my employ and has no authority to speak at this meeting."

Donovan pressed his lips tightly together for a moment, willing God to take control of the situation. Bennington spun on his heel and faced the crowd. "You people know me. I'm here to bring commerce and opportunity to this backwoods, and I know you'll all be happy as soon as I've completed negotiations with the Weaver family so we can get on with building this mill."

A few of the farmers exchanged glances. "I don't know him. Do you know him?"

"Heard about him but never met him."

"Anybody here know this fella?"

"I know he just insulted us by callin' us a backwoods community."

Grumbles rolled through the crowd, and Myron Snead stood. "Mr. Bennington, it has come to our attention that the property where you wanted to build isn't even for sale."

Bennington's face flushed red and the veins in his neck extended. The people in attendance continued to raise their voices.

Pastor Parkin took the platform. "Brothers and sisters, let's all calm down."

The muttering quieted, and Donovan spoke up. "Part of what Mr. Bennington said is true. I am no longer in his employ. But I feel you folks deserve to know what's happening in your community."

Pastor Parkin nodded. "So do I."

Mayor Gilbert took a step forward. "I agree. Mr. McNeary is right. You all deserve to know, and he is the one with the answers."

Bennington blustered. "Well, I'll just go build my mill somewhere else."

Nora grimaced. As much as she didn't want to see the burial ground dese-crated, neither did she want to see the people of Pine Ridge disappointed if Bennington followed through with his threat. She held her breath and waited as Donovan turned to his former boss.

"Where is that, Mr. Bennington?"

All eyes turned to Donovan.

"What other locations are under consideration? As your former assis-tant, I happen to know several other towns...um, declined your offer." He stepped down from the platform and extended his hands outward. "But I'll leave it up to the people who will be impacted the most. Do you folks want to hear what I learned when I visited with Ellis Weaver?"

One of the cotton farmers, Judd Wingate, poked his hand in the air. "Seems to me that Bennington fella's had plenty of opportunity to tell us what's goin' to happen. I think I'd like to hear from this McNeary fella."

"Me, too."

"He's the one who says there's another option."

"Let the young fella talk."

Pride for Donovan spiked through Nora, and a bubble of encouragement rose in her chest.

A hint of doubt colored Bennington's eyes as he scanned the people sit-ting in the pews. He planted his fists on his hips and curled his lips into a snarl as he glared at Donovan, but he kept silent.

Donovan turned so he was facing the people instead of Bennington. "El-lis Weaver is very willing to sell another parcel of land about a thousand yards downriver. The current isn't as swift there, but there is a solid rock ledge where a spillway can be built which would guarantee consistent water power for the mill."

Bennington shook his head. "Too expensive to build a spillway. I say put pressure on Weaver to sell the original plot I offered to buy."

A muted growl rumbled in Grandpa's throat. He pushed forward on his seat. Nora sucked in a sharp breath, and she tightened her grip on Grand-pa's hand. If he mentioned protecting the burial ground, some would support him, but there would be others who wouldn't see the need, and she couldn't bear to see him hurt. She leaned close to his ear. "Wait, Grandpa. Let Donovan speak."

A scowl deepened the creases in Grandpa's brow, but he sat back and patted her hand.

Donovan folded his arms across his chest. "Ellis Weaver was adamant. That land is not for sale." He walked partway down the center aisle. "The mill would be of great benefit to everyone in this community for several reasons—convenience to the farmers, jobs, commerce and growth for the town. I've already spoken with a respected member of your community." He arrowed a look at Grandpa. "He has given me the names of a dozen men who would be willing to volunteer their time to help build a spillway."

He turned back and approached Mr. Bennington. "Not everyone responds the way you want them to when you make threats or use intimidation. Pine Ridge wants your mill for their community, and they're willing to pitch in and help do what is necessary to make it happen. But if you bully them or the Weaver family, or if you try to force your will on them, you'll be looking for another location, all right, but we've already established the other towns have closed their doors to you, Mr. Bennington.

"And one more thing." Donovan reached into his coat and withdrew a folded paper. "I have here a letter of intent signed by Ellis Weaver to sell the parcel of land he and I spoke about, for a fair price. You see, Mr. Bennington, these folks aren't ignorant. They are hard-working people who want to provide for their families and see their community grow. They have honor and respect for each other, and they value honesty and faith above business savvy."

Nora looked over at Grandpa. A tear was sliding down the old man's cheek. She squeezed his fingers. The resting place of his love, his Eve, was safe.

Mayor Gilbert cleared his throat. "Mr. Bennington, I'm asking you right here in front of all these folks if you will please consider this other piece of land Mr. McNeary spoke about. He's right, you know. We do want the mill, but he's right about another thing. Nobody likes being bullied. So will you look at the letter from the Weavers?"

Every eye in the place focused on Bennington, and Nora bit her lip, afraid to breathe. Finally, the man nodded, an expression of resignation falling across his face. "McNeary, let's have a look at that letter."

The room erupted into applause and whistles, and the people filed out, slapping each other on the back. Pastor Parkin and Doc Guthrie shook Grandpa's hand. Nora gave him a quick hug and whispered in his ear. "Grandma's resting place is safe, Grandpa." She turned to the other two men. "I have to go back to the courthouse. Doc, will you please make sure Grandpa goes home and gets some rest?"

"I will. C'mon, Hosea. You heard her." The trio headed for the door, leaving Nora to wait and watch Donovan, Mr. Bennington, and Mayor Gilbert conferring over Ellis Weaver's letter. Did that mean Donovan was re-hired? She'd have to wait to find out.

With one more glance over her shoulder, she turned toward the courthouse.

Nora glanced at the clock. It was past time to close up, but the men's voices still droned behind the mayor's door. Attorney Lawrence Templeton and land agent Wilber Dorsey had joined Asa Bennington, Mayor Gilbert, and Donovan in the mayor's office more than three hours ago. She needed to go home and check on Grandpa and feed him supper. Should she tap on the mayor's door? Indecision halted her feet.

At that moment, the door opened and Nora's breath hitched. Donovan stood before her. They both spoke at the same time.

"How is it going?"

"You're still here."

They laughed, and Donovan tipped his head toward the office door. "They're finishing up in there. May I walk you home?"

The depth of his eyes robbed her of speech, but she nodded. She retrieved her reticule and accompanied Donovan to the door. He looped her arm through his as they made their way toward her home.

"It appears I'm employed again."

She looked up at him. "I suppose that's good. Are you happy about it?"

He nodded. "I am, especially since it means I'm going to get to stay in Pine Ridge."

She widened her eyes and halted. "You are?" Chagrin sent a warm flush to her face, but she didn't care if her reply sounded too eager. "For how long?"

He took both her hands. "Permanently. Mr. Bennington just made me the overseer of the building project, and when it's completed, I'll be the mill manager. So I suppose you could say I'm happy about it. After all, I couldn't very well ask your grandfather for permission to court you if I didn't have a job."

He wanted to court her? Tears clogged her throat and her pulse galloped like a horse that had just broken free of the pasture.

"Nora? Did you hear what I said?"

She moved her head silently up and down.

"Have I upset you?"

She shook her head.

"Will you say something?"

A smile that began deep within bloomed over her entire being. He glanced around at the nearly empty street before his eyes took on a twinkle. He lowered his face to hers and brushed a soft kiss across her lips. "Now will you say something?"

Joy flooded her being. "Yes."

BETTER TOGETHER THAN APART

ROSE ALLEN MCCAULEY

This book is dedicated to my
oldest granddaughter *Natalie Brooke Kinney*,
and my two daughters, *Christy Kinney* and *Mandy Thornberry*,
and to all those who have stepped out into the wide,
wonderful world of mission trips
for God's use and His glory.
It is truly a life-changing event for all! Right, girls?

"By yourself you're unprotected.
With a friend you can face the worst.
Can you round up a third?
A three-stranded rope isn't easily snapped."
ECCLESIASTES 4:12 THE MESSAGE MSG

CHAPTER 1

Natalie Brooks slipped out of bed then slid open the door to the balcony on the ship. She winced at the grating sound and glanced over her shoulder toward her roommates. Good. Jenna and her mom, twin images lying on their right sides, didn't stir.

Natalie sat down in one of the two orange and purple-striped deck chairs. She pulled up her legs and wrapped her extra large University of Kentucky T-shirt around them as she watched the morning sky morph from gray to purple to pink. With a burst of orange, the sun peeked over the horizon, illuminating the vast ocean surrounding them.

You are awesome, God.

Tap, tap. At the noise, she turned to see Jenna's smiling face through the glass door, so beckoned her friend to join her.

Jenna flopped into the empty chair, her navy blue eyes wide with wonder. "I can't believe we're here, can you?"

Natalie's emotions mixed in her head. "I know. It's hard to believe we left Florida last evening. Now, we have a whole day at sea, and we'll arrive in Jamaica tomorrow morning."

"Mind boggling," Jenna agreed. The morning light glinted off her auburn curls. "I hope we'll get picked for the same mission trip tomorrow. When mom and I went on the K-Love cruise last year, we visited a place for handicapped children. One girl lay flat on her back in a wheelchair bed all day, but she prayed aloud for some of us. Can you believe it? We thought we were there to bless them, but they blessed us even more."

"The same thing happened on the mission trip I went on while in high school." Natalie cocked an eyebrow. "Did I ever tell you about the guy I met on my trip to Jamaica?" She'd been so impressed with Ken and his selflessness and commitment to God—the kind of guy she hoped to marry someday.

Jenna rolled her eyes. "You mean the tall, dark, and handsome one whose parents ran the orphanage there?"

"Yes, and with eyes so blue you could drown in them. We exchanged letters for several months, but after we both got busy with college, they fizzled out." A forgotten ache surfaced.

Jenna's perfectly arched brows knitted together. "You don't even know if he's still in Jamaica?"

"No, but it doesn't matter anyway." Natalie shrugged, portraying an indifference she didn't feel. "I've got another year and a half of law school ahead of me, and he's probably still doing mission work." For months, a still small voice had nagged at her. Like before, she fought back with the same argument she'd used on Ken. As a successful lawyer, she could support these mission outreach efforts financially. Without taking any risk.

Time to change the conversation. "I'm so glad it worked out for me to room with you and your mom on this cruise. When my mom needed to stay home to help my aunt and her new baby I worried I'd have to cancel, too."

"Sorry she couldn't make it, but I'm glad we get to room together." Jenna reached over and squeezed her hand.

Gratitude for her kindred spirit swelled her heart. "Yeah. Now, we can share everything on the trip. Like Mom always says, 'All things work together for good.'"

Another peck on the glass. Jenna's mom, Bobbi, opened the door enough to stick her head out. The wind tousled her blonde curls. "Good morning, girls. I'm going to take my shower first if you all don't mind."

"Go for it, Mom. We took showers last night while you were at the Matthew West concert. We'll get dressed, so we can head to breakfast together. "

"Good plan. I'll grab my clothes and head for the shower." Bobbi disappeared into the cabin.

Jenna popped out of the chair. "My mom takes short showers, so we better get ready."

Natalie took one last glance across the rippling surface of the ocean before she followed Jenna inside the cabin.

When they were all dressed for the day, they ambled to the staircase leading to the breakfast bar.

Natalie took the steps two at a time. "It's cool we're on the floor right under the buffets so we can work off some calories by using the stairs."

Jenna kept up with her. "We would've burned more calories if we'd had ten flights to climb."

"No." Bobbi smiled. "Because then I would've used the elevator."

They were still chuckling as they entered the huge dining room. The scents of bacon mingled with waffles and syrup made Natalie's stomach growl. The power of suggestion drew her to the waffle line. Next she added a boiled egg, some juice, and a cup of hot chocolate before scanning the crowd. Jenna and her mom were sitting by the windows. Natalie weaved her way between tables and joined them.

"Couldn't resist, could you?" Jenna teased.

Natalie made a face. "No, but at least I'm not eating *pizza* for breakfast."

"What's wrong with pizza?" Jenna held up a finger. "I remember in health class studying that it contained all the food groups."

"And lots of fat. But it does smell good. I may choose that tomorrow morning." Natalie's eyes gleamed. "We *are* on vacation."

"Let's pray." Bobbi bowed her head and blessed the food.

Natalie took a bite of crisp bacon. "Mmmm, delicious. What's on the agenda for today?"

"We can swim or sunbathe or go for a walk around the decks," Jenna suggested.

"Or read in a lounge chair, or check out the silent auction room, or wait and watch an artist on deck at ten o'clock," finished her mother.

"That's just the morning!" A tall, bearded man in a baseball cap strode by. Natalie's gaze followed him and then swung around to stare at Jenna. "Was that Crowder?"

"Yep, I can't wait to hear him again. Last year, his concert was so awe-inspiring and worshipful I thought I'd died and gone to heaven. I believe he's on the schedule for tomorrow night."

Natalie couldn't believe one of her fave singers was on the same boat with her. "Want to walk around with me, Jenna? Maybe we'll see more singers."

"Sure." Jenna stood. She gave her mom a hug. "We'll come to the room to get you for lunch."

"Great. I plan to catch up on some reading, but if the boat lulls me to sleep, you can wake me up." Bobbi grinned.

The girls climbed to the top level where they didn't need to dodge so many people. They stood at the railing, the sea wind tossing their hair. Natalie breathed in the salty ocean air and was drawn back to the time she stood on the beach with Ken—the last night of her mission trip to Jamaica almost six years ago.

The breeze had whipped a piece of her hair into his face. He leaned over to brush the lock away then kissed her lips so softly she wondered if it even happened. Joining hands, they walked some more. Both promised to write, and they did for several months—until they had a major disagreement by mail over her desire to become a lawyer and his to stay in Jamaica as a missionary. Neither would concede.

By the time her freshman year of college ended, months had passed since she'd heard from him, so she threw his letters away when she packed up to move home that summer. A pang twisted her heart. How could something so sweet have gone so wrong?

Ken Worth paced the mission compound while awaiting his parents' return from the doctor's office. Concern for his mom twisted his stomach into a giant knot. She'd been having night fevers for weeks now, so bad that neither she nor his father slept much. *What will I do if my parents need to fly back to the States?* Maintaining the mission, keeping up with all the staff and children, was hard enough for the three of them. He couldn't imagine staying here and trying to run everything on his own.

Shouts from the gatekeeper announced someone's arrival. The children ran to the sides of the dirt road and waved their hands in the air as the familiar vehicle came through the gate, "Mada! Fada!"

Ken noted his parents' smiling faces and prayed they weren't pretending to keep the children from knowing anything was wrong. He'd be lost without his parents' presence, but most of these kids would be on the streets starving without them.

As some of the other helpers gathered the children for story time in the rec hall, he jogged behind the car to their house on the back of the property. His long legs covered the ground as he hastened to meet his parents and help his mother out of the car. She'd been so weak this morning, he and his father had walked on either side to support her.

Taking her arm, he helped her to the house while his dad locked up the vehicle. "Feeling better, Mom?"

"I most certainly am. The doctor said there's nothing wrong with me except I'm becoming a *mature* woman." She gave a wry smile.

"Mature? You're already the most mature woman I know."

"Thanks...I think." She laughed. "The doctor said we'll need to run an air conditioner in our bedroom or at least a fan at night to help me sleep. He also gave me some thyroid medicine and wants to keep a watch on my blood pressure. It's probably just hormones so I should be fine."

He whooshed out a sigh as he sent up a silent prayer of thanks. "I'm so glad. I don't know what we would do without you."

His father joined them. "You can't keep a good woman down, and your mom's the best of the best."

She blushed. "This woman better go see what she can find for a quick supper—without using the oven." She turned toward the kitchen.

Dad motioned for Ken to join him outside, and Ken's heart boomed against his eardrums as he followed. What did Dad need to say without Mom around?

His father smiled, and some of the lines disappeared from his face. "I know we've both been worried, but the doctor thinks she'll be fine until our next visit to the States in a couple years. He says it's just a normal thing called peri-menopause, and it should run its course in a few years. We need to make sure she gets more rest and keeps her blood pressure monitored. I still want us to help out all we can, especially during most of the outside activities."

Ken's gut unknotted a little. "Sure. I better grab my guitar for the sing-a-long we usually have after story time." He hoisted his instrument from a corner of the porch then walked to the rec room.

As he strolled to the hall, the assignment for the online class he needed to finish that night came to mind. He'd soon have enough classes finished to do his last thirty-two hours in residence at Asbury Theological Seminary. Would his mom's health mean he'd need to postpone getting his degree? He'd postpone things in a heartbeat if that's what it took. Could he get a scholarship to cover at least part of the cost?

Pray about it, My son, and trust Me to work it out.

He knew to listen when God spoke to his heart. What kind of miracle would God work out this time? He hadn't known how he would ever be able to afford a degree in missions until Uncle J.T. offered to foot the bill for the online work at his alma mater. Now, only six more hours of online classes and several thousand dollars for two semesters stood between him starting classes on campus, the final requirement.

I know You are faithful, God. Please help me to be faithful to follow Your lead.

CHAPTER 2

The next morning, Natalie, Bobbi, and Jenna boarded the small bus in the Jamaican terminal. They chatted as they slid into a double seat. Bobbi snagged a place behind them.

The tall, muscular missionary in charge of the trip walked up the aisle counting everyone before taking his seat behind the driver. He hefted a microphone. "My name is Brad Hammond. My wife Susan and I will be leading this tour to the SonShine Orphanage outside Kingston."

The words hit her like a sucker punch. Was that the name of Ken's parents' orphanage? Even if it was, that didn't mean he would still be there.

She stared out the window as they sped down city streets then soon turned onto a country road. Nothing looked familiar, but almost six years had passed. They drove by several ramshackle buildings then onto a road so narrow the green leaves on the branches from the bushes scratched the sides of the windows.

The man spoke again. "We'll arrive at the orphanage soon, so I need to share some important info." He glanced at his watch. "It's almost ten thirty now, and we all need to be back on the bus before four o'clock in order to board the ship by five. Susan has an assortment of healthy snack packages like peanut butter crackers, raisins, and nuts. Please help yourself to a couple from her basket to give you some nourishment until we get back on the ship to eat dinner."

The dark-haired woman carried a wicker basket of treats to the back of the bus then started her way to the front as her husband continued to talk. "Don't drink any water except bottled while here. In this cooler," he pointed underneath the front window, "is enough large bottles of water for each person to take one as you get off the bus. We'll refill the cooler with ice and water bottles for the return trip so no one will get too hot or dehydrated."

When his wife reached the front of the bus, he handed the microphone to her.

She smiled as she scanned the crowd. "We're so glad to share the beautiful country of Jamaica and its wonderful people with you. Please keep these safety tips in mind. Always use the buddy system and never leave the fenced-in compound. Let either of us know if you're unsure about anything. If you're comfortable reading or playing with the children, please do that. Or ask one of the workers if they know a job you could help them with. Also, there is a building project going on toward the back of the property, so if you don't mind getting dirty, volunteer there. We want you to have as much a taste of the missionaries' lives as you would like, so long as no one gets hurt." She looked at her husband. "Did I leave out anything?"

He grinned. "There are two bathrooms in the first building you'll see when we get off the bus, and also two more portable ones near the back building project where most of the men are working. Meet us here by the gate at ten till four. Any questions?"

Natalie's eyes surveyed the property outside her window, and she sucked in a breath at the memories this place evoked. Her pulse fluttered and she bit her lower lip. What would she say if she came face to face with Ken again after so many years?

The group filed off the bus. Bobbi wanted to stop by the restrooms, so the girls waited for her. They'd make a group of three buddies today.

As they waited, Natalie's gaze roamed over the dusty paths, a few palm trees, and several cinder-block buildings. Two small girls approached them. One put her arms around Jenna's waist like long-lost friends while the other one gave a shy smile and reached out a hand for Natalie.

Natalie took the girl's hand. "Hi, y'all."

The child sent her a confused look and gave a fake yawn with her hand and mouth. "Yawn?"

Natalie laughed as she squeezed the child's hand. Understanding the girls wasn't a problem, but getting the Jamaicans to understand their Kentucky slang was a little harder.

Bobbi came outside and put on her hat. "Did you girls apply sunscreen while on the bus?"

"Yes, Mother," they said in unison.

The two Jamaicans chimed in. "Yes, Mada."

Nat listened, then answered Mr. Hammond. Ken wished he could hear the whole conversation. He didn't want Natalie to leave so soon. "Yes, Mrs. Worth invited us to spend some time with her. Could you also find Bobbi Lee and tell her where we are so she won't worry?" She paused again. "That would be great. Thank you." She hung up the phone and smiled at Ken's mom. "He said if you're up to it, visiting with you would be a wonderful use of our time. I also asked him about Jenna's mom and he promised to bring her here to join us."

His mother beamed a radiant smile.

Ken's heart soared, and he nodded. "So, it's settled. Mom, this is Natalie Brooks who came here five or six years ago, and her friend, Jenna. Let's sit down in the big room where the fan is." He led them into a large room with a couple of couches and several stacks of folding chairs set against the wall. "We hold meetings and sometimes church in here during the rainy season."

"I remember a service in here last time. You didn't have as many buildings then." Nat smiled at his mother.

"Yes, all mission compounds are works in progress. Like the building Ken and the other men are working on now. It's a dorm to house groups that want to stay here for a couple weeks so they won't need to travel back and forth like you did, Natalie."

"That makes sense. They'd have more time to do things here rather than spend an hour or more each day traveling."

"Indeed." Mom settled into the sofa cushions. "Were you in high school the first time you came, Natalie?"

"I'd just graduated."

Mom nodded. "So, are you out of college now?"

"I'm in my second year of law school."

"A lawyer. I'm sure God can use you to do a lot of good with that degree."

Ken noted Nat's eyes flickered to his before answering. "I hope to, although I'm still not sure what specialty of law I want to pursue."

"I'll add that to my prayer list."

Ken agreed. He planned to do the same.

A knock at the door brought Ken to his feet before his mother got up to answer it. "Come in, Brad, and this lady must be Jenna's mom."

"Yes, Mrs. Bobbi Lee." Brad shook Ken's hand then waved to the others. "Good to see you, Tina. Better go keep an eye on things."

Jenna moved over to make space for her mother.

Bobbi smiled. "Thanks for sending Mr. Hammond to find me. I would've been concerned if I hadn't seen you both by now." Bobbi turned to speak to Nat. "I didn't realize you'd already been to Jamaica, Natalie. Did you know that, Jenna?"

Jenna nodded, and her cheeks reddened as she glanced at Natalie whose face glowed to match.

Ken noted their embarrassment. Did Nat tell her friend about him? If so, what had she said?

His mother stood. "Ken, would you help me get some cookies and tea ready?"

"Sure, Mom." He followed her into the kitchen, hoping she wouldn't pepper him with questions. He had too much to think about. Did Natalie remember their disagreement? Their kiss? He'd never forgotten her. Had she forgotten him?

Natalie had gone from anticipation to apprehension in a heartbeat. Now that Ken left the room, maybe she could corral her racing thoughts and galloping pulse. She wished she could read Ken's mind. Was he as conflicted as she? What if he brought up their past disagreement? Was she ready to give up all her fears to do what he'd asked her to do before?

Natalie stared at Jenna, who turned to stare at her mother.

She looked at the girls and whispered, "Mr. Hammond told me anything Mrs. Worth offered would be fine to eat and drink."

Jenna sighed. "That's a relief."

"Yes." Natalie agreed.

Ken and his mother returned. She carried a plate of cookies, and he held a tray filled with glasses of tea. His fingers brushed Nat's hand as she reached for a glass. Goosebumps travelled up her arm.

She raised her head and smiled. Had he felt it, too? Was he as sorry as she was about their lost years?

CHAPTER 3

Ken's heart accelerated as he pondered being alone with Nat, but he had to take the chance. He couldn't stand the idea of not getting to talk with her in private before she left. Who knew how long it might be before they connected again? "Nat, could I speak to you outside a few minutes before I go back to the building project?"

"Sure." She set her glass down on a coaster and stood. Was that surprise in her eyes or happiness?

He held the door open for her then closed it behind them. Now what to say? Words eluded him. This whole day had been such a surprise—like a do-over, one he didn't want to mess up.

As he stared into her huge brown eyes, he knew where he needed to begin. "Nat, I owe you a big apology." She didn't turn aside. "I shouldn't have tried to change your mind about becoming a lawyer. Who am I to tell you what to do? It was selfishness on my part. I wanted you to take Bible courses or teach or something that would lead you back to the mission field...back to Jamaica." *Back to me.* He wiped the sweat from his brow. "Will you please forgive me?"

"Of course, Ken. I was eighteen and you were nineteen. We both had a lot to learn and a lot of growing up to do." The golden flecks in her eyes twinkled.

He dug the toe of his shoe in the dirt. "I must say, you've grown up quite nicely."

She blushed then gave him a sideways glance. "You, too."

He took both her hands in his. "I can't believe you're in Jamaica. I want to hear all about what you've been doing, how long you plan to stay..."

Her head jerked up. "We're leaving at four o'clock."

"Today?" His insides twisted like he might be sick.

"Yes, the boat is only in Jamaica one day before heading to the Grand Cayman Islands."

His stomach sank, but he rallied with an idea. "I'd like to escort you and your friends around the compound. If it's okay with you?"

"I'd love it!" Her smile lit up her face.

"Wonderful. And, is it still okay to call you Nat like I did when you were here before?"

"I'd like that."

They went back inside, and he told the others his plan.

After eating their cookies and getting the go-ahead from his mom, Ken and the three ladies from the cruise ship set off on a grand tour of the mission compound. With God's help, he would make the most of this day, then he would release the results into the Father's hands.

First, they explored the building project behind his house. As they approached, several shouts of "Mr. Ken" peppered the air. The men must've saved up their questions for him while he was in the house.

A tall Jamaican man approached them and slapped Ken on the back. "Where you been, bredda? We need you to tell us what pitch to make da roof."

He sighed. "Okay, Peter, but only for a minute. I've got guests." He didn't want to miss one minute of his short time with Nat.

Ken shot Nat an apologetic look. "Sorry, this won't take long."

Natalie studied Ken as he pointed, measured, then drew lines on the plans. She glanced at the time on her cell phone. One o'clock. Guilt swept over her for keeping him from his work, but she couldn't bear to tell him to stay, not when she'd be leaving in three short hours. Meeting him again had resurrected her memories of the good times they'd shared, and she didn't want to leave so soon.

He returned. "I want to show you our school."

She and the other ladies followed him down the path to an older building with two doors. The tin roof was rusting and needed a paint job. When they entered the first door, the three dozen or so students all sat up straight and quiet.

Ken smiled at the teacher. "Please continue your lesson, Mrs. Brenda."

She nodded then called out mental math problems. All of the students from youngest to oldest answered aloud and got every problem correct.

Ken complimented the children and then thanked the teacher.

In the next room, the teacher read a story to another thirty plus students. After she closed the book, she began to ask questions. Most hands were raised, and many questions answered correctly by the eager students.

"Well done," Ken said, and the ladies clapped for the students. The students repaid them with their own round of applause.

The next building they approached was quieter than the first. Ken held up a finger to his lips. "Let me stick my head in the nursery to see if any of the babies are awake. If not, we'll come back later." His head disappeared then reappeared with a smile across his face. "Two of the babies just woke from their naps and are being diapered. Would any of you ladies like to feed them their bottles?" He cocked an eyebrow.

Natalie wanted to, but Jenna and Bobbi volunteered first. Nursery workers pointed to two rockers where the ladies could sit. The helpers placed the babies into their arms, then handed them the bottles. She whispered into Ken's ear, "Is it okay if I snap a picture of them with the babies?"

"Sure." Ken motioned toward the room in the back of this one. "There are the remaining cribs and more sleeping babies."

Bobbi placed the baby she was feeding on her shoulder and patted the child until a burp erupted. She stood and, holding the baby in one arm, motioned for Natalie to sit in the rocker. Bobbi then put the warm bundle and half-full bottle in Natalie's shaking arms.

Her nervousness soon turned to contentment. She'd never had much opportunity to rock or feed a baby since her sister was only two years younger and her brother had been adopted when he was five. She would never forget this moment when everything else faded away as she looked into the baby's sweet face and watched the child's mouth suck in the nourishment.

When the babies finished feeding, the nursery workers lifted the bundles from their arms, and the women followed Ken out the door. Nat's arms ached with an emptiness she'd never experienced before. She wanted to hold the child again. Or move here and do nursery duty every day.

"Would you like to see the girls' dorm? The one for the boys is on the other side of our home."

"Yes," Jenna agreed, and the others nodded.

He opened a door, and they entered a colorful room with large cots. As they continued on, smaller beds appeared, until the last room held a dozen or so cribs. "You saw the nursery building where the babies sleep until they are at least a year old with someone who stays there around-the-clock. This room is for those who have passed their first birthday and can walk. One house-mother sleeps in this room with them, and another one sleeps in the front to be available for any of the older children who might need help during the night. It doesn't happen often, but we thought it best as our numbers grew."

Bobbi turned a thoughtful frown on Ken. "How many boys and girls live here?"

"We keep beds for ninety, and when someone leaves, that cot fills very soon. Some of these children have families who can't afford to keep them, but over half of our children are true orphans with nowhere else to go."

Jenna's forehead pinched. "How many of them will ever be adopted?"

Ken hung his head. "That's difficult to say, but not many. Maybe a dozen or so. Jamaica has its adoption regulations, and America, or any other country pursuing an adoption here, has their own laws. Most adoptions take a year or more to finalize."

Natalie barely recalled her own brother's adoption since she was only six, but it had been a joyous time for her family. "I remember my parents telling me there were home visits in the States."

Ken nodded. "Yes, and the adoptive parents must satisfy the qualifications for both countries, so it's even more complicated to do an international adoption. But it's well worthwhile for those who are ready to do what's required. I hope you've seen the love these children share with others, and the love they need. It's hard for less than twenty adults to give them all lots of individual attention, but we try."

Natalie pondered what she'd learned as they moved on to a large kitchen and dining room combination. This newer building had been built since her first trip. The children and adults had eaten outside on the ground then, trying to find shade under a tree if possible.

Shiny bright appliances gleamed, and the sinks and countertops were all scrubbed clean, as well as the tile floors. Ten or more tables of varying sizes covered the dining hall, with chairs enough for everyone. A few high chairs for the youngest babies sat at the corners of some of the tables.

Ken led them to the next building. A smile teased the corners of his mouth. "Nat, I hope you will find our latest building to your liking."

He didn't give her any other clues, so she was flabbergasted when they entered a room that held shelves loaded with books covering almost all the walls. Ken smiled at her. "Do you remember telling me we needed a library for kids like you who never had enough books to read?"

Her cheeks flushed. "I do. But, where did you get so many books?"

"I told my mother about your request. Over a dozen churches sponsor our mission, so Mom wrote letters to each of them asking the ladies to hold book drives for new or gently used books to send to us." He pointed to some lower shelves under colorful pictures on the wall, and another small table with six chairs around it. "We received puzzles and other games which we keep in that area."

Next, he pointed to several taller shelves. "These are books for the teen-agers and young adults. The workers even enjoy checking out books from here because most of them don't have much to read in their homes. So, thank you for your idea. I'm glad you get to see how it came to life."

Tears filled her eyes. Heart overflowing, she thanked God.

Ken glanced at his watch. Already after three. Where had the day gone? Today had been the most enjoyable afternoon he'd experienced in months, and he could already sense a letdown at the idea of Nat leaving soon. *God, please give me a chance to talk to her about writing again, even with so many people around.* "Would you like to stop by the boys' dorm, then say good-bye to my mother?"

"Since you said the boys' dorm is similar to the girls', I'd like to spend these last few minutes with your mom. Her wisdom impressed me." Nat smiled. "Not that we haven't enjoyed our time with you as our special guide, too."

Ken laughed. "I agree. My mom is much wiser than I am, so let's go visit her again."

They trooped off to the Worth home.

His mother greeted them with big hugs like long-lost friends. "I hoped you would stop by before you left. Please come in and sit down for a few minutes."

Bobbi turned to Mrs. Worth. "Could you drop me a note now and then to keep us abreast of what's going on? I'd love to pray for you and your family and for the work here."

"Certainly, and you can fill me in on your family and how I can pray for you, too."

"I'd appreciate that." Bobbi smiled.

Thanks God, for Your fast answer to prayer. Ken handed Nat, Bobbi, and Jenna copies of the latest newsletters from the mission with the address and email on it. "Nat, I hope we can keep in touch, too. Email out here in the boonies is kind of erratic sometimes, and long distance is very expensive, so we connect much of the time through the slow-but-sure, inexpensive mail system.

She tore off a blank corner of the newsletter, scribbled her address and email on it, then handed it to him. "I won't have email or phone service until I get back to the States in five days. It was too expensive for me, too." She turned to his mom. "I'm certainly impressed with all you've done here in the five and a half years since I left. The compound has grown so much, and I love the library."

His mom raised an eyebrow. "Were you the gal who put that great idea in Ken's head?"

"Yes, she was." Ken winked at Nat.

"I trust you enjoyed it." Mom grinned.

"I certainly did. The children and the babies were my favorite part of the day, but the library was my favorite building."

"I hope you can return again and see more changes in a few years." Mrs. Worth smiled.

A warmth filled Ken's heart, but he hoped she wouldn't wait years to visit again. "We'd better be going so you won't be late."

After another round of hugs and well-wishes, the ladies were ready to depart. Ken accompanied them, and his steps grew slower as they approached the front gate.

The bus was nearly filled, and Brad was waiting in the open door. "Thought maybe you'd kidnapped some of our team, Ken." The man chuckled.

I wish I could. "No. They're all here." He opened his arms. "One last group hug?" They obliged, and he felt Jenna push Nat closer to him. That would have to do for...how long?

CHAPTER 4

Natalie heard very little of Mr. Hammond's wrap-up of their trip. Instead her mind overflowed from her day at the SonShine Orphanage. Her admiratio for Ken had soared with each completed project he explained. His imprint glowed from the finished buildings to the plans he'd shared with them for more ventures when the funds came in. He was a fount of wisdom on the land and the people, too. The special love he and the children shared brought a smile to her face. They'd called out "Mr. Ken" over and over again, always with respect and love.

Jenna touched her hand and brought her out of her reverie. "Natalie, Mr. Hammond is passing around the microphone for anyone who wants to say something about the trip today."

Could she share anything? It was all so personal. *God, please give me the words You want me to speak.*

Jenna took the mic. "Mrs. Worth, the missionary's wife, had a health scare lately, so I hope we'll all remember to pray for her and also for the babies we held and fed." She glanced at Natalie. "I'll never forget their faces and their dark eyes staring into mine." She passed the microphone to Nat.

Natalie sniffed and blinked her eyes to stop the tears. "It wasn't until we arrived here today that I realized it was the same place I'd spent two weeks after my high school graduation. I'm amazed at what the Worths have accomplished in the years since I was there. I'd like to go back again after I graduate law school. I'm praying about how God wants to use me, so I would appreciate your prayers also." She passed the mic over her shoulder to Bobbi.

She leaned against the window and stared out at the riotous greenery. *God, I want to pray as Jesus did, "Not my will, but Yours." Please show me what You want me to do.* The next thing she remembered was a gentle shake.

Jenna grinned at her. "You must've fallen asleep. We're back at the dock."

Natalie climbed out behind her friend, her dream of Ken surrounded by the Jamaican children fresh on her mind. What was he doing now?

Ken had taken the time for a quick, early supper with his mom before he returned to the worksite. The other men were locking up their tools to leave. He hollered at Peter, "Can you stay a few minutes and catch me up on what you did and what I can do now?"

"All right, mon, me no 'ave a hot date like you."

Ken laughed. "It wasn't a date, but I wish it had been."

"Pretty gal wid pretty brown hair an' brown eyes dat spark like da stars." Peter's smile flashed merriment.

Nat indeed had eyes that sparkled like the stars—eyes he would never forget. "We better get busy or I'll still be out here tonight when the stars come out."

His friend chuckled and picked up the plans. "See here? Dat pitch neva wuk out wid da porch so we did haffa shorten it some."

Ken studied the paper then nodded in agreement. "So how did you modify it?"

Peter talked and gestured, explaining the changes to him.

"Thanks, I'll measure and cut a few rafters this evening so we'll be ready to start in the morning."

"Okay, see you den." Peter whistled as he left.

After Ken worked a few minutes alone, his father joined him. "Pretty busy day, huh?"

And fun. He nodded. "Super busy, and I took off part of the day to walk around with some of the group that came with Mr. Hammond."

"Your mom told me one of the girls was from a trip several years ago." His dad's gaze bored into his.

"Yes, Natalie Brooks. We wrote a few times, but it fell through. I don't plan to let that happen this time." He grinned at Dad.

His dad chuckled. "Let me give you a hand with the boards so you'll have time to write her tonight."

"Thanks, Dad."

The work went twice as fast, and Ken's heart gladdened at the faithful support of his parents.

That night as he lay in bed praying, Ken wished he'd mentioned to Natalie the scholarship he hoped to receive, but why get her hopes up when he hadn't heard anything? He needed to stop by the post office when he went to town tomorrow. *God, not my will, but Yours, and help me to be patient as I wait on You.*

As the gentle waves rocked the boat that evening, Natalie lay in her bed, her brain on overload. The whole day had rocked her boat, especially meeting Ken Worth again. Their short summer romance fizzled out years ago, but her heart wouldn't let that happen this time. His bright blue eyes told her he wouldn't either.

She'd missed the evening concert tonight to stay in the cabin and write to him. The words flowed through her pen as her heart poured out many personal feelings—her desire to seek God's direction above all else, and her increased love for the orphans she'd met and rocked today.

Her internal musings turned into a petition to God to help her discern His will for her career and life, to show her what He wanted her to specialize in her last year of law school, and how He wanted to use her. She also prayed for all the orphans in Jamaica and all the missionaries, especially Mr. and Mrs. Worth and Ken. Slumber claimed her mid-prayer.

Someone calling her name and the light shining through the balcony doors awakened her at daybreak. She glanced over at Jenna and her mom, but both still slept. Natalie recalled the boy Samuel hearing God's voice. She responded as he'd done.

"Speak, Lord, for your servant hears."

She slid her Bible from the table, and tiptoed out to the balcony for some quiet time with God, her favorite part of the day. The spectacular sunrise again brought words of praise to her tongue. "O Lord, our Lord, how majestic is Your Name in all the earth." She stilled her thoughts before Him, read a chapter in His Word, and basked in His glorious presence around and within her.

Half an hour later, Bobbi opened the sliding door. "Good morning, Natalie."

"Yes, it's a beautiful one again." She waved her hand toward the rippling ocean waves and sky bursting with color.

Jenna joined them. "Are you partying without me?"

"Never." Natalie smiled. "Are y'all hungry?"

"Let's go." Jenna pulled her up from her chair.

In less than ten minutes, they were climbing the stairs to the buffet. Thankful for her Christian companions, Natalie tried the pizza.

When she finished eating, Bobbi stood. "I want to run to the cabin and brush this syrup off my teeth, but I'll meet you all down on deck 2 where we de-board for our trip to Grand Cayman in about thirty minutes."

Natalie arose. "Sorry to bail out on you all, but I need more quiet time with God. I'm going to stay in the room or on the balcony most of the day."

Bobbi cocked her head. "Are you sure?"

"Yes. When I awoke, I heard Him calling my name. Then I read Matthew eleven in my Message Bible and understood why when I reached the end of the chapter." She quoted, "'Are you tired? Worn out? Come to me. Get away with me, and you'll recover your life.'" She smiled. "I love this part at the end: 'Learn the unforced rhythms of grace.'" She looked up at Bobbi. "I think God wants to teach me something, and I need quiet to take it all in."

Bobbi bent over and gave her a hug. "Who am I to argue with God? I'll pray for you today, and in the days to come."

Jenna added a hug of her own. "Me, too."

Natalie inched toward the buffets. "I'm going to grab some fruit for my lunch, so you go on up to the room. I'll be waiting to hear about your trip at supper. And, will you mail the letter on my bed while you're in Grand Cayman?"

Jenna raised an eyebrow. "If you tell us who it's for."

"Ken Worth."

Bobbi nodded. "Sounds like you plan to stay in touch this time."

Natalie watched them leave before gathering her food for the day. She desired this day to be only about her relationship with Him. She stored the food in their little refrigerator before grabbing her Bible again and returning to the balcony. She read the last verse in Matthew eleven aloud.

"'Learn the unforced rhythms of grace. I won't lay anything heavy or ill-fitting on you. Keep company with me and you'll learn to live freely and lightly.'"

She bowed her head. "God, that sounds so good to live freely and lightly.

You know how uptight I can be at times, especially about school and being secure. Help me to be still and let You speak to me about how to change and follow You in unforced rhythms of grace."

The sound of the waves overtook her conscious thoughts, and she opened her heart to God and wherever He led.

After lunch, Ken drove to town to pick up the mail and some groceries to supplement their farm produce. Raising chickens and a garden year-round helped to cut expenses in order to aid more of their people.

He riffled through the mail in the box. Mostly for his father, but one envelope with Asbury Theological Seminary in the left-hand corner set his heart to beating faster than the steel drums the natives played. Ken hurried to the truck, and all thumbs, tore open the envelope and read.

> *Mr. Worth,*
>
> *We regret to inform you that all scholarship money has already been allotted for the coming school year, but we hope you will try again next year or perhaps take out a student loan.*

His heart took a dive. He bowed his head. "God, You know there's no way for me to pay back school loans. I don't understand this, but I will trust You to supply the funds or give me peace about not going on in school."

As he drove back to the compound, he tried to prepare the best way to tell his parents the bad news. They wanted what was best for him. They would probably tell him to accept this as God's will. He would have more time to work on building projects. Maybe take some of the preaching load off Dad's plate, although Ken was more comfortable on the job site than in the pulpit.

His mom met him with a questioning gaze and carried in some of the lighter groceries while he brought in the rest. "Any mail?"

He handed her the stack. "Mostly for dad and one for you." He swallowed down the lump in his throat. "I didn't get the scholarship I applied for. They said all the funds were gone this year, so they suggested I apply again next year or take out student loans."

"How absurd. What missionary could afford to pay back student loans for a private university?"

No surprise his mother was in his corner. "I'll go tell Dad unless you need me to help put the groceries away."

"Shoo." She waved her apron. "I can pray while I do that. God will make a way."

His father stood surveying the building site behind the house.

Ken stopped next to him. "Hey, Dad, got a minute?"

"Of course."

"I picked up the mail. You've got a stack at the house."

His father's eyebrows rose. "Any word from Asbury?"

"Yep. No funds this year, so I guess I'll be here another year at least."

"I prayed it would be this year, but don't give up hope yet, son. God knows what we need better than we do, and He always supplies it in His perfect timing. Right?" He put an arm around Ken's shoulder.

"Right. What can I do here?"

"If you can take over, we might be able to get the rafters up before the men leave for the day. I need to look at the washing machine for your mother. It stopped in the middle of a load while you were out."

"Sure thing." *It will keep me so busy I won't have time to dwell on my disappointment.*

CHAPTER 5

Natalie, Bobbi, and Jenna walked to breakfast the following morning. Suddenly Jenna groaned. Natalie and Bobbi gave her puzzled looks.

"I can't believe this is our last full day on the ship. It's flown by."

"I agree." Natalie sighed. "But I'm eager to get back to real life and make some changes based on what God's been teaching me this week. Who knew I'd have to come on a cruise to get closer to God?"

Bobbi grinned. "God did. What do you two plan to do today?"

"I want to get in the pool this morning." Nat gave a mock shiver. "It might be too cool by the evening when we're approaching the U.S. again."

"Great call. I'll join you. How about you, Mom?"

Bobbi shook her head, making her curls bounce. "I have a book I haven't finished, so today's the day."

"Why don't we find chairs around the pool, so you can join us later, Bobbi."

"Sounds like a plan. Maybe we can even eat lunch out on the deck."

"I love it." Jenna smiled.

After breakfast, they all dressed in their swimsuits and cover-ups then found three chairs together on the deck. Jenna and Natalie swam and even went down the slide a few times before climbing out to sit beside Bobbi.

While Jenna went to get some ice cream, Natalie pondered what she wanted to say to Ken. Could she share something as intimate as what God showed her yesterday? She'd barely touched the surface with Jenna and her mom last night at supper. It was all so fresh, she didn't quite understand it herself. But she was certain God was calling her to walk closer with Him in her identity as His child and to trust Him to help her release the fear that had bound her ever since she and her mom were trapped in a creek when she was five. Her own dad had saved them, and now she had to grow in her trust that her Heavenly Father would always save her, too.

She would wait to write again when she was home. By then, she could gather her thoughts. She trusted Ken to understand them.

Dear Ken,

I hope you and everyone else at the mission are well, especially your parents. It was a pleasant surprise that this trip brought me back to your compound. I came on this cruise not knowing why, except to have a good time with other Christians and get a little sun before heading back to winter and law school. Yesterday I spent the day alone in my room with God. He showed me so much at SonShine.

He's continuing to teach me how to live life with Him and wait on Him for direction in the decisions I need to make in the coming weeks and months.

Please pray for me to be willing to follow wherever He leads. He also showed me I need to let go of fear. Please let me know how I can pray for you and your family. Waiting on Him with expectancy, Nat

Ken re-read his letter from Natalie then sat down and answered it so he could mail his reply while in town today.

Dear Nat,

I was so happy to receive this second letter from you. Your first one, mailed from Grand Cayman, arrived in three days, but this one took almost two weeks. Everyone is fine here, and the progress on the mission guesthouse you saw us building has it now under roof.

God is teaching us both to wait on Him and His timing. I had been accepted to a university in the States to finish my Master's in Intercultural Studies. For several years, I've been taking online classes, but I need a scholarship to take the remainder on campus. They informed me there isn't any more scholarship money this year, so my master's will have to wait. I have determined to do as you said and wait with expectancy on where He leads now.

Thank you for sharing your fear with me, and I will pray for Him to show you that you can always trust your Heavenly Father.

Your friend, Ken

He debated about changing the ending to something more personal, but it might not be appropriate. Only God knew if their paths would ever cross again. He placed the letter in the addressed envelope as he walked into the kitchen.

"Hey, Mom, is your grocery list ready?"

She glanced over her shoulder at him from the sink. "It's on the table."

"Thanks. Anything else you need while I'm in town?"

"Stop by the post office if it's not too much trouble." She winked.

"If you insist." He placed a kiss on her cheek.

As he drove the Rover into Kingston, Ken mentally made a list of the things they needed for the guesthouse. That would be his last stop, but no contest for which would be his first. He entered the post office and couldn't miss the grin on the postmaster's face.

"Hey, mon, why you be here so soon again?"

"Mom and Dad needed some things, so I thought I'd stop by and see you."

"Sure ting. You no want dis letter den?" He waved a short envelope.

Ken reached over the counter and snatched the letter. "Thanks. Anything else for us?"

His friend handed him a bundle of mail banded together. "And some for your mada and fada."

"Thanks, mon." Ken waved as he left, whistling his happiness. When he reached his vehicle, he opened the two-page letter from Nat and hungrily scanned the lines of her handwriting, smiling at her report of helping people at the free law clinic where she volunteered. He related to her complaint about not liking to be stuck in front of a computer instead of being face to face with people, and wished he could talk face to face with her instead of reading her thoughts from a sheet of paper.

The letter mentioned she'd been dating a fellow law student but she'd broken it off when she learned their values differed. Ken's teeth clenched at the thought of her dating someone like that. Should he write and ask her to go steady with him...or whatever they called it now?

Farther down the page, her request for prayer in seeking a specialty tugged at his heart. He hoped she knew he already prayed for that every day. Her description of wanting sun after all the snow in Kentucky produced a chuckle. Would it be nice to bottle up some Jamaican sunshine and send it to her? Or, better yet, deliver it in person?

With her letter in his pocket, he was ready to purchase groceries and other supplies before heading back. He loved what he did and knew that God had prepared him for the mission field by giving him the chance to grow up on the ministry compound and learn from his mom and dad. He prayed for God to show Nat what He wanted her to do. Would it be something she could do in Jamaica, too? Would she be willing to move there if it was where God called her?

Natalie drew in a deep breath of air as she passed some fragrant dogwoods on the way to the Law Library. Spring had finally arrived in Kentucky, lifting her spirits.

She was certain another guy from church she'd been dating wasn't the one for her. Was Ken? His rare calls and frequent letters and emails had become the highlights of her week. They'd been apart for years except for the day she spent at Sonshine Orphanage in January. But, from his letters and her past experiences with him, she'd seen his heart for God and His children.

Could God use us better together than apart?

From where had that question come? Her grandmother had shared advice when Nat started dating. She'd written those words on the back of her photo to Pappaw when they dated in college, and they were still serving Him together almost fifty years later.

Thank You, God, for reminding me of Mimi's words. Please help me to marry the person You know is best for me—the one with whom I can serve You better together than apart.

How could she use a law degree from Kentucky in Jamaica? She wasn't sure, but was certain God could bring it to pass if it were in His plans. As she entered the library, she shot up a prayer for God to guide as she chose a topic for her final term paper for her International Law class.

Two hours later she'd read about international laws on marriage, divorce, property, and banking, but none of them interested her. Weary and bleary-eyed, she wanted to quit, but something nudged her to continue, so she did.

Education intrigued her, but how could she narrow the broad topic down? She scrolled farther until she came to a new heading—International Adoption Laws. Her heart squeezed. That's it! Why hadn't she thought of it before now?

Your heart wasn't ready until now, My child.

The words He spoke to her inner being rang true. Before the trip, so many other things competed for her attention and her heart. Through her experiences on the cruise and the letters she and Ken had shared, she now sought to live a life with God in every part of it.

Images of the babies she'd rocked in Jamaica and all the other children at the SonShine orphanage came to mind. She could make a difference in their lives and give purpose to her own—God's purpose for all of them. After printing the pages she'd need, Natalie paid, then floated out the door like she was walking in Air Jordans. She would go home and call Ken later. They couldn't afford to call all the time, but this was too good to wait to share.

Ken sat in his bedroom in front of his computer, thinking about emailing Nat. His cell phone rang, and his pulse accelerated at the sight of her number on the screen.

"Hey, Nat. What's the big occasion? Did you ace that test on financial law?"

"Better than that."

"Really? Are you flying down here tomorrow?"

She chuckled. "I wish, but it's almost as good." She paused then heaved a big breath. "God showed me today how I could use my law degree in Jamaica."

His heart climbed into his throat, and he swallowed. "How's that?"

"Did you know there are international adoption lawyers? I can spend the next year learning about all the different laws in the U.S. and other countries, especially in the Caribbean, and Jamaica in particular. I might have to travel some, but…" A nervous laugh came across the line. "Sorry, I'm so excited I'm rambling."

"I like the sound of your rambling, especially the words. This would be great. Several adoptions fell through at the last minute this past year when all the regulations weren't completed on time. Multiply that by all the orphanages in Jamaica, and you'll have more than a full time job."

"Please ask your parents for their opinion, and I'll check with my advisor in the morning. She knows I've been searching for an area to specialize in, and I have a whole year to do the work. I can't think of any more fulfilling way to use my law degree than to help families who are eager to adopt and especially help the children who need a family."

"I agree. I love the verse in Psalm 68 that says, 'God sets the lonely in families.'"

"I love that verse, too."

"How did this all come together?"

"We've both been praying for God to lead us, and I was trusting God to work it all out when something my Mimi told me a few years ago popped into my head."

"What was it?" He held his breath.

"It's pretty personal to share over the phone, but I'll tell you in person when the time is right."

"I can live with that, as long as it means you'll be coming to Jamaica soon."

"I wish you were coming to the States even sooner."

"Me, too, and we'll keep praying. In fact, let's pray now. Dear Father, we thank You for this answer to prayer for the direction You're leading Nat in for her specialty. Please continue to go before us and guide us every step of the way."

Natalie continued, "And, Lord, please make a way for Ken to finish his degree in the States if it's Your perfect will. We trust You and leave that in Your hands also. In the mighty name of Jesus we pray. Amen."

"Amen." He cleared his throat. "I'll go talk to Mom and Dad about this. I'm sure they'll be excited. I'll write you tomorrow."

"Ditto, and, tell your parents hi from me."

As he hung up, a wave of sadness enveloped him. What if Natalie moved to Jamaica in a year, and then he received a scholarship to the States? What if he had to choose between being with her and completing his degree?

God, please help me trust You even when I don't understand. No turning back.

CHAPTER 6

Natalie wanted to fly to Jamaica to see Ken as soon as school was out, but being knee-deep in research books and papers on international adoption kept her grounded. The project took much longer than she'd thought, so her teacher agreed to give her an incomplete as long as she finished before the first summer term ended. She had one month to complete her paper, so she was working late again, surrounded by books and papers spread all over her living room furniture.

Not how she'd planned to spend her summer, but this was too important to do halfway. Her parents had promised to travel to Jamaica with her over the Independence Day holiday, so they could meet Ken and his family. She and Ken had never discussed any serious plans about their relationship, but she was falling in love with him long distance. Together they'd decided for both families to meet before things did become more serious.

When the phone rang at almost ten o'clock, she scrambled to search for it under a pile of papers on her desk. "Hello?"

"Nat, it's Ken. I hope it's not too late, but my uncle J.T. just called me."

Her mind drew a blank. Why would he be phoning her to say his uncle had called him? "Is everything all right?"

"It's better than all right." He paused. "He's going to pay my way to Asbury Seminary this fall."

"To finish your degree?"

"Yes." His excitement crackled over the line.

Joy filled her. "That's wonderful."

"I agree, but I have a question to ask you."

Bewildered, she gulped. *Over the phone?*

"Asbury has two campuses where I can finish my Master of Arts degree. One is in Florida, and the other in Wilmore, Kentucky. I wanted your input on which one to choose."

He's asking me to decide? "I would pick Florida, but I hope *you* will choose Kentucky. Did you know Wilmore is less than thirty minutes from my apartment?"

Ken laughed. "No, but my uncle did mention it was near Lexington."

Tears filled her eyes. "It's what we've been praying for, so why am I so surprised?"

"Exactly. It's like the verse in Ephesians 3 that says God has given us 'immeasurably more than all we could ask or imagine.'"

"How true." She wiped her eyes. "What did your parents say?"

"They were in on the plan. My dad called his brother a few weeks ago to see if he had any ideas to help me get to school this year, and he said his business had a stellar year, so he'd be glad to send me. I need to finish everything possible here before I leave in two months to fly to Kentucky. I hope you and your parents will still come next month, so they can meet my folks."

"We're looking forward to it. I just have to finish my paper before then."

"I'll let you get back to it. Remember, I'll see you here in July, and in Kentucky in August. Bye for now."

"Bye." She glanced at the clock as she sank to her knees on the floor. Only five minutes had passed, but her world had turned on its axis, and her head was spinning. She needed to call her parents and Jenna, but first she wanted to thank the One who'd answered their prayers beyond her wildest dreams.

Natalie turned in her paper a week early so was catching up on some things while watching a little of the news. One of her college friends had mentioned last night about a storm brewing in the Caribbean. The announcer said something about Jamaica, so she turned up the volume.

"A category two hurricane is heading for the island of Jamaica. Winds are increasing, and they expect it to reach landfall near Kingston by this evening, then hit Cuba the following day."

Her cell phone rang with her mom's name on the screen. Natalie snatched it up. "Hi, Mom."

"Have you heard the news, dear?"

"Yes, just now. Channel 27 said a hurricane is expected to hit Kingston by tonight."

"Channel 36 said the same thing."

Natalie rubbed her temples, trying to fight off a headache. "What are we going to do, Mom?"

"Pray and keep an eye on things. We may have to postpone or delay our trip."

"I want to call Ken, but I'm sure he's extra busy now with all the storm preparations."

"Why don't you call his mom to see what she knows?"

"Great idea."

Natalie dialed the house phone at the mission. It was noon in Kentucky, so would be eleven in the morning in Jamaica. Ken's Mom would probably be inside. "Hello?" Static distorted Mrs. Worth's voice.

"Hello, Mrs. Worth. It's Natalie. We wanted to check on you all because of this storm coming."

"Hi, Natalie, the men are working outside trying to batten down the hatches. I'm collecting water in jugs, the tub, and in sinks. The latest reports have the storm turning to the east, so it may not be as bad as predicted." Interference swallowed up some of her words. "...keep praying."

"We will. Tell Ken I'll try to call again tomorrow."

The line went dead.

Natalie relayed the call to her mother then called her prayer chain at church for additional prayers before sinking to the floor and crying out to God. "Lord, I feel so out of control in this situation, but I know You are in control. Guard our hearts, Lord, and keep our trust in You. Please protect all those in the storm's path. I will praise You in the midst of the storm." She quieted her heart and let His love wash over her.

A still small voice spoke to her heart. *I am with you and with all those in the storm. Trust Me.*

Trusting Him, she stood, then went to the bedroom to pack for her trip to Jamaica, trusting it would come to pass.

Ken wiped his sweaty face with the tail of his shirt. Too many things to do before the encroaching darkness covered them. He lifted the hammer to pound more nails in the shutters on the dormitory windows, then went around to the other walls, and did the same. A wail pierced his ears, and his heart caught. Was someone crying, or was it only the wind?

A hand on his shoulder spun him around. His dad hollered into his ear. "I need you to help me set up the generator in case the electricity goes out tonight."

Ken nodded then followed his father to the shed where they stored the machine. Together they rolled it to the building outside the garage and filled it with gasoline so it would be ready to start within minutes of the loss of power.

His dad nodded. "Let's go in and eat supper. It may be our last chance to relax for awhile."

They washed in the kitchen sink. Ken was glad to see the water still flowed. Sitting down at the table, they bowed their heads while his dad prayed. "Lord of all things, we ask You to keep us safe from all the storms of life. We thank You for this food and ask You to use it to strengthen us to do the tasks You set before us. Please help everyone to find shelter from the storm, and their ultimate shelter in You. In Your Son's name. Amen."

Ken chowed down. "Great sandwiches, Mom, and the rice and beans, too."

His dad nodded with a full mouth.

His mom rose. "And there's ice cream for dessert. If the electricity goes out, it won't re-freeze well, so we'll enjoy it tonight."

"Good thinking, dear." His dad patted her hand.

Watching his parents, Ken hoped God would bless him with a marriage like theirs. Funny, he'd only started having those kind of thoughts since re-connecting with Nat. Was she the one God meant for him?

He needed to pray about it, but there was no time to think about it now. As soon as he finished his dessert, he carried his plate and bowl to the sink. "I plan to make sure everyone is in their dorms for tonight. I'll tell them the generator is hooked up, so to give us a little time to get it started if the electricity goes out. But I'm praying it will stay on at least through the dark hours."

"Me, too, son." His dad rose. "I'll check all the shutters to make sure none have blown loose. Make sure you tell the workers to keep all the children inside in the morning until one of us comes to give the okay to go outside." He kissed his wife. "Remember, until last year's Hurricane Matthew, there hadn't been a major hurricane hit Jamaica since Gilbert in 1988 when I was getting ready to go to college in the States, so it will likely go east and out to sea."

Mom nodded. "Yes, I remember because we met that year, so Matthew was my first real experience with a hurricane. God kept this compound and us from major harm last year, and I'm certain He can do so this year. But it never hurts to do our part by being prepared." She ran water into the dishpan and began to wash the dishes.

Ken started out the door then came back in for his slicker. "The rain is coming down in sheets, Dad, so cover up." He went back out to fight his way to the other buildings. No telling how long this would take.

He found several minor repairs to make and didn't arrive home until almost midnight. He took off his boots and crawled into bed, hoping this storm and its aftermath wouldn't keep Natalie from coming down next week.

To his relief, he awakened the next morning to sunshine streaming in his windows. On his way to the kitchen, he picked up the house phone to call Natalie and let her know they were all right, but he didn't get a dial tone. He'd forgotten to charge his cell phone last night. When he went to plug it in on the counter, there was no current.

Mom came into the kitchen, wrapping her robe around her. "Your dad is almost ready. The power went out a few minutes ago, so you'll need to help him start the generator."

His dad headed for the back door. "Lots of wind and rain last night, but no major damage. We'll get the generator working, then go do a quick check on everyone before we come back for breakfast."

Ken followed his dad to the outside building. They quickly got the generator running before they split up to check on the people and buildings. The workers had everything under control, and most of the kids had slept through the night.

Finally back at their house, Ken noted why their phone line was down. A tree behind the house had fallen on it. It could take a week or more to be repaired, depending on how other parts of the island fared. All the more reason to re-charge his cell pronto while the generator was running.

Natalie had awakened at five the next morning to check the news. She'd tried to call Ken several times, with no success. Channels 18 and 27 said the reports of the hurricane were slowly coming in from Jamaica due to most power lines being down. She kept praying.

After nine, she phoned her mother. "Have you heard anything, Mom?"

"The most recent report said there were no deaths reported so far in Jamaica, just power outages. The worst of the storm is over, so hopefully you'll hear from Ken soon. Let me know when you do. I'll keep praying."

She tried Ken again and received the same dead air space. Memories of her and her mom trapped in the car with the water rising around them filled her head.

Pray and praise Me. And trust Me.

Yes, that's what she needed to do. She put in a worship CD and walked around her apartment singing as loudly as she dared with close neighbors. When it ended, she chose one of her favorite old hymns.

Praise to the Lord,
The Almighty, the king of creation!
O my soul, praise Him,
For He is thy health and salvation.

After singing all the verses she could remember, she sang several choruses from her childhood. She was still singing when the phone interrupted. She hoped to see Ken's name on her screen, but it was Mom.

"Another report says the hurricane went to the east, so all they received were high winds and rain."

The thoughts of high winds and rain swept over her, again reminding her of her childhood fears. She shuddered. *God, please cover my mind with Your peace.* A strange calmness came over her.

Her mom's voice spoke. "Have you tried Ken again?"

"No, but I'll try right now and let you know when I hear something." She found the number for the house and punched in the numbers. A busy signal buzzed, so she speed-dialed it again and again. While trying it, someone beeped in on her phone. Her heart gave a leap. Ken's cell number!

"Nat, are you okay? I've been trying to call you for several minutes, and all I got was a busy signal."

She laughed with relief. "That's because I kept calling your two lines."

"Sorry, our house phone is still down and may be for several days, but I was so tired when I got in last night, I forgot to charge my phone. It's plugged in as we speak."

Tears of happiness spilled out. "I'm sorry. I've been praying for you and the people down there."

"Dad and I have checked every building and everyone's okay. We didn't get anything more than a bad rainstorm."

"I'm so glad." What would she have done if he'd been hurt or— She wouldn't go there. *Thank You, Lord, for the storm turning, and everyone being all right.*

"Nat, are you still there?"

"Yes, I was thanking God for keeping you all safe."

"We've been praising Him, too, but there's a lot of work to do today, so how about I call you tonight around ten before I go to bed?"

"Okay." Her hands and voice shook with pent-up relief as she called her mom to report the good news.

CHAPTER 7

Natalie peered down at the myriad shades of blue and green surrounding Jamaica as they approached Kingston from the air. She was reminded again of the greatness of God—the One who created this whole earth and its many marvelous features.

She leaned over to whisper in Mom's ear, trying not to wake Dad sleeping in the aisle seat. "Can you see all the blues and aquamarines?"

"Sometimes, when the plane dips. Maybe I can sit by the window on the way back?"

"Sure." She smiled, but Natalie didn't want to think about going back to Kentucky in less than a week.

The landing gear came down, and her dad shifted in his seat and opened his eyes. "Are we there yet?"

"Almost," Mom answered. "I'm glad you napped. Too many late nights this past week."

"Part of the job when you're the boss." He winked at his wife.

The wink reminded her of Ken winking at her last January, and her insides flipped. Would he wink at her again? Would he kiss her again? There hadn't been any opportunity last time with the tour bus waiting. Her mind wandered back to their first and only kiss when they were in their teens...

The jolt as the tires of the plane hit the tarmac pulled her back to the present.

As soon as the plane taxied to the terminal and came to a stop, her dad retrieved their overhead bags. He let her and Mom exit the row in front of him. She picked up her carry-on and placed it on her shoulder.

Finally, the bell dinged to signal they could depart. She set off as if a fire chased her. Her parents followed her off the plane. As the bright sunlight struck her eyes, she squinted and wished for her sunglasses.

Customs went smoothly. Natalie heard Ken's voice and looked up to see him waving at her, a big smile across his face. She ran to meet him, and he caught her in a snug embrace.

After several seconds, Dad chuckled, and she pulled away. "Mom, Dad, this is Ken Worth. Ken, these are my parents, Christy and Chris Brooks."

They all shook hands, then Ken and her father rolled the suitcases to the parking lot. The guys stowed the luggage in the back of the Land Rover, then they all got in, her up front by Ken.

He angled a grin into the backseat. "I hope you enjoyed a nice flight."

"Yes, wonderful," Mom said.

Dad yawned. "I even slept, and I can't wait to see this place Natalie loves so much."

Ken nodded. "I've already done some errands, but before we leave Kingston I'll need to buy some perishables." He pulled into another parking lot. "Do you all want to come in with me or wait?"

Natalie couldn't bear to stay away from Ken for one moment. "I want to go inside."

Her parents joined them. They enjoyed perusing the merchandise, especially the local brands. As they approached the checkout, Ken added four green bottles to his basket. When they reached the car, he distributed one to each of them. "I want you to try Ting, our local Jamaican drink—it's tart and sweet all in one bottle."

They enjoyed the cold drink on the ride.

"I don't usually like pop, but this is on my buy-again list now," her mom said.

Dad nodded. "I like the tartness of the grapefruit. I wonder if we can have some shipped to our house."

"Probably." Ken kept up a running travelogue about the flora along the way as they drove to the compound.

The guard opened the gate, and Ken waved before driving to the house.

His parents came to the door to greet their guests. Natalie introduced her parents again, and Ken did the same. "These are my parents, Mickey and Tina Worth."

His mother smiled. "We're so happy to have you visit us along with Natalie. She's a lovely girl inside and out."

A blush tiptoed into Nat's cheeks, and a longing grew within him to brush his lips across the rosy glow.

Mom eased toward the kitchen. "Supper is almost ready, so Ken will show you to your rooms. Take a few minutes to settle in then we'll eat in about ten minutes in there."

Two suitcases in hand, Ken started down the hallway. He pointed out the bathroom on their left and then opened the door to the guest room. "Mr. and Mrs. Brooks, this is your room." He pointed across the hall. "That's my room, but for this week it'll be Nat's, and I'll bunk in the older boys' dorm."

"We could have stayed at a hotel, Ken," Dad said.

Ken frowned. "We wouldn't have wanted that."

Nat nodded. "That would have taken a lot of driving time, Dad, so I'm glad we're staying here." Her support thrilled Ken.

"Me, too," her mother added.

He already liked this beautiful, older version of Natalie. "I'll leave you all to settle in, then meet us back in the kitchen when you're ready."

In less than ten minutes, they joined his family and sat down around the table. They all joined hands before Dad prayed a blessing. Ken noted Mom had set the table with his grandmother's special dishes that his parents had brought from the States. The china, only used for special occasions, gave the dinner a festive feel. They passed around the fried chicken, mashed potatoes, gravy, green beans, and rolls.

Mr. Brooks bit into his chicken, and his eyes widened. "This tastes just like my grandmother's chicken used to when I visited their farm."

Mom smiled at him. "That's because we raise our own chickens free-range like she probably did. Your eggs in the morning will be home-grown, too."

Nat's dad grinned. "I'm sure glad we stayed here. Can I gather the eggs like I used to do for Granny?"

Mom laughed. "That can be your job all week if you want."

After supper, they went on a tour of the compound. The Brooks made many complimentary remarks about the mission. Ken loved the affirmation Natalie's parents spoke to his. Fears of them not finding anything to talk about proved unfounded, and he could tell where Natalie got many of the qualities he loved. Yes, he loved her. It shouldn't surprise him, but he was glad to finally admit it to himself. Now when would he tell her?

Ken had told his parents he wanted to take Nat on a tour of the island—alone—since they hadn't spent time by themselves since her visit to Jamaica six years before. They understood. When he mentioned a day to themselves, she threw her arms around his neck.

"Great idea!"

He winked, then gently disengaged himself. "Dress in something nice to start, but pack a swimsuit, a change of clothes, and beach shoes since we might get wet later. "

Her eyes sparkled. "Will do."

Ken started the morning with a drive around Kingston. He pointed out several sites.

Her gaze scanned the area. "Everything looks so historic."

"It is. Kingston was founded in 1692."

"Wow." Her neck twisted from side to side. "I wish we could get out and walk around."

"That's the plan. We're almost ready to stop."

He pulled off into a parking area and pointed to a sign that read Norman Manley School of Law. "We don't have to get out here unless you want, but I thought you might want to get a look at the law college while you're here."

She stared at the campus. "It looks pretty small...especially compared to the University of Kentucky."

His stomach sank to his toes. Had he made a mistake bringing her here? Of course, it was small compared to a school in the States but it was the training and credentials she would obtain that were important.

She reached for her door handle. "Might as well get out and see it while I'm here."

"We don't have to." He exited, but stood by the car. "Are you sure?"

"Yes, it would be silly to not look while I'm in Kingston."

They walked up the pathway to the building bearing the sign with the name. He held the door for her, and she entered.

A receptionist looked up. "May I help you?"

Ken glanced at Nat, but she didn't speak. "My friend is visiting from the States and would like to get some information on the program here for those with an American law degree."

The lady looked up at Nat. "You already have a law degree?"

Nat nodded. "Almost. I'll graduate next May."

The receptionist stood. "Follow me, and I will see if I can find one of our professors to speak with you." She led them down a short hallway to an office. "Sit please. May I bring you some bottled water?"

Nat shook her head, and Ken answered, "No thanks."

They sat in silence for several minutes until the woman returned with some pamphlets and brochures. "Here is some literature for you to peruse while we wait for one of our instructors to come to talk with you." She left again.

What he'd planned as a fruitful time together was turning sour. Ken reached for her hand. "Sorry for surprising you. If the teacher doesn't come soon, we can leave." He squeezed her hand.

She squeezed back. "It's not your fault." At least she didn't seem upset with him.

"I thought next we could drive to Ocho Rios and spend some time at Dunn's Falls."

A tall Jamaican entered the room. The man extended his hand. "I'm Professor White. Which of you is interested in our college here?"

Ken shook the man's hand then swiveled in his chair toward Nat. "This is Miss Natalie Brooks from the United States. She will graduate with her law degree next spring."

Mr. White smiled at her. "Have you heard of our six month certification program for lawyers from other countries?"

She held up a brochure. "Yes, sir. In this."

Ken cringed. He shouldn't have sprung this on her.

Mr. White gestured to the brochure. "Do you have any specific questions about the program?"

They spent the next fifteen minutes discussing the certification and how it could work for Nat. Mr. White leaned back in his chair. "Do either of you have any more questions?"

"No," Nat said.

Ken stood. "I live on a mission compound about an hour from here. I will contact you if Miss Brooks or I have any further questions. Thanks you for your time and the information."

Natalie drew in a deep breath when they reached the outside air. Her chest ached as though she'd been holding her breath the whole time they were there. She'd anticipated a day of getting to know Ken better, but now it seemed he was trying to direct her future.

Ken touched her hand. "I'm sorry I didn't speak to you beforehand."

"That would have been nice." She hurried toward the car.

He trotted after her. "I realize now I should have. Will you forgive me?"

"All right."

They reached the car and settled into the seats. He started the ignition. "Ready to go to Dunn's River Falls now?"

"Yes."

She stared out the window as he drove. She wanted to push aside the uncomfortable feelings holding her captive so the day wouldn't be ruined.

After several silent minutes, Ken spoke. "Do you want to talk about it?"

"No, I just want to stare out the window and think. My mind is on overload right now."

"A day at the beach should be just what you need, then."

Yes, a day at the beach should help her forget all the decisions she needed to make, but she wouldn't be able to enjoy the day unless they cleared the air first. She prayed for courage and faced Ken. "Ken, I don't appreciate you taking me to the college without even asking me if I wanted to go. My mom and dad don't make important decisions without talking about things first. I'm not comfortable with you trying to make that decision for me."

He pulled off at an overlook and put the car in Park. "I'm sorry, Nat. I wanted this whole day to be a nice surprise for you without you having to do anything. I was so excited, I didn't think about how you might feel. I promise I'll try not to do it again, if you'll forgive me." He took her hand in his. "Please?"

Her heart melted. "Yes, of course I'll forgive you."

"Thank you." He pulled back onto the road. "Besides Dunn's River Falls, do you have any place you want to go?"

"Can we find a candy store? When I was here six years ago, I sampled some coconut drops. They were so yummy. Do you know where we can find them?"

"I certainly do. There's a store named The Coconut Shop in Kingston and we can stop there on our way home."

Natalie awoke on their last day in Jamaica with a prayer of thanks on her heart for the special week she and her parents had shared with Ken and his family. She hurried to the kitchen to assist Mrs. Worth, but her mom was already there. "Where's Dad?"

"Gathering the eggs, if you want to help him. We're almost ready to cook them."

She headed out to the henhouse and peeked her head in the door of the dark coop. "They're ready for the eggs, Dad." She squinted. "What are you doing in there?"

He emerged with a basketful of eggs and a sheepish look on his face. "I remembered my Granny named her laying hens, so I did the same. I've been telling them each good-bye until I come back."

She loved this seldom-seen side of her dad. "You realize the same chickens might not be here, right?" She grinned. "They might end up in a meal."

"Granny always said you keep the good ones until they quit laying, then you boil them and use the broth in soup as medicine."

Longing to know the granny who died before she'd been born washed over her. "I wish I'd known her."

"Me, too, but I can share some stories about her on the trip home."

She hugged his waist. "I'd love that."

"Ditto, kiddo."

They both laughed at his familiar saying from her childhood. This trip had brought the whole family closer, not just to Ken's family, but also to each other.

After breakfast, they packed and loaded the mission vehicle for the trip to the airport. Natalie and Ken stole a few moments alone outside while waiting for their parents to say their farewells. They walked behind the house for some privacy.

Ken drew her into his arms for a long hug then kissed her lips. Electricity tingled up her body clear from her toes to her hair. She reached up and put her arms around his neck, drawing him closer, then kissed him.

When they came up for air, his eyes locked on hers. "Natalie, I love you. I know we haven't spent that much time together but..."

She placed a finger across his lips. "I love you, too, Ken. And, we've known each other for over six years now, just lived on different continents and different worlds."

"I hope we can solve that problem in the future." He stroked her cheek.

Chill bumps raised on her arms. "I agree. I'm trusting God to work it all out how He plans."

He smiled and kissed her nose. "That's the best way."

Their parents called for them, so they went back to the front yard where his mom was kissing her mom's cheek and the dads were sharing man-hugs.

Natalie sat up front again. The next four weeks would drag, but she and Ken each had lots of work to keep them busy. They probably wouldn't see each other every day after he moved to Kentucky, but at least they'd be in the same state and country. *Keep drawing us closer, Father, even when we're apart.*

After leaving Nat and her parents at the airport, Ken ran his regular errands, then drove back to his home for the next month. He didn't begrudge the precious time together, but he would miss her even more in the coming weeks. He hoped time would pass super fast, but how could he get everything done in that short time? Driving through the mission gate, the first idea came to him—delegate.

As soon as the groceries were stowed away, he requested a pitcher of tea from Mom, then went outside and found one of the workers. He asked him to gather up the other four men who worked there and meet him at the unfinished dorm.

Peter slapped him on the back. "Hey, mon, long time no see." The other three nodded.

Ken smiled. "Yes, I've been busy with our guests this past week. Plus, I'm going to be so busy the next month before I leave that I need all of you to help me get things done and come up with ways to keep them running smoothly around here while I'm gone." He pointed to a long strip of paper he'd tacked to the inside wall. "On the left I've posted some of the areas that need to be taken care of. At the top are your names, plus Toby who isn't here today."

Micah studied the chart and frowned. "More jobs dan people."

Ken chuckled. "You're right, so we'll need more than one person on many jobs just like you all helped build this dorm. Right now, I'd like you to study the chart, and when I come back in a few minutes I'll have you take turns choosing which job you want to be in charge of while I'm gone, then others can volunteer to help when you need it. Understand?"

"Yea, boss."

Ken went to the kitchen and picked up a tin of cookies he'd purchased at the grocery, the tea in a plastic pitcher, and six plastic cups. He carried them out to the dorm and set them on a barrel before pouring the tea. "Help yourself."

The men stood there for a few seconds before Peter took a cookie and a cup of tea.

"Okay, Peter, you get to choose the first job you want to be in charge of."

His friend's eyes gleamed as he chose finishing the inside of the dorm. "Me say we need everyone to sign up to help wid dis project."

The other four men scrambled to collect their cookies, tea, and jobs.

Thank you Lord for giving me this idea. What's next?

CHAPTER 8

Natalie finished her last class of the day but couldn't recall much. Excitement at seeing Ken in a few short hours coursed through every heartbeat. She called her mother on her drive to Bluegrass Airport.

"Hi, dear, is his plane still on time?" Mom sounded as eager as Natalie felt.

"Yes, as far as I know. I'll check again when I get there."

"Is he renting a car?"

"No, we decided there was no need, as he'll mainly stay on campus during the week. On weekends, I can pick him up, or he should be able to catch a ride to Lexington."

"That makes sense. Your dad and I want to take you both out for supper tonight. How about we meet at Ramsey's on Harrodsburg Road?"

"Great. That's right on our way to Wilmore. I'll call you when he arrives. Bye."

Natalie parked in the cell phone lot and waited for Ken's call. She attempted to read a chapter for her international law class but gave up and sang along to the music on K-Love until her phone buzzed.

Ken's text read *On the ground.* Her heart galloped. She texted back for him to let her know when his luggage arrived, then she phoned her mom to head to the restaurant.

After another twenty minutes, a second message dinged. *On my way.*

Nat pulled out and drove toward the baggage claim area. Ken was coming out the door as she parked along the curb. Her heart thumping, she jumped out and ran to meet him. He dropped his bags and enveloped her in a hug. When they broke apart, she noticed several people staring and smiling at them. She didn't care.

"Ready to ride? My parents are taking us out for supper tonight." Natalie popped the trunk of her Camry, and he stowed his luggage there.

He held her door then slid into the passenger seat. "Good, I'll be glad to see them again." He touched her hand. "I'm overjoyed to see you, Natalie. May I have a kiss?"

"I thought you'd never ask."

After a couple of minutes, she heard a tap on her window and looked up. A smiling policeman pointed to his watch. She flushed, pulled back from Ken's arms, and waved at the officer as she left the curb. "I'd hate for you to get cited on your first day in the States."

He grinned. "What would be the charge?"

"Accomplice to kissing in a 'no parking' zone."

They laughed as she drove to the restaurant, happy they were in the same country.

Ken lazed on his dorm bed on his first morning in Kentucky. Was he really at Asbury Seminary and only thirty minutes away from the love of his life? *God, You are the only One who could've orchestrated all of this. Thank You.* He should get up, but his body resisted. The last few weeks' work and lack of sleep had caught up with him. But it was all worth it. He didn't want to be anywhere else.

His phone rang. He picked it up, grimacing at the low battery signal. "Hello?"

"Good morning."

Nat's voice startled him wide-awake. "Just woke up. What time is it?"

"Nine."

He jumped out of bed. "I'd better run. I'm supposed to be in the dean's office at nine thirty. I'll call you when I'm done."

He dressed, brushed his teeth, then loped down the stairs and across the campus, glad he'd asked Natalie to drive him by the building last night.

When Ken returned to his dorm a couple of hours later, he dialed Natalie, but she didn't answer so he left a message. He should've asked when would be a good time to call her. Since it was almost eleven, he decided to walk around campus instead of looking for some breakfast.

At a quarter till noon, his growling stomach led him to the cafeteria. After eating, Ken checked out the library on campus, where he'd spend much of his time. Next, he went to the dorm to get his phone so he could try her number again. He counted three messages from her before dialing the number.

"Hello, Nat. Sorry I needed to leave my phone here charging."

"That's okay. Are you off the rest of the day?"

"Yes, but I need to scout out the location of all my classes. They start tomorrow."

"My classes are over for today, so how about I pick you up and we can explore together? Then we can eat supper before I head back."

His heart skipped a beat at the chance of seeing her again so soon. "That would be great. But I'll need to eat at the cafeteria since Uncle J.T. already paid for my meals."

"I understand. I'll buy something there to eat with you. We can compare our schedules and work out study dates."

"Great idea. See you soon."

By October, the road to Asbury Seminary had become an old friend to Natalie as she wound her way around the curves. The trees stood in their fall glory, the variety of oranges, yellows, reds, and purples waving their praise to God.

Ken met her at the cafeteria at six, their regular Thursday study-date night. "Hello, beautiful."

Her heart melted at his usual greeting. "Hi, yourself."

They went through the cafeteria buffet, then Ken led them to a table apart from the others.

She raised an eyebrow. "Everything okay?"

"We only have a couple of months until our last semesters start. We need to make plans for next year. Do you plan to move to Jamaica after graduation?" His brow furrowed, and his eyes locked on hers.

She blew out a breath. "It's a lot more complicated than I first thought. In my class on international adoption we learned that each country in the Caribbean has its own laws. To set up a law office in Jamaica, I'd have to take and pass the six-month conversion course at the Norman Manley Law School, but I'm not sure if that would be the best route. I've been thinking about starting out with an international agency here in the States that would send me to whichever countries need adoptions finalized."

"So you'd live in the United States then just travel to the Caribbean when needed?"

She nodded. She'd be so much more secure at a U.S. agency. "I can live anywhere I meet the residency requirements, but I would have to obtain up-to-date visas, as you and your parents do to travel into or out of the country. I'd also need a work permit any place I was on the job."

He gazed at her with wide eyes. "I hadn't imagined all that with a law degree. We don't travel out of Jamaica very often except to go on furlough every five years when our mission board sends another missionary to take our place for twelve months."

Natalie frowned. "Sounds like we both have a lot to learn."

"I'll ask my advisor in my intercultural studies class if he has any ideas about handling international adoptions."

"Okay. Let's talk again this weekend. Can your friend bring you to Lexington for church or do you need me to drive here?"

"Neither. Our class is taking an overnight trip to Appalachia, so we'll stay in people's homes and go to their church on Sunday morning. We'll return late, so I guess our next date night will be Tuesday."

Her chest went tight. "That'll be the longest we've been apart since you moved here."

"You're right. I've heard absence makes the heart grow fonder, so we'll see how much you miss me."

She sighed. After all their months apart, she already knew how much she'd miss him.

The next morning Ken packed his duffel bag for the trip. The bus would leave right after his last class ended at four. He'd spent the night wrestling with Nat's uncertainty, and he still wondered why life had to be filled with wrinkles and roadblocks. He tried turning it all over to God in prayer, but he couldn't concentrate on his other classes.

What if this was a problem they couldn't agree on? Would God want him to give up his dream of the mission field? Would Nat be willing to give up her hope of helping orphans be adopted into loving homes?

As the van drove out of Lexington on I-66, and then turned on Mountain Parkway, he continued to brood. When they left the Parkway, he began to read signs for Quicksand, Lost Creek, and Dice. Even the town names depressed him.

The group stopped in Hazard to eat at an Arby's, one of his favorite restaurants in the States. While they ate, Dr. Smith told them since there were five students and one professor, one of them needed to share a room with him. Ken volunteered. What better way to have his teacher all to himself for some advice?

It was already dark by the time Dr. Smith dropped off the other four guys then drove to a home up another "holler," as the locals called them. Mr. and Mrs. Yancey welcomed them into a very warm living room and offered them some apple pie and ice cream, which proved delicious. They sat around the woodstove and talked an hour before climbing upstairs to the guest bedroom where twin beds sat on opposite sides of the room.

After he and Dr. Smith prepared for bed, his teacher spoke, "What's bugging you, Ken? You've been happy as a lark all semester until today. Did you get bad news from home?"

"Not home, but my girlfriend told me yesterday that she doesn't know if our idea for her to use her law degree to help with Jamaican adoptions is going to work. There seems to be too much red tape to go through."

His teacher cocked his head. "Are you all engaged yet?"

"No. I'd planned to ask her next May when we both get our degrees, but now I wonder if I should ask her this Christmas so we can go on and make plans. But what if she says no since we don't know how things will come together?"

"Are you sure she's the one for you?"

Ken nodded emphatically. "Definitely." Then he shook his head. "No one else."

"Then I suggest you step out on faith and ask her. If she says yes, then you'll both need to do some serious praying and surrendering to God. Do you believe He can work it out—even if it's not the answer you want or she wants?"

He searched his heart. "Yes, sir, I do."

"Smart answer. Then ask her."

"I better buy a ring first."

Dr. Smith smiled. "That's your second smart answer. Let's get some sleep now, and I'll add this to my prayers. Your mission station is in Jamaica, right?"

Ken nodded, although he didn't see how that could solve his problem.

"My wife and I've been talking about taking a group of students on a summer mission trip. Do you think your place might work?"

"We'd love to have you. We're just finishing a dorm for groups like that."

"Great. We'll talk more when we get back to campus. I'll check with the dean to see what else we'll need to do."

Thank You, God, for answering that prayer before I even thought of asking it. I know I can trust You with everything else, including Nat and our future.

CHAPTER 9

When Ken returned to Wilmore on Sunday evening, he phoned his parents and told them his plan to propose to Natalie over Thanksgiving.

"Way to go, son." Dad's happiness came through loud and clear.

"I'm so happy for you both." His mother spoke with tears in her voice. "Don't mind me. These are tears of joy." Then she told him about her mother's engagement ring she'd left with her brother in the States. He should call Uncle James in Louisville to see if they could meet up somewhere before Thanksgiving.

Ken called him right then, and the uncle he'd only seen a few times during furloughs delivered the heirloom ring to Asbury the weekend before Thanksgiving. It was more beautiful than Ken had remembered.

On Thanksgiving morning, Nat picked him up for a tour of the Arboretum. Her mother's meal wouldn't be ready until two that afternoon, so she asked if he'd like to visit the Arboretum for an hour or so before the big dinner. He'd jumped at the chance for some time alone with her. They would stay at her parents' home the rest of the day since both her siblings would be home, too.

"Before we hit the Arboretum," she said, "I need to stop by my apartment and change into some warmer clothes. This cold spell arrived overnight, and I don't want to cut our walk short."

Inside her apartment, she headed for the hallway. "I can't wait to see Dani and Keith and for you to meet them, too. Make yourself at home while I change."

"Okay. And I can't wait to meet the rest of your family." He walked around her living room, looking at pictures on the shelves. Would he and Nat someday have their own family pictures?

The CD player switched to a lively Celtic Christmas tune. He sat on her couch and laid his head back. He'd looked forward to this long weekend all semester. Now nervousness about popping the question to Natalie had his stomach dancing. Not the decision itself. He was certain of that. They still hadn't agreed on how to work things out concerning her job. Was there some way they could both compromise? *God, please show us the way.*

Nat returned wearing leggings with a long sweater and boots. She looked good enough to kiss. She made some hot chocolate and poured it into travel mugs, then they donned their jackets and headed for the car. "Arboretum, here we come."

Natalie held the car keys to Ken. "You've mastered driving on the right side of the road, so do you want to drive in Lexington now?"

"Sure." He took them from her hand and kissed the tip of her nose.

After buckling in, he maneuvered the car out of the parking area. "You'll need to tell me the turns."

"Take a right onto the road up ahead then go about a mile. Or almost two klicks." She liked being the navigator to his driver. They did many things well together. But how could she be sure they could serve God better together than apart like her Mimi and Pappaw had?

They approached an intersection, and they had the green light. Ken didn't slow. A truck careened up the street on Natalie's right. It showed no indication of slowing. She shrieked, "Stop!"

Ken stomped on the brakes so hard she would've hit the windshield if she'd not been wearing a seat belt. The truck sped through the red light, almost hitting another car on its way, then continued out of sight.

Ken gripped the steering wheel, panting. "Whew. I'm glad you hollered. We could've been part of a pile-up. Not a good way to start a holiday weekend." He looked at her. "Are you okay?"

She glanced at his white knuckles on the steering wheel. "Yeah. How about you?"

"I'll let you know once my heart slows down to normal." The car behind them honked, and he eased the Camry through the intersection.

They made it to the Arboretum without any further mishaps and enjoyed their walk together. When they came to the rose garden, Natalie darted ahead. "Oh, these are so lovely, aren't they?" She glanced over her shoulder, but Ken wasn't there. "Ken, where...?"

He stepped from between bushes and went down on one knee.

She raised a hand to her mouth.

He smiled so sweetly it took her breath away. "Natalie Brooks, would you come here?"

She walked toward him as if in a trance. Was this really happening?

He took her hands, but then he let go and pulled a box out of his pocket. He reached for her again, grinning. "I should have practiced this."

Natalie giggled.

He flipped the box open with his thumb, revealing a twinkling diamond encircled by smaller diamonds.

She gasped. "Ken, it's gorgeous!"

"I'm glad you like it. It was my grandmother's, and my mother saved it for it for me to give to the one God chose for me. I believe that woman is you, Natalie, and I hope you feel the same way."

She looked into his blue eyes. "Oh, Ken, yes, I do. I will marry you. As long as we can serve God better together than apart. That's what my mimi told my pappaw years ago, and they'll celebrate their fiftieth anniversary next year."

"I agree with that wholeheartedly." He slipped the ring on her finger.

A perfect fit. And a perfect ending to a perfect morning.

Hand in hand, they strolled to the car, Natalie's excitement bubbling out in laughter. He offered her the keys, but she held up her shaking hands. "I'm too excited. Besides, how can I stare at my ring and drive?" She held her hand out and gaped at it.

He laughed and kissed her again.

She took her eyes off the ring only long enough to direct him to her house. After he parked, she turned toward him. "Is it okay if we wait until after the meal to announce our engagement? Not only is it Thanksgiving, it's my mom's birthday, so let's get all that hoopla over with before we spring our surprise."

"Sure, but you better put the ring in your pocket then."

She hated to take it off, but agreed. As she tucked the ring in her jacket pocket, her sister, Dani, came running down the sidewalk. Her long blond hair swung into her face as she leaned down to open the door. Her squeal echoed.

"It's been so long since I've seen my big sis, I couldn't wait."

Natalie got out and gave Dani a big squeeze. Ken rounded the car and Natalie smiled. "Ken, this is my excitable sister, Danielle. Dani, this is Ken." She swung an arm around Dani, and they walked arm-in-arm into the house.

"We're here," Natalie announced. "Where's the rest of the family?"

Mom hollered from the kitchen. "Your dad and brother are in the basement. Why don't you take Ken down there to meet Keith, then you and Dani come back to help me finish up."

After the introductions, the girls climbed the steps to the main level of the house. Natalie hugged Mom. "What needs to be done first?"

"The dressing is ready to go in the oven for thirty minutes, but set the timer for fifteen, so we'll remember to put the rolls in next. Set the table for eight. Mimi and Pappaw are on their way."

Mom buttered the rolls then began the gravy. By the time the buzzer went off, the girls had the table ready. They slid the rolls in the oven.

The familiar smells and voices brought happy memories to Natalie's mind. She was overjoyed to be able to share her family and their traditions with Ken.

The kitchen door opened, and Mimi appeared, bearing her famous German chocolate birthday cake. She gave her daughter a kiss on the cheek. "Happy birthday."

"Thanks, Mom. Where's Dad?"

"He's carrying in the pecan pies."

Natalie's dad appeared at the top of the basement steps, followed by Keith and Ken. "Sure smells good in here."

Mom stirred the gravy. "Yes, dear, the turkey and ham you sliced earlier are ready to be placed on the table because this gravy's done."

Pappaw came in, and Nat took one of the pies from him. She followed him to the buffet to set them down. "Pappaw, I want you and Mimi to meet Ken, but I don't know where he is."

Mimi walked into the dining room, escorted by Ken. "Is this handsome stranger the one you're looking for, Natalie?"

"Yes, ma'am. I should've known you'd find him. Ken, this is Mimi and Pappaw. The ones I told you about." He winked, and she knew he remembered what she'd told him.

She nodded to the man she loved. The delicious secret of their engagement swept over her. "And, this is Ken."

Ken battled waves of uncertainty during dinner. Her entire family had welcomed him as family, too, and they'd fed him until he felt like a stuffed pig with an apple in its mouth. Could he take Nat more than a thousand miles away from all these she held dear? Not just the distance, but also the different customs?

She caught his eye, and his heart began to pound when she slid the ring on her finger. Then she waggled her hand in the air.

Danielle squealed.

Keith sat up straight and stared at Dani. "What's wrong with you?"

Flapping her hands, she smiled. "Look at Natalie's left hand."

They all gasped. Mrs. Brooks and Dani left their chairs and hugged Nat.

Her dad asked, "When did this happen?"

"Today," Ken and Nat answered together.

Mimi beamed at her granddaughter. "When will the wedding be?"

Nat laughed. "We haven't discussed that yet."

"Where will the wedding be?"

Ken shrugged. "We didn't discuss that either."

Dani placed both hands on her hip. "Am I going to be your maid of honor?"

"Of course," Natalie said. "Who else?"

They all laughed.

The rest of day disappeared between wedding talk and playing board games around the dining room table. Ken bested them all at Scrabble, and he confided, "Comes from growing up playing against my parents."

Natalie's dad said, "Let's invite them for next Thanksgiving. It will keep me studying all year."

"Great idea." Ken glanced out the window. The sky was dark. "What time is it?"

Nat sighed. "After seven. I better drive you home, Mr. Scrabble Champ."

Mrs. Brooks returned from the kitchen toting several plastic containers in a bag. "I've packed up some leftovers for a snack tonight or tomorrow, Ken."

"Thank you very much." Ken bent and kissed her on the cheek like he did his own mother. More family to love. He hoped they wouldn't all be disappointed if he took Natalie far away from them.

The closer they got to Wilmore, the slower Natalie drove. She parked the car in the lot beside his dorm but left it running to keep them warm. She took Ken's hand. "We need to talk."

He squeezed her fingers. "You're right. I'm willing to compromise, even if it means you need to stay in the States for part of the time."

She loved that he was willing to compromise. "I've been reading online about the Norman Manley Law School. I want a break from classes after seven years of college, but if we got married soon after we graduated, classes wouldn't start there until September. So I'd have several months' break from school and time to acclimate myself to marriage in my new country. Plus, I found out my credentials from there would cover most all of the Caribbean Islands, which is great."

His mouth was hanging open.

Her heart sank. "Am I rushing you? Maybe you don't want to marry that soon."

He burst out laughing. "Of course I want to marry you that soon, or even sooner if you want to. Let's pray about it and discuss it on Tuesday evening. Graduation is less than six months away, but we can trust Him to work it all out so we can serve him better together than apart."

She leaned toward him. "Let's stop talking and kiss good-night."

"I won't argue with that."

EPILOGUE

On a beautiful Friday afternoon in May, Natalie drove to Wilmore and picked up Ken. Then the two of them drove to the airport to meet Ken's parents. While the car tires hummed on the highway, her mind whirred with everything crowding the calendar.

Their last semester of graduate school had passed even faster than the first, and this coming week would be jam-packed. Tomorrow morning at ten o'clock was Ken's graduation from the seminary, followed by her own from UK College of Law at two in the afternoon. Mimi and Pappaw had invited both sides of the family to a graduation supper Saturday evening.

Sunday afternoon, Dani and Jenna were hosting a personal shower for Nat at Bobbi's house, and Keith had planned a cookout for the other groomsmen and Ken. The following Friday they'd have their rehearsal and dinner.

On Saturday afternoon, she and Ken would pledge their vows to one another at her home church in front of God and a couple of hundred others. A reception would follow in the church hall, and she would officially be Mrs. Ken Worth of Jamaica.

After their honeymoon on a Caribbean cruise, where they would meet several of the orphanage missionaries she might be working with in years to come, they would return to Jamaica and stay at Ken's parents' home for a week. During that time, the mission team from Asbury would arrive to assemble their small pre-fab home, a wedding present courtesy of Uncle J.T.

They parked at the airport parking lot, and she settled her gaze on Ken's adoring face. "Do you think our lives will ever return to normal?"

He covered her hand with his. "As my dad once told me, 'We serve a risen Savior. He wasn't ordinary or normal, and neither should we expect to be.' As long as we let Him lead us, everything will be fine. You remind me if I forget that, and I'll remind you."

"Agreed. And, we'll always serve Him better together than apart."

"Amen." He sealed his promise with a kiss.

ACKNOWLEDGMENTS

Thanks: Special thanks to *Kim Sawyer* and her fabulous team at Wings of Hope, especially *Connie Stevens*, lead editor, for all the help and hope they share with me and others. And for *Kim and Don Sawyer* inviting my husband and me to go on a K-Love cruise with them in January 2016, which gave Kim and me the ideas for our stories in this book. I thank our *Father in Heaven* for leading us both to do this book together after encouraging and praying for each other for over fifteen years!

To *Bobbi and Jenna Graffunder*, whom we met on the K-Love cruise in 2016, and who graciously allowed me to use their first names as roommates for my character. Also for their suggestions and Bobbi's offer to do a critique. Thanks to *Christy Kinney* and *Mandy Thornberry*, who also read over and helped edit this book, as well as *Joy Liddy*, who critiqued all the chapters and *Loretta Gibbons*, who critiqued the first three chapters.

Plus a big thanks to present-day missionary in Haiti, *Susan Ross Hammond* (HammondsinHaiti.com) who came for a visit and shared with me such wonderful details of Caribbean culture, some which I've used in this book. Also to *Allen Arnold* whose book and class on *The Story of With* at the ACFW conference in August, 2016, worked their way into my heart to stay and also into this story which I began soon after. I highly recommend both the book and class to all.

Thanks to *Maria Koppelberger* in the Admissions department at Asbury Theological Seminary who answered my three phone calls and helped me choose the right educational pathway for my fictional hero. Any mistakes are my own.

Humongous thanks to all my readers and prayer partners who are always so encouraging and want to know when the next book will be out!

As always, a huge thanks to *my husband* who does dishes, driving, and all the details it takes to promote me as a writer—my biggest fan who always reads the book aloud with me as the last step before it goes to the publisher.

Foremost, to my *Father in heaven* who is the Giver of ideas!

A SHELTER IN A
WEARY LAND

JULANE HIEBERT

To Him,
who is my constant shelter,
my Lord and Savior, *Jesus Christ*

"For thou art my rock and my fortress;
therefore for thy name's sake lead me, and guide me."
PSALM 31:3 KJV

CHAPTER 1

CASS COUNTY, MISSOURI
LATE AUGUST, 1863

Heavy with child, Charlotte Teasdale widened her stance to balance on the uneven terrain of the Missouri hillside. "I can't believe you made me do this, Lafe Teasdale. I'm sweating, I'm thirsty, and you'll be lucky if I don't have this babe right here on the side of this rocky hill."

Lafe put his arms around her. "You'll thank me one day." He kissed her nose. "Besides, it's for your own good—yours and the babe's. Now follow me. We've only a bit farther." He grasped her hand and gave a tug.

She groaned with the effort of another step. She'd never questioned her husband's reasoning before now, but this entire plan frightened her. Her husband was one of the few young men in Cass County who'd not ventured off to war. But of late, Lafe went riding off to meetings he said he couldn't tell her about, with people he wouldn't identify. Middle-of-the-night visitors had become more frequent. There'd be a loud bang on the door, and Lafe would grab his gun and disappear into the dark, always with a command that she *stay put and under no condition follow him*. And at times he'd be gone for days.

He rode off in the night three days ago, and this morning he returned and insisted she follow him...and *don't ask questions*. Something deep inside her warned of trouble.

She yanked her hand from his. "Lafe, I'll not take another step until you tell me why this is so all-fired important. My back hurts, my legs hurt, and frankly, you're scaring me."

His eyes darkened. "Don't fight me on this, Char." He leaned against a nearby tree and pulled her to him. "Look, I'm scared, too. Bad things are going to happen. Bad things *have* happened. You're not safe in our cabin."

"What kind of bad things?" Her heart skipped a beat. "Lafe, where have you been? What have you done?"

"I told you, no questions."

She stomped her foot. "No, Lafe. You're wrong. I *will* ask questions. You leave me with no explanation, and now you're dragging me up the hill to hide in some cave like an animal. And I'm not to ask questions? We promised. Remember? No secrets—ever."

"It's not safe to stand out in the open like this, my love. Trust me, that's all I'm asking. Please."

"Out in the open? Lafe Teasdale, if you were to move ten feet from me I couldn't find you in this brush and timber."

"You could if you had a spy glass. Please, Char. Just come with me."

He locked his fingers around her wrist so hard it hurt, but she knew better than to utter one more complaint. She'd go with him. But if he left her again, she'd make her way back down to their cabin, and he couldn't stop her.

The remainder of the climb was grueling. If Lafe hadn't held her wrist so tight, she wondered if she could manage to carry her growing body up the steep hill by herself. For sure, it wasn't something she could do in a hurry. Perhaps she should reconsider her self-pledge to disobey her husband.

"We're here." Lafe loosened his grip at last. "Now, see if you can find the opening."

She turned in all directions scanning the hillside, but as far as she could see there were only rocks, brush and trees. Nothing that resembled anything close to a way for her to enter a cave was visible.

"So am I going to have to hunt for this place every time I come up here?"

He turned her toward the rugged face of the hill, and wrapped his arms around her waist, his fingers splayed across the bump that was their unborn child. "You're not going to climb up here over and over again. You're staying here and not leaving until I come for you. Do you understand?"

She tried to wiggle loose but he held tight. "Now? You want me to stay now? Lafe, I didn't even clean up breakfast makings because you wouldn't let me. The food will rot. I can't just stay up here."

He tightened his grip even more. "Look, there are troops of Union soldiers at John Hook's farm right now, and rumor has it General Ewing is mad enough to clear the border of any and all so-called enemy."

"And who is the enemy?"

"Depends. But Ewing considers anyone not loyal to the Union an enemy, and that includes both men and women. You can't trust anyone right now. Royal Weathers answered a knock on the door the other night and was shot dead right in front of his wife. Mrs. Weathers says Lyle Ford is the one who shot him. But right now, Ford isn't anywhere to be found."

"Turn me loose. I want to look at you when we talk. Please."

He gave her tummy a pat, turned her around and pulled her against his chest.

"No, don't smother me." She leaned away from him. "Tell me why Lyle Ford would shoot Mr. Weathers? They're friends. I want to know, need to know, why would a friend kill a friend?"

"Weathers was considered a southern sympathizer."

"But he doesn't own slaves. Neither do we. Why would anyone want to kill him over an opinion? Besides, Royal Weathers is an old man, too old and crippled to be of any use to the war effort."

"No, he didn't own slaves. But neither did he believe those Union people should be able to come into these hills and tell us what to do...what to believe. I think Ewing figures age don't make a difference if a man believes different than him."

"What do we believe, Lafe?" Her heart pounded.

"I don't believe it's right for one man to own another, but it ain't right for one part of the country to tell another part what to believe, what they can and can't do. If it means taking a stand, then I'm prepared to—"

He couldn't mean he'd be willing to die? What would happen to her and the babe? She put her hands over her ears. "Don't say it. Please. I don't want to hear you say you'd be willing to—to—"

He traced her eyebrow with his finger. "I gotta say it, my love. If it ain't worth dyin' for, then it ain't worth livin' for. You want our child to be brought up believin' one way but forced to live another? No, Char. Whatever it takes, I have to follow my conscience. That's why I fixed this place for you and the wee one. You can't trust no one. Royal trusted his neighbor, his friend, and look what it got him."

"Poor Mrs. Weathers. What will she do now?" She hid her face against Lafe's chest. His heartbeat vibrated against her cheek. This was always her safe place, in his arms with her head against his chest. The steady thrum of his heart meant all was well—until today.

"She has people back east. I reckon that's where she'll go, once she gets things packed up. But don't you see? That could happen to me, too, and then what? You have no people back east, or north, or south, or any direction."

A cold chill shivered through her body and tied a knot of fear in her belly. The kind of fear that in the past meant being left alone, forsaken, forgotten. She pulled away from him and stood with her hands on her hips. "So you're saying I need to stay up here in this cave."

"That's exactly what I'm saying."

"For how long? How long am I supposed to live like an animal?"

He shook his head. "I don't know. Until this is over, I reckon."

"Over? Until what is over? This—this awful time of hate and mistrust? What if this child decides to be born when you're off doing whatever it is you've been doing when you ride off into the night? What if something happens and there's no one to go for Granny Wilson? What then? I don't want this son or daughter to come into this world without a pa."

He pulled her to him again and pushed her head against his chest. This time his heartbeat thrummed wild and uneven. He smelled like sweat and horse and lye soap all mixed together. She clung to his sleeves as hard as she could.

"How will I ever know if you're coming back, Lafe? How long do you want me to wait before I come out of your hiding place? I can't do it. I won't do it. They won't harm a lone woman, will they? Isn't there a code or something that declares women to be safe? Whoever they are, aren't they men like you? Don't they have wives and families? Look at me. I'm big as a barn. They wouldn't harm me. Beside, maybe—maybe it won't come to that. Maybe—"

He grabbed her shoulders and held her away from him. "Look at me and listen to me. It has already come to that. There's an order—order number ten they call it—that says any woman or head of household who gives aid to any confederate will be ordered out of the territory. Not only that, they've already jailed women and girls just because their husbands or papas or brothers are fighting for what they believe in. You aren't safe. No matter the code, there's always them what think they don't have to go by any rules a'tall. I've heard tales of what them kind do when they find a woman alone, and believe me, it will make little difference what shape you're in."

She tried to shrug away, but he held fast. "You're scaring me."

He nodded. "I know. That's what I want to do. I want to scare you enough you'll listen to me for a change."

"I listen to you." She took his face in her hands and gazed into his eyes. "Even when you don't say words, I hear you."

He bent and brushed his lips against hers. "Don't need words, huh? Don't tease, Char. There isn't anything I want to do more than hold you right now. But there's no time for that, and if you'd really been listening to me, you'd know I have to leave again...soon."

"How soon? Where? Why? When will you be back?" She pushed her face against his chest again. "Why can't I stay in our cabin? I'll lock the door. I won't even light a lamp. No one can see our place from the road. If anyone comes, I'll hide in the root cellar if need be."

He grabbed her shoulders and gave a little shake. "No! Doggone it, Charlotte, stop trying to talk your way out of this. There's nowhere on our place you can hide where they won't find you. They'll look. I guarantee you, they'll look. You've got to promise me you'll stay here. I'll find you, but you have to promise to do what I've asked."

She sighed. "Show me this cave then."

"You promise? Char, look at me." He tipped her head back. "Look at my eyes and promise me you won't try to be brave. Promise me you'll stay right here and wait for me."

Tears streamed down his face. How could she deny him this request? He'd never asked her to do anything that would harm her. But her once smiling, happy-go-lucky husband had changed, and she hardly knew this determined, hardened man he'd become. He no longer whistled as he went about his daily chores. No longer grabbed her to show her a pretty cloud or asked her to listen with him as the mockingbird trilled through its repertoire. Even at night, while holding her, he seemed to always be listening, his body taut as though waiting for the knock that would signal him to leave.

"I promise, Lafe. And I promise to wait for you. But you promise to come back to me, you hear? I need you. This babe needs you. Can you promise you'll come back? Can you?"

"All I can promise you, my love, is if I don't, you'll know I died tryin'."

She pounded his chest with her fists. "That's not funny, Lafe Teasdale."

"I know. But it's all I can do for now."

She stood on tiptoes and pulled his face down to hers. Lafe could always kiss away her fears. And he tried. She knew he tried.

This time it didn't work.

CHAPTER 2

Charlotte eyed the narrow opening between two large rocks that obscured the mouth of the cave. "And just how am I supposed to fit through there?"

Lafe grinned at her. "You'll have to side-step through here, my love. I'm afraid there isn't enough room for you and the babe to go straight through." He gripped her hand as he went ahead of her.

"It's your fault, in case you have any more smart observations." Charlotte held tight to his hand as she wiggled between the rocks.

Once inside he relaxed his grip and slipped his arm to her shoulders. "Let your eyes adjust to the darkness before you go any farther. During daylight hours, enough sunlight'll sneak through that high crevice to let you find your way around."

She squinted through the shadows and her heart dropped. "There's nothing here. It's empty." How could he do this? Surely he didn't intend for her to live like this.

"I know, and I'm hoping that's what anyone else who might happen onto this place will think. But follow me." He grasped her hand again.

She tugged against his grip. "Lafe. Stop. I can't do this. I can't live like some kind of wild animal while you're off to wherever it is you're going."

He drew her to him. "Just a bit farther, my love. It isn't as bad as you think. You'll see. Trust me."

The lump in her throat prevented her from uttering one word, but she managed a shrug and a nod. She'd go along with his plan...for now.

Beyond the first chamber, through another narrow passage, was a second, smaller room. A bed of coals, surrounded by flat rocks and topped with an iron grate, supported a pot of simmering stew. The glowing coals sent weak light over the room. Charlotte blinked against tears. Logs topped with a crude plank made a table. Cushions made with grain sacks would suffice for seating.

She crossed to the warmth of the coals and hugged herself. "Is it safe?"

He put his arms around her and grinned. "Safe? You mean my cooking?"

She pushed away from him. "No. I mean, is it safe to have a fire in here?"

"You really think I'd hide you away up here and not make sure it was safe? The cave goes deep into the hill. And it's well vented. I made sure of it."

"And I suppose you've thought about food, too?"

He pulled a wooden barrel from the shadows against the wall. "There's salt pork in here. I dug what was left of the carrots and turnips while you was a sleepin' this morning. They're in the sacks along the wall, along with the potatoes. If all else fails, you know how to make rabbit traps." He pointed to a small crate next to the sacks. "There's candles in there, and matches, too, but use'em sparingly so they'll last."

Her mind swirled, but she knew better than to ask more questions. She lifted one of the cushions and burrowed her face against the rough burlap. This man, who insisted she not ask questions, had remembered how much she loved the fragrance of pine. She took a deep sniff of the pine needle stuffing and smiled. "They'll be a bit stickery to sit on, but thank you for remembering."

He hugged her close to his side. "I remember you every minute I'm away from you. If I close my eyes, your face is ever before me. At night, I imagine you in my arms. Even when we're far apart, you're so close to my heart I can even smell you...the sweetness of wild roses and everything good." He bent and brushed his lips against hers.

He turned her to face the other side of the room. "See? I didn't forget the most important part." A quilt-covered mattress lay atop a bed of pine boughs. And her good pillows, the ones meant for company—though seldom used—and stuffed with the goose feathers she'd saved over the years, were plumped and encased in the white covers with the lace edging she'd crocheted herself. Heat seeped through her body, and she dug her elbows into his ribs. Of course he'd remember a bed.

"And that box there at the end? Well, I packed up what clothes I thought you wouldn't miss...your weddin' dress, your goin'-to-town dress, and a couple of night shifts. Oh, and your slippers. Figured you'd get real tired of wearin' your boots all day."

"Where did you— How did you—"

"No questions. Remember?" He perched on the edge of the mattress and pulled her down beside him. "I know it's crude, my love. But it will keep you safe." He pointed to a branch that was propped against the wall. "See that?"

"The branch?"

He nodded. "It looks like a branch, but you'll use it as a broom. Make sure you take it with you should you go into the front chamber. Drag it behind you when you come back here. Don't leave any tracks for someone to follow. If you hear anything at all, come back into here." He pulled a gun from beside the makeshift bed. "You know how to use this. Don't hesitate if need be."

"You want me to shoot someone? Dead?" The heat she'd experienced before, now changed to cold fear.

"No, I don't want you to, but if you're in danger I don't want you to hesitate. I've never been more serious. Don't let anyone in here except me. I will call your full name, Charlotte Mae Teasdale, before I enter. Are you listening?"

"I'm listening, but I don't want to hear this. Are you leaving me here tonight? Alone? What am I to do if this child of yours decides to be born?"

"I don't know when I'll leave, but I'll be back before the babe comes. You said the middle of October. Right? I'll be back, or die trying."

Tears rolled down her cheeks before she could stop them.

He thumbed them away. "I'm sorry. I shouldn't have used those words." He kissed her forehead. "You have no idea how difficult this is, my love. You have to believe me."

She shifted away from him and stood. "I know this is hard, and I've made it harder." She swiped the tears from her face with the back of her hand. "But you have to know how hard it is for me, too—how frightened this makes me. I'll not argue. I'll stay here, as you've asked. But if you're not back in three weeks, I'll come looking for you."

Lafe jumped to his feet. "You'll do no such thing. You wouldn't have the faintest idea where to start looking, and I can't tell you where to find me."

"Can't? Or won't?" She moved her hands to her hips.

"Can't, because I don't know. All I know is I'm to catch up with—"

"Who? Catch up with who?"

"I won't tell you because, God forbid, should any of Ewing's men find you, I want you to honestly be able to tell them you don't know where I am or who I'm with."

She stepped toward him. "I...I thought you said I'd be safe here. Now you're worried Ewing's men might find me. What am I to believe?"

He gathered her in his arms. "You are safe, at least as safe as I can possibly make you. Much safer than many of the wives who are still on their farms, alone. But this is war. Ewing is determined to get rid of what he calls 'vermin' in these hills. They'll scour the area. His men don't know these hills and hollows, but there's always that one lone renegade who might decide to take matters in his own hands. I can't promise you that skunk won't find you." He held her and rocked back and forth, rubbing her back, caressing her hair. "I love you, Charlotte Mae. Love you more than you'll ever know. I gotta do this, though. What kind of a man would I be if I let others dictate how we was to live? What we can believe? Please, please, my love, try to understand."

She couldn't answer. There were no words. No more tears. No arguing. But she clung to him so tight her hands hurt. She'd been left too many times over her nineteen years, by people who loved her and those who didn't. Now he was the culprit, and it pained her too deep to tell him.

THREE DAYS LATER

Charlotte stretched and knew before she opened her eyes that Lafe was gone. She hadn't heard him leave. There'd been no knock at the door, because there was no door. Somehow he'd managed to leave the bed without making the dried cornhusk stuffed mattress crackle loud enough to wake her.

She rolled to her side and opened her eyes. Coals sent out a faint glow. Enough for her to find the hollow in the pillow where he'd laid his head. She buried her face in it, savoring his fragrance, yearning for his arms.

How was she to know if he wasn't coming back? Had he told her? She thought she listened, but had she missed that one vital bit of information? One day? Two days? A week?

The babe kicked, and she rubbed her stomach. "Hey, there, little one. You awake, too? Your papa went away, you know. But he'll be back." She tried to talk past the terrible dread that threatened to overcome her.

She rolled to her other side and pushed herself to her feet. Only a man would think a pregnant woman could get up from the floor without help. Somehow she had to make it through this day without dwelling on Lafe's absence. Surely he'd be back. Wouldn't he?

"If I don't come back, at least you'll know I died trying. I love you, Charlotte Mae. Don't ever forget how much I love you. And tell the babe his papa loves him, too."

A shiver snaked down her spine, and she hugged her bulging stomach. He wasn't here. She knew he wasn't here. But why did she hear his voice? Why did she feel his breath on her neck?

She grabbed Lafe's pillow and, with the broom in hand, made her way to the opening of the cave. Fresh air. She needed air. She was still in her night-shift, but who would see her? For now, she had to get out of this place.

Wincing, she picked her way through the brush. Her thin slippers did little to protect the bottom of her feet from the small acorns that littered the timber floor. A deadfall log not far from the cave offered her a place to sit. There wasn't room to stretch her legs without being in the tangle of undergrowth, but if she sat sideways she could get comfortable. The faint blush of dawn was just beginning to color the eastern sky in front of her, and the thin layer of early morning fog that lay farther down the hillside gave an eerie, pinkish hue to the area. Robins chirped their morning songs, and a whippoorwill sang its benediction. All comforting signs no one was intruding nearby.

She hugged the pillow close to her breast. If only she had a spy glass. How she longed to go back to the cabin and gather a few things, but her hilltop view also made her realize how difficult it would be for her to climb back up carrying anything but the babe already cradled in her womb.

What would she do all day? If only he'd told her his plan. There were things a woman needed, perhaps not to survive, yet to live. Things like combs for her hair, the sugar bowl with the gold rim, and the rag rug she'd made with her old dresses and Lafe's old shirts. Had she known he was going to make her stay, she would have gathered her knitting.

At least he'd bundled the flannel she'd purchased to make diapers and shifts for the babe. She'd found it while going through the box of items he'd sneaked out of the cabin. But he'd not thought of her knitting, or her Bible.

Oh, Lafe, where are you? His loving had been urgent but gentle last night. She should have sensed he'd be leaving. She wrapped her arms tighter around his pillow. A sudden sense of dread, a presence she couldn't explain, filled her breast and instinct told her to go back to her cave. Get out of the open. Go back into the cleft of the rocks. She stood and sidled back into her hiding place. To call it a living space took more imagination that she could muster. It was more like a tomb.

A tomb? She leaned against the rock wall. All this time and she'd not given one thought to praying. But now, thinking of this cave as a burial place, caused her to pause. They put Jesus in a hole like this. All because he was willing to die for the likes of her. Lafe had provided this place of safety because he was willing to die. She supposed a preacher would argue the comparison. But it helped. Oh, how it helped.

Charlotte straightened her shoulders. Jesus died for her, and Lafe was willing to do the same. How could she do less than choose to live for them?

I can do all things through Christ which strengtheneth me.

Her Bible. She could live without the combs and the sugar bowl or the rag rug. But she did want her Bible. Pressed into her hands as a parting gift from the one woman she could remember being kind to her, it was her most prized possession.

Somehow, she'd find a way to get it.

CHAPTER 3

Sitting atop his horse, hidden among the still lush timber of the Missouri hillside, Union Sergeant Robert Stallings scanned the ground below with his spy glass. Only moments ago he'd spotted a lone figure. A young woman with an expanded belly, dressed only in a nightshift. The white gown stood out like a flower in a desert. He'd cleaned the glass and looked again, but now he couldn't find her.

Why would a woman be out here alone? The only reasonable explanation was that she was in hiding. Placed there, perhaps by a father or husband, though by her obvious pregnancy, a husband would be the more reasonable supposition. She'd be fair game if others in his company spied her. He'd better draw attention away from the area.

"Saddle up, men. Time to move out. You've likely had your rest for the day." Robert lowered his field glasses, praying the men would be too busy to question his observation. He'd seen action in this terrible conflict that pitted brother against brother. Truth was, he'd rather fight his own brother than carry out General Ewing's latest order.

Fitted with notices to be presented to every home he found in Cass County, his job was to make sure the orders were carried out. He detested the assignment. He pulled the missive from his pocket and snapped his wrist to open it. Had he missed something? Was there some way to avoid carrying out such cruelty?

General Orders No. 11
Headquarters District of the Border
Kansas City, August 25, 1863

1. All persons living in Jackson, Cass, and Bates counties, Mis-

souri, and in that part of Vernon included in this district, except those living within one mile of the limits of Independence, Hickman's Mills, Pleasant Hill, and Harrisonville, and except those in that part of Kaw Township, north of Brush Creek and west of Big Blue, are hereby ordered to remove from their present places of residence within fifteen days from the date whereof...

He clenched his jaw and took a deep breath to quell the anger. There was more. Much more. No matter how many times he read it, he couldn't find a loophole. They were to confiscate anything of value left behind and burn what they didn't take. Revulsion filled him. It was one thing to fight against soldiers like himself, men who readily joined their respective armies believing in the cause and anticipating a short war with each side sure theirs would be the victor. But this order put a new face to the so-called enemy, targeting men too old or infirmed to fight as well as women and children. It wasn't right, and he swallowed against the bile that seemed permanently lodged in his throat.

"Saddled, *sir*. You want us to go ahead of you?"

Robert chose not to collide with the snide address from the pimply faced youngster who seemed determined to push against authority. "That would be the idea, *Private*."

"A notice on every post or door, right? And what if they argue? Do we shoot 'em?" Private Garvey pulled his gun.

Robert rankled at the sneer on the younger man's face. Some thought they weren't soldiers unless they could shoot or kill. This brash youngster was far too eager to do both.

"Holster it, Garvey. Listen up, men. Our job is to give them the notice. You shoot without provocation and you better have the next shot aimed at me. I'll tell you right now, there's isn't a one of you who can outdraw or outshoot me, so don't even consider it. You understand, Garvey?"

A salute of sorts accompanied Garvey's nod. For now, Robert would let it pass. But he'd address it in private at the first opportunity.

"Carry on, then. I'll stay here on top and keep lookout for awhile but will follow shortly. Keep your eyes peeled for rebels, too, but we're not to engage unless threatened. One lone man doesn't constitute a threat."

He waited for his men to get far enough down the hillside they wouldn't be as likely to double back, then looked through his field glass again where he'd seen the glimpse of white near an outcropping of rocks. He fixed the position in his mind, using the jagged rocks as a focal point. He'd have to take a chance that somewhere in the nooks and crevices of the hillside, she'd found a place of refuge.

Despite his caution, there was enough dry underbrush to crackle with the weight of the horse. Besides that, the birds had stopped singing. If this lady knew anything about the world around her, she'd know someone—or something—was in the vicinity and would thus likely draw deeper into her place of hiding. He didn't have much time or his men would wonder at his lagging behind.

Choosing stealth over time, he tied his horse to a nearby bush and proceeded on foot. Perhaps he could cushion his footsteps enough. He'd folded a notice and stuck it in his pocket in the chance he'd find her, or at least locate her hiding place. She might not believe him, but perhaps she'd read the notice and realize he had no intention of harm. He didn't want to frighten her. In fact, he only intended to warn her to stay hidden. If she were truly alone, and with her obvious condition, her safety was foremost in his mind.

His downward pursuit would have been in vain had he not spied a crude form of a broom lying on a deadfall trunk. Had it been on the ground, he'd have dismissed it as part of the undergrowth. But this seemed a deliberate fashion of a tool, and he could only surmise it had been forgotten by the lady he'd observed earlier.

He retrieved the broom and, with some scouting, finally found a tall, narrow opening behind a large rock. He squeeze through and entered a cave. Close inspection revealed small footprints in the dust although the room itself was quite large and empty. Instinct cautioned him not to go any deeper into the cave. After all, he wasn't there to subdue her, but rather to assure her he meant no harm and would do all he could to prevent any intrusion. He took the notice and a pencil from his pocket and scribbled a quick note, then picked a stone from the floor of the cave to weigh down the flyer. He'd leave it. She'd surely find it.

He advanced only far enough to be able to wipe out any of her footsteps, then backed out of the cave, brandishing the broom to clear his as well. He left the broom leaning against the entrance in hopes she'd see it as another sign he meant no harm. By his watch, he was a good fifteen minutes behind his men. Now, if only he could proceed without questions from Garvey.

Charlotte chided herself for forgetting the broom. How could she be so careless? Would she ever get used to this new way of living—like an animal always on alert to danger?

She turned to retrace her steps to retrieve it, but caution stopped her. Not a noise, but a presence she couldn't explain—like when she could feel Lafe's breath even though he wasn't there. Fear constricted her chest, and her legs trembled. This couldn't be, could it? Had someone found her? The first day Lafe was gone?

She lost track of how long she stood, barely breathing. Ten minutes? Fifteen? Long enough for the babe nestled in her womb to let her know he was there, and for awhile she allowed herself to enjoy its antics as it moved her tummy beneath her thin nightdress. It was safe now, this wee one, but what would happen when it decided to make its entrance into this cruel world?

With her hand over her mouth to muffle any sound, she took a deep breath. She'd learned that tactic as a child, attempting to escape from abusive overseers masquerading as loving caregivers. It didn't always work, but it never failed to give her new resolve—the tenacity to face whatever the future held. But as a child, she had only herself to protect, by any means she found necessary. It was different now, what with the babe.

At last she felt safe enough to poke her head around the rocks that protected her. A stone-weighted paper was present, and her forgotten broom leaned just inside the entrance. With steps slow and tentative, she made her way to the paper. Once retrieved, she opened it against her cotton gown to diminish the crackle, then leaned against the rock wall and angled the paper to the shaft of light streaming from the opening.

According to the paper, there was a new order—number eleven, the simple title making it sound impersonal. She shoved her knuckles against her mouth to stifle the scream that fought its way through her whole being. They would confiscate her property? They would destroy anything left behind? All she and Lafe had worked so hard to achieve—their crops, their animals, and all their worldly goods still in the cabin—would be lost?

She couldn't let it happen. The notice said they had fifteen days from the date of issuance. She scanned the paper again. The issue date was August twenty-five. She ticked the days off on her fingers, but it was no use. She couldn't even remember what day of the week it was. But no matter—she couldn't wait in a hole in the side of a hill while every vestige of their sweat and tears were threatened. Lafe wouldn't want her to. He said bad things were going to happen, but he didn't know about this. He wouldn't have left had he known. He'd have stayed and fought against the forces of evil men who dared take away all they called their own.

She reread it, and only then noticed a note at the bottom. *Take no chances. Stay hidden. Don't forget broom.*

This wasn't from Lafe. It wasn't his handwriting. But why would he send someone to warn her when he was so determined to keep her whereabouts hidden? A terrible, crushing weight bent her shoulders, and she slid down the rock wall to a sitting position. She would not break. She'd known fear before, and she'd been forsaken many times over. She didn't break then, and she wouldn't break now. *"Be strong and of a good courage, fear not, nor be afraid of them: for the LORD thy God, he it is that doth go with thee; he will not fail thee, nor forsake thee."*

Lafe had laughed at her when she quoted from the Bible. He claimed he couldn't trust what he couldn't see. She'd tried—oh, how she tried—to convince him he couldn't depend on his own strength or his own knowledge. Despite his lack of faith, he always loved her. Just as she loved him.

The memory of his love made her more determined. She'd survive. If need be, she'd have the babe alone. But she wouldn't, she couldn't, give up hope Lafe would return soon.

CHAPTER 4

Robert rode into the clearing in the midst of bedlam. Chickens, held by their feet, squawked and beat their wings against their captors. One large ewe bleated in protest and braced its legs against the drag of the rope around its neck, and a sow waddled and grunted as it was being driven by one of his men brandishing a stick. A pile of household goods grew as items were tossed from the open door of the cabin. Beside the mound of confiscated goods stood Garvey, methodically tearing pages from a Bible and shoving them under the bottom items.

Driven by anger and disgust, Robert drew his sidearm and shot three times into the air. The scene before him came to a momentary halt, but the heat of anger surging through every fiber of his being didn't cool. "What in thunder is going on here?"

Private Garvey lifted his head slowly and gave a one-sided grin. "Obvious, ain't it, Sarge? Carryin' out orders, like ya said."

"No, Private, you are not carrying out orders. The orders specifically state these people are to be given fifteen days from the date of issuance to vacate their property. Until then, you and every last man-jack of you involved in this fiasco can be arrested for insubordination." His hand holding the gun shook, not from fear but rather from rage. He hated this war and what it was doing to people. Where was the decency?

Garvey straightened and jabbed the air with the Bible. "Yeah? Well, look around, Stallings. Ain't nobody in sight. I'll swear on this supposed holy book I'm holdin' that some dirty reb is hidin' in the timber, probably got his ugly wench with him. Breakfast still on the table, bacon cold in the fryin' pan. Somebody knowed we was comin' and done warned their lowdown hides."

"Hey! Lookee what we found." A shout from the small barn at the edge of the clearing took Robert's attention away from the sneering private. He hipped around in his saddle in time to see two soldiers stride toward the pile of belongings carrying a cradle.

A wad of spittle from Garvey landed in the dirt beside Stalling's horse. "Like I was tellin' ya...somewhere out in that timber there's a reb and his wench. Don't reckon we can stop 'em from breedin', but sure as shootin' we can keep 'em from droppin' more of their kind in this county. Fire it up, men!"

The image of the pregnant woman flashed across Robert's mind, and instinct told him this was her cabin. Her cradle. Her Bible. All her earthy goods. He stood in his stirrups, his gun still drawn. "Put a match to that pile and you get a bullet. You understand?"

Garvey didn't move, but the two with the cradle set it in the dirt where they stood.

Robert breathed a deep sigh of relief. He didn't doubt the loyalty of his men. Except for the firebrand private, and that one had wrestled against orders from day one. Apparently Garvey decided today was the day to exert his rebellion. "Every last one of you, drop what you have in your hands, mount up, and get on down the road. Now!"

"I'm sayin' torch it." Garvey widened his stance and put one hand on his sidearm. "What're you doin', Stallings? Ewing ain't gonna be happy when he finds out you ordered us away from here. Not when we didn't follow his orders."

"My orders, Garvey. You follow my orders, and I'm telling you and every soldier in this company one more time—drop what you have in your hands, mount up, and get moving." He fixed his gaze on Garvey. "Private, I'm warning you. One more display like this and I'll put you afoot. You can be sure Ewing will hear of this."

Garvey drew his gun and pointed to the soldier nearest the mound of goods. "Who ya gonna listen to? Stallings or me? We both got our guns out, but mine is on you."

Robert nudged his horse closer to Garvey. "And mine is aimed at you."

Garvey swiveled and pointed his gun at Robert's chest, his face contorting. "I been wantin' to do this for a long time, Stallings."

Shots rang out, and something hot seared into Robert's left shoulder. He pulled his trigger one more time as he tumbled backwards from his mount and hit the ground. He tried to sit up, but pain shot through him like shards of glass, and he bit his lip to quell the moan.

"Lookee here, men. If anybody asks, this one was shot by a dirty reb."

Though he could barely focus, Robert made out Private Garvey's face bending close to his.

"This is what happens when ya ain't got the guts to do what them orders said we was to do. Here." Something heavy hit his stomach. "You need this worser'n me. Course, it ain't all together no more. Had to use some of it to start the blaze. I hear that there Holy Bible says somethin' 'bout the fires of hell. Well, you can bet those shiny boots of yours them reb-lovin' people around here is gonna have them a little taste of that place once we get to fol-lowin' orders. Best be sayin' your prayers, Stallings. I'd shoot ya again but no need to waste another bullet. You're gonna die anyway."

The ground shook with the pounding of horses' hooves as his company of men departed. He waited until he could no longer hear them, then he allowed himself to succumb to the pain while a veil of darkness obscured his sight.

Charlotte's heart thrummed. She'd heard shots—echoes, really—but she'd been in the hills long enough to know gunfire when she heard it. Below her was all she had. Her home, her belongings, and...and Lafe. She sank to her knees. Did Lafe fire the shots? There were too many to be only a warning. She shut her eyes against the other possibility. Was Lafe the target?

"If it ain't worth dyin' for, if it ain't worth livin' for."

She groaned behind her fist. *Oh, Lord, I promised my husband I'd not leave this place. But what if he's hurt or...or—*

She couldn't say it. Not even in the silence of her thoughts could she ut-ter the words that would mean an end to her world.

The babe kicked against her ribs and she wrapped her arms around her stomach. "I know, little one. I want to kick, too. Kick and scream and fight my way down this mountain to see if your papa needs help."

What if someone else, not Lafe, needed help? She'd taken risks many times before, but those risks never included the life of anyone other than her-self. Did she dare risk the life of this babe—the one thing that would remain of Lafe should he not return? If he did come back and she'd been foolish and lost the babe, he would know she defied his orders and her promise.

She leaned against the crude broomstick to help her to her feet, then with one last look to make sure her footprints were obscured, she made her way to the inner safety of the cave. She changed into her brown muslin dress and lowered herself to the rough mattress. How would she ever survive the terrible hours of fear and worry?

Oh, Lafe. Please come back.

Robert stumbled to the safety of the timber and leaned against a tree. He'd been in battle often enough to recognize the odor of blood, gunpowder, and smoke. But not until he'd attempted to sit up did he realize the blood was his own. That revelation brought the happenings of the day fresh to his mind.

Judging from his cracked lips, the congealed blood on the front of his uniform, and the smoldering remains of what at one time had been a thriving homestead Garvey had torched despite his command, he must have lain in the open at the mercy of the scorching sun for several hours. How could he have been so careless as to let a brash, undisciplined, hotheaded private take him down?

Anger, that's what.

He rubbed his wrinkled forehead. He'd always prided himself in his ability to stay calm and levelheaded while others around him allowed anger or fear or any other number of emotions distract them from the reality of the moment. But here he was, pain throbbing through his left shoulder with each pump of his heart—that arm useless—and nothing but a Bible he'd found lying in the dirt beside him with which to defend himself against whatever might be in the surrounding timber, man or beast. All because he was so blinded by anger he didn't see what was coming.

His legs trembled with the effort to remain standing. He slid down the trunk of the tree until his rear met the forest floor, then he drew his knees to his chest and laid the Bible on top of them. He'd gotten himself into this mess by sending his men ahead of him so he could scope out the lone woman. If he'd stayed with his men, he'd have maintained his charge instead of setting up Garvey to take control.

Or would he have stayed in charge? While the orders did say to give the occupants of any given property fifteen days to vacate, he knew the likelihood of that happening was slim. It was like being handed the keys to a candy store, only it wasn't the want of something sweet that motivated the soldiers. Fear and hate and a taste of power heretofore unknown to the men—boys really—who made up his company drove them. Maybe, had he not taken the time to warn the woman, he could have prevented his present situation.

Then again, maybe taking the time to warn her would be his salvation. He couldn't stay here. If sympathizers hid in the timber, they'd find him long before he knew they were there. If a man didn't find him, the scent of blood would be an invitation to wild animals. He needed to get somewhere safe, and the cave was his best choice.

But what if the woman he'd seen wasn't alone? What if she had a gun? Surely, if she was hidden there by a loving husband, he'd have given her a firearm with orders to use it against any intruder. What if the babe she was carrying wasn't her first? What if there were other children safely ensconced in the belly of that hillside? His mother would have fought like a mama bear if anything or anyone threatened her children. Could he convince this woman he meant no harm? If there was a husband hiding somewhere, as Garvey intimated, he'd not blame him to shoot first and ask questions later.

Robert opened the Bible. His mama penned all things important in the pages of the family Bible—names of those married and when, who was born and who had passed. Maybe this was something all women did.

He tried to raise his left arm to help steady the Bible while he turned the pages but was met with searing pain. He bit his lower lip to keep from yelling and prayed he would stay conscious. He drew slow, deep breaths and leaned his head against the tree. Eyes closed, he battled a wave of nausea, and his heartbeat swooshed in his ears like wind whistling through the timber.

Finally he opened his eyes and settled his gaze on the Bible. Even after finding the page he was looking for, it took a bit for his eyes to focus. At last he made out the inscription.

Presented to: Charlotte Mae Bowers.
By: Isabelle Miller
On this date: September 23, 1855.

A childish scrawl added *12 years old* after the date. On the next page, he found only one entry—the marriage of Charlotte Mae Bowers to Lafe Adam Teasdale on January 1, 1860. Nothing was recorded on the pages that had space to list births or deaths.

Robert scrunched his forehead. If the woman at the cave was this Charlotte Mae Bowers Teasdale, and she was twelve years old in September of 1855, that would make her—he counted on his fingers—twenty next month. Since no births were listed, he assumed the child she carried was her first. Only the sacrifices of war would entice a man who loved his wife to leave her and their unborn child in a hole in the side of a hill.

Now the same sacrifices left him with no choice but to seek shelter among the same rocks. He unbuttoned his shirt and slipped the Bible inside, then groaned as he grabbed the nearest branches of a bush to pull himself to his feet. The top of the hill might as well have been a day's march into enemy territory. Both were senseless to try to achieve. But the climb to safety of the rocks was essential if he was going to survive.

CHAPTER 5

Darkness set in early on this side of the hill, and while the shadows gave Robert needed cover, they also impeded his climb. He grimaced in pain as he grabbed yet another branch laden with thorns in his effort to reach the cave and hoped-for refuge. How safe he'd be would depend on one Charlotte Mae Teasdale—if indeed she was the woman he'd observed—and his ability to convince her he meant no harm. He could only pray he'd not encounter an enemy on the way, or find one already entrenched within. But then, who was the enemy? His own men had left him for dead.

A shaft of light caught his attention as it swayed toward him—above him, to the left, now to the right. Was someone coming, swinging a lantern? He threw himself prostrate among the brush, ignoring the thorns and praying he'd not encounter a snake. His shoulder throbbed with the sudden impact on the ground, and he feared it would cause new bleeding, which would only serve to further weaken him and make him more vulnerable to the nocturnal hunters roaming the hills.

He burrowed his face into his bent arm and forced himself to take deep breaths. The Bible in his shirt dug into his ribs, but to roll away from it now would cause movement he didn't want detected. How easy it would be to just lie where he was and succumb to fatigue and perhaps death. What difference would it make how he died? For that matter, who would care?

He fought against the image stalking through the shadows of his mind—one gravestone which bore the names of all he loved and had left behind. *Margaret Elizabeth Stallings, beloved wife of Robert Andrew Stallings.* Underneath Molly's name, the chiseled replica of a lamb and *Robert Andrew Stallings, Jr.* He'd buried the stillborn babe in Molly's arms, then rode away from his ranch where even the walls cried out her name and the hills echoed the lament.

Some would call him a coward, leaving like he did. If coward could be described as pain with every breath, every minute of the day, from the memories that were so bittersweet he could hardly bear to think, then he'd agree—a coward he was. The ranch would still be there. He'd left it in good hands with his brother, Luke. But whether he returned remained to be seen. He'd joined the army not caring if he lived or died. Now, three years later, he still didn't care.

He swallowed. He could give it all up right there and no one would know it was by his own choice. Some might even think he'd died a hero, with the gunshot wound as evidence. So why was he trying to find refuge now?

He had no answer for the question that reverberated like a shot in the hills. Perhaps the will to survive was stronger than the desire to die, even when he didn't care one way or another. Or was it seeing the young pregnant woman seemingly alone that somehow resurrected his past, buried so deep he'd not recognized the implication, urging him forward?

He turned his head and rested it on his arm. The light that swayed back and forth continued to throb through the trees, but didn't appear to be advancing. He squinted, hoping he could get a clearer view. He did, and he collapsed in relief. He was a military man and should know better, although caution was the better part of valor. The light was no more than the full moon, now high in the sky, shining through the timber. The wind swaying the branches made it seem to dart hither and thither.

He'd identified the enemy, and it was his imagination. He'd viewed the light as something from which to hide. God sent it to show him the path. Taking a deep breath, he pushed himself to his feet with his good arm. Weak...so weak... The effort of standing brought a new round of dizziness, but if God provided the light, then it was up to him to follow it even though more light, however slight and patchy, would also make him more vulnerable.

One step at a time, Robert. Go with the light, one step at a time.

A faint lightening of the eastern horizon and the occasional twitter of an early bird signaled morning by the time Robert reached the rocky outcrop that overshadowed the entrance to the cave he sought. His hand was raw from pulling himself forward by tugging on rough tree trunks or various underbrush that surrounded him. He'd lost count of how many times he'd ripped his sleeve away from thorny branches that seemed intent on thwarting him.

211

His ribs were sore from the Bible jabbing into them every time he tripped and fell over hidden tree roots among the debris of the timber floor.

As far as he could ascertain, the mouth of the cave was only a few yards above him, but now a bigger dilemma faced him. Was the woman alone? Did she have a gun? If she did, would she use it? Of course she would use it. He would have told Molly to use hers in such a situation.

Molly had seldom been left alone, but each time he had given her clear instructions concerning strangers arriving at her door. He'd taught her how to use a gun. He had learned—after she inadvertently mistook him for an intruder and sent a warning shot way too close to his ear—to call her name. Neighbors knew her as Molly Stallings. Only he knew her real name was Margaret Elizabeth O'Brien Stallings. Calling it out saved him injury on other occasions, and he smiled at the recollection.

Charlotte Mae Teasdale. Maybe—even if her husband was present—calling her name might indicate he meant no harm. It was worth a try. If he got shot in the doing? Well, at least he'd see Molly again sooner than expected.

The last few steps took nearly all his strength. Once inside the cave, he stayed on his feet long enough to pull the Bible from his shirt, then his knees buckled and he slid down the rock wall.

A lump caught in his throat. He'd made it. His shoulder throbbed. His hands were raw and bleeding. His legs were too weak to hold him upright. And he must smell like a goat. But for the time being—even if only for a short time—he was still alive...and safe.

Fear prickled along Charlotte's spine, and she curled her fingers around the shotgun. She'd grown somewhat accustomed to the skittering of rock lizards across the walls and the squeaks and scratches from beneath the makeshift table. This sound was different. There was no mistaking the *thud* she'd heard, as though something or someone dropped to the floor inside the cavern entrance. She blew out the candle and aimed the shotgun at the opening to her refuge, ready to shoot should there be real danger present.

"Charlotte? Charlotte Mae Teasdale?"

Lafe! Lafe said he would call her full name. If he had been the target of the shots she'd heard yesterday, then he was injured and needed her help. Yet it wasn't his voice. Why did it sound like a question, as if whoever called was not sure?

She shuffled slowly toward the opening to the passageway. "Lafe?"

There was no answer, but perhaps he was too hurt to reply. She kept both hands on the gun and used her hip to trail along the rock wall until she reached the narrow opening that would require her to leave the safety of her interior cave to enter the larger chamber.

"Who's there? Lafe? Is it you? Whoever it is, I have a gun and I'm not afraid to use it."

"No, ma'am. Please...don't shoot. I—I need help. I've been shot."

Charlotte's heart beat faster. "Who are you? How did you find this place?"

"Sergeant Robert Stallings, ma'am. I saw you through my field glasses yesterday. I left you a note."

She gripped the gun even tighter. An injured man... Was he friend or foe? Should it matter? Didn't God's Word say that whatever one did unto the least of these, they were also doing it unto Him? How could she refuse to help? But what if it was a ploy? Now she understood why Lafe wouldn't tell her where he was going or who he was with. "How did you know my name? Did Lafe send you?"

"I found your name in a Bible, yours and your husband's."

"How do I know you're telling me the truth?"

"Please. I need help."

"Who shot you?" Could it have been Lafe?

"A man by the name of Garvey shot me, ma'am. If you're not going to help me, could I please at least have some water?"

It was against everything Lafe warned her about, but she'd been in need of help too many times to ignore this man's plea. Besides, he sounded weak, and she had a gun. "I'll get a light."

"No. No light."

"Water then. I'll go for water. Don't move."

He groaned. "Don't have the strength to move, ma'am."

Charlotte held a cup of water to the man's lips. Morning light was beginning to seep through the entrance, and she was able to get a better look at him. He was a soldier, and judging by his uniform, a Union soldier at that. However, his obvious weakness gave her a small measure of confidence that he'd not harm her. "Do you think you can stand and walk? It's not safe to stay here." She moved the cup away. "Not too much at one time or you'll be sick."

"How far?"

"Not far, but you have to squirm around a boulder."

He motioned to the gun. "Can I use that to lean on?"

She rolled her lips. What if he turned it on her? Yet nothing in the man's demeanor suggested he would do such a thing.

He shook his head and a faint smile crossed his lips. "Won't shoot you." He picked the Bible from the floor and held it toward her. "I promise."

Her Bible. She took it from him. The cover was crusted with blood, but otherwise it appeared unharmed. She held it against her breast. This was one of the reasons she'd been tempted to go against Lafe's orders. Now this man, a supposed enemy, had brought it to her. How could she refuse him help?

She handed him the gun. "I don't reckon shooting me would help you any."

He struggled to his feet, and beads of perspiration gathered on his forehead. "Lead the way."

Charlotte made sure he was still on his feet when they entered the safer interior, then hurried to light a candle. "You better lie down." She motioned to her bed. "I need to look at that wound."

He leaned against the near rock wall. "Can't take your bed, ma'am. I'm dirty, and there's blood—"

"Please. Don't argue. That blood is the very reason you need to be on something besides a dirt floor."

"I—"

Sergeant Stallings slumped and fell sideways onto the bed before Charlotte could catch him.

She folded her arms across her stomach and prayed the man would stay unconscious long enough for her to assess the wound. She could move his feet to the bed—could even pull his boots off while he was awake. But except for Lafe, she'd never looked on another man's bare torso, and she certainly didn't care to do it if he could watch her.

Charlotte straightened and gave her shoulders a shake. She'd do what she had to do. The same as she'd want someone to do for Lafe.

CHAPTER 6

Stalling's hand closed around Charlotte's wrist. "The broom."

The broom? Was he delirious? He'd not even twitched when she pulled his blood-crusted shirt away from the wound, bringing a fresh flow of blood with it. He'd remained unconscious while she probed and scrubbed. All the while she'd made every effort to focus only on the man's injury. She'd even kept her eyes from his face, telling herself over and over that it was Lafe she was helping and not the enemy. But now his grip was so strong it hurt, and she found herself staring into eyes black as coffee—very strong coffee—and she couldn't look away.

"Please, let me go. You're hurting me."

A frown creased his forehead, and his grip loosened. "I'm sorry. But you can't forget the broom." His gaze never wavered.

She rubbed her wrist. Were his eyes always this dark? Except for those eyes and a dark, whiskery stubble, his face was devoid of color. She nodded toward the wall. "The broom is right here. I didn't forget it."

He licked his lips. "But you didn't use it, did you? "

Was he scolding her? "Since you can remember the broom, then you will also remember there were more important things to tend to at the time."

"No." His gaze hardened. "Go. Do it now."

"I'll go when I finish here, unless you care to bleed to death." She tore a strip from the precious flannel she'd saved for the babe—the only thing she had available to use for a bandage—and pressed it against the wound.

"That's an order, ma'am."

Had she been able to tear her gaze from his, she would've rankled over his assumption that he could bark orders and expect her to follow them. But his demeanor was not one of superiority—rather a plea. Lafe would have given her the same edict.

She tore another strip, folded it to make a pad, and laid it on top of the previous one, then took his hand. "You need to put pressure on this."

His fingers folded around hers. "I'm sorry I sounded harsh. I don't much care if I'm found or if I bleed to death. Believe it or not, I'm thinking of you and the—your babe. I don't know where your husband is, but if he shows up, I want him to know I did my best to keep you from harm. Even if I die trying." He gave her hand a gentle squeeze. "Please. I promise I won't bleed to death while you're gone."

Charlotte pulled her hand away, but their gaze remained locked. *Die trying.* The very words Lafe used and she fought against hearing. Did this Sergeant Stallings realize that her husband was somewhere off waging war against the likes of him? Yet, his thoughts were not for his own safety but for hers. Hers and Lafe's unborn babe.

He was weak, with one arm completely useless, and he wore an enemy uniform. At least Lafe would label him an enemy. But was he? If Lafe were in the same situation, weak and injured and at the mercy of some strange woman, he'd never cause that woman harm. When one man was willing to stand for what he believed against another man who had the same conviction, only an opposing view, which was the enemy?

She willed herself to look away and pushed herself to her feet. Words wouldn't get past the lump in her throat, so she'd not even try. Rather, she'd focus on what needed to be done.

Stallings was either asleep or unconscious again when Charlotte returned, but his hand still lay on the bandages. She was thankful she wouldn't have to meet his gaze, and she hoped he wouldn't awaken when she moved his hand so she could finish binding the wound. The memory of the gentle squeeze haunted her. It was difficult to pretend this man was her husband and not respond to his touch.

"Did you make sure you wiped them all away?"

She jerked her hand away. "I thought you were— Your eyes were closed, so I thought—"

He opened one eye, and a hint of a smile crinkled the corner of his mouth. "Have a habit of closing my eyes when I hurt. I don't suppose you have anything for pain?"

"I...we have laudanum in the cabin. I—"

"No!" Both eyes were open now, wide and threatening. He grabbed her wrist again. "You'll not think of leaving this place. It's not an option. Promise me. Even if I pass out again, you must not leave here."

She pulled against his grip. "I wasn't going to try to get down the hill, but only because I promised my husband I wouldn't, not because you're shouting orders at me. I'm not one of your soldiers, Sergeant Stallings."

Remorse slid across his countenance. "I apologize, ma'am. Would you finish binding the wound?"

Charlotte pointed to her wrist. "I can't very well do that with one hand."

He released his hold and closed his eyes again.

"Are you hurting worse? Your eyes are closed again." If only he'd let her explain. She had no intention of trying to make it down the hill on her own. Not now. But she would have ventured outside the safety of the cave to look for willow bark or dandelion leaves to make a strong tea. But then, he'd probably have resisted that, too.

He shook his head but didn't open his eyes. "I caused you pain, and I'm so, so sorry. Please forgive me."

She didn't answer. She should have. Good manners dictated she at least acknowledge his apology. Except for Lafe, few people had ever apologized for causing her pain of any kind, and Lafe had to teach her how to respond. Words were easy, but trusting those words came hard. Over the years, she'd learned that Lafe didn't utter one syllable she couldn't believe, whether it was declaration of love, an apology, or a promise. So she knew—although she hated to acknowledge it—that if he didn't come back, he died trying.

While this man said the right things, he had yet to prove himself. Thankful his eyes were closed, she studied his face. A small wrinkle lay between his brows, and from time to time his jaw rippled. Was that a sign of pain he didn't want to admit? Or was he deep in thought. Did he have a wife somewhere? Someone who missed him and wondered if he were all right, just as she worried over Lafe? Did the woman have his babe nestled in her womb? Should she ask? Would he tell her?

If Lafe was injured and lying on another woman's bed, would she study Lafe's face as he slept? Would she ask him questions about his wife? Would he admit he'd left her in a cave high on a hillside? Would he tell her about their unborn child? Would he—

Cast down all imaginations...bring all thoughts captive to the obedience of Christ.

The babe kicked against her ribs and jolted her back to the task on hand. She took a deep breath and lifted the bandages. No fresh bleeding. Good. Now to get the wound bound before he opened his eyes again. Those eyes—like candles in a window—invited her to seek shelter within. But she dare not accept the invitation.

Robert clenched his teeth, determined to keep his eyes closed while Charlotte continued to care for his wound. It was true that he shut his eyes against pain. But there was more than the pain of his shoulder involved.

Molly was not the first woman to ever catch his attention. But she was the only woman to capture his heart. Before Molly, he hadn't known how much love a heart could contain—full, sometimes, to the point of hurting. Even when he thought it could hold no more, she'd find a small crevice, the tiniest of cracks in his ordinarily well-guarded seat of emotions, and pack it even tighter.

He fisted his good hand at his side, determined to concentrate on now, to forget the then. Forget? How was he to forget when the now was nearly as unlikely as his meeting Molly? Sure, he'd observed the Teasdale woman from afar, but how could he have known seeing her face could evoke such comparison? He, a Union soldier, at the mercy of a woman who sought safety in the cave from the very likes of him.

Theirs had been an unlikely meeting, too, his and Molly's. She a banker's daughter and he a cowboy. They'd met when he went to her father's Kansas City bank to sign the papers for his ranch. There she sat, dressed in pink and looking for all the world like a wild rose.

He'd learned to drink wine and use the correct fork, all while wearing stiff-collared white shirts and silk bowties. She, over the objections of her parents, had climbed into his buggy and headed west after their wedding. They'd slept under the stars on their wedding night and one short year later danced under the stars when she told him he was to be a papa.

Then with the labor of birth came the swiftness of death, and his heart broke. The break released all the love it once held. He'd survived. Against his will, he'd survived, but with survival came a new kind of agony. The agony of bittersweet memories.

An involuntary moan escaped from his lips.

"I'm sorry. I'll try to be more gentle."

The woman's voice was soft and tender. How could she know his moan wasn't from pain from the now, but hurt from the past? Her compassion couldn't help the ache that went deeper than the bullet lodged in his shoulder.

The army had helped, somewhat. Days could now pass without his every thought occupied by Molly. Over the past three years, his heart had begun to patch itself together again. But he'd vowed it would never again hold love. He'd reveled in the discipline it took to be a good soldier. He'd chosen a side and prided himself on his loyalty—until now.

Now, with order Number 11, the seams of his patchwork heart began to come apart. Into the crevices crept bitterness and a loathing for what man could do to man—and a hatred for what he, as Sergeant Robert Stallings, was instructed and expected to fulfill. While he was fully aware of that internal war, he'd not anticipated the battle he now fought.

What he felt for the woman tending his wound wasn't love. Not even close. He'd not allow it. Could not fathom it. But the sighting of Charlotte Mae Teasdale, alone and with child amidst the rock and timber of this Missouri hillside, instigated a skirmish that quickly escalated. It wasn't like he was unaware of the danger involved. What made it worse, in debriefing the situation, was how he'd convinced himself the only way to save himself was to reach the very doorstep of the imagined foe. He'd crawled and pulled his way for hours and now lay helpless in both mind and body.

He was too weak to even sit up by himself. One arm was useless. His shoulder throbbed. And as for his heart—

"Are you about done?" His resolve was melting fast, and he had to fight to keep his eyes closed.

"Almost. Just need to tie the ends of this bandage and then you can rest."

He groaned when she secured the dressing.

"I'm so sorry, I've hurt you again. I don't want this to wiggle loose."

Cool fingers brushed his forehead.

"I don't think you have fever, but if you're a praying man this would be the time to do it. Would you like another drink of water?"

He nodded. "I am, and I would."

She didn't answer him, but he sensed her absence, and it only added to his angst. He could always sense Molly's presence and would know if she left the room, even without hearing or witnessing either the coming or going. He'd never asked another man if it was normal, and perhaps it wasn't so unusual. Yet it was the one thing that haunted him after her death—he could no longer *feel* her. He'd walk from room to room, night after night, begging her to come back, longing to catch a whiff of the rosewater she always dabbed behind her ears and on her wrists.

He'd been in the army long enough now to almost forget. Nighttime was a noisy time among men, and their presence or leaving was never a mystery. It helped. He no longer woke with a start when a fellow soldier entered a darkened room after answering the call of nature. He'd learned early that rosewater was not among the various fragrances a fellow encountered in a camp of men.

But now...now Charlotte Teasdale had left his side without a sound, and he sensed her absence. His chest tightened, the way it often did right before going into battle. The sensation that came with the uncertainty of the outcome. He turned his head to the side. He was thirsty, but he couldn't chance looking into her eyes—eyes as clear and blue as a summer sky. Not yet. She was a married woman with another man's child in her womb.

Oh, God, I am a praying man. Please don't let me succumb to anything that is not in Your perfect will.

CHAPTER 7

Robert side-stepped his way down the steep hillside. One thing was sure, it was much easier going down than his climb uphill a month ago had been. He paused and rotated his shoulder.

Though still tender, he'd regained the use of his arm and no infection had hindered the healing process. Charlotte was a good nurse. Too good. Although his britches still bore the evidence of a Union soldier, the war he fought was one of the heart and mind—and he was his own worst enemy.

What was it about Charlotte that made it possible for her to penetrate the wall of memories and unanswered questions that had become his hiding place? Few people—and those only a handful left behind in Kansas—knew of Molly. Just as he would never have dreamed to share his wife with another man while she was living, he couldn't share her memory, either. But then, he'd surrounded himself with men and had stayed deliberately detached, and no one pried. Charlotte didn't pry, either. Yet, somehow she'd managed to chink away at the mortar of his memory bank and steal his reserve.

A squirrel scolded him from a branch high above. Evidently he'd stayed too long in the bushy-tail's domain. He gave a mock salute. "I got the message, kind sir, and will continue on my way."

He gave one more furtive glance through the timber. Though birds still sang, and squirrels chattered, his military training cautioned him to be alert. So why had he let down his military guard when it came to Charlotte Teasdale?

The truth was, he had no answer. Whether it was weakness from the loss

of blood, or perhaps the anonymity the cover of darkness of the cave provided, the end result was the same—they'd both shared openly about their
mates, and they'd also shared tears in the doing. Yet, he'd not felt shame or
embarrassment.

But while he was now able to release the pain of Molly's passing, he was
not free to claim Charlotte's heart. She had a husband...somewhere. His
name was Lafe, he'd hidden her in the cave to protect her from Ewing's men,
and she had no idea where he was or when he would return, only that he
promised to be there for the birth of their child...or die trying.

He stepped forward and allowed gravity to pull him down the hill for
a short distance, making sure his shoulders stayed well behind his feet lest
he topple head over heels. While he managed to keep his body upright, he
couldn't stop images of the past weeks from tumbling through his mind with
each downward tread. They'd talked no further of that night of revelation but
in the following days and weeks, theirs had become a comfortable existence.
This morning, when he told her of his plan to return to the clearing, her eyes
spoke words her lips didn't utter, and his arms ached to pull her to him. He
wanted to hold her and assure her he'd return soon, that she'd be safe until
then.

But it was wrong. Laughing and crying and the sharing of private matters
made it too easy to have vain imaginations. If he had any sense at all, he'd hit
the clearing and keep on going. *Flee from youthful lust.* Isn't that what God's
Word required? He couldn't leave her. Wouldn't leave her. But neither could
he continue to occupy the same space, even if separated at night. This was not
a nocturnal skirmish he was in. It was a full-out battle, and one he couldn't
afford to lose.

Charlotte folded her arms on top of her rounded belly, and leaned against the
entrance to the cave. A slight breeze lifted a strand of hair and she pushed it
behind her ear. The dense foliage had long ago swallowed Robert, and while
she could no longer see him, she didn't move from her vantage point. Had he
sensed her angst at his leaving?

It wasn't that she was afraid to be alone. She wasn't. She'd become quite
accustomed to her cave dwelling. Although she missed her cabin and the trea-

sures it held, she'd found a sense of satisfaction making-do with what she had.

No, it wasn't being alone that frightened her. Still no sign of Lafe frightened her. The prospect of his never returning allowed fear to run rampant. All the what-ifs she'd experienced in childhood reared their ugly heads. Lafe had rescued her from them, but who was to rescue her if Lafe didn't return? Her tummy tightened, a different sensation than what signaled the babe's movement. It didn't hurt, and it subsided quickly. Had she been busy with something she doubted she'd even noticed. But she wasn't busy, and she did notice.

She took a step outside the opening and shielded her eyes against the sun. If only she could catch a glimpse of Robert. Aside from begging him to stay, what more could she have done to prevent his going? She wiped her hands across her eyes. To be truthful, Robert frightened her, too. Rather, he elicited feelings she'd heretofore only experienced with Lafe—and that scared her. She couldn't allow herself to describe it as love, but rather that of safety, of being able to share her heart and know he wouldn't laugh. Of knowing he felt safe enough to shed tears and not apologize.

But it was wrong. All wrong. And that's what frightened her the most. God's Word was plain about such things—*flee youthful lusts...thou shalt not covet...cast down imaginations.*

Another twinge tightened her tummy, and this time waltzed its way around to her lower back. She wrapped both arms around her unborn child. "Getting restless, little one? Well, you go ahead and wiggle. At least I know you're there. But you wait for your papa, you hear me?"

She scuffed back to the inner chamber and lay down. She'd not slept well last night, and there was little to do today but wait.

Oh, Lafe. You rescued me once. Please, please come home.

She gulped.

And, Robert...stay safe.

Robert stood at the edge of the timber. Except for piles of ashes and burned shells of what were once buildings, little was left in the clearing. He'd sift through the remains in hopes of finding something—anything to take back to Charlotte. In all their talking, he'd not mentioned the mound of household goods he'd witnessed being tossed from her cabin, nor the smoldering pile of ashes he'd noticed when he regained consciousness that terrible day.

Even more obvious than the destruction, more telling than the remains of what at one time had been a thriving homestead, was the awful stillness. Death had a silence all its own, but this went beyond that. Death stilled a voice, while the clamor of life continued around it. But this kind of silence seeped into his mind and his heart. It shouted and cried and moaned until he put his hands over his ears to quiet it. Bent corpses of trees, as though they still writhed in pain, stood stark and black around the remains of what had been Charlotte's home. Even after all this time, he still remembered the bleating ewe and the squawking chickens that had been taken as spoils, their agonized voices of terror echoing over the terrible void of life that permeated the area.

Oh, God, what awful destruction man has done unto his fellow man. Why? How long will this hate continue? How will the generations to come view this terrible time? As surely as fire consumed the hopes and dreams and livelihood of the peoples along these borders, it is by Your mercy that we, Your people are not consumed.

With heavy feet, he shuffled to the remains of the cabin. How strange that the doorframe still stood, and even stranger that he felt compelled to enter through it, though there were no longer walls. Dishes lay, still stacked, where once a cupboard must have been, but they crumbled in his hands when he touched them. A corner of a picture frame, a blackened spoon, the buckle from a man's belt, like bones of a once-upon-a-time life, lay buried among the ashes of all else reduced and returned to dust. It was like walking through a burial box, and his stomach heaved.

He turned to leave, again through the blackened door frame, this time out of reverence to the home that once was, but his eye caught a small glimmer. He bent and dusted away the ash that covered it. A sugar bowl, still intact, one tiny speck of a gold rim visible. Willing it not to break, he used both hands to scoop it up, as gently as one would lift a newborn from its mother's arms. The bowl became one fragile, tangible piece of hope, and he cradled it against his cheek and let his tears flow, not ashamed of the sobs that tore the silence.

His shoulder ached and his hands were raw, but he worked his way through the tangle of burned trusses where once the barn stood. His search yielded a length of leather harness, the head of an ax, and a dented tin bucket. Well after noon he ceased his efforts, satisfied he'd found all he would deem usable among the ruins. If they were forced to stay hidden in the cave for the winter, he'd have to scour the countryside, but for now he'd take his spoils and make his way back to the cave and Charlotte.

Maybe handing her the sugar bowl would soften the pain that was sure to come with the knowledge that all she'd known as home was gone.

Charlotte cradled the sugar bowl against her heart. She'd never had a lot of pretty things, nothing from her childhood to remind her of a loving family, but Lafe had given her the sugar bowl for their first Christmas. He'd sold a pig and bought the piece of gold-rimmed china and ten pounds of sugar. She'd never felt so fancy or so rich.

Now all that was left of home was the sugar bowl and her memories. She had a sweet tooth, and Lafe had teased her every time she spooned the sweetener into her coffee. Had even threatened her at one point, saying if his kisses weren't sweet enough he'd have to find another to bestow them upon. They'd laughed amidst the loving, and she'd made him promise to keep them all for her. He'd taken her face in his hands—those big, calloused hands that were gentle as a kitten—his eyes bright with unshed tears.

"Charlotte Mae Teasdale, don't you ever think for one minute I'd favor another over you. You're all this man wants. You understand?"

She'd answered him with a kiss. The memory of it made her close her eyes against a wave of guilt. Just this morning she'd fought the urge to beg Robert Stallings to stay at the cave. Even resisted the temptation to fall into his arms—arms she knew would welcome her. Even as she stood at the entrance, watching until he disappeared into the timber, she'd wondered if she laid her head against his chest if his heart would thrum against her cheek, its rhythm telling her more than words.

She bit the tip of her tongue lest she cry out. How could she entertain such thoughts when Lafe might be coming home to her right this moment? If he stepped around the rocks and into the inner chamber, what would he see? Robert sat in front of her on one of the stuffed grain bags, but one hand rested on her arm. Would Lafe understand Robert was only trying to comfort her? That's all. Wasn't it?

"Charlotte? You've not said a word. You know, it's all right if you want to cry or ask questions, or—"

She averted her eyes. "Thank you, Robert—for everything. I...I can't think of anything you could have salvaged that would mean more to me. But if you don't mind, I'm really very tired. For now, I'm not ready to think over what all you've told me. I only want to sleep. You understand, don't you?"

He squeezed her arm, then stood. "I do understand. Sleep well. If you do want to talk, you know where I am."

"I know."

She waited until he was gone, then blew out the candle in the holder on the floor beside her bed. Maybe in the dark the images of the past would go away. Maybe without light the imaginations of the present would disappear.

CHAPTER 8

Robert propped his back against the rock wall and laid the gun across his lap. Weary as he was from the day's events, he wasn't ready to succumb to sleep. Charlotte's reaction to the news that she no longer had a home concerned him, though he wasn't sure what he'd expected. Maybe what he anticipated was nothing more than a desire—that she'd throw herself into his arms, thankful he'd returned safe, pleased he'd found the sugar bowl, needing the comfort of his embrace after she learned the horrible news. He would not have been surprised or shocked had she screamed a litany of the years of toil and sacrifice or blamed him or his men for the destruction of all she and Lafe had worked so hard to build. He would have had a better sense of what to do had she railed against God for allowing such atrocity.

No, it was her silence that bothered him. Even though she didn't move away from him while he told of his findings, he'd sensed her retreat, pulling within herself, hiding behind the sugar bowl.

He stood and moved to the mouth of the cave. There was a peace that accompanied nighttime that belied the destruction daylight revealed. Distant thunder rumbled, and the smell of rain sweetened the air. Robert closed his eyes and took a deep breath. Tomorrow, perhaps tomorrow Charlotte would be ready to face reality. Maybe tomorrow she'd want him to stay...allow him to hold her and comfort her.

Or maybe tomorrow her husband would return to keep his promise to be there for the birth of their babe. He wanted her to face reality, and he needed to do the same. Could he face reality if it meant admitting he'd fallen in love with another man's wife?

He moved to his pallet. Sleep. Deep sleep was the only way he'd escape the truth. Wasn't truth supposed to set him free? Why, then, did he feel so trapped?

Robert jerked awake. Something wasn't right. He could sense it. A quick scan of the interior revealed a stone he didn't remember being present before. Rocks littered the cave floor, but this one was larger than most and lay just inside the entrance. If it been present last night, he would've stumbled over it. He bent to retrieve it and his chest tightened. Attached with a hank of string was an envelope addressed to Charlotte.

Only Lafe Teasdale would know where to find his wife. If he wrote the note, why not deliver it himself...in person? Was her husband crouched somewhere in the timber? Did he know Sergeant Robert Stallings was present? Would he give him a chance to explain his presence?

With the note gripped in one hand and the gun in the other, Robert sidled his way past the boulder separating the two chambers. "Charlotte? Charlotte, are you awake?

Charlotte's hands shook as she untied the string holding the envelope to the stone. She turned the missive over several times, caressing her name—more precious because it was in his handwriting and she knew how he loathed to write. "Will you read it to me, Robert?" She held it out to him.

He shook his head. "It's addressed to you. I—I wouldn't feel right."

She looked up and met his gaze, those dark, dark eyes boring into hers. "Please. I can't. I just...can't.

He took the letter and unfolded it. "Are you sure this is what you want?"

"Yes, just...just do it. Please."

His shoulders heaved with a sigh. "'My Charlotte, my love. If you are reading this, please—'"

"No!" She grabbed the letter from him. "No, I'll—I'll do it myself. I'm sorry." She didn't want to hear what she felt in her own heart—Lafe was gone. Especially didn't want to hear it from Robert. It was her fault. She'd allowed wicked imaginations and now God was punishing her. Lafe was her husband, but she'd entertained thoughts of another man. And now... Now...

"Please, leave." She couldn't look at him. Not now. Maybe never again could she look into those dark-coffee eyes.

"Are you sure? I'll not say a word, Charlotte. I'll just *be* here. You know, in case—"

"No. I need to be alone. Please. Go."

His feet dragged through the dirt, and she was almost certain he went no farther than behind the rock that guarded the narrow entrance into the inner chamber. But at least he was gone.

She smoothed the letter on her knee, and turned toward the candle light.

My Charlotte, my love...

She bit her bottom lip. She could hear him. As plain as his handwriting, she could hear him. How often he would say those very words—my Charlotte, my love.

> *Don't step outside the cave to look for me, I'll not be there. This note will be delivered by a trusted friend. I know I promised to be home when our babe is born. But my love, you have to know by now that is impossible. I'm sorry. I'm so sorry. As I write this, there's little chance I'll ever be home again. And if you're holding this letter in your hand right now, know, my Charlotte, my love, that I died trying.*
>
> *Kiss our babe for me and tell him his papa loved him. And Charlotte, love again. Promise me you'll not raise this babe alone. That's my wish, my deepest need—to know that you and our child are loved and cared for. Hold me always in your memory. And stay strong, my love. Stay strong.*
>
> *Lafe.*

A scream went the air and shot through Robert like the bullet that hit his shoulder. He was by Charlotte's side before a second one could leave her throat. This was not the piercing cry of a woman whose absent husband would return any time soon. No, he recognized agony, the sheer tortured sobs of a heart broken into a million pieces. He'd experienced the same when Molly died, only then there was no one present to wrap their arms around him, to comfort him, to assure him that someday, somehow the sun would shine again, that life could and would go on. It would never be the same, but it would continue.

She sank to her knees, and he went down with her. He wrapped her in his arms, cradled her head against his chest, and rocked her. No words were needed. There were no words to soothe this deep, deep pain. They would come later. Later when the whys and if-onlys, and what-ifs clamored for attention, maybe then words would soothe. But not now.

It seemed hours passed, but he had no way of knowing. The front of his shirt was wet from tears, but it would dry. His shoulder ached and he needed to stretch his legs to ward off a cramp, but he held her until at last she no longer cried Lafe's name.

"Robert?"

"I'm here, Charlotte."

"Lafe is—"

He caressed her hair, tresses that shone like copper in the candlelight. "I know. I know."

"He won't ever—" A sob caught on her breath

"I know."

There was a long silence, and he felt her relax against him. Good. She needed to rest, but only when she was ready. He continued to rock.

"I'm so scared." Her voice muffled against his chest.

"What are you afraid of, Charlotte?"

"Life without him." She tilted her head away from his chest. "Tell me, Robert. Tell me how to keep living. How can you go on? I don't want to forget him. Ever. But tell me how to keep living without him."

Her eyes bore deep into his, no longer summer-sky blue, but dark and troubled, reflecting the storm he knew brewed within. He thought there would be days before the questions came...not hours. He wasn't ready. This was not the time to tell her he loved her and that he'd help her live, one day at a time...without Lafe. That he'd wait for her to love him, but would never leave her side. He'd not had time to think how, when or where they'd go from this cave. Home to his ranch in Kansas, to be sure. But they had no mode of travel, and until he could deem it safe to travel west, they dare not leave the safety of their rocky hideaway.

What if she refused to go with him? In all his imagining, had he considered she might not want a life with him? She might not love him? Had he considered—

Maybe if he clenched his teeth hard enough the roar in his ears would drown out his conscience. No, as a matter of fact, he'd not considered anything other than he loved her and could wait for her to love him. He hadn't allowed himself to contemplate she might never come to love him.

"One minute at a time, Charlotte. One minute, one hour, one day at a time."

She began to sob again, and his tears fell freely, too. God's Word never lied...hope deferred did make the heart sick.

A familiar tightening of her tummy accompanied a spasm that grabbed Charlotte's low back, and she caught her breath. It couldn't be the babe, could it? Not now. Not without Lafe. What about Granny Wilson? If all Robert told her was true, there was no one left in Cass County. Not even the old midwife. Only Robert.

She gasped. No! Never! Never could she allow another man to help with the birthing of Lafe's child. She bit her lip and willed whatever was happening to stop. *Please, Lord, don't let this babe come now. Not now. Not yet.*

She pushed from Robert's embrace. What was she thinking? How could she seek comfort in another man's arms, when her Lafe would never hold her again? "I need to lie down, please."

"Of course." He slipped to his knees beside the bed. "Rest if you can. I'll be right here."

"No. Please—please leave me alone. I need to be—" Another pain grabbed her. She tried to twist away from it, but it followed her and a groan escaped her lips before she could stop it

"Charlotte?" He took her chin in his hand and forced her to look at him. "Is it the babe?"

"Please leave. I need...I need to rest." She lay back against the pillows as another wave of pain gripped her. She couldn't let him stay—couldn't allow him to take Lafe's place. "Go, please."

Now the pains were coming in waves. This isn't how it was supposed to happen, was it? Didn't Granny Wilson say Lafe would have plenty of time to fetch her once she felt pain? What was wrong? Is this what it meant to travail?

Even with her eyes closed, she knew Robert was still there. She could sense it. Hadn't she told him to leave? "Robert. Go. Please. I just want to be alone."

Another pain rolled through her and she arched her back against it. Too fast. It shouldn't happen this fast.

Robert gripped her shoulders. "I'll not leave you."

"Yes, you will." She flicked her wrists, but he grabbed them and held tight. "Look at me, Char."

She couldn't. She couldn't bear to look into those dark eyes and tell him to leave. Neither could she allow him to stay. This was Lafe's child. Her's and Lafe's. No other man should be privy to this occasion. And why was he calling her Char? No one ever called her by that name except Lafe. No, it was all wrong.

"Char, look at me. All right, don't. But I'm not leaving. You need my help. Please. I've done this before and you haven't. Once this babe is here, I'll leave you alone. But for now, like it or not, I'm staying. We'll do this together. Look at me, Char. Do you understand?"

She nodded. What choice did she have? Instinct told her she couldn't do it alone. *Oh, Lafe, how could you let this happen? Why? Why did you leave me? You knew. You knew the chance you took. But you promised. You promised...*

"Do you have a name for her?"

"Lydia. Lydia Ruth. It's the name Lafe chose before he—" Charlotte gulped. "Before he went away." He laid the babe in her arms, and something sweet flooded her. Her travail was over and she no longer remembered the anguish—only joy, a deep contentment.

"It's a good name. She's beautiful, Charlotte." He smiled and his eyes crinkled at the corners.

"She is, isn't she?" She cupped her hand under the tiny, fuzzy head. She looked up and her gaze met his. "Thank you, Robert. Lafe would be—"

"Shh." He shook his head. "You did all the work, you know. I'm just glad I was here." He gave her hand a gentle squeeze. "Now, I shall retreat to my chamber and leave you two alone to get acquainted."

Shadows danced along the rock wall as the flame of the candle flickered with his leaving. Only the soft little grunts and suckling noises of the babe at her breast broke the silence. It was always dark in the interior chamber, and Charlotte had lost all sense of time. But it didn't matter. The babe was here and now time could stand still. If only Lafe could see her.

Robert stepped out of the cave and leaned against a tree. Every groan, every tear that slid down Charlotte's face, every time she squeezed his hand so hard it hurt, memories of his desperation to help Molly and save their child had haunted him. Although thankful the ordeal was over for Charlotte, grateful she'd delivered a healthy, beautiful baby girl, his heart ached to the point of tearing out of his chest. He had no idea what it was like to be in the throes of bringing life into this world, but could it possibly be more painful than watching life slip away? Could anything hurt worse than holding the promise of the future embodied in one tiny human being and realizing it would never take a breath, never run and play, never say Papa?

A new layer of pain threatened to swallow him. Would he ever be able to declare his love for Charlotte? Could he bear caring for her and tiny Lydia, knowing that one day they'd part, perhaps never to meet again?

He turned his face against the trunk of the tree and cried deep, gulping, sobs. Some for what had been, and was no longer.

Some for what was now, but perhaps never could be.

CHAPTER 9

"Charlotte, you have to let me help." Robert wasn't sure who he'd be helping the most—Charlotte or himself. His nerves were frazzled. Tiny Lydia's cry belied her size. Or maybe it was the effect of echoes within the cavern walls. But at this rate, no one was getting sleep, day or night.

"What's wrong with her? Why can't I get her to stop?" Dark circles under Charlotte's eyes spoke of her exhaustion. A constant stream of tears ran down her cheeks. Still, she steadily refused to allow him to take the child from her arms.

He knelt beside her. "You're exhausted and the babe can sense it. You're not eating, thus probably not producing enough—"

"Stop! Why would you talk to me about such—"

"Because, in case you haven't noticed, it's just you, me, and this baby in this hole in the side of the hill. And none of us are sleeping." He ran his hands through his hair. "I know about such things. I was the oldest of a whole passel of brothers and sisters." He reached for the babe. "Please, at least let me try. I promise to stay right here. She'll not be out of your sight." He knew he sounded harsh, but something had to be done.

"You can't feed her. I don't know what good you think it will do, but whatever I'm doing isn't working." She loosened her grip and allowed him to take the babe from her.

A wave of emotion he'd not expected swept through him when he cradled the babe. "What is it, little one? Why are you so angry? Shh, shh. You're safe." He jiggled her, and she opened her eyes. "Look at you, pretty girl. You know, you don't have to cry to get our attention." She stiffened her legs and

234

one tiny foot poked from the flannel blanket. "Already kicking against your boundaries, aren't you?"

He cupped the warm little foot in his hand and swallowed against tightness in his throat. He'd cradled his tiny son like this, but he'd never seen the color of his eyes or felt the warmth of his tiny body against his.

He refolded the blanket around her and traced one finger along her pink cheek. "You know you've kept your mama awake, don't you?"

A tiny wrinkle settled between the baby's eyes, and her bottom lip puckered.

He chuckled. "No, no, you can't use that pouty face on me, little miss." He shifted her to his shoulder, pressed her head against the side of his face and began to rock to and fro. She gave a little hiccup. "I know. Crying is hard work isn't it? Shh... All is well, baby Lydia."

The baby relaxed against him, and little puffs of air against his cheek suggested she might be sleeping. He'd not stop moving—not yet, anyway. It was a small price to pay for a measure of quiet.

"How did you do that?" Charlotte whispered.

He winked at her. He mouthed, "My charm."

She gave a small chuckle, and it was like music to his ears.

Charlotte lay against her pillows and observed Robert with Lydia. She had no idea the sight of a grown man sleeping with a babe nestled against his shoulder could evoke such a mix of emotions. Her heart still ached for Lafe, and she longed to see his face again, to feel his heart beat against her cheek, to reach across the bed and touch him. Yet, there were times when anger ruled. He'd left her without saying goodbye. He knew the danger. Otherwise he wouldn't have left her in a hole in the side of a hill. He chose to leave. Oh, maybe he hadn't meant to leave her forever, but he knew how it could end, and he left anyway.

Then along came Sergeant Robert Stallings, the enemy. The enemy who managed to quiet hers and Lafe's screaming child. How could she ever forget Robert's quiet words of encouragement while she was in the throes of labor, or the tender hands that swabbed her face with cool cloths, and allowed her to dig her fingernails into his palms, never pulling away? How gentle he'd been when he handed her newborn Lydia. How discreet he'd been in his care for her since giving birth.

"Robert?"

He turned sleepy eyes toward her "Hmm?"

"I think she's sleeping. You want me to take her?"

He kissed Lydia's head. "No, she's fine. You try to sleep if you can."

"What about you? You need sleep, too. I'm sorry I've been so stubborn."

"Not stubborn, Charlotte." He smiled. "Well, maybe a little bit stubborn. But I understand. I do. You sleep. I can sleep right here. This little one will let us know when it's time to wake up again."

Did he understand? Could he know the reason she'd not released her hold on Lydia was that she was afraid of this very thing—that Lafe's child would be quieted in another man's arms?

Lafe had penned that he wanted her to love again—to promise that she'd not raise their child alone. But could Robert know that?

"Charlotte? You still awake?"

Oh, if he only knew. "Yes. Is something wrong?"

He stood and brought the baby to her. "Nothing wrong with me. But— well, I think you might need to show me how to change a diaper."

She reached for Lydia. "I thought you had a whole passel of experience."

He shrugged, and a smile crinkled the corners of his eyes. "I reckon I have a lot to learn. In case you wondering, I'm a fast learner." He kissed his finger-tips and touched Lydia's cheek. "I'm also...more than willing."

She busied herself with the task at hand. Was this his way of letting her know he'd read Lafe's letter?

LATE OCTOBER, 1863

Robert stacked another layer of deadfall branches against the rock wall just inside the mouth of the cave. The nights were cooler, and he didn't want to be caught with no dry wood once winter weather set in. As much as he hated the thought of spending the winter in this place, it was still much too early to try to get to his ranch. If he were alone, he might risk it, but not with Charlotte and baby Lydia. And he couldn't leave them behind.

Against his training, he'd read the letter Lafe penned to Charlotte. How hard it must have been for the man to know he'd never again hold his wife, or see his babe. Had it not been for his plea for her to love again—and to promise she'd not raise their child alone—he'd have risked anything to get her somewhere other than a hole in the side of a hill, somewhere among people she knew.

He'd never told her he knew what the letter contained, and she'd never offered to share the contents. Yet their existence together had become more comfortable. Maybe it was because he no longer felt the terrible guilt he'd experienced before he knew Lafe would never return. He was free to love her, although not yet free to tell her. He was not at all sure how much longer he could keep up the ruse. Discretion said he should wait until he came up with a plan to get them safely to Kansas before he revealed his love for her. But his heart said it was foolish to keep pretending he had no feelings other than a desire to keep her safe.

He stopped before entering the inner chamber. "Charlotte, may I come in?"

"Of course. I think you need to work your so-called charm on this little girl. She's fussed ever since you left this morning." She met him with the squawking baby. He was always amused how much noise one so small could produce. But it pleased him that Lydia quieted in his arms. He had no explanation but always answered Charlotte's pleading looks with the same teasing, *My charm.*

"What's the matter, Lydie-punkin?" He lifted her from Charlotte's arms. "Did you miss your—your Uncle Robert?" Heat flooded his face. How close he'd come to calling himself her papa. He shook his head. "I'm sorry, Charlotte. I—"

She gripped his arm. "It's fine. Really, it is. Uh...did you check the rabbit traps?"

"What?" He laughed above Lydia's cries. "You have competition, Mama, you'd better speak a bit louder."

She stood on tiptoe. "The rabbit traps. Did you check them?"

He snuggled Lydia against his cheek, which seemed to be her favorite spot, and patted her bottom. She burrowed her little head against him and soon quieted.

"Don't you dare say it, Robert Stallings."

He laughed. "Ah-ha! You don't want to hear it's my charm, do you? You have a better explanation?"

She plunked her hands on her hips. "Hmmph. I think you put some kind of potion on your face that puts her right so sleep."

He bent toward her and turned his other cheek. "Want to sniff for yourself?"

She slapped his arm. "Stop it! You're mean. Now, did you check the rabbit traps?"

"I did, and we have one rather scrawny looking rabbit, but it will add a bit of meat to the pot."

Charlotte turned away, but not before he saw tears puddle in her eyes.

He moved in front of her and tipped her chin. "What's the matter?"

She tilted her head. "Do you really want to know?"

"Of course I do. Was it something I said? Was it because I teased about my charm?"

She shook her head. "Could you lay Lydia down, please?"

"You can't talk with me holding Lydia?"

"No. No, I can't, as a matter of fact."

He gave the babe a gentle squeeze and laid her on the bed. She stretched and opened one eye, but quickly settled back into sleep. He turned to Charlotte. "All right. I'm listening."

She took his hand and led him to the table. "I don't know how to start."

His heart dropped. This was obviously something very important, and he feared she was going to ask him to leave.

She reached into the pocket of her dress and withdrew Lafe's letter. "I guess you should read this first."

He took her hand. "I don't need to read it. I read it the night Lydia was born. I'm sorry. I should have told you."

"You read it? You know what it says about—about, you know."

"About you loving again? About Lafe not wanting you to raise Lydia by yourself? Yes, I know."

She jumped to her feet. "Then what is stopping you?"

"Stopping me?"

"Yes, stopping you. Robert Stallings, the day you went down that hill to check on our cabin, I watched you until I couldn't see you any longer. I thought sure you could hear my heart beat and I was ashamed. Ashamed that I was a married woman and had such feelings for—"

He got to his feet. "For me? Charlotte, are you telling me you have feelings for me?"

"Then you held me and let me scream and cry after I read Lafe's letter, and you stayed with me while Lydia was born. After all this time you, you act like there's— And I felt so guilty, and I was sure God punished me for...for—"

"Come here." He pulled her to him. "Do you have any idea how hard it's been for me to not tell you how I feel? I love you, Charlotte Mae Teasdale. But until I read Lafe's letter to you, I was not free to say one word."

She pounded her fists on his chest. "But you read it a long time ago, and you didn't say a word. Where's your so-called charm?"

"What would you have said had I admitted my love for you before this very moment?"

"I would have said I love you, too. And for someone who can quiet a babe in no time at all, you're mighty slow with—"

He held her face in his hands and kissed her forehead, her eyes, her chin, and finally, at last, her lips. To think he'd wondered how and when he should tell her.

With baby Lydia cradled in one arm, Robert pulled Charlotte close to his side as they stood at the mouth of their hideaway and gazed across the timber. He kissed the top of her head. "You do know we can't leave here until spring, don't you?"

"I know."

"And you know that we can't—"

She smiled up at him and giggled. "Sergeant Robert Stallings, you're blushing."

He winked at her. "You do that to me, woman."

"It's my charm." She giggled again and lay her head against his shoulder.

How could she ever have known back when Lafe insisted that she hide in a cave that it would one day shelter an unlikely love in this oh, so weary land?

COTTON CANDY
SKIES

K. MARIE LIBEL

CHAPTER 1

The stale scent of pretzels wafted under Danica Stewart's nose, and she turned her head toward the window in a feeble attempt to escape it. Her stomach rolled as she tried to focus on anything but the nausea threatening to overtake her. She would not throw up in front of strangers. She firmly chanted the command to herself for the umpteenth time.

Danica closed her eyes and tried to let the sounds around her distract from her queasy stomach. Wrappers crinkled, a baby several rows back fussed while its mother made frantic shushing sounds, someone's high-pitched giggle painfully pierced the air, and the oversized gentleman sitting next to her hummed off-key. Plenty of sounds to divert her attention, and yet her nausea still overpowered. Ugh. How she hated flying.

Just as she was sure she wouldn't make it much longer, a perky voice echoed over the speakers. "We're about twenty minutes from our destination and your pilot is preparing to land. Please find your seats and buckle your safety belts. We will arrive shortly; thank you for flying with Express Airlines. Enjoy your stay in sunny Jamaica."

"Thank you, Lord, the end is in sight," Danica mumbled.

"You say something?" The gentleman beside her turned his head her direction, his jowls jiggling with the movement.

Danica forced her lips to lift in what she hoped was less of a grimace and more of a polite smile. "I'm glad the flight's almost over. I'm not a very good flyer."

"Hmm. Yeah, come to think of it, you do look a little green. You're not going to, you know . . ." His eyes drifted toward the air sickness bag.

"I'm trying very hard not to, sir," Danica replied through gritted teeth and turned to gaze out the window.

Below her, the ocean spread out in an endless carpet of sparkling turquoise with patches of deep blue woven in. The colors alone blew her away. She'd never seen any color in nature like what she was seeing now. Her nausea temporarily forgotten, she gasped at the beauty of her first glimpse of the ocean. No wonder people spent their hard earned money to see this . . . it was *stunning*.

Before she'd had her fill of her from-above ocean view, the plane lowered its altitude over palm trees and rundown buildings. The abrupt change in altitude reminded her stomach why she hated flying, and she felt herself break into a cold sweat. No, not now. She'd almost made it. She could hang on a little longer.

She closed her eyes tightly and sang her favorite praise song in her mind until she felt the bumpy landing and the rapid slowing of movement. With slow, controlled breaths she waited until the plane came to a stop and the attendant instructed everyone to remove their safety belts and exit the plane in an orderly manner. When someone finally allowed her seat partner to exit into the aisle, Danica stood slowly and reached for her carry-on. Her shaking hands couldn't keep their grip, and her bag repeatedly slipped from her grasp.

With a frustrated grunt, she reached again but a tanned pair of hands snaked in front of hers and grabbed the handle on her bag.

"Hey!" Danica tried to bat the stranger's hand away. "That's my bag."

"Yeah, I figured since I've watched you try to grab it four times now. In the interest of the rest of us getting off this plane, may I please help you get it down?"

She turned toward the smooth, deep voice and her gaze collided with a pair of chocolate brown eyes. Her knees quivered slightly—curse her, she'd always had a thing for deep brown eyes—and she shakily leaned against the nearest seat.

The stranger raised an eyebrow in question, his lips turned up in an amused grin, and he jerked his head toward her bag. "So . . . ?"

She nodded mutely and then immediately wished she hadn't as her stomach rolled with the motion. She felt herself break out into another cold sweat and dizziness made her vision swim. Oh, no...

"Whoa, there."

Her knees gave out. Strong arms wrapped around her and held her in place. "I'm fine," she muttered, but even she heard the weakness in her voice.

"Uh-huh, sure you are. You're white as a sheet, you're shaking, and—"

Panic flashed through her and her hands blindly searched the back of the seat. "Bag! I need a bag!"

With lightning reflexes, the stranger held her up with one arm and plucked an air sickness bag with the other, shook it open, and held it in front of her in time for her to lose what little breakfast she'd managed to choke down before her flight. The stranger muttered soothing words to her as he— bless him—held the bag steady until she finished being sick. Without a word, he handed the bag to the flight attendant who, Danica noticed, was standing just outside of the danger zone.

"This is not happening," Danica moaned, humiliation crawling up her spine.

"You okay to walk now?"

Danica's senses grew acutely aware of the fact that she was being held against a solid form, which smelled amazing, by the way. Her skin tingled with goosebumps. She nodded, too embarrassed to speak, and attempted to right herself.

She smoothed her hand over her hair, subtly checking to make sure it hadn't gotten in the way during her episode, and attempted to regain some of her dignity. "Sorry for the holdup, everyone," she told the remaining line of passengers, unable to look her rescuer in the eye.

With what little poise she had left, she lifted her chin and spun around to march confidently off the plane. Or, at least that's what she would have done if her spin hadn't brought back the dizziness. She felt herself wobble, and again those strong arms came to her rescue.

"Ooookay, I think I'd better help you all the way off the plane." He spoke so close to her ear that her scalp tingled and the hairs on the back of her neck raised with the soft rush of air accompanying his voice.

He half-led, half-carried her off the plane, and it wasn't until they were halfway through the terminal that she remembered her carry-on. "My bag, I left my bag," she rasped, her voice not wanting to cooperate with the sensory overload.

"Don't worry, I've got it. Let's just get you to a chair." He led her out of the terminal and then abruptly stopped and let out a groan.

"What's wrong?" Danica looked around and immediately realized the problem.

In front of them was a long walkway, followed by a wide set of stairs which led down into a large, open room where lines and lines of people waited for their turn to go through customs.

"I'm afraid we've got a long wait ahead of us before I can get you to that chair."

Danica tried to gently extract herself from his arms, even though a small part of her didn't really want to. Which was silly, of course. She didn't even know this man. But he was being so nice to her, and it had been so long since a man had held her like this . . .

Snap out of it, Danica. He's not sweeping you off your feet. He held you up while you puked. Not exactly a recipe for romance.

"I'll be fine, really." She reached for her carry-on and tried to avoid eye contact. Those eyes of his were far too tempting, and she was way too humiliated to see what he must really think of her.

"All due respect, I disagree." He looked around and then snapped his fingers. "Wait here, I'll be back."

Danica stared after him. How had she gone from being sick in a stranger's arms to letting that stranger boss her around? Some start to her vacation this was. She sighed and stepped to the side to let people pass her, and then found a space near the stairwell where she could lean against the wall without being in the way. But she wasn't staying there because he told her to. She wasn't ready to tackle the stairs yet.

Her skin still tingled where he'd touched her.

She rolled her eyes at herself, knowing she'd stay put until he came back.

Twenty-two minutes later—not that she was counting—he returned, pushing a wheelchair and being followed by a dark skinned young man in an employee uniform.

The stranger helped her get settled into the wheelchair and then handed her a granola bar. "Here, you need to get something in you to get your strength back up."

She took the granola bar, and her face heated as her fingers brushed his. "Thank you, but is all this really necessary?"

The airport employee stepped forward. "My name is Jamal and it would be my pleasure to escort you down on the elevator and assist you through customs to make sure you are healthy and safe."

Before Danica could respond, Jamal stepped behind the wheelchair and pushed her toward the elevator door.

"Wait!"

Jamal paused. "Is there a problem, madam?"

"I—I just—I don't even know his name." She craned her neck to look behind her. The stranger was still standing where they'd left him.

He smiled at her, gave a little wave, and then joined the throngs of people flowing down the stairs. She watched until he disappeared and then sighed, disappointment dulling the ache in her neck from her awkward position.

"Thank you, whoever you are," she whispered as Jamal pushed her onto the elevator.

CHAPTER 2

The waves crashed gently along the shore and splashed sand over Danica's ankles. The water felt heavenly against her skin, flushed hot from the sun. She wriggled her toes into the wet sand and smiled at the sensation of the sand being pulled back out from under her feet by the retracting waves. The sun was high in a brilliant blue sky and glittered over the surface of the water like diamonds. Danica couldn't get enough of this view or of the carefree, relaxing aura it created around her. God sure created a beautiful world, and she was finally getting to experience more of it than just her little corner of Wichita, Kansas.

Now *this* was what she'd saved tirelessly for over the last year. This was her gift to herself—two full weeks of no responsibilities, no boss hanging over her shoulder, no well-meaning but irritating mother nagging her about when she would start dating again, no running into her ex-boyfriend and his new wife and faking smiles and small talk, no reminders of the future she could've had but lost.

She drew in a deep breath, letting her lungs expand to the max with the salty air. *Thank You, Lord, for making this possible.*

The waves lapped at her feet and, in a spontaneous burst of giddiness, Danica flung her arms wide and spun in a circle, not caring if those on the beach thought she was crazy. This trip was her liberation, her cry to the world that she was done feeling sorry for herself. So her life hadn't turned out the way she'd thought. It was time to pick up the pieces and form them into a new and different future. A life-makeover of sorts.

Gazing out over the crystal water, no end in sight, Danica embraced the change. This Danica wouldn't be so timid—where had that gotten her anyway? She would no longer be afraid to say *yes*. Yes to a new job, yes to blind dates, yes to new possibilities. Seeing as she was quickly falling in love with the ocean, maybe she'd even say yes to relocating. Who said a new start couldn't include a move to somewhere where she could walk along the beach every day?

Anticipation coursed through her. "The sky is the limit!" She laughed into the breeze.

She lightheartedly kicked at the waves until an aggressive wave flung a large piece of petrified coral against her ankle bone. Wincing, she grabbed her ankle and began hopping on the other foot. "Ouch! Ow ow ow!"

Between the unsteady footing of the sand and the increasing strength of the waves, her balance was already precarious. Hopping around on one foot didn't help, and soon she was flat on her backside in the sand.

"Oh, good grief." She huffed and glared at the waves. "And just when I thought we had a true bond."

A muffled laugh startled her, and she craned her neck upward to find the source. A familiar hand reached down and helped her up, and before her muddled brain could process what was happening she was staring into melted chocolate.

"It's you," she whispered breathlessly. "I mean . . . what are you doing here?"

"Vacationing, same as you, I imagine. You look to be feeling better."

His eyes crinkled in the corners when he smiled, and Danica resisted the urge to trace the tiny lines with her finger. When his smile widened she realized she was staring, and her cheeks warmed. At least if she was visibly blushing she could blame it on the heat.

"I'm feeling completely normal now," she managed to stutter.

"So splashing around in the water, talking to yourself, and falling down is a normal day for you? Now, the falling down part I can somehow believe." His voice was teasing and she felt her lips threatening to tug into a grin.

"Oh, ha-ha." She playfully punched him on the arm. "No, I'm not normally this clumsy. Only when I'm sick from flying and when the ocean attacks me."

She pointed to her ankle where the skin was swollen and already turning purple.

He shook his head. "Ah, I've been a victim of the killer coral myself. Gotta watch out for those evil attackers."

Danica moved farther from the water, trying not to limp on her throbbing ankle. "So . . . you've been here before?"

He took her elbow as if it were now completely natural to help her walk. Should she shake him off and tell him she was more than capable of taking care of herself? Maybe, but she liked his warm fingers on her arm. Besides, the gesture was rather sweet.

He pulled his sunglasses off his head and slid them back down over his eyes. "This is my fourth visit to Jamaica but my second time to this resort. There's something about this piece of ocean that keeps drawing me back. I've never been anywhere so beautiful before."

"I know what you mean. I've never even seen the ocean before, but I think I'm in love. I never want to leave."

He smiled warmly at her. "I'm Aaron, by the way. Aaron Neilson. Considering the adventure we had together I can't believe I never did catch your name. I've just been thinking of you as the pretty girl on the plane."

"You've been thinking of me?" The words were out of her mouth before she even realized they were coming, and her face burned with humiliation. "I mean, I'm Danica. Danica Stewart."

Aaron reached out his hand and she grasped it in a firm but gentle handshake. "It's nice to officially meet you, Danica Stewart." He held her hand a few seconds longer than necessary and then slowly released her.

"Likewise." She chuckled sheepishly to cover her nervousness. "I didn't exactly make the best first impression, did I?"

"Well . . ." He shrugged, the corner of his lip tugging upward with the rise of his shoulder. "You made *some* kind of an impression."

Danica tried to glare at him but found she couldn't keep a straight face against the orneriness of his teasing grin. "So is rescuing damsels in distress a normal day for you, or did I catch you in a particularly charitable mood?"

"How about we say my mother raised a gentleman, and I couldn't let someone who obviously needed help go without it. Even if she *was* being too stubborn to accept it at first."

"Yeah, well, nothing will strip a woman of her pride quite like throwing up and nearly passing out in front of a bunch of strangers." Danica rolled her eyes and laughed. "Seriously though, I never got a chance to thank you. I really do appreciate you helping me."

He waved his hand in a dismissive gesture. "It was my pleasure, honestly. It's kind of funny how we ended up at the same place." He paused, seeming to carefully consider his next words. "Do you think . . . well, would you maybe be up for another adventure together? This time one that doesn't involve air sickness bags and wheelchairs." This time his grin stretched wide enough to reveal a dimple in his left cheek.

Her heart sped its tempo, and she tried to push down her growing attraction for him. "Considering the circumstances under which we met, I'm surprised you'd even consider having another adventure with me." She laughed lightly.

Aaron lifted one shoulder in a casual shrug. "I'd like to get to know the girl behind the barf bag."

Danica let out an exaggerated groan while he grinned cheekily. "That has got to be the worst pickup line I've ever heard."

"But did it work?"

She laughed, her nervousness fading away with his playful approach. Hadn't she decided she would start saying yes? "Okay, why not? What have you got in mind?"

The soft fabric of Danica's skirt twirled around her knees as she spun in front of the full length mirror in her room. The sundress was a gift from her mom to bring on the trip, and Danica loved the way the deep teal color made her eyes look two shades brighter. The silky fabric brushing against her skin made her feel decidedly feminine. The loose curls into which she'd coaxed her hair fell softly down her back, completing the look. No jewelry, minimal makeup—Danica liked things simple. If Aaron didn't appreciate that about her, well then . . . too bad for him.

She smiled at her reflection and then reached for her sandals. Her stomach fluttered as she readied herself to meet up with Aaron in the resort lounge. She placed a hand over her belly button and released a nervous laugh into the room. She couldn't even remember the last time she'd had butterflies!

Aaron had refused to tell her his plans but suggested she wear something comfortable and loose-fitting. Her mind had managed to concoct all sorts of scenarios, and she hoped she was dressed appropriately for whatever adventure he'd planned for tonight.

Checking the clock and confirming she was right on time to meet him at 6:00, she grabbed her purse and made sure she had her room key—she'd already locked herself out once and didn't want to have to ask a staff member to let her back in again. When she stepped off the elevator and entered the lounge, she spotted Aaron immediately, and a smile tugged at her lips. She should try harder to play it cool, but there was something about him that made her want to let down her guard.

Aaron turned and caught her eye, and an unabashed grin made his dimple appear again.

Adorable.

"Hi." His brown eyes glowed in approval. "You look beautiful."

Danica's cheeks warmed. "Thank you." She cleared her throat to cover her pleasure at the simple compliment. "So what are we doing tonight?"

"It's a surprise, but are you up for some dinner first?" He held out his arm for her to take his elbow.

"I'm starving." Her stomach emitted a growl as if to drive home the point.

"Do you mind eating outside? I thought we could try the outdoor restaurant overlooking the ocean."

"Perfect." She smiled contentedly at him and let him lead her through the resort.

Once they were seated in a gazebo-type area facing the water, Aaron leaned his forearms on the table and looked at her intently. "So, as cliché as this sounds on a first date, tell me about yourself."

"This is a date?" she blurted, immediately wishing she could stuff her words back into her mouth. Who came right out and actually asked if they were on a date? Way to play it cool.

Aaron's smile was slow and lazy. "That was my intention."

Her face grew hot again, and she fidgeted with the edge of the tablecloth.

"Blushing is very becoming on you." Aaron's teasing coaxed her to relax. "But you shouldn't be embarrassed about anything. Not with me, anyway. I find it refreshing how you say whatever's on your mind."

Danica let out a self-deprecating laugh. "Refreshing, huh? My mom would say it's unseemly."

"Not at all." His face showed his sincerity. "You're straightforward and refreshingly genuine. That makes me think you're not the type to play games, you're just . . . you."

"Don't know who else to be." She shrugged one shoulder. "Life is too short to play games, don't you think?"

"I couldn't agree more." Aaron leaned back in his seat. Something dark flashed in his eyes, fast and hot, but as quickly as it came it was gone and the ornery sparkle was back. "If it will make you feel any better I'll be bluntly honest with you, too."

"That would be a nice change of pace from my life back home."

His eyes caught hers and held them captive. "I don't think it's a coincidence that we ran into each other again, and I'd really like to get to know you. As you now know, I'm not into playing games and I respect honesty and integrity. From what little I know about you, I suspect those are both qualities I'll find in you. This *is* a date, and I'm hoping there will be a second, but I don't want to take over your vacation so I'll let you take the lead from here."

Taken aback, Danica leaned heavily into the chair's backrest. She'd never had a man be so straightforward with her—in fact, in her experience they were anything but—and she found that she liked it. A lot.

"I'd like to get to know you, too." A slow smile pulled at her lips. "And I'll get back with you about that second date."

It was official. Aaron was smitten with the caramel-haired beauty seated across from him. As they shared a meal, the music of the waves serenading them, Aaron discovered Danica was only a year younger than his twenty-eight years, an only child, and was a Case Manager for mentally ill adults. He also learned she was warm, funny, genuine, and completely clueless as to how gorgeous she was. He loved how she laughed with abandon, how she didn't pick at her food, and how she blushed whenever their eyes connected. His infatuation strengthened when the waiter placed their food in front of them and Danica immediately bowed her head and closed her eyes in prayer over her meal.

Could this woman be the reason you called me back here, Lord?

Aaron wasn't typically one to put any stock in "signs," but he couldn't deny that God had wanted him in Jamaica for some reason. Not only had he felt the calling, but the plans seemed to flawlessly fall together. The job had been easy to line up, and he'd even managed to get a last minute room at his favorite resort. He'd thought perhaps he was supposed to witness to someone, but maybe, just maybe, he was supposed to meet this enchanting, vivacious, irresistible beauty. Everything about his time spent with Danica so far felt completely natural, yet exhilarating.

She'd laughed when he called her refreshing, but she was. His last serious relationship still left a bitter taste in his mouth. Unfortunately he'd found out the hard way that Stacey was anything but the Christian woman she'd claimed and pretended to be, as evidenced by her unexpected pregnancy. Since they'd never been intimate it wasn't too hard to figure out she'd been cheating on him, and the betrayal was a brutal slap in the face.

Aaron wanted a woman who was real—real in who she was, real in how she loved, real in her walk with God. He was ready to settle down if only God would answer his prayers and lead him to the right woman.

He let his gaze rest on the curve of Danica's cheek as she stared serenely at the ocean. It was too soon to be having these thoughts, of course, but he already felt a connection with this woman that he couldn't deny. Still, he'd take it slow, not let himself get his hopes up—or scare her off by trying to move too fast. He didn't want either one of them to get hurt. He suspected she'd had her own heart broken not so long ago as well.

Danica laughed lightly. "I can feel you looking at me."

"Sorry." Now it was his turn to blush.

She smiled softly at him, and a silent moment passed between them before she spoke. "Thank you for dinner. It was amazing."

"Trust me, it was my pleasure." Flipping his wrist over, he examined his watch. "Are you ready for what comes next?"

"Are you going to let me in on the secret?"

He scooted his chair back and extended his hand to help her up. Her small hand fit so nicely in his that he didn't want to let go, but he also didn't want to be presumptuous, so once she was out of her seat he released her fingers. Besides, he'd get to hold her hand plenty once they got to where he was taking her.

"Do you like to dance?" Nervousness struck. He'd taken a gamble on what he'd planned for them, and he hoped Danica would be up for the experience.

She looked sideways at him. "I'm not sure I'm much of a dancer . . ." His face must have reflected his quick flash of disappointment because she quickly smiled. "But I'm always up for a new adventure. As long as you don't mind your feet getting stepped on."

Aaron chuckled and led her back through the resort to a large, open hall surrounded by an outdoor garden area. A live band played music in one corner and couples were grouped up around a dark haired woman in an eye-catching red dress and a tall, reed-thin man who stared at the woman with puppy dog eyes.

"What is this?" Danica bit the tip of one finger and looked nervously around the room.

"How do you feel about taking salsa lessons?"

Her eyes lit up as she looked at him. "Really? I saw this on the resorts activity list and I've always wanted to learn, but I didn't have a partner, so . . ."

"Well, now you do." He bent in an exaggerated bow and held out his hand. "Would the lady do me the honor of being my dance partner for the evening?"

Danica giggled and dipped into a curtsy. "It would be my pleasure."

Laughing, they joined the group around the instructors, and within fifteen minutes they were on the dance floor, awkwardly working through the steps the instructors demonstrated. Danica stepped on his feet several times, and he even stepped on hers once or twice, but before too long they were twirling around the room with more ease.

Danica's laugh was the perfect accompaniment to the band's music, and he loved how her aqua eyes brightened with each laugh. Aaron couldn't remember the last time he'd had this much fun or laughed this much. Too soon the class was over and, breathless, Aaron led Danica outside to walk through the garden and cool off.

"That was so much fun, but man, I'm pooped!" Danica plopped down on a white painted bench, pulled off one sandal, and rubbed her foot.

"How about a walk along the beach then, instead of the garden? The sand will be softer, and the water will feel nice and cool."

"Sounds great."

They walked in silence until they reached the sand, and then they both stopped to remove their shoes and strolled casually to the water's edge.

Aaron playfully bumped her shoulder with his. "So how'd I do for a first date?"

She shot him a heart-melting grin. "I can honestly say it's the best first date I've ever had. You took me totally out of my comfort zone. And I loved it!"

"I'm glad you had a good time. I know I did." He tentatively reached to take her hand in his.

She gently twined her fingers through his. The sensation was both adrenaline-charged and comfortable, and his heart raced with the headiness of new possibilities. They chatted easily as they walked slowly along the shore line until Danica gasped and dropped her sandals and pointed at the sky.

"This has got to be the most gorgeous sunset I've ever seen." Her face was bathed in complete awe.

The sky had exploded in color, turning the fluffy clouds into various shades of coral and lavender with fire-rimmed edges, only touches of soft blue remaining high in the sky. Danica was right. It was a stunning display, but he wasn't sure which sight he enjoyed more—the beautiful sky God had painted this night, or the beautiful woman God created who stood captivated next to him.

As if sensing his thoughts, she looked up at him and smiled demurely. "Is it always like this?"

"Often, but not always." He gently squeezed her hand. "I've photographed sunsets all over the world, but my favorites by far are the sunsets over the ocean. The way the water reflects the sky, it's like the sunset has no beginning or end."

"It must be amazing, getting to take pictures all over the world. You must see so much more than most people ever do in a lifetime." Danica sighed. "There's so much I want to see and experience . . ."

Not for the first time, Aaron marveled at how lucky he was to work for a major travel website. Not only did he get paid to see the world, but he got to follow his two passions—taking pictures and meeting new people with whom to share the love of his Savior.

"Why don't you come with me tomorrow? I'm taking a private boat out to a shipwreck site and taking some underwater pics. I'll be scuba diving, but you could snorkel, or even just stay in the boat and enjoy being out on the water. There's still plenty to see."

"Really? I could do that?" The excitement in her eyes was apparent.

"Sure, if you're up for another adventure." His smile stretched wide, anticipation growing at the prospect of Danica joining him.

She did a little dance in the sand. "I'd love it!"

His heart swelled. Putting that excited smile on her face made him feel like the biggest man in the world. "Consider yourself officially invited then."

"I can't wait!" She bent to pick up her sandals. "I should probably head back to my room then and get some sleep . . ."

He understood the reluctance in her voice. He wasn't ready for the evening to end either, but tomorrow would be a long and draining day and required a good rest. "Sure, let's turn around and head back."

They changed direction and aimed their feet toward the resort, their fingers still linked together. Aaron continued to sneak glances at her. He couldn't help himself. Her hair blew softly around her face as she continued to gaze at the sky.

"I wish you had your camera," she said suddenly.

So did he, but he doubted he'd be taking pictures of the sky. Already in his mind he had framed out a perfect picture—Danica standing at the water's edge, silhouetted against the bright background of the setting sun with the clouds bursting behind her, her hair twirling around her face, skirt blowing around her knees, arms outstretched in abandon like this morning when he'd seen her playing in the water.

Danica pointed up, pulling him out of his thoughts. "See how the clouds are so full and fluffy and colored light pink and purple? It reminds me of cotton candy."

He smiled at her description. "A cotton candy sky, huh? I like that."

She blushed prettily. "Maybe one of these nights you can capture a picture for me to take back home?"

"I'll take as many pictures as you'd like," Aaron promised. He pointed to the outdoor spigot and they rinsed their sand-covered feet, then slipped back into their shoes. "May I walk you back to your room?"

A shadow of hesitancy crossed Danica's features and she twisted her hands together. "Um . . ."

"I'm not trying to come into your room, Danica." Aaron intuitively understood the reason for her reluctance. "I'll be a perfect gentleman, I promise. I don't feel right ending our date by leaving you alone at the elevator."

Her shoulders relaxed and she nodded up at him. "Sorry."

"No need. There are a lot of pushy guys out there who give the rest of us a bad rep." He motioned for her to enter the elevator ahead of him as the doors slid open.

"But I didn't mean to assume you were that kind of guy." She didn't meet his gaze. "I'm not used to— Well, I mean—"

Aaron put his finger over her mouth to stop her rambling. "Danica, it's okay. I'm not offended. We've only met, and honestly you don't know me that well yet. There's no way for you to know what to expect from me. So I'm going to make it easier for you, okay?"

She raised her eyebrows as he removed his finger from her lips.

"I am a gentleman. I'm also a Christian. I'm not going to try to come into your room or pressure you into anything because I've vowed abstinence until marriage." He chuckled as her eyes widened in obvious surprise. "Yes, there are still men out there who do that, and I happen to be one of them. That being said, I can't promise I won't try to kiss you at some point, depending upon how things develop, but I'm not going to tonight. I'm simply going to walk you to your door because that's what a gentleman does, and then I'm going to tell you goodnight, and I will see you in the morning. Okay?"

"You really are an honest one, aren't you?" Her voice sounded breathless.

"I think it's fair to be upfront with people."

"No games." She smiled up at him.

His lips tugged upward, and he gave a perfunctory nod. "No games."

"I think I really like you, Aaron Neilson, photographer extraordinaire, rescuer of damsels in distress, gentleman through and through." Danica threw him a sassy grin as they reached the door to her room. "And the answer is yes."

He stared at her blankly. "Yes?"

"To that second date."

Now his face stretched into a full-out grin. He probably looked like an over-eager teenager but he didn't care. He lightly squeezed her fingers and wished her sweet dreams, then waited until she'd locked herself securely in her room before he headed back toward the elevator, resisting the urge to happy dance his way there.

Tomorrow was going to be a great day.

CHAPTER 3

Cold water sprayed over the side of the boat as it raced across the top of the water, skipping over the crests of waves and bouncing Danica in her seat. She laughed out loud and pushed her sunglasses more securely onto her face. Stealing a glance at Aaron, she found him watching her with an amused smile on his face, and she shot him a giant grin.

"This is great!" She had to yell over the roar of the boat's engine.

Aaron gave her a thumbs up and laughed. "You act like you've never been on a boat before." He yelled, too.

"That's because I haven't."

"Never?"

Danica shook her head and made a futile attempt at shoving loose strands of hair back into her ponytail. She'd been invited out to the lake with friends a few times over the years, but there'd always been some reason she couldn't go. Now she was glad for her lack of experience. She couldn't imagine a better "first time" than this.

The boat began to slow and the engine quieted, making it easier to talk. Aaron bumped her arm. "Something tells me there's an adventure-loving girl inside of you that's never gotten the opportunity to come out and play."

She placed a hand over her abdomen where excited butterflies danced, and she hungrily took in the view around her. "I think you might be right."

"Then I know exactly what we're going to do for our second date." Aaron's eyes sparkled as he spoke, and she found it hard to look away.

Clapping her hands in excitement, she leaned forward. "Oooh, tell me!"

"Sorry, nope. I think it'll be more fun as a surprise." He mimicked locking his lips and throwing the key out into the water.

Danica crossed her arms and tried to scowl, but she was too giddy to pull off the sour expression. "Oh, fine. So far you haven't disappointed, so I'll trust you."

"Good. I won't let you down."

The boat driver subtly cleared his throat, and then started unravelling the rope to drop the anchor. "We've arrived, Mr. Neilson. I'll be right here in this spot until you are finished."

"You ready for this?" Aaron extended his hand to help her up.

"I think so." She bit the tip of her finger. "You're sure it's safe? There aren't, like, any sharks around here or anything, right?"

"You'll be safe, I promise. We're in pretty shallow waters still. But trust me, this coral reef is one of the best snorkeling spots around. You're going to love it."

Aaron helped her slip into her life jacket and pull the snorkel over her face, then showed her how to position it in her mouth. "All you have to do is float on the surface with your face down in the water."

Danica put the mouth piece in her mouth and pulled her lips over the outer ridge. "Ike is?"

Aaron laughed and took a step back. "Yes, just like that."

"I eel ike a oohall."

"I'm sorry, what?" He raised one eyebrow as he chuckled at her inability to speak clearly around the snorkel mask.

She removed the mouthpiece and made a circling motion around her face. "I said, I feel like a goofball."

Aaron's smile softened and he gently brushed her cheek with the back of his fingers. "But you're an adorable goofball."

The heat rose in her cheeks, and Danica inhaled a sharp breath. The butterflies began to flutter again.

With a knowing wink, Aaron began donning his scuba suit and securing his oxygen tank. Once he was all suited up, he turned to her and motioned for her to sit on the side of the boat. "Okay, we're going to swim a short distance out from the boat. Just follow me until I motion for you to stop. I won't be able to talk once I've got my mask on, so let me show you some basic gestures we can use to communicate."

As Aaron demonstrated the hand motions they would use once in the water, Danica did her best to commit them to memory and prayed there wouldn't be any problems. Her stomach was a giant ball of nerves but her heart raced in anticipation.

"I'll stay with you for a few minutes to make sure you've got the hang of things, and then I'm going to swim a bit farther out and go deeper to get the shots of the ship, okay? I won't be far, but if you need help you'll have to holler at Beau." Aaron jerked his chin toward the boat driver. "You'll watch out for her, right, Beau?"

"Ya, mon. I'll be right here, Missy. You stay close and you'll be fine." Beau flashed a toothy grin and saluted.

Aaron joined her on the edge of the boat. "Ready?"

Danica nodded, too nervous to speak, and together they slid into the water. Aaron immediately reached for her to steady her, and she shot him a thankful smile. "I'm good, don't worry."

He reached up and took his water proof camera from Beau's outstretched hands, and then tilted his head to indicate which direction they'd be swimming. Danica inserted her mouthpiece and followed Aaron until he stopped and motioned for her to put her face in the water. When she did, she involuntarily gasped and was immediately thankful for the attached tube which kept her from inhaling ocean water.

Below her, the ocean floor shifted softly with the gentle rolling of the waves and green plants stretched upward as if reaching for the sun. Bright colored coral decorated the ocean floor in a haphazard pattern, and Danica's gaze roamed right and left trying to take it all in. But what really stole her breath were the hundreds of fish that swam beneath and around her feet. She'd never seen so many colors and patterns in nature, and the complexity of this underwater world filled her with wonder and appreciation for the details God took the time to add.

A bright yellow fish with black stripes brushed her ankle as it swam by, tickling her skin, and she giggled into her mouth piece. Nearly dizzy with all the visual stimulation, Danica lifted her head from the water and shifted her eyes to Aaron, who floated a few feet away from her. He gave her a little wave to indicate he was leaving her now, and she nodded her understanding. She wished she could see the shipwreck he was photographing, but she'd ask to see his pictures later. Right now she had enough to keep her busy taking in the majestic beauty of the sea.

Danica floated on the surface and gently kicked her flippers to navigate the perimeter of the reef, taking it in from different angles and trying to interact with schools of fish which either ignored her or quickly fled as she came near. An hour later she was as much in awe of how many different types of fish and coral there were as she'd been the first moment her eyes had captured the underwater view. She could do this all day, every day, and never grow tired of it.

Another piece of her heart gave itself to the ocean, and she began to dread returning to Kansas. Not that Kansas didn't have its own kind of beauty, but this... She felt as if she'd been yearning for the ocean long before ever seeing it and now suddenly a piece of her felt complete.

Too soon she felt a tap on her shoulder and she lifted her face to find Aaron had joined her. He'd removed his mask and gifted her with an ear to ear smile. "I take it by the look on your face you're enjoying yourself?"

Danica removed her mouthpiece so she could talk to him and rubbed at her aching jaw. "Oh, Aaron, it's...unbelievable. Thank you so much for bringing me with you today."

"I got some great shots. It was a perfect day to come out. Have you had your fill yet, or do you want to spend a little more time in the water?"

"Is it okay if I have a few more minutes?"

"Of course. I'll give Beau my camera and trade out for a snorkel mask and join you. Just give me a few."

Danica waited while Aaron returned his gear to the boat and acquired a snorkel mask, then pointed to an area on their left. "I saw the most beautiful sea shell over there. You've got to see it."

She led him to the spot and then pointed into the water. "Do you see it?"

Aaron dipped his face in the water and nodded. He lifted his head back out of the water and removed his snorkel mask. "Can you hold this? I'll be right back."

"Wait, what do you mean be right back?" She grasped his outstretched mask. "Where are you going without this?"

"Down there," he told her matter-of-factly.

"Wait!" She grabbed his arm. "Isn't that dangerous?"

"It's not that far, Danica. I can hold my breath long enough, don't worry."

Without another word he dived into the water, and she nervously watched him from the surface. When she realized what he was doing, her heart swelled. He retrieved the shell she'd been ogling and swam back to the surface with it, making the whole thing look as effortless as breathing.

"Here you go." Aaron took his mask from her and handed her the shell. "A souvenir of our adventure. So you won't ever forget it."

Something in his eyes made her heart pound forcefully, and she was glad she was wearing a life jacket because she didn't think she'd be able to hold herself afloat in this moment. "I don't think I'll ever forget this." *Or forget you,* her heart whispered. And in that still moment she fell heart first into an emotion as vast as the ocean.

A soft breeze ruffled the pages of Danica's journal, causing her to grunt in frustration. Sitting here on the beach, soft sand under her toes, unspotted sky above her, waves breaking gently against the shore, she felt more inspired than ever to write. If only she could keep the pages from fluttering under her pen. She smoothed her hand over the page, holding the corners in place, and read over what she'd written so far.

> *Like a song, the ocean calls to me*
> *Beckoning me closer with its turquoise swells.*
> *Soft sand and gentle breeze*
> *Capture me completely in their spell.*
> *My heart hears the music,*
> *The cymbal crash of water on shore,*
> *The symphony of birdsong,*
> *The crescendo of waves completing the score.*
> *In the music I feel a longing*
> *I've never felt before;*
> *The sea, it's part of me now,*
> *Embedded down into my core.*
> *When the music plays its melody*
> *I finally feel where I belong;*
> *I want to live forever*
> *In the beat of my ocean song.*

Danica bit her lip, reciting the words over again to herself. A shadow fell over the page and she quickly slapped the journal closed. She looked up into Aaron's tanned face, and her heart fluttered at the sight of him. Oh, the things he did to her insides.

"I didn't know you were a writer." His eyes held pleased surprise.

"I'm not, really." She shrugged. "I mean, I like to write, but I don't know that I'm any good at it."

"Would you let me be the judge of that?" Aaron tipped his head inquisitively and looked pointedly at her journal.

Danica's stomach clenched. "Oh, I don't know . . . I don't usually let people read my writing."

His eyes held disappointment, but his smile was gentle. He softly stroked his thumb over her shoulder. "I understand. Writing is very personal. Pictures are, too, you know. Each picture I take seems to have a little piece of myself in it. Knowing how many people end up looking at them is like exposing a little piece of myself to the world each time."

He held her gaze, and she realized he'd just revealed a part of his soul to her. Something in his eyes reassured her that she could do the same, and that he would guard it carefully. Gathering a deep breath of courage, she gripped her journal with both hands, slowly stood up, and handed it to him.

Aaron took it carefully from her hands and flipped to the last page on which she'd been writing. She watched his eyes scan left to right as he took in her most recently written words. When he looked up from the page, his dimples reappeared.

"I knew it would be good, but it's even better than I expected."

Danica released a breath she hadn't even realized she'd been holding. "You really like it?"

"I take pictures with a camera for a living. You create pictures with words. It's a talent I don't possess, but one I very much admire." He held the journal to his chest. "Is there any way you'd let me have a copy of this?"

He really liked it. A rush of pleasure flooded through her at his request. "I guess that would be okay." She took the journal from him, flipped to an empty page, and copied the poem in her best handwriting. Hesitating for a moment, she scrawled a quick note at the bottom of the page and signed her name before ripping the page out and handing it to Aaron.

He skimmed his eyes down to the bottom where she'd signed her name, and smiled as he read out loud, "'To Aaron, thanks for all the adventures. I'll remember them always as part of my ocean song.'"

Danica's face heated, and she covered her cheeks with her palms. "Oh, that sounds so lame when you read it out loud."

Aaron gently tugged her hands away from her face. "Not lame at all. It's perfect. Just perfect."

His face hovered close to hers, and for a breath of a moment she thought he was going to kiss her. Would he? Did she want him to? Oh, who was she kidding? Yes, she wanted him to.

Heart pounding, her eyes darted between his lips and his eyes, and she swore she could see a battle waging in his chocolate irises. His soft sigh fanned her face as he took a reluctant step back, and her heart sank. Clearly he wasn't as interested as she was. Her chest thudded, still anticipating a kiss that wouldn't come, and she looked down, breaking their eye contact.

Ever so gently, Aaron lifted her chin so she was forced to look at him again. "I'd like to take you on that second date. Are you free on Friday?"

Confusion swirled, making her dizzy. He didn't want to kiss her but he wanted to go on another date? She wracked her brain for an intelligible answer. "Um, no, actually. I've signed up to go on the catamaran cruise Friday."

His eyes lit with pleasure. "So have I! I was already looking forward to it, but now I have a whole new reason to be excited."

His sincerity was genuine, and Danica chastised herself for thinking he wasn't interested in her. He'd told her he was a gentleman, and he had certainly proven that to be true. He'd also told her at some point he would probably try to kiss her. Right now wasn't that moment. After all, they'd only spent a few days together. Granted, they'd gotten to know a lot about each other in those few days, but it was probably still too soon to be thinking about kissing.

It was probably way too soon to have the feelings she was developing too, but she couldn't seem to convince her traitorous heart.

"You know, the cruise is only a few hours. We'll still have most of the day available." Aaron pulled her out of her thoughts. "Unless you have other plans besides the cruise?"

Still distracted by his dimples—had she ever found dimples on a man so charming before?—she blinked. "Sorry, what?"

His chuckle was deep. "What's got you so side-tracked?"

Her cheeks flamed. "My mind just wandered for a moment. Sorry."

A fire lit in his eyes, and his knowing smile seemed to hint he knew exactly what she'd been thinking. He leaned closer until she could feel his breath on her lips. "I want to kiss you, Danica. More than you probably know. But I'm not going to. Not yet." He tucked a strand of hair behind her ear. "The best things in life are worth waiting for, don't you think?"

A tingle traveled all the way down to her toes. "I do," she whispered, nearly breathless.

"Good." He eased back an inch. "Now, how about dinner after the cruise?"

Danica nodded mutely. Her ear still tingled where his fingers had brushed it a few seconds ago.

"Good. Then it's a date." He smiled and took another step back. "I don't want to hog your whole vacation, so I'm going to go. I've got a couple places to visit with my camera, but I saw you and couldn't resist saying hi."

"I'm glad you did."

"I'll see you day after tomorrow on the catamaran." He winked, threw her a disarming grin, and sauntered off.

Danica watched him walk away, and then fanned herself with her journal. As much as she was looking forward to tomorrow's excursion—horseback riding in the mountains, followed by a shopping trip in town—she found herself wishing tomorrow would hurry up and be over.

CHAPTER 4

Danica tried to inconspicuously rub her sore backside as her horse worked hard to climb without stumbling on rocks that littered the trail. She'd ridden before, but today's ride was taking saddle-sore to a whole new level. As her horse found level ground again, she let her gaze sweep around her and then inhaled sharply as another formerly-unknown missing piece clicked into place inside of her. From her mountain top position, she had a three-hundred-sixty-degree view. High above the tall trees floated fluffy white clouds in a brilliant blue sky, and down below the edge of the cliff where her horse had stopped, palm trees lined the glittering aqua ocean which stretched out before her as far as her eye could see.

Unconsciously stroking her horse's neck, she was all at once overcome with the sensation of how her smallness compared to her surroundings. And yet, as small and insignificant as she was in the grand scheme of this great big world, God still held her esteemed and knew even the number of hairs on her head. It was a humbling and empowering thought, and she whispered a prayer of thanks for the opportunity to see this piece of His creation and to feel deep in her heart how much she was loved.

Pulled out of her thoughts by the call of her name, she reluctantly pulled her gaze from the majestic view and tugged the reigns to coax her horse into joining the rest of her tour group. Never before would she have had the courage to not only take a vacation by herself, but to experience some of the things she already had on this trip. While at first she'd felt way out of her comfort zone, she now realized she was finally finding a part of herself that she never knew existed. The realization left her with a heady sense of liberation and satisfaction.

Wouldn't Rob be surprised to see her now? She shook her head and gently kicked her heels into the horse's flanks to get him to speed up a bit. Rob's biggest complaint was she was always too reluctant to try anything new. She'd argued she simply found comfort in routine and there was nothing wrong with that. But a restless energy had begun to fester after Rob called off their engagement, forcing her to take a good hard look at her life.

Sure, there was security in routine—but where had routine gotten her? Her fiancé had retracted his proposal after deciding he wanted someone less boring, she lived alone and had no social life of which to speak, and she knew exactly what each day would be like—the same as the one before it.

She'd become overwhelmed with the urge to do something out of character—to escape the security of her safe little world. Thus . . . Jamaica. And so far, it seemed like the best decision she'd ever made for herself.

What would happen when she returned home from this trip? Would she revert to her old self, afraid to take chances, resigned to follow the same routine day after day and only dream of the places she wanted to see and the things she wanted to do, but never have the courage to go after what she wanted? Or would she forever set aside the restless yet safe little world she'd created for herself back home?

No, she wouldn't revert. She'd been permanently changed and she'd never again be content to spend the rest of her days in the same town, doing the same job, seeing the same people. While she still didn't find complete fault with the security of a routine, she now realized the need to shake things up every now and then. She smiled to herself, amused at her own transformation. Something within her was changing and she readily embraced the metamorphosis.

Perhaps this new sense of self was what attracted her to Aaron. He brought out her adventurous side—a side she never knew existed until she came here—and she felt free to be this new and improved version of herself with him. Meeting him was definitely a happy bonus—one she hadn't been expecting, but one for which she was extremely grateful. Even if she never saw him again, she credited him with helping her with her transformation, and she'd never forget him for that.

Danica flipped her reins to keep up with the rest of her group as they began to descend the mountain, and she cringed as she bounced lightly in her saddle. She'd be sore for a while, but she still wouldn't trade this experience for anything in the world. As much as she enjoyed her adventures with Aaron, she was glad she had today for herself to reflect and let her thoughts flow freely without the distraction of his chocolate eyes and endearing dimples.

A slow heat filled her face at the thought of him, and she let out a self-deprecating laugh. Yes, she was thankful for today, but she'd be a straight-out liar if she said she wasn't looking forward to spending the day with him tomorrow . . . and the day after that.

Boy, was she in deep.

Aaron placed his hand on the small of Danica's back and guided her toward the exit ramp, admiring how his hand fit in that spot as if it were made for him.

"That was crazy!" Danica exclaimed, laughing, as Aaron grasped her hand to descend the ramp off the catamaran. "These Jamaicans are wild!"

Aaron helped her off the ramp and into the sand. "They know how to have fun and forget their worries, that's for sure."

"They're always smiling, always laughing, like they don't have a care in the world. It's amazing to me." Danica rambled on about the boat crew teaching everyone the Dollar Dance and joking around with everyone on board as if they were old friends. "Then again, if I lived here I'd probably be the same way."

Aaron gaped at her in mock surprise. "You mean you're not always this happy and carefree?"

Danica playfully swatted at his arm. "You know what I mean. Life can get...well, difficult and frustrating, and it's hard not to worry or stress sometimes."

"Sure, I get that." Aaron steered them toward the resort. "But I think the people here may be on to something. Nothing changes by us worrying or stressing over it—it only affects how we feel."

"True enough." Danica kept in step beside him and he made a mental note talk to her more about on the subject of worry later.

"So, dinner?" Aaron asked as they approached the resort.

"Yeah, but give me time to shower and change first." A yawn stretched her mouth wide. "And maybe a short nap."

Aaron elbowed her teasingly. "All right, Sleeping Beauty, wanna meet up around 6:30?"

"Sounds good." She wiggled her fingers in a flirty wave. "See you then."

Aaron watched her disappear onto the elevator and then made his way toward his room in the opposite tower. Truth be told, he could use a nap, too, but even though his body craved rest, he suspected his racing mind wouldn't allow it. He hadn't told Danica yet he was leaving in two days. He'd have to tell her over dinner tonight that they'd have one more day together, enough time for him to take her on their third official date, and then the next day he'd have to get on a plane and leave her behind.

Already the thought made him sick to his stomach.

As he unlocked the door to his room and slipped inside, he mentally ran through how he would tell her. Would she be disappointed? Would she want to keep in touch after he left? He already knew he wanted to stay in touch with her. He felt a connection with her that he couldn't leave behind on this island without a serious dose of regret and what-ifs. He didn't doubt she had feelings for him. Whether she knew this about herself or not, her face was an open book and he had little trouble reading her. He liked that about her. It went well with her straight-forward nature and left little to the imagination. He believed he could trust her, and he very much liked that, too.

The real question would be if she wanted to continue this relationship after they parted ways. Did they even have a relationship, or was this some vacation fling? He ran his fingers through his hair and flopped onto his bed. This wasn't a fling for him—his feelings were real, and he wanted to see where things could go for the two of them. It would be difficult, trying a long-distance relationship, but he was willing to try if she was.

His mouth pulled into a slow smile. He couldn't wait to see her reaction tomorrow when he took her zip lining. He suspected she'd never been before, but wouldn't she love the adrenaline rush she'd experience as she flew over the trees? He loved watching her face flush with pleasure, her eyes light with excitement, as he introduced her to new and thrilling things. In a way, it was like experiencing them all again for the first time. He'd grown accustomed to the unique experiences that came hand in hand with his profession, but Danica brought a new light to things he'd done a dozen times before, and he again experienced the thrill of a simple boat ride or the surge of waves slapping against his legs as he walked the beach.

His thoughts wandered lazily over the last few days, recalling little details that stuck out in his mind, reliving his favorite moments with the girl who had managed to capture his attention so effortlessly. He always had a difficult time leaving Jamaica—it was one of his favorite places in the world—but this time it would be markedly harder. He didn't want to go, but it couldn't be helped. His plane ticket was already booked and he was due to present the pictures from this trip to his editor in a week. He'd need the in-between time to edit the photos and select the best ones for submission.

"Ugh!" He smacked his hand to his forehead. "I haven't gotten any pictures of Danica yet!" He made a mental note to do that tonight after dinner.

Speaking of dinner, he realized time was slipping away and he needed a shower before meeting back up with Danica. Aaron jumped off the bed, gathered a pair of khakis and a white button up shirt, and quickly made it through his shower. Making sure to grab his camera and portable tripod, he dashed to the elevator. Ten minutes later he was seated comfortably on a plush sofa in the resort lobby when he saw Danica step off the elevator. He nearly let his jaw drop open as he took in her appearance. Her hair fell in loose waves over her shoulders and down her back, and he caught a hint of auburn highlights as she walked under the chandelier. Her gauzy white dress, with its tiny straps clinging to her shoulders and fitted waist, floated softly down to hover over her sandal-clad feet. Not only did her look appeal to him as a man, but it caught his photographer's eye as well.

He could have sat gazing at her all night, but she caught his eye, smiled, and headed toward him. Aaron rose and greeted her with a chaste kiss on the cheek. She even smelled amazing—like lilacs. His favorite.

"You look beautiful, as always." The blush he loved stole across her cheeks as she thanked him. He offered her his arm. "Shall we?"

Danica slipped her fingers around his arm and smiled up at him. Lord help him, his heart actually fluttered. How was he going to tell this woman goodbye?

Conversation came easily through their dinner of shrimp, vegetables, and decadent desserts that Aaron was certain would never be found in America. Finally Danica pushed her plate away, laughing.

"It tastes so good it's hard to stop, but I think if I eat one more bite I may burst."

Aaron checked his watch. "How would you like to walk some of it off, then? I was hoping to get some pictures of you tonight, like you asked. I could get some shots with the sunset."

"Oh, yes, that would be great!" Danica scooted her chair back.

Again he offered her his arm, and again she took it with a giggle.

"What's so funny?"

"It's not so much funny as it is sweet." Danica squeezed his arm. "You're the only man who has ever offered his arm to me as we walked. It's such an old school thing to do, but I love it." She graced him with a sincere smile. "You truly are a gentleman."

Right now, if he were honest with himself, he didn't feel much like being a gentleman. The way Danica looked up at him, her bright eyes framed with dark lashes, full lips tilted alluringly, he felt overcome with the urge to pull her close and cover her lips with his own. He reminded himself to be patient and took a steadying breath as he led her outside.

Once on the beach, he lowered his arm and reached his hand for hers. She took it willingly, and he laced their fingers together as they walked. There was only a slight breeze tonight so the waves were calm and serene as they gently swished against the shore.

"Danica?"

She pulled her gaze from the water. "Yes?"

"I have to tell you something." He swallowed the lump in his throat. "I'm leaving the day after tomorrow to go back home."

Her face fell. "Oh."

"I wish I didn't have to, but…"

She squeezed his hand lightly. "It's okay. We both knew we'd have to leave. You're just the one to leave first." She turned her head but he saw the disappointment in her eyes.

Aaron released a heavy sigh. "I had no idea when I came here I'd end up falling for someone and it would make it so hard to leave."

Danica's chin jerked back toward him and her eyes lit with timid hope. "I couldn't have guessed it would happen for me, either. But now that it has… where do we go from here?"

He didn't hesitate. "I'd really like to stay in touch. Emails, phone calls, hopefully some visits?"

"You really want all that?" Her voice sounded breathless and she searched his eyes for truth.

"Danica, it's hard for me to explain my feelings for you. I know we just met, but I have this connection to you I can't ignore. All I know is I don't want this to be some short-term vacation fling. I want to continue getting to know you. I want to take you on more adventures, read more of your poems... I know it's asking a lot, with you in Kansas and me in Florida, but I want there to be an *us*." He stroked her palm with his thumb. "Do you feel the same?"

Her lips trembled as she offered him the sweetest smile. "I do. I've never been in a long distance relationship before so I'm not really sure how it will work, but we'll figure it out as we go. I'm willing to try."

He couldn't control the crazy grin that he felt tugging at his cheeks, nor could he any longer control the urge to kiss her. He eased his camera and tripod down to the sand and then gently pulled her against his length. A small gasp escaped her lips as her hands came to rest on his chest. He told her with his eyes what he planned to do, and her eyes granted him permission. He brought one hand up and gently tangled his fingers in her hair as he wrapped his hand around the back of her neck and pulled her face close. He watched in fascination as her eyes closed, waiting and ready for his kiss.

He planned to remember this moment forever. Slowly he lowered his lips to hers and his heart swelled with the sweet feeling of homecoming when their lips finally met. Danica leaned into him and wrapped her arms around his neck, and he marveled at how well they fit together. After several long, glorious seconds—or was it minutes?—Aaron ended the kiss.

A blissful sigh flowed from Danica's lips and fanned his as he leaned his forehead against hers. "Wow."

He chuckled. "My thoughts exactly."

She tickled her fingers across the back of his neck. "That was definitely worth waiting for."

"So are you," Aaron whispered. "I want you to know that I won't date anyone else. I don't care how many miles separate us. For as long as you want me, there won't be anyone else."

"Thank you for saying that." She slid her hands from his neck and rested them on his chest. "Same for me. No one but you."

"Good to know." He grinned and kissed her forehead. "I hate to end this moment, but the sun will be setting soon and if we're going to get some pictures we should probably do that now."

Reluctantly, they stepped apart and he collected his equipment while Danica collected herself. He spent the next half hour alternating between telling her how to pose and taking some candids as she walked along the shore and threw flirty winks over her shoulder at him. The sun began to set behind her. The picture he'd first envisioned taking of her would now become a reality. He asked her to stand with her feet in the water and look out toward the skyline. Her hair and skirt floated softly in the breeze, and Aaron moved around her, taking pictures of her from different angles until he was satisfied he'd made the best use of the remaining light.

"Okay, one more and then we'll be done." He mounted the camera to the tripod, then angled the lens toward her and set the timer. Quickly jogging over to her, he stepped behind her and wrapped his arms around her middle. She laughed happily and angled her head to look at him, a joyful smile lighting up her face. Aaron's heart thudded as he looked into her eyes, and he felt himself freefall as the camera clicked, capturing this most perfect memory forever.

CHAPTER 5

The sun peeked through the curtains, tickling her awake, and Danica stretched lazily across her mattress with a massive yawn. It had taken her forever to fall asleep last night, she'd been so hopped up on adrenaline. She sleepily rubbed at her eyes, and her lips eased into a slow smile as she remembered the reason her heart had kept her up with its insistent pounding.

Suddenly energized, she bounced out of bed and picked out her clothes for today—a pair of yoga pants, a loose fitting tank, socks, and sneakers. Aaron had carefully instructed her on what to wear today and advised her to pull her hair into a ponytail. She still didn't know where he was taking her on their last Jamaican adventure together, but at least she'd be comfortable.

Her face heated as she anticipated seeing him again this morning and spending the day together. That kiss last night was...*wow*. No one, in all of her twenty-seven years, had kissed her so tenderly, filling her both with excitement and leaving her feeling so cherished. A pang stabbed in her chest—this would be their last day together. She quickly dismissed any negative thoughts. She would not let the cloud of Aaron's impending departure ruin today. Today she would enjoy the time they had together to the fullest and wait until he was actually gone to start missing him.

She showered and dressed quickly, pulled her hair into a ponytail, and then headed down to meet Aaron for breakfast. Her stomach danced with butterflies when she saw him and her lips tingled with their own memories. Judging by the look in his eyes, he was as affected by the sight of her.

Breakfast went quickly, Danica's anticipation growing with every bite. "Are you finally going to tell me where we're going?"

Aaron shook his head. "Not yet. But you'll see soon."

"The anticipation is killing me!"

He chuckled and lightly traced his fingers over her wrist. "Didn't we already establish the best things in life are worth waiting for?" His eyes hinted at the memory of their kiss.

Her gaze automatically flicked to his lips. They stretched into a knowing smile and brought a rush of heat to her chest. "Yes, I suppose we did."

"Just a little longer," he whispered as he pulled her out of her chair and kissed her softly on the cheek.

Weak in the knees, she let him lead her to the front of the resort where they caught their ride. They rode over rough terrain and pulled up to a line of bright orange, windowless Hummers. She gave Aaron a questioning look, but he only shrugged, and she rolled her eyes at him. They climbed into a Hummer and bounced up the mountain until they reached a stable where several large mules were being prepared for riding.

Danica drew back. "We're riding mules?" This was Aaron's idea of one last great adventure?

"Will you just trust me?" He helped her out of the Hummer and led her over to the rest of the group.

Following instructions, they sat on a hard wooden bench and listened to the guides explain what was about to happen. Danica tried not to think about her still saddle-sore backside and muster up some enthusiasm. As she listened and it became clear where they were heading, her excitement grew and she promptly forgot her soreness.

"Zip lining?" She whispered into Aaron's ear. "That's what we're doing up here?" Her voice squeaked. "Oh, my goodness, Aaron, I can't believe it!"

The guide shot her a pointed look and she clamped her mouth shut, but her foot bounced in eager anticipation. Even as they mounted the mules and began their trek the rest of the way up the mountain, Danica barely registered her surroundings. Her mind continued to conjure images of flying through the air, wind rushing past her face. Her heart raced at the thought of it.

After what seemed like ages, they finally reached the top of the mountain and Aaron quickly dismounted. He helped her off her mule and her feet met the ground, but her hands still rested on his shoulders and his hands still spanned her waist. For a moment they stood gazing into each other's eyes. A shrill whistle broke their spell, and they obediently—if not reluctantly—followed the group to a covered pavilion where the guides handed out what looked like repelling gear.

Before she knew it, she and Aaron were approaching a platform on the edge of a steep drop. The guides began giving instructions. Danica did her best to listen attentively, but her gaze kept trailing to the gaping valley below them. Goodness, they were high. The tops of the trees looked no bigger than the plastic trees from the Lego set she'd played with as a kid. What if she fell? What if her pulley wasn't hooked up right or something went wrong and she fell through all that open air until she finally reached the far, far away ground?

Her heart pounded painfully, nearly rocking her back and forth with its force. Her breath came out in short bursts, and a wave of dizziness overtook her. She grasped blindly for Aaron's arm and dug her fingernails into his skin.

"What's wrong?" Aaron searched her eyes. "Do you not want to do this? It's okay if you don't."

"I—I thought I did, but now…" She gulped as she took another look at the drop. "I don't know if I can go through with this. What if I fall?"

"You won't fall. I've done this twice before and there's never been a problem. I promise you they take every precaution for people's safety." He spoke confidently, but his reassurance did nothing to ease her anxiety.

"It's so far down. Look at all that open space, nothing there to catch you." Her voice came out strained and she tried unsuccessfully to clear her throat. "Aaron, I'm sorry but I'm scared."

He rubbed his hands up and down her arms as if trying to warm her up, and she realized she was covered in goosebumps. When she shivered he pulled her to him and wrapped his arms around her.

"It's okay." His voice rumbled next to her ear. "You don't have to go through with it if you don't want to, but I also really think you'll regret it if you don't."

"Why?"

"Because I saw how excited you were when you figured out what we were doing. You couldn't wait to get on that zip line. It wasn't until you saw how high up we were that you got scared. But everything you're afraid of was there when you were excited. Seeing it doesn't make the reality any different than what it was before. Only your perception has changed."

Danica mulled over his words as he rubbed his hand in slow circles on her back. He was right—she had been excited. She'd pictured herself flying through the air, free and wild like a bird, and the thought had filled her with a longing to experience the uninhibited release. She hadn't thought about the ground being so far below her until she saw it. But that risk had still existed, even when it hadn't been the focus of her thoughts. Being aware of the risk didn't make the task any more dangerous.

She opened her eyes, and her gaze travelled across the wide expanse to the far side of the valley where the other end of the zip line disappeared. Could she be brave enough to do it, to face the risk for the reward of reaching the other side?

Aaron pulled back and brushed a strand of hair behind her ear. "Let your faith be bigger than your fear. You won't regret it, I promise."

Danica reached down deep and summoned every ounce of courage she possessed. "Okay. I'll do it."

Aaron's smile was almost reward enough. He took her hand. "Come on. I'll go before you. That way I'll be waiting on the other side for you, okay?"

The tour guide attached his harness to the pulley system with thick, sturdy clips. The guide tugged hard on it when he was done, convincing Danica everything was connected securely. Then he stepped back and signaled for Aaron to proceed. Aaron turned his head to meet Danica's gaze and shot her a reassuring smile then, before she could even return his smile, he stepped to the edge of the platform and pushed off the edge.

Her breath caught in her throat as she watched Aaron soar across the open valley at an alarming speed. Her hands clenched into fists until her fingernails became sharp razors against her palms, but she wouldn't relax until he landed safely on the other side. He grew smaller and smaller until finally he slowed and came to a stop on the other side, landing on another platform barely visible from this distance.

She let out a huge breath as relief coursed through her veins. He'd made it! And now—she gulped—it was her turn. Heart pounding in both fear and anticipation, she approached the platform and allowed herself to be hooked up by the skilled guide.

"Okay." The guide patted her solidly on the back. "You're all set. Just step to the edge and push off."

The ability to draw a complete breath suddenly seemed impossible. She sucked air in desperate gasps as she moved to the edge of the platform and looked straight down. Another wave of dizziness rocked her balance and she took a frantic step backward.

The guide's eyebrows dipped in concern. "You okay? Wanna back out?"

"No!" The word burst out of her and she forced herself to calm. "No, I'm going to do it. I just need a minute."

The guide offered her a comforting pat on the shoulder. "In my experience it's best to not overthink it. Just...jump."

Danica looked straight ahead at Aaron's tiny form. "Let your faith be bigger than your fear," she whispered. "Just jump."

And then she was flying.

Exactly as she'd imagined, the wind rushed past her face, giving evidence to how fast she was moving. She looked down and gasped in surprise. What she hadn't been able to see from her vantage point on the mountain now stretched below her like a Thomas Kinkade painting. Trees of all different sizes and shades of green—some dotted with bright yellow, orange, and fuchsia flowers—swayed softly in the breeze, bringing to mind the gently rolling waves of Kansas grain. A waterfall spilled topaz water from its place tucked into the mountain in between the trees.

How many people got to see something like this? This was special, and she'd nearly let herself miss it. Her fears leapt from her chest and disappeared behind her in the breeze, and she spread her arms wide and threw her head back. She whooped at the top of her lungs. "Yeeeaaaahhhhh!" Her eyes greedily took in every detail she could catch, and she laughed as a bird flew under her. She was soaring even above the birds! She couldn't believe she'd almost let her fear keep her from this.

How much of her life had she missed out on because she was too afraid to step outside of her comfort zone? Her heart filled with sadness for her past self, and she resolved to never let go of this feeling, to take more chances and let herself fully live her life, not merely float through it.

Too soon she saw the platform at the end of the line drawing close, and she put her gloved hands on the line the way the instructors had demonstrated and squeezed to slow her descent. Her feet hit the platform, and the waiting guide steadied her before removing the hooks from her harness.

As soon as she was free, Aaron's arms encircled her, and he spun her around. "You did it!" His eyes sparked with jubilance in the face of her accomplishment.

"Aaron, that was the most incredible experience of my life! I felt so . . . *free!*" In a burst of euphoria, she flung her arms around his neck and kissed him firmly on the lips. "Thank you for talking me into it."

"If that's the thanks I get each time, we will definitely be doing more of this." He winked, and she giggled happily.

The guide chuckled under his breath and pointed to an area where they could wait. "Okay, you two love birds, clear the deck for the next person coming in, please."

Aaron took her hand and kissed her knuckles as they stepped off the platform. "Tell me your favorite part."

Danica drew her bottom lip between her teeth and tried to think of how to answer. "The view was stunning. I've never seen anything like it. But I think my favorite part was how I *felt* up there, looking down on a part of the world I never would've seen otherwise." She wrapped her fingers around his. "This might be hard for you to understand, what with all the places you get to see and capture with your camera, but I've never been anywhere or done anything. I've spent my whole life in Wichita, Kansas, and never thought I'd venture outside my little corner of the world. Coming here was a huge step for me, but I needed it. I needed to get outside of myself, if that makes sense."

He nodded and his eyes glistened with understanding. "It does."

"All the things I've done here in Jamaica have been..." She struggled to think of the right word. "Redemptive. Like with each new experience I've grown and discovered something about myself I never knew before, and it's changed me a bit each time. When I was up there flying above that valley, having faced my fear and letting go, it felt like I finally became *me*. The me I was meant to be but never let myself be."

She stopped and shook her head. "I'm rambling and probably not making an ounce of sense, am I?"

Aaron's smile, so tender, tugged on her heart. "You're making complete sense. I'd hoped it would be that way for you. It was for me, too, the first time."

For reasons Danica couldn't explain with words, learning they'd shared the same soul-changing experience bonded her more firmly to him, and she leaned up on her tip-toes and kissed him lightly. "I'm not going home the same person. Part of that is thanks to you."

Aaron shook his head. "You started this journey on your own. I was just privileged enough to get to come along for the ride."

"I did, that's true. But the old me was still there and might have held me back even after I took the step of coming here." She squeezed his hand. "You pushed me along, gave me opportunities I might not have sought out on my own, and in the process I grew and I won't ever be the same. So thank you. It's the most precious gift anyone has ever given me."

Something indefinable flickered in Aaron's eyes, and he swallowed hard before leaning his forehead against hers. "I'm really going to miss you."

Danica felt a lump form in her throat. "Me, too."

He bent his knees until their eyes were level. "I'm going to work on making my next job in Kansas. So don't get too used to not seeing me." His smile was teasing, but she saw a sadness in his eyes that touched her heart. This really was as hard for him as it was for her.

Imagine it... Someone she'd met only a week ago showed more reluctance to be apart from her than her fiancé of two years had when he ended their relationship. Then again, Danica hadn't exactly been shattered by the breaking of their engagement either. She'd been more upset about having to start over and missing out on the logical next steps of her life which she'd had all planned out. She'd been comfortable and safe in her plans with Rob, but she hadn't been excited by them. Apparently he hadn't been either.

And she was okay with it. Because now she finally understood.

Life was about so much more than being comfortable, than the security of routine. She'd gotten complacent. There was no pleasure in her life, only the same thing day after day. But complacency was over. God created this great big world for His children to enjoy. There was so much joy to be had in life, so much of the world to see and experience, and she wanted to do it all.

Danica met Aaron's gaze. "Promise this won't be our last adventure together?"

He tightened his arms around her and kissed the top of her head. "Promise."

CHAPTER 6

It was no use. How in the world was he going to get all these photos edited and submitted to his boss when he couldn't stop thinking of the woman who appeared in so many of them? Aaron pinched the bridge of his nose and shoved his chair away from the desk.

Thirty-seven hours had passed—not that he was counting—since he'd kissed her goodbye at the door to her room after their last date, and he missed her like crazy. He got up and grabbed a bottle of water and a banana, then went back to his desk. He'd check his email one more time to see if she'd written yet, and then he'd get back to work and actually focus this time.

Pulling up his email, his stomach actually fluttered when he saw a new email from Danica, sent just four minutes ago. He read her message, unable to squelch his smile, and typed out a quick reply.

Danica,

I was just thinking of you and then your email came in. Nice to know we were thinking of each other at the same time. :) Thank you for your email—I miss you too. I'm actually having a hard time focusing on my work because I keep thinking of your sweet smile. I hope you know what a wonderful time I had with you over the last week. You're a very special woman, Danica. (I hope that doesn't sound too cheesy! I can't seem to help myself when it comes to you.) Once you're back home, let's make a plan to Skype? In the meantime, how about sending me a poem?

Fondly,
Aaron

He hit send and then made a concentrated effort of going through his photos with a critical eye, deleting the ones that didn't meet his high standards, and carefully editing the ones he thought would make the best impressions. Only when his back began to ache did he realize hours had slipped by while he was absorbed in his task. He stood and stretched, and his stomach growled, reminding him it was well past lunch time.

Satisfied he'd made enough progress to justify taking a break, he wandered into the kitchen and made himself a sandwich. Now that his mind was free to wander again, he absently munched on his sandwich and checked his email again. Nothing from Danica. He suppressed his disappointment and then chastised himself. She was still on vacation. She had more exciting things to do than hang out at the public computer all day and write to him. Besides, if they were going to do this long distance thing, he was going to have to learn to be patient.

He swallowed the last of his sandwich, downed a glass of milk, and resolved he would not check his email again until this evening.

Danica walked alone along the shore and watched the setting sun paint the sky with pink and purple streaks. She'd kept so busy over the last week, it had felt really good to have a day to relax and enjoy the salty ocean air from her lounge chair. But now that the day was coming to an end, she was really starting to miss Aaron's company. She must be crazy. She'd only known the man for a week, yet his absence left her with an empty ache in her chest.

Overhead a seagull cried out, and the sound seemed to echo the lonely cry in her heart. How could she miss someone so much when she barely knew him? But no, that wasn't really true. Aaron had revealed himself to her in ways he probably didn't even realize. He'd told her that writing was deeply personal, that you could see a person's soul from the words they put on a page. She'd discovered the same applied to what Aaron was able to capture in the pictures he took. When she looked at his work, she felt like she was seeing who he really was, all the way to his core.

His talent for catching couples in loving, intimate moments showed his softer, romantic side. He captured people's expressions in a split second and exposed a glimpse of who the person really was without even knowing them.

And the pictures of buildings or nature invited Danica to look at ordinary objects in a whole different way, as if they had somehow taken on a personality of their own. She'd never thought that a dying tree or an abandoned stone fort could have a history, a story to tell. Yet somehow Aaron not only recognized their story and captured it with his camera, he was so masterful the image let her see it, too.

Aaron looked at the world differently than most people, and he'd helped her see the world differently, too. He even saw something in her that she didn't know existed until she came here, and now she viewed herself in a different light. The question was, who would she be once she was back home? It was easy to be New Danica in Jamaica where no one knew her, where she didn't already have a life established. At home, back into her routine, she wasn't sure how she'd make sure New Danica would stick around. But one way or another, she'd make sure she did. God had given her an opportunity to grow as a person, and she wouldn't let this experience go to waste. She was still a work in progress, and she prayed God would keep working on her once she traded her beloved ocean waves for the familiar amber waves of grain.

Again, a seagull's cry pierced the air and seemed to intensify the longing she felt for Aaron's hand in hers, for his smile and his voice as he told her about his adventures around the world. Like a flash, words started assembling themselves in her mind, and she quickly ran to the resort and up to her room. She was panting by the time she got to her door—running on sand was exhausting—but she let herself in and scrambled for her journal. She flipped to a blank page as she grabbed a pen off the nightstand.

Lying on her stomach across the bed, she let the words pour onto the page and then scrutinized them as she arranged them into an order that made sense. When she finished, she placed her journal on the nightstand. Tomorrow she would email Aaron and, since he'd asked for another poem, she would send him this one. She hoped he would understand why she wrote it.

Suddenly drained, Danica undressed, turned off the lights, and let the sound of the waves through her open balcony door soothe her to sleep with their lullaby.

Despite setting his alarm, it was mid-morning before the sun finally teased Aaron's eyes open. Glancing at the clock, he groaned. Two hours behind schedule already. He flung the covers off his legs and rolled from the bed.

Despite the freedom to work from the comfort of his home, he still had to stick to a routine if he wanted to have his work done by the deadline his boss had imposed. He'd learned early on he needed to keep himself disciplined or he wouldn't get everything accomplished on time. Being punctual with his assignments—along with his God-given talent with a camera—kept him in good graces with his employer.

A quick shower and a banana muffin later, he was engrossed in editing his photos—and deliberately avoiding the ones with Danica in them so he could stay focused—when his email alert dinged. He finished the photo on which he was working and then clicked over to his email. He smiled as he saw Danica's name and eagerly opened the message.

She'd written, *Thinking of you*, and a poem followed.

Ask Me Why the Seagulls Cry

As I walk across the sand, it turns a glittering gold.
I long for him to hold my hand and tell a story he's never told.
But as my thoughts wander away, as the waves quietly sway,
His hand I no longer feel, his voice I no longer hear;
The quietness, the loneliness—the sign of no one near.
The sadness drifts into the sky...
Now ask me why the seagulls cry.

Aaron leaned back in his seat and rubbed the back of his neck. His chest ached, and he missed so acutely the feel of her hand in his. After a long deliberation, he hit reply and typed, *I miss you, too.* He hit send and then released a sigh. This long distance thing was going to be harder than he thought.

Lord, I really believe You brought Danica into my life for a reason. The distance between us will make things harder, but please...help us figure out how to make this work, to give this a real chance to see where it might lead.

He picked up the picture he'd printed of the two of them together on the beach. Danica looked blissfully happy, and he looked like a man in—

"Whoa." Aaron dropped the picture and clamped his hands over his thighs.

He wasn't in love. That was crazy. Wasn't it? Sure, he had strong feelings for her already, but didn't love take time to grow?

With shaking hands, he picked up the picture and examined it. Okay, true, when he looked at Danica's pictures or thought of her beautiful smile, he couldn't help smiling himself. And when he remembered how naturally their fingers intertwined he couldn't help marveling what a perfect fit they were. And yes, he missed her like crazy. He couldn't wait to see her again, to hear her voice again, to hold her hand again, to kiss her again.

He traced his finger across the picture. "Lord, I am falling..., aren't I?"

CHAPTER 7

THREE MONTHS LATER…

The air became hazy as they passed through a low hanging cloud, and Danica laughed as Aaron took the opportunity to steal a kiss. "This is much better than our last trip in the air, huh?"

Aaron wrapped his arm around her middle and looked over the edge of the hot air balloon. "I can't believe I've never done this before."

"It wasn't easy, but I finally found something we could *both* experience together for the first time." Danica grinned. "And what better way to show off my neck of the woods than from the air?"

They looked down at the patchwork of corn fields, wheat fields, and meadows interspersed with small rivers, ponds, and dirt roads. Danica leaned lightly against his frame. "It looks like the coverlet my grandma quilted for me when I was little. It really is beautiful."

Aaron raised his camera and took several shots from around the perimeter of the large basket. "These will be great for the website. From up here, Kansas looks so peaceful and homey."

"So this was a good surprise?" Danica asked, deliberately injecting a teasing lilt.

"The best." Aaron kissed her again, and then cleared his throat. "Actually, I have a couple surprises for you, too."

Danica snuggled close to his side. "Lucky me."

He squeezed her gently and then eased away, clearing his throat again and swallowing hard. If she didn't know any better she'd think he was nervous. But he'd been fine with the hot air balloon ride so far. Why would he be nervous now?

She put her hand on his arm. "You okay?"

He nodded and looked somewhere past her, and she wrestled down the urge to turn around and see what he was looking at.

"Aaron? What's going on?"

He finally brought his gaze back to her face, and a soft smile appeared on his lips. "Do you know how amazing you are?"

"Aaron . . ." Her face heated with pleasure at his simple yet sweet words.

"The last few months, writing and calling each other, your trip out to Florida to visit me that one weekend... The more I've gotten to know about you, the more I've come to—"

She waited, but he didn't finish the sentence. She searched his eyes. "Come to what, Aaron?"

For a couple of seconds he looked terrified, but then he exhaled slowly and smiled. "Come to love you," he whispered. He reached for her hands and enfolded them in his own. "I'm in love with you, Danica."

She gasped, and a hot rush of joy raced from her toes to her face. "You—you are?"

Aaron lifted her hands and kissed them one at a time. "With all my heart."

Danica nearly wilted, her trembling knees suddenly feeling like wet noodles. But then she looked into his eyes and found strength there. "I love you, too."

She could almost swear the already brilliant sky brightened with his smile. He pulled her to him and kissed her with more tenderness than she'd known a kiss could possess. When he pulled away long seconds later, he brushed a strand of hair behind her ear, stroked her cheek with the gentlest touch, and then sank down onto one knee.

For a moment she thought he'd gotten dizzy and she reached for him, but then she noticed what he held in his hand. The sun threw sparks off the diamond and white gold band.

Her heart beat faster. Oh, boy, now she was dizzy. She fumbled for something to hold onto and drew in a sharp breath. "Aaron?"

"Danica, I know a lot of people would probably think this is too soon, but I know what my heart wants, and it's you. I'd been praying for God to bring the perfect woman for me into my life, and then I got onto a plane headed for Jamaica and there you were." The sweetest smile of remembrance lit his face. "I think I started falling in love with you that first night, under your cotton candy sky. I want to go back there, to the spot that will always hold a special place in my heart, and marry you under another cotton candy sky like that one. Meeting and falling in love with you has been the greatest adventure of my life, and I want to have a million more adventures with you by my side."

He took her trembling fingers and slid the glittering circle of gold over the ring finger on her left hand. Danica's breath caught in her throat. The ring fit perfectly just as Aaron fit her so perfectly. He was right—it was soon. But she didn't need more time to know he was the one God had chosen for her. How she loved this man! And he wanted to spend the rest of his life with *her*. Hot tears filled the corners of her eyes as love for him filled her entire being.

"Danica?" Aaron's whisper carried deep emotion. "Will you marry me?"

She sank onto her knees and threw her arms around his neck. "Oh, Aaron . . . yes! Yes, yes, yes!" She laughed giddily and pulled back to look at him, and then playfully swatted him on the arm. "And here I thought I was the one surprising you today."

"I was surprised. I had no idea I'd be proposing to you in a hot air balloon. I was just going to take you on a walk!" Aaron chuckled and kissed her, his lips forming into a smile against hers. "This was way better."

He helped her up and they stood with their arms around each other, watching the sun set while the pilot urged the balloon to slowly descend. Danica rested her head on Aaron's shoulder, and her mind filled with thoughts of their future together.

"Aaron?"

"Hmm?"

"Where will we live? I can't really see you moving to Kansas."

He kissed her temple. "I was kind of hoping you might want to move to Florida. We could look for a place closer to the ocean."

Danica pulled back, her interest piqued. Oh, to wake up every morning to that salty sea air would be heaven on earth. "I'd love that." Then reality nudged its way in, and she frowned. "You know, I've been considering a career change, maybe going back to school, or pursuing my writing, like you've encouraged me to do. Can I still do that once we're married? Will we need me to bring in a steady income?"

"That's actually the other surprise I had for you." Aaron turned his body so he faced her and took both her hands in his. "What if I told you that you could pursue your writing and get paid for it?"

"Well, as incredible as that would be, you know it takes time to establish yourself as a writer. It could be years."

"What if I already had a job offer for you?" He tilted his head, his mouth quirked in a crooked grin.

Her head tilted, mirrored to his. "What do you mean?"

"I had this idea. I ran it past my boss and, well, he loved it. As long as you agree, it's a done deal." Now Aaron's smile stretched wide across his face.

She shook her head. "I still don't understand. What idea?"

"A travel blog. You do the writing, I take the pictures. We travel together as a team and present as a team. The company is going to do some major promotion on it since I've already got a bit of a following. They think it'll be a big hit."

Danica's jaw dropped open, and she made a concentrated effort to pull it closed again. "Are you serious?"

"Absolutely. I showed my boss some samples of your writing, and he was really impressed. All you have to do is say yes."

She stared at him mutely, too overwhelmed to form words.

Aaron's eyebrows dipped and uncertainty clouded his eyes. "Unless . . . you don't like the idea? We don't have to do it. It's just a crazy idea, a way for us to be together and go on more adventures, a way for us to both do something we love and actually make a living doing it. But if you don't want to, I understand. I know it's asking a lot—"

Finally Danica found her voice. "Aaron." She put her hands on his cheeks and stared into his eyes. "I'm so surprised. I never expected an offer like this in a million years."

She laughed, still a bit frazzled at the abrupt turn her life had just taken. It was funny in a way. For so long she'd craved routine because she thought routine equaled security. And now, here she was agreeing to travel the world with her soon-to-be husband on someone else's schedule, yet she'd never felt more secure than she did knowing she and Aaron would be doing it all together. God must have a sense of humor.

Feeling more confident about her future than she ever had before, she linked her hands around his neck and smiled up at him. "It sounds absolutely perfect."

The relief and love reflected in his chocolate eyes as he pulled her close was all she needed. They sealed the deal with a sweet kiss.

EPILOGUE

The welcoming breeze was gentle and lightly fluttered the long skirt of Danica's white dress as she walked barefoot on the sand toward her groom. Aaron's eyes reflected so much love and tenderness, her eyes pooled with happy tears. Oh, how far God had brought her. It only seemed right to start her new life as a wife in the very place God had begun her transformation.

Aaron had wished to marry her under a cotton candy sky, and apparently God was a bit of a romantic Himself because He'd painted a perfect canvas for their backdrop on this most special day.

In only a few short steps she reached the love of her life, and Danica released her dad's arm, kissed him on the cheek, and turned to face the man who would soon become her husband.

Aaron leaned close. "You are so beautiful."

She smiled and winked. "You're not so bad yourself."

His answering smile was mischievous. "Are you ready for the greatest adventure yet?"

Their love and their life together would be the greatest adventure she could have ever imagined. She grinned. "Let's do this."

If you enjoyed this compilation of stories,
please look for these other novella collections
from Wings of Hope Publishing.

Threads of Time

A collection of seven Christian romantic novellas about a very special quilt—one intended to grace the marriage bed of a young couple but never fulfilling its original purpose—which travels through many hands and decades, lending comfort to its temporary owners before being passed on.

FEBRUARY 2014

A Place of Refuge

A cabin constructed by Scottish immigrants in the mid-1870s becomes a place of rest, restoration, and refuge for weary travelers over the decades. Enjoy seven stories featuring one log cabin in the beautiful mountains of Wyoming, and find your place of refuge, as well.

MARCH 2015

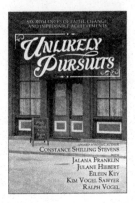

Unlikely Pursuits

Embark on six exciting journeys following the adventures of unique heroes and heroines—from the 19th century to the present day—who dare to pursue unusual occupations in order to do what they love, including a newspaper editor, a dress maker, a hangman, a carousel painter, and a veterinarian.

APRIL 2016

www.wingsofhopepublishing.com

Est. 2013

Wings of Hope Publishing is committed to providing quality Christian reading material in both the fiction and non-fiction markets.

CPSIA information can be obtained
at www.ICGtesting.com
Printed in the USA
LVOW13s2331030817
543784LV00006B/147/P

9 781944 309183